ARI GRAY

Shadow in the Ward

Copyright © 2024 by Ari Gray

All rights reserved. No part of this publication may be reproduced, stored or transmitted in any form or by any means, electronic, mechanical, photocopying, recording, scanning, or otherwise without written permission from the publisher. It is illegal to copy this book, post it to a website, or distribute it by any other means without permission.

This book is a work of fiction. Names, characters, businesses, places, events, locales, and incidents are either the products of the author's imagination or used in a fictitious manner. Any resemblance to actual persons, living or dead, or actual events is purely coincidental.

While this book does refer to certain existing products, services, or entities, these references are for the purpose of contextualizing the narrative and do not constitute an endorsement or critique of such products, services, or entities. They are used nominatively for purposes of realism and not to imply any association or sponsorship.

The author and publisher disclaim any liability to any party for any loss, damage, or disruption caused by the use or interpretation of this work. Readers should not infer any medical, legal, professional, or personal advice from the contents of this book, and any actions taken based on the events or characters in this book are the sole responsibility of the reader.

By proceeding beyond this page, the reader agrees to these terms.

First edition

This book was professionally typeset on Reedsy. Find out more at reedsy.com

To all the devoted clinical educators who generously carve out moments from their demanding schedules to nurture the minds of the next generation: Your unwavering belief in the promise of a brighter tomorrow not only shapes the future of healthcare but also ignites the spark of knowledge and hope in countless hearts. With deepest gratitude and respect, thank you.

Acknowledgement

To my wife and son, your love and support are my greatest strengths. Thank you for being my steadfast companions on this journey. Additionally, I extend my gratitude to my colleagues and family members who provided invaluable insights and contributions. Your belief in this project has been a source of inspiration.

* * *

Should you enjoy this work, please consider leaving a review on your preferred online platform. Your feedback is greatly appreciated.

Chapter 1

He struggled to establish a coherent stream of thoughts. One memory raced past another—his twenty-third birthday, his marriage, and the birth of his son. Each recollection arose spontaneously, then quickly disappeared into the darkness. Murky shadows loomed above him as he lay supine on a cold, hard surface. Was he dreaming? Dead? Was this another memory? Unable to focus long enough to consider all the possibilities, he was essentially reborn every few minutes. Consciousness was impermanent.

He had goals and aspirations. He wanted to go back to school, maybe even buy a house one day, but he could not recall any of the day's events preceding this moment. Memories eluded him like a thief in the night. Every thought was a fleeting apparition, harshly disrupted by a searing agony on the right side of his face, a pain that cut deep like a sharpened blade.

A sudden realization jolted him: his jaw was no longer under his control. It dangled there, slack and disobedient. The muscles that he had taken for granted all his life now refused to cooperate, leaving his face in a state of disarray. If not for the intense throbbing, he might have thought his mandible had vanished altogether.

If he could just turn his head to the side, he might orient himself to this unfamiliar environment. Instead, a heavy object bound his movements, forbidding even the slightest turn. Mustering all his strength, he pried open his eyelids. Light careened past him in a dizzying blur. Was he in motion? The shadows coalesced into humanoid shapes. Were they responsible for this? A tide of anger and frustration swept over him. Struggling to move, he discovered that his limbs were restrained to a table, and an intravenous catheter was protruding from his arm. He must have tried to escape before.

He wanted to speak to and negotiate with his captors, but he couldn't open his jaw. A pool of liquid was collecting in the back of his throat. Unable to cough or gag, the viscous fluid dripped into his respiratory tract. He tasted iron. It was blood. It trickled through his vocal cords, moistened his trachea and bronchus, and settled deep in his lungs. Tiny air sacs, crucial for exchanging oxygen and carbon dioxide, were now impaired, putting his life in danger.

Before this evening, he had been a prosperous business owner. A proud alpha male driven by materialistic pursuits, he reveled in showcasing his success. Gold and firearms were symbols of his idolization. Swanky clubs, illicit stimulants, and opulent automobiles were his playgrounds of indulgence. In his mind, he was an invincible conqueror, and even committed to tattooing the word *fearless* above his ribs and sternum.

But tonight, he lay naked on the stretcher—exposed, humbled, and emasculated. Despite never believing in God, he found himself praying. The concept of death had never

CHAPTER 1

crossed his mind. It was a distant concern, an abstract possibility that happened to other people. But like the crack of thunder interrupting a warm summer day, he was immediately confronted by the fragility of his existence and the notion that the world might go on without him. A single moment of poor judgment plunged everything he loved and cherished into peril. Frightened and remorseful, he felt helpless in determining his fate.

The lights were no longer moving, and the hum of engines halted abruptly. He hadn't noticed the noise until it stopped. Chaos surrounded him, a frenzied language foreign to his ear, yet the fervor of their movements spoke volumes of the dire situation. Beads of sweat streamed down their faces, reflecting the intense pressure they carried. The atmosphere was heavy with tension, something had gone terribly wrong.

He was being transported from one sector to another. Was he coming or going, and was this his final location? A shiver ran through him as the cold air gave way to warmth, and he felt protected by the feeling of being indoors. Automatic doors closed behind him. As he passed by, he made out eight ominous letters on the wall: *ER/Trauma*.

"Twenty-eight-year-old anonymous male status post motorcycle accident," shouted a disembodied female voice, speaking in staccato clips. "No helmet... Significant head and facial trauma... AOB, likely ETOH."

He tried to process the words, but AOB meant nothing. ETOH, even less so. But the speaker was familiar with these acronyms, enabling swift and precise communication. These were medical professionals, and their manner instilled confidence. The paramedic was pointing out the scent of alcohol on the patient's breath. ETOH, an abbreviation from organic chemistry, suggested the presence of ethanol in his bloodstream.

His rescuers were knowledgeable and experienced, having likely executed this operation numerous times before. At this point, his best chance at survival lay in the hands of these emergency medical technicians. Their expertise was his beacon of hope, their unwavering dedication a testament to the selflessness of society's heroes. These skilled rescuers, with their humble hearts and tireless spirit, answered the call of duty with unwavering professionalism. They were ready at a moment's notice to bring comfort to those in need.

"Multiple lacerations to the face and scalp... Combative en route."

The room buzzed with the energy of high-stakes medicine. He could hear the precise, clipped tones of the medical team, their words slicing through the air with urgency. The numbers were foreign, yet they spoke of a dire situation, his situation. He was a bystander in his own emergency, a witness to the battle for his life.

"Hypotensive... heart rate 140... SpO2 88%."

Under normal circumstances, he carried five liters of blood, an essential fluid that exerted a pulsatile force against his arterial walls. This force, known as blood pressure, was a crucial indicator of overall health. A significant decline suggested severe blood loss, or hemorrhage. Based on his vital signs, the patient had lost more than two liters.

The medical team also monitored his oxygen levels using pulse oximetry, indicated by SpO2. Normal levels ranged between 95-100%, and any deviation indicated an issue with his airway, breathing, or circulation.

He had never actually stepped inside a hospital, but this

CHAPTER 1

room was unlike anything he had ever imagined. The walls were painted with crowded circuitry that flashed and shimmered like an aerial view of a vibrant city at night. Particles of light darted across the electronic map, bouncing back and forth like they were communicating secret messages. Tinted drawers for storage were scattered amidst the electronic chaos, creating a labyrinth of hidden treasures waiting to be unveiled.

Heavy, robust medical machinery lined the perimeter of the room. One appeared to be a rotatable light structure, while another was a hinged stand with a large protruding metal beam. Possibly an X-ray machine? A donut-shaped apparatus with a diameter wide enough to effortlessly accommodate a human body occupied the front of the room.

"Do you need anything else?" inquired the lead paramedic. There was a noticeable quiver in her voice, a departure from her earlier tone.

The atmosphere in the room had shifted dramatically, leaving the patient to wonder if he was dead. He assessed his bodily sensations, but nothing seemed different. Who was she speaking to? Nobody answered, and no one spoke. He had a strange feeling that no other people were in the room. But that wasn't possible, was it?

An unfamiliar presence entered the chamber. The deep tone of revving and whirring machinery echoed through the resuscitation bay as the patient struggled to open his eyes.

The shadows above him were no longer cast by humans. Instead, a mammoth, towering contraption, about seven feet tall, loomed overhead. A triangular, forward-facing, metallic head-like structure sat atop a sturdy metallic case. Light beams emanated from a protected glass encasement in a 180-

degree arrangement. There was no mouth, and it did not speak. The entire cephalad complex rested on an articular pivot joint powered by thick cables that moved similarly to human muscle.

Beneath that, broad shoulders, composed of overlaid plates, were flexibly fused by fibrous connective material, allowing for twisting, turning, and bending. Four appendages emerged beneath its armor, each linked to the central segment via a ball-and-socket mechanism. The elbow and forearm areas were replaced by an array of cables wrapped in a spiral configuration. On the left, a hand-like structure with multiple digits and an opposable hook allowed for grasping objects. On the right, fluid-filled canisters housed various solutions and a pressurized injector, a sharp 18-gauge needle at the tip.

Interwoven wired connections veiled the front of the thoracic cavity, reminiscent of the circuitry on the resuscitation room's walls. A bulky canister was attached to its back. Hundreds of tiny coils reached around the flank to connect to the anterior motherboard. The torso and abdominal area hung suspended by a stack of twisted cords. Moving downward, two more appendages branched out with ball-and-socket connectivity. These powerful limbs supported the upper structure, enabling bipedal locomotion in an upright position and rotation, flexion, and extension near the hip. Proprioceptive sensors laced the external surface for monitoring speed, location, and orientation in space.

Within nanoseconds, a myriad of data points from the physical world was wirelessly transmitted to a sophisticated neural network. The interconnected web of digital nodes swiftly synthesized the incoming data stream, and through

CHAPTER 1

the use of algorithms, initiated the resuscitation process. By employing cutting-edge machine learning techniques, the system's capacity to collect and integrate information, develop predictive models, choose interventions, and adapt to real-time feedback surpassed any human's cognitive capabilities.

As he drifted in and out of coherent thought, the patient suddenly knew where he was. He heard about this place on the news. It was at a one-of-a-kind institution developing a self-sufficient system for robotic medicine. The technology was called ALDRIS: *Autonomous Learning for Diagnosis, Resuscitation, Imaging, and Surgery.*

It was a strange sensation, being cared for by something that was neither alive nor dead, a creation of human ingenuity that held his fate in its metallic hands.

Under the glaring lights of the resuscitation bay, he lay trapped in a haze of pain and confusion. His voice, once robust, was now a mere whisper, stifled by the cocktail of alcohol, brain trauma, and the metallic taste of blood in his throat. In a primal response, he raised his left arm, a feeble attempt to fend off the looming, mechanical behemoth beside him. But the machine, with its cold, unyielding claw and hook, was unrelenting, pinning him to the table with strength that he had never encountered in his life.

"Is that legal?" whispered a junior paramedic to his partner.

"Yea. When a patient's judgment is impaired, the law permits intervention," the senior explained, her eyes fixed on the scene. "If he's a danger to himself or others, restraint is necessary."

An automatic hatch on the wall unfastened. A door lifted, unveiling a shelf of blood products for trauma patients. As the room's warm air met the refrigerator's chill, water vapor condensed, releasing a misty gust. Simultaneously, a slender metal pole descended from the ceiling, stopping next to the stretcher. A robotic arm selected a bag of dark maroon fluid, hanging it on the pole. As the blood began its journey through the tubing, a sense of vitality, a distant memory of strength, began to seep back into the patient's veins. The sensation was comforting. He was receiving a transfusion.

"O negative blood. The universal donor," the emergency technician commented.

But this momentary relief was short-lived. The trickle in the back of his throat became a steady flow, overwhelming the entranceway to his esophagus and respiratory tract. His pharyngeal reflexes and epiglottis, which typically protect the larynx from food and liquid during swallowing, were failing him, causing him to slowly suffocate from an accumulation of his own blood and dismembered tissue.

Recognizing the compromised airway, the emotionless device quickly took action. One extremity after another propelled it to the head of the stretcher. Using articulated digits to probe the remnants of the man's face, it grasped his cheekbones and effortlessly lifted them. The accident had disconnected the patient's facial bones from his skull.

At that moment, he felt a new, unexpected sensation. A numbing comfort flowed through his veins, mesmerizing him. His vision tunneled, and the world's edges faded into a hazy embrace. It felt as if he hadn't slept in weeks, and he had never been so relaxed. He instinctively tried to reach for his face, but his brain couldn't communicate with his arm. Helpless, he lay paralyzed, a prisoner in his own body. He could not command even the slightest movement, and his

CHAPTER 1

limbs were frozen in a statuesque stillness.

Everything went black, consciousness faded, and there was only nothingness—the end of the experience.

"It just gave him etomidate," the senior paramedic announced, referencing a medication that obliterated consciousness by suppressing neural activity. When coupled with succinylcholine, there was a temporary twitching throughout his body, followed by complete paralysis.

"It's going for the airway."

"Man, it's going to be difficult with all that blood and facial trauma."

At this juncture, the patient was fully sedated. He had once been a vibrant, outgoing persona, but now he was reduced to a lifeless, flaccid shell of his former self. Lying on the stretcher, completely vulnerable, his chances of survival relied entirely on the mechanical contraption looming over him with a blank expression.

The robot was preparing for endotracheal intubation, a fundamental skill for any emergency physician or anesthesiologist. When performed correctly, a curved metal blade, called a laryngoscope, was inserted behind the tongue to facilitate the placement of a breathing tube.

"Here it goes."

The hulking machine bent at the waist and repositioned the patient's head. Articulated digits extended deep into the mouth, manipulated the soft tissue, and depressed the tongue. Infrared light beamed over the neck, while a specialized laryngoscope unfolded and entered the mouth. It scanned back and forth, seeking carbon dioxide through retrograde transillumination. A blinking light showed the pathway to the trachea.

But something was off; the process was not proceeding as smoothly as it should have been. Blood splashed upon the camera, obscuring the detector. Unable to initiate respirations and still without a breathing tube, the patient's oxygen levels dropped to dangerous levels.

"It can't ventilate or intubate," added the paramedic. "This is bad, real bad."

Managing airways was often routine, but this was the exception that defied training, the kind of nightmarish ordeal that some practitioners, despite years of rigorous preparation, never encountered in their careers. Even the most skilled providers could fall victim to adrenaline surges during these high-stakes situations, leading to muddled judgment and impaired performance. But at this particular institution, human error was all but eliminated.

"Now what?"

"Cricothyrotomy."

Unphased by the turn of events, the contraption swiveled to the side of the stretcher, its claw-like appendage gripping the patient's neck with precision. It carefully aligned itself with the patient's anatomy, and after a quick spray of disinfectant, a retractable scalpel emerged. The device expertly carved a three-centimeter vertical incision through the patient's neck tissue, followed by a horizontal cut through the underlying cartilage. His trachea was now exposed to warm air, and blood flowed freely from the surrounding tissue.

The ALDRIS system quickly inserted a breathing tube and secured it to the skin. A robotic limb connected the opposite end of the plastic tubing to a nearby mechanical ventilator, and the patient's oxygen level began to rise, indicating that the procedure was successful.

CHAPTER 1

In the rear of the room, the paramedics let out a sigh of relief. They stood frozen against the wall, honored to witness such revolutionary technology. The crew was speechless, filled with awe but fearful of disrupting the automated resuscitation process with an accidental movement.

The automated device then retreated from the stretcher. A donut-shaped cylinder descended from the ceiling and engulfed the patient, obscuring him from view. Probes attached to his chest wall transmitted vital signs to a wireless receiver on the wall, designed explicitly for cardiac monitoring. Several minutes later, when the patient emerged, a brief written report appeared on the digital screen, providing information for human observers.

Multicompartmental acute intracranial hemorrhage, including acute bilateral subdural hematoma, acute epidural hematoma, and bilateral subarachnoid hemorrhage. Multiple bilateral displaced/depressed calvarial fractures. LaForte Type III fracture.

"That's one of the worst injuries we've ever seen," the medical team whispered among themselves. The radiology results were nothing short of devastating. The brain and facial injuries were beyond repair in most hospitals.

But the ALDRIS system had already initiated its next step. The patient was swiftly transported to the therapeutic hypothermia unit for suspended animation, where his body would be cooled to a staggering fifteen degrees Celsius. This groundbreaking process would induce metabolic standstill, providing a glimmer of hope for the patient's recovery.

Despite initial optimism from animal trials, randomized controlled clinical studies in the early part of the century revealed that induced hypothermia in trauma cases worsened neurological outcomes. Although human brains could survive cryopreservation, the subsequent reanimation stage led to severe degradation of proteins and synapses. Unable to endure the return to normal temperature, these minds resembled those of Alzheimer's patients. In contrast, the neurons of other animals repaired themselves well, showing no neurological damage after reemergence.

In the lab, scientists reduced inflammation in mice by injecting them with hydrogen sulfide. However, due to its toxicity in humans, researchers explored other options. At this groundbreaking facility, it was discovered that iodide, a related element, could act as a protective shield. When introduced to the body, it converted hydrogen peroxide into oxygen and water, effectively reducing inflammation. This element averted free radical oxidative damage and was successfully used in human subjects for the first time in 2037.

Now in 2042, the process of suspended animation provided essential rest and neuroplastic healing. A robotic surgeon would perform delayed resuscitation and reconstruct the patient's facial structures later.

As the paramedics began moving toward the exit, one glanced upward and gestured to his partner.

"Look, there he is."

"Who?"

"The guy who built this place."

Behind a glass enclosure that separated an observation deck from the resuscitation suite, the hospital's founder leaned back nonchalantly in his reclining chair, a nonverbal show of approval. His eyes were weathered from years of clinical experience and bold experimentation. Despite his advanced age, he was ahead of his time, consumed by innovation, with a passion for creating new technologies and

CHAPTER 1

pushing boundaries. His unwavering faith in the machinery was evident as he gripped his cane and slowly exited the room. In his mind, the patient's survival was never in doubt.

Chapter 2

"Your eardrum is red and bulging. It looks like an ear infection," said Dr. Seth Kelley, his voice confident as he examined the patient. The woman frowned, clearly unhappy with the diagnosis. But Seth, a seasoned emergency physician with 15 years of experience, didn't let her reaction faze him. This clinical diagnosis was obvious.

He stood in the cramped and cluttered emergency department hallway at Bayshore General, surrounded by stretchers and the sick and injured who lay upon them. The moans of the afflicted echoed in the tight confines. He couldn't help but feel frustrated at the circumstances in which his patients were forced to receive care, but he couldn't offer them better privacy.

The hospital was simply too small for the growing population it served. Overcrowding had become the norm. Admitted patients were left for days, waiting for beds on the upper floors. Imaging was backlogged for hours. The triage process was haphazard at best, and medication reconciliations were a rarity. Despite the challenges, Seth and his colleagues did their best to provide adequate care. The charge nurses worked tirelessly to manage the chaos, but he couldn't shake the feeling that his patients deserved better.

CHAPTER 2

The clientele came from various backgrounds and had different reasons for seeking treatment. Socioeconomic factors precluded access to adequate primary care, let alone an expensive specialist, so some came several times per month for minor or chronic complaints. Seth's heart sank a little each time he saw a familiar face return, their conditions unchanged or worsened.

Many were well-known to the hospital system, repeatedly admitted for the same diseases or complications of therapy, with severe underlying comorbidities and convoluted treatment courses. Despite their differences, all patients were protected by an unfunded federal law—the Emergency Medical Treatment And Labor Act (EMTALA)—that mandated hospitals to provide a screening exam and stabilization, regardless of their ability to pay.

Seth was tasked with sorting through the endless cascade of new, undifferentiated patients pouring into the department through the ambulance bay and triage. The pace was overwhelming at times. At a minimum, he was responsible for the expeditious diagnosis and treatment of life-threatening conditions, but he frequently went beyond that. With a crowded waiting room full of patients, speed was essential to ensure that those with serious conditions were not left waiting for care. He felt a duty to make space available for them, too.

"Don't you think I need a CT scan?" asked the patient, her voice tinged with frustration. Her words implied a sense of incompetence on his part, suggesting he overlooked something important during his examination. Seth stepped back abruptly, taken aback by the accusatory line of questioning. "My brother thinks I should get one. He's in nursing school."

The patient was a twenty-four-year-old female who presented with ear pain and headache that gradually worsened over the past three days. Her physical exam was consistent with uncomplicated otitis media, easily treated with oral antibiotics and anti-inflammatory medication.

Seth offered a slight smile, the embodiment of professional assurance. "I hear your concerns, truly I do," he began, his tone soothing, "but let me assure you, a CT scan is not needed in your case. Yes, it's a powerful tool in detecting major abnormalities, but it also exposes you to a substantial dose of radiation—we're talking the equivalent of around 2,000 x-rays of an extremity. We need to be careful with that kind of stuff. You're suffering from an ear infection. Uncomfortable, I know, but it's also quite treatable."

"But I just want to make sure," she fired back.

The veteran physician knew there were negative consequences to excessive testing and inappropriate resource utilization. Clinicians who overtested rarely missed a diagnosis; however, this resulted in more harm than good, such as unnecessary exposure to radiation, unintended adverse effects, and departmental congestion. Through years of practice, he honed his clinical gestalt and nearly perfected the delicate art of determining when the benefits of imaging outweighed the risks.

"It could be dangerous for your brain, especially at a young age," Seth warned, his words saturated with genuine concern. However, her mind was already made up, and she seemed visibly irritated. Despite his efforts, the patient's opposition persisted.

"I am not leaving here without that scan. And don't think I'm scared to post about this online," she retorted. "What's

CHAPTER 2

your name again? Dr. K-e-l-l," she spelled out slowly, her eyes squinting to read his identification badge, emphasizing her threat.

"I understand that you're upset, but...."

"Actually, I might just call my lawyer."

Emergency room providers were held to a high standard of never missing a dangerous diagnosis in patients with undifferentiated symptoms. With fleeting patient interactions, they lacked the luxury of conservative management before opting for additional testing. This created a high-risk environment where many clinicians were incentivized to perform low-utility workups to avoid potential litigation and professional sanctions, resulting in higher costs, repetitive testing, and time spent addressing inconsequential incidental findings.

Her threat of a lawsuit didn't bother Seth. He understood that it was common for emergency physicians to be sued, as they often had to make quick decisions with limited information and a high volume of critical patients. Many legal teams lacked medical expertise, relying on paid and biased testimony from non-emergency doctors. Juries with limited scientific literacy awarded compensation to plaintiffs in cases of adverse outcomes, regardless of whether the standard of care was met.

"I'll prescribe Amoxicillin. You should start feeling better in a few days," Seth said, ending the conversation. By remaining firm, he was satisfied with his decision and felt confident in the resolution.

As a scholarly and seasoned provider, Seth consistently aimed to integrate the latest clinical guidelines into his practice, deliver top-quality care, and always advocate for the best interests of his patients. He firmly believed that evidence-based practice should trump defensive medicine and the need to accommodate unreasonable patient expectations. Consequently, he was willing to embrace uncertainty in situations where the risks were minimal. Through deep contemplation of the world's intricacies, Seth had developed a profound understanding of the complexities involved in medical decision-making. As a result, he was ready to face the potential of his own fallibility, willing to admit his mistakes if he believed a course of action served the best interests of his patients at that particular moment.

In the latter portion of his career, he frequently contributed to medical journals, writing on communication techniques and methods for improving the hospital experience. He was a sought-after speaker at conferences to present strategies to enhance the doctor-patient relationship. Since the compensation was meager, he pursued it out of enthusiasm for the subject matter and was dedicated to principles beyond personal gain.

"In a couple of years, I won't need you anymore. I'll just go to the hospital where the robots are," the patient said sharply. The words stung like a thorn in his side.

As he listened, Seth remained the embodiment of professionalism. Yet, in his mind's eye, he was struck by the weight of her words. He considered the possibility that doctors, like so many before them, may one day become yet another profession replaced by the relentless march of artificial intelligence.

Eight years ago, the first theoretical blueprint for a robotic physician was developed by a graduate student, who later sold the patent to a private industry. Soon after, an actual prototype was constructed, and proof-of-concept was established. At first, experimental models were mostly relegated to viral videos and technical trade shows, but the future of healthcare quickly became apparent. Despite Seth's initial reservations, phase one clinical trials examining the safety of new interventions and therapeutics demonstrated no statistical difference in adverse events. Early data from phase two clinical studies, designed to investigate efficacy in small sample sizes, showed non-inferiority in patient-oriented outcomes when treatment was facilitated by a robotic caretaker.

He was now considered a *provider* more than a physician, and the label implied that his role was to meet patient expectations, as misaligned or unrealistic as they may be. Additionally, only discharged patients were given satisfaction surveys, rather than critically ill patients who required more attention, care, and vigilance. For these reasons, Seth knew that continuing to engage with this contentious patient would be self-sabotaging and counterproductive. With increasing competition in the space, he was under immense pressure to meet customer demands or risk being replaced by a mechanical alternative.

"I'll order the scan," he replied reluctantly, turning away from the patient. He felt utterly demoralized.

* * *

Seth was tall and lanky, standing nearly six feet and three inches. Though this gave him an advantageous perspective, allowing him to detect subtle medical findings on the head or back, it also presented its own set of challenges. His stature, coupled with relentless bending, had wreaked havoc on his lower back. It was challenging for him to intubate unless he correctly aligned himself in parallel with the patient's airway.

Years of stress and long shifts had carved deep lines into Seth's face and drained his cheeks of their fullness. But he wore the evidence of his life's work with quiet dignity. Though his hair had begun to thin some six years prior, he had compensated by growing a subtle beard. He used to play sports, but nothing was left physically to show for it. He wasn't the type of doctor who spent his days off rock climbing or running marathons. Instead, he preferred spending time at home with his family, even if it meant being labeled "boring" by his more adventurous colleagues. Seth was reserved at social gatherings, content to let others do the talking, and sidestepped small talk whenever possible.

As he meandered back to his desk, Seth took in the unit's ethos, using his instincts and observations to aid in departmental stewardship. He was attuned to the department's pulse, reading the nurses' faces and the speed of their steps to gauge its overall acuity. The number of stretchers lining the hallways was a surrogate marker for patient volume, and the general temperament of the unit would oscillate with each successful or failed resuscitation. He was understanding of delays in imaging and medication delivery during consecutive trauma alerts and toward the end of long shifts. As an overnight physician, he was privy to the invigorating effects of a midnight meal delivery and the draining pull of exhaustion in the predawn hours. Robotic caretakers, slated to gradually replace human labor in the

CHAPTER 2

coming years, promised to eliminate these shortcomings.

As Seth strolled down the hallway, his eyes were drawn to a disturbing scene. An elderly woman, whose mind had been ravaged by Alzheimer's dementia, struggled to escape the confines of her hospital bed. Due to a recent functional decline, her family could no longer care for her at home, so they dropped her off at the emergency room and refused to pick her up. With the hospital short on ancillary staff, the patient was placed in a protective vest for safety and left unattended as she muttered unintelligibly. The bedsheets were stained with remnants of her soiled diaper. The nurse was occupied with more pressing matters.

In the next room, there was a morbidly obese patient. Her health was a litany of misfortune, a catalog of chronic diseases, including congestive heart failure, pulmonary hypertension, chronic kidney disease, atrial fibrillation, and diabetes. And if that wasn't enough, she had recently undergone a complex aortic valve replacement, further complicating her recovery. A triangular mask was securely fastened to her mouth and nose. Her cardiac function had decompensated to total dependency on respiratory support. Accounting for social determinants of health, she couldn't function independently for more than a few days outside the hospital. Her lifeless eyes rolled back into her head as she inhaled every breath.

He caught a glimpse of a disheveled drug addict, picked up by paramedics on the side of the road after injecting fentanyl, who was given an intranasal spray to reverse her overdose. Her matted, unkempt hair spoke of a life lived on the fringes. Untrimmed fingernails left smudges of black eyeliner as she fiercely wiped away the remnants of a hard night. Despite cheating death, she now shouted obscenities at the nursing staff for not providing enough pain medication. Seth was struck by the cruel irony of it all, by the beautiful potential that lay within, amidst the wreckage of a life lost to addiction. He couldn't help but wonder, what kind of world will her child be born into?

A younger version of himself found the pace exhilarating. Seth was once enthralled by the sights and sounds of the department: sirens wailing in the distance, cardiac monitors beeping over the hum of air conditioners, and the staff shouting precise medical jargon over the whispers of anxious family members. Telephones constantly rang over the sound of unit secretaries typing loudly on their keyboards. Intoxicated patients ranted about their rights to an attorney. The groaning, dry heaving, and nonsensical babble of the delirious were drowned out by consultants chatting about their call schedules. At first listen, it was a symphony of chaos and disarray. But beneath the surface, a secret song of justice played, governed by etiquette, that was only audible to those with the training to hear its framework. The stream of patients was like an eternal river, ebbing and flowing with the weather and day of the week—but never running dry.

At long last, Seth made his way to a small, confined space, about the size of a walk-in closet, and sat down at one of the two computers. The pulsating rhythm of trance music echoed from a portable speaker in the room.

He was not alone in this struggle. His trusted colleague, the seasoned Dr. Kabir Gupta, sat at the adjacent workstation, his fingers dancing across the keyboard fervently. In the dim room, the only source of light came from the flicker of the computer screen. The glow highlighted the rugged outline of Kabir's scruffy beard, and his blue scrubs, once crisp and clean, were now stained with the toil of countless long nights.

The cluttered state of his companion's desk spoke to how he coped with the demands of the profession. Amongst the sea of candy wrappers, popcorn kernels, empty soda cans, and crumpled napkins, Kabir's workspace reflected the varying coping mechanisms employed by medical professionals. Each person had their own way of dealing with the stress and pressure, and the littered desk before him was Kabir's way of staying afloat.

"Hey, where's the med student?" Seth inquired.

"Oh, he asked to go home early," explained Kabir. "Said something about applying for dermatology. He's just checking a box by being here."

Seth grumbled with animosity, "That's not the point. It's about commitment, dedication. Seems like students nowadays lack a solid work ethic."

"You know, my folks used to say the same thing. You're just a bit old-fashioned, Seth. You place your patients above all else, but that's not how it works anymore."

Kabir's mother and father were retired physicians who practiced during an era when the doctor-patient relationship was sacred. Unlike his friend Seth, however, Kabir was not burdened by the weight of financial obligations. This afforded a more harmonious work-life balance, while a significant portion of Seth's paycheck was deducted each month to repay the government.

Seth sighed. "I'm not sure how long I can keep going like this. I know, I say it often, but this time it's different. The volume and acuity are draining."

"Well, it's the fourth time you've said that *this week alone*," replied Kabir. His colleague paused, looking up from his disorderly workstation while chewing on a piece of gum. "Someone's gotta save lives with me at four o'clock in the morning."

"I feel like I haven't made a real impact in weeks. We're just staving off the inevitable, prolonging suffering. And the healthcare system is too broken to truly help anyone in a lasting way."

Privately, Seth struggled with emotional scars from his work. Despite his focus on healing the community, he couldn't help but feel frustration and anger at the systemic issues affecting this profession. In his opinion, the maladjusted individuals who accessed the emergency department at nighttime for non-medical complaints, particularly those who repeatedly returned, suffered from undiagnosed personality disorders and complex socioeconomic determinants. They were casualties of a broken community that he couldn't fix. Each had succumbed to personal demons in different ways and was trapped in a perpetual battle between rehabilitation and relapse.

At times, when the seemingly endless parade of traumatizing encounters accumulated and felt as suffocating as a black cloud, he struggled to repress the frustration and anger at a country that could so casually leave people behind. He was immersed in an underworld preferentially overlooked by the rest of society. As a result, he had become numb to picking up the pieces of violence, exploitation, poverty, discrimination, homelessness, addiction, and undereducation that plagued his workplace. At times, Seth questioned whether he was damaged himself for being well-suited for such a pathological environment.

CHAPTER 2

Despite his heavy burden, Seth pressed forward, driven by a sense of purpose. He channeled the tumultuous emotions into a force for change, using medical activism and health promotion as a way to improve the flawed systems that perpetuated cycles of suffering. Despite the seemingly insurmountable odds, he remained steadfast, driven by an unwavering belief in the inherent goodness of humanity.

He reminded himself, time and time again, that the individuals he encountered each night were but a small and self-selected slice of society. Their struggles and self-destructive behavior should not be used to paint an entire population with a single brush. Night after night, he donned his mantle of duty, arriving early for his shift with stoic resolve, determined to make a difference in the lives of his patients. He guarded his inner demons fiercely, never allowing them to seep into the care he provided. His private turmoil remained just that, private, as he stood as a bastion of strength and compassion, a beacon of hope in a world that often seemed devoid of it.

"Do you remember the day you got accepted to medical school?" Seth inquired.

"Not quite, I was too busy celebrating," joked his colleague.

"Everyone was so proud," Seth went on, his voice full of nostalgia. "All my friends were going into accounting and finance, but there I was, committing to the life of a student for another four years. A diet of ramen noodles and a stack of credit card bills. My family thought I was on my way to change the world. But now, it's a battle just to get out of bed because I know I won't make a dent."

Kabir sighed heavily, his eyes reflecting the same weariness Seth was feeling. "But, Seth, changing the world doesn't exactly pay the bills, does it? And to be completely honest, I haven't felt like I was making any difference for quite some time now. I'm here to do a job, that's all."

His friend was an exceptionally knowledgeable physician who always provided exceptional medical care, but Kabir's bedside manner lacked empathy. He was often straightforward with his patients, particularly when discussing a poor prognosis and palliative treatment options.

In some ways, Seth envied his friend's ability to detach himself emotionally from the job, as it allowed him to make difficult decisions objectively. Yet, even as it allowed Kabir to make tough calls with ease, it also kept him from truly connecting with his patients, from being a source of comfort and solace in their hour of need. In that way, the two friends complemented each other in their strengths and weaknesses, bound together by their shared passion for the art and science of medicine.

"Maybe a transition to urgent care or administration might do the trick. Or even... switching to days?" Seth muttered to himself as he contemplated his options.

"You, on day shifts?" Kabir retorted with a chuckle. "You wouldn't last a week, buddy. And urgent care? How many cases of upper respiratory infections can you tolerate in a day?"

"Five or six," Seth quipped back swiftly, a spark of humor in his eyes as if he had genuinely weighed the monotonous alternative. "And in administration, well, I'd have to say goodbye to the beard, and we both know that's not happening."

The two men shared a laugh and continued typing. Seth reached for an energy drink, hoping the sharp taste would jolt his weary senses awake. Yet, despite his best efforts, his

CHAPTER 2

eyelids were becoming heavy with sleep, his concentration wavering in the early morning hours. This marked his eighth consecutive night of work.

"You know, a friend of mine struck gold by dealing robots on the black market," Kabir offered, his voice casual. "Selling to affluent families, private clients who can't be bothered to wait for FDA approval."

"That's not for me," Seth asserted, his voice firm. "I went into emergency medicine to help anyone, anytime, irrespective of their financial means or the life choices that brought them here."

Kabir nodded, adding in a softer tone, "But you can't help those who aren't willing to help themselves, Seth."

With groundbreaking advancements on the horizon, the implications were far-reaching and profound. The elites of academia and venture capitalism marveled at the limitless potential of these technologies, their imaginations running wild with the possibilities. But while they rejoiced, others decried the unequal access to these life-saving innovations, reserved only for the wealthy and privileged. The Food and Drug Administration faced a storm of criticism for their sluggish approval process and limitations on access to care, leading to a thriving market for off-label use in the homes of the wealthy. Without widespread authorization for use in hospitals and clinics, these machines became symbols of economic disparity, coveted objects of luxury only attainable by those with the means to purchase them from exorbitant, unregulated vendors. The divide between those with access to cutting-edge healthcare and those without only grew wider, a constant reminder of the imbalance in our society.

In addition to robotic physicians, industrialized nations

embraced a plethora of innovations in the field of medicine, including the use of robotic physicians, nanomedicine, gene therapy, augmented reality, remote monitoring, and even the printing of three-dimensional organs. Thanks to these breakthroughs, infectious diseases and genetic disorders were nearly eradicated in society's most educated, affluent, and scientifically-literate segments. This resulted in a staggering increase in life expectancy, with the average person living almost 100 years. Many elderly patients were cared for by their still healthy and functional parents.

Conversely, small splinters of the population emerged that were mistrustful and hesitant about cutting-edge treatments. The winds of misinformation whipped through social media and biased news outlets, fanning the flames of ignorance with polarizing snippets. A mob of unqualified opinions was led astray by self-serving leaders with simplistic answers to nuanced conversations. The fervor of populism swept through communities unschooled in the intricacies of science, leaving a trail of illness and poverty in its wake. Frequently sick with preventable diseases and unable to work, this subset of the population plummeted into destitute living conditions, their potential for prosperity lost in the shadows of their own misconceptions.

As wealthy patients privately sought the precision and convenience of robotic care, hospitals saw a declining number of paying customers. Still burdened with the unfunded mandate of universal care, many institutions suffered non-sustainable increasing financial losses as emergency departments were overrun with uninsured and impoverished patients. In anticipation of the widespread adoption of automated care, management firms cut back on staffing,

CHAPTER 2

leading to overworked human providers and deteriorating working conditions, reduced demand, declining salaries, and uncertainty about the future.

Seth clicked through his computer and opened a new chart to document his latest patient encounter. He took his time, carefully crafting each word and recording every detail with purpose. Nearly fifteen minutes of charting time was needed for every five minutes of patient interaction—another inefficiency that could be resolved by implementing robotic doctors. He typed slowly and methodically, which disadvantaged him compared to more recent, tech-savvy residency graduates, let alone a fully-automated physician. The clock ticked away as Seth labored over his documentation, fully aware that the threat of automation loomed larger with each passing day.

There was a vibration in his pocket. It was a peculiar hour to receive notifications. Seth assumed it was too early for a text message, so he glanced at the screen on his cell phone. With a gentle touch, he unlocked it and beheld an email that would alter the course of his life forever.

Job Opening. Premier West Hospital. Overnight Physician Needed.

He had heard whispers at department meetings about a private investment company building a new hospital on the city's outskirts. They spoke of robotic care and advanced technology, but Seth remained ignorant of the details, making the extent of progress a mystery.

Just as he was lost in contemplation, an electrocardiogram appeared before him, jolting him back to reality. With a steady hand, Seth signed the document with practiced ease, passing it back to the waiting technician. Kabir looked over without making eye contact. He hesitated before speaking, taking a minute to consider his words carefully.

"How's your wife doing?"

"We've got an appointment with the neurologist this afternoon, so sleep isn't on the agenda," Seth admitted. Exhaustion pulled at his eyelids, but he shook off the fatigue. "Ah, the urine results for Room 5 are back."

The doctor rose from his chair after abruptly ending the conversation. He was reluctant to continue this line of questioning and eager to discharge one of his remaining patients. With automation on the horizon, short disposition times were an important metric and essential for job security.

The patient in Room 5 was a 65-year-old female with an extensive list of comorbidities. She had a heart that had undergone bypass surgery, a body that battled diabetes, a liver that fought hepatitis, lungs that had once struggled with pneumonia, a stomach that had bled, a conduction system that danced to the irregular beat of atrial fibrillation, and a chest that had been drained of pleural effusions. Seth had been eagerly awaiting the results of her urinalysis, the key to unlocking the mystery of her fatigue and weakness. It showed 6-10 white blood cells and +1 leukocyte esterase.

Every medical practitioner understood the two components of urine testing: a urinalysis and a urine culture. A urinalysis screened for surrogate markers of infection, while the culture took several days to yield results by observing microbial growth in a laboratory.

Seth knew that no test was absolute, and the art of diagnosis was a delicate balance between sensitivity and specificity.

CHAPTER 2

Sensitivity was about catching every case of a disease. A urinalysis fell into this category, a screening test prone to false positives. On the other hand, specificity was a measure of how well a test correctly identified individuals who did not have a disease. A urine culture, with its precise methodology, was best used to confirm a diagnosis. In the fast-paced world of emergency medicine, sensitivity reigned supreme. The priority to avoid missing a severe diagnosis outweighed the risk of false alarms.

Urinary tract infections existed on a spectrum of disease, much like other pathological states. Even the simplest diagnostics, such as a pregnancy or flu test, reduced a qualitative finding to a binary result. It was a necessary compromise for both patient understanding and the practicalities of billing. Yet, the ambiguity of a urinalysis often left room for interpretation, causing a chasm between what was certain and what was merely a possibility. Seth longed to bridge this gap, to provide diagnoses that would truthfully reflect the intricacies of his profession, to speak not in absolutes, but in gentle nuances like *possible migraine* or *unlikely appendicitis*.

With incomplete data and the impracticality of re-evaluating the patient later, the decision to initiate treatment based on the results of a urinalysis was an imperfect science. The clinician had to weigh the benefit of starting empiric treatment against the dangers of unforeseen consequences. In the case of pharmaceuticals, consideration needed to be given to possible reactions, adverse side effects, and antimicrobial resistance. Every patient was unique, every situation different, and the management was variable between providers, patients, and circumstances.

Seth sat down with the patient to discuss the results of

her urinalysis. Given her absence of urinary symptoms and allergies to many common oral antibiotics, he considered it appropriate to hold off on initiating treatment. He advised her to follow up with her primary care provider as an outpatient and return to the hospital for persistent or worsening symptoms. He then opened the conversation for any questions the patient had.

"What are some symptoms that I should watch… " the woman began to ask, but her question was interrupted by the ringing of Seth's zone phone. He answered it and was summoned to the trauma bay. Paramedics were transporting two gunshot victims, and he had precious few seconds to prepare the trauma bay before their arrival. Although he felt remorse for not having enough time to fully address her concerns, Seth's duty was to optimize the odds of survival for the incoming patients in dire need. As he rushed off, the woman freed herself from the cardiac monitor, leaving behind the comfort of her bed, and limped out of the department before receiving her discharge paperwork.

Chapter 3

After enduring the grueling twelve-hour shift at Bayshore General, Seth found himself unable to surrender immediately to the beckoning comforts of home. An ever-growing backlog of charting shackled him to his workstation for another hour, as he dutifully completed his documentation before signing off.

For Seth, stepping into the outside world was like surfacing from the depths of a disturbing nightmare. He would inhale deeply and relish in the sweet summer air as it filled his weary lungs. It was an invitation for him to remember that beyond the pale, fluorescent lights, there existed a reality much more diverse, rich, and invigorating. Now, distanced by hours and miles from his trying ordeals, the refreshing breeze served as a vibrant counterpoint to the weighty remembrances he bore.

Despite the exhaustion, his mind would relentlessly review the night's events, searching for gaps in his care or areas for improvement. Such contemplation was a double-edged sword; it meant revisiting the shadows of the night, the suffering, and the violence that inhabited the hospital corridors after sunset. Memories would storm back, raw and urgent, refusing to be dismissed. The horrors of the overnight events retained a chilling realism that he couldn't shake off, knowing that the abhorrent and melancholic scenes were as authentic as the ground beneath his feet.

As the sun crept above the horizon, his plantar fascia throbbed from treading on withered insoles crying out for replacement. There was no feeling comparable to the release of tension that accompanied the removal of his shoes after a draining shift. He felt the burdensome weight of the day lift from his shoulders as he crossed the threshold of his home, hurriedly discarding his sneakers and hospital-issued scrubs. The remnants of his taxing profession, marked by blood stains and the lingering scent of illness, were unceremoniously cast into the washing machine without a second glance.

But as his body found temporary respite, his mind and spirit remained drained, leaving him incapable of offering his family the warm, effusive greetings they deserved. Once a man brimming with life and energy, he had been whittled down to a mere shadow of his former self. While the rest of the world basked in the warm embrace of the morning sun, savoring cups of coffee and hearty breakfasts, Seth was preparing himself for the closing act of his day. A creature of the night, his routine had, by necessity, become a mirror image of the diurnal world.

"Hello? Anyone up?" Seth bellowed upon entering. The interior of his two-story home was a tapestry of modern bohemian decor, its walls woven with rich textures and earthy hues. He added to the towering pile of mail on the dining room table. It was a haphazard collection of unpaid medical bills from a never-ending barrage of clinics and hospital stays.

CHAPTER 3

"Daddy!" The exuberant shout echoed through the house, and there at the head of the stairs stood his daughter, her hair cascading around her shoulders, glowing with the radiance of the morning sun. Abigail was his mirror image, from the shape of her nose to the curve of her smile. But it was her bright hazel eyes that told a different tale—they were a gift from her mother.

"Abigail!" Seth's voice softened at the sight of her, a smile forming on his weary face.

At just ten years old, her insatiable curiosity and surprising intellect were already beyond her years. She descended the stairs, her small arms open wide for an expected hug. "How was work, Daddy?" she asked, tilting her head to one side.

"It was a long one, Abby, and busier than usual," Seth confessed. His gaze softened as he looked at her. "But I'm home now. Let's have breakfast together, shall we?"

With a joyous skip in her step, Abigail made her way to the dining room. Seth followed her, reaching for the cereal box and a carton of milk, and pouring a generous serving for his wide-eyed little girl.

"Daddy, will you be awake when I come home from school?"

His heart clenched at the hopeful note in her voice. "I'll be home, sweetheart, but probably catching up on sleep. I have to work again tonight."

As Abigail lost herself in the world of morning cartoons, Seth quietly withdrew from the room. He climbed the spiral staircase, each step bringing him closer to the sanctuary of the bedroom. There, he was met by the sight of his wife, Rebecca, reclined amidst the tangled sheets of their bed. Once an avid runner, her legs were now atrophied, and her eyes sunken.

"Hey." Her voice was soft, carrying a hint of fatigue.

"How are you feeling, Bec?" Seth asked.

"Tired, but okay," she answered. "I don't want to complain. I'm always your last patient of the day."

Their shared laughter was soft, a bittersweet melody that played through the room, a reminder of the love they shared and the challenges they faced together.

About two years prior, Rebecca had been blindsided by a sudden, distressing distortion in her central vision. Over the span of a few disconcerting days, predominantly red hues began to blur. Objects in motion seemed to approach her in unsettling elliptical paths, while her once graceful coordination became awkward. As an emergency physician, Seth's instincts were honed to seek out the most pressing dangers, and with a mounting fear of an occipital stroke or a lurking malignancy, he whisked her away to the hospital in a frenzy of concern.

At Bayshore General, she underwent a magnetic resonance imaging (MRI) exam, a non-invasive procedure that produced high-resolution images of the body's tissues. During the scan, she lay stationery within a large cylindrical magnet. Radio waves briefly knocked her hydrogen nuclei out of alignment, while a watchful computer compiled cross-sectional pictures of her internal structures. Although the MRI was generally considered safe because it avoided the use of ionizing radiation, it was not suitable for individuals with internal metallic objects like pacemakers. This was because the intense magnetic fields could interfere with their functionality and pose risks to nearby metal objects.

"Has Abigail finished getting ready for school?" asked Rebecca. Her kindhearted personality persisted despite her

CHAPTER 3

physical limitations.

"She's having breakfast as we speak. I'll take her to the bus stop once she's done," Seth assured, shouldering the responsibilities at home in addition to his demanding job.

He could vividly remember when he read the impression from the radiologist's report of Rebecca's MRI. *Multiple white matter lesions that are consistent with demyelinating disease.* The on-call neurologist diagnosed her with multiple sclerosis a few hours later.

In a state of disbelief, Rebecca absorbed the neurologist's diagnosis. Once a protective entity, her immune system had turned against her, viciously attacking the core of her nervous system—the myelin sheaths responsible for cellular communication. Signs and symptoms varied widely, contingent upon the type of nerve affected and the severity of the damage. While disease-modifying therapies existed, a definitive cure remained elusive.

Over the course of the subsequent year, Rebecca's condition fluctuated erratically. She had both good and bad days, but a constant decline loomed. The exacerbations became progressively more severe, each more debilitating than the last. High-dose bursts of steroids offered a glimmer of hope, but even with physical therapy, she could never fully recover her previous level of functioning. At her current point in the disease's progression, chronic motor weakness in her lower extremities had taken hold, rendering her wheelchair-dependent.

Despite her immunosuppressed state, Seth continued working to pay medical bills. Day after day, he donned the suffocating mask, a symbol of the pandemics that plagued their world, as he worked tirelessly to provide for her.

With a tender touch, Seth reached under her legs and lifted her, putting his already-strained muscles under further duress. Carrying her down the stairs, he was a symbol of strength and love, determined to care for her every need. He flipped the television to the morning news as she settled into her wheelchair.

"Mommy helped me with my homework last night," Abigail proudly proclaimed.

"Is that so?" Seth responded, a warm smile on his face. "What are you learning about?"

"The solar system! Did you know that Jupiter is the biggest planet and Mercury is the smallest?" Abigail looked expectantly at her father, eager to share her newfound knowledge. But Seth's attention had already shifted to the television.

"Yet another protest was held yesterday at city hall, as local citizens are demanding early access to robotic doctors. So when can we expect approval? We'll cover that story and more, right after the break," announced the news anchor, slightly stumbling over the teleprompter script.

Seth's patience snapped—a rare departure from his usual composure—and he hit the mute button with more force than necessary. At the sudden movement, Abigail flinched, her excited chatter fading away. Quietly, she abandoned her half-eaten breakfast, placed her dish in the sink, and slipped on her shoes by the front door.

"Seth." Rebecca's voice cut through the tension. She looked at him, her eyes soft and pleading. "She doesn't understand."

He shot back, a frustrated edge to his words, "I don't know what we're going to do, Bec. I heard there are some private equity firms hiring in more remote areas of the country.

CHAPTER 3

Maybe we should consider moving... to Nebraska?"

"We can't pull Abigail out of school now, Seth," Rebecca argued gently. "She's at a crucial age. She's just starting to make friends."

Seth took a seat and powered on his laptop. The day's tasks loomed before him. It was a never-ending list of responsibilities and obligations. Fees for his professional organizations were long overdue, but he was reluctant to pay the exorbitant charges. Their leadership was sheltered from the front lines, far removed from the visceral struggles of tending to critical patients. Administrative status had rendered them out of touch with the grueling realities of the profession.

But as he scrolled through his emails, the job opening at Premier West Hospital again caught his eye. Unlike the barrage of irrelevant job postings cluttering his inbox, this one seemed personal. Now free from the distractions of his demanding shift, Seth could give the posting the attention it deserved.

Job Opening. Premier West Hospital. Overnight Physician Needed. Dear Dr. Kelley: We seek a medical director for nocturnal administrative oversight. You meet our minimum requirement of board certification in emergency or internal medicine with 5+ years of clinical experience in direct patient care. Hands-on training in artificial intelligence operations will be provided. We look forward to hearing from you.

Artificial intelligence? The institution was rumored to be exploring robotic medicine, but he assumed that the machine's actions were following preprogrammed scripts. *If this, then do that.* But as he dug deeper, a hint of something more tantalizing caught his eye. The email hinted at autonomous thinking, suggesting a future where computers could make their own determinations, unshackled from the constraints of algorithms.

Seth sat in awe, his mind grappling with the unfathomable concept of true artificial intelligence. The rapid advancement of automation had already transformed countless industries, seamlessly weaving its way into the fabric of the modern workplace. Still, he assumed robots would always operate under the guidance of humans, serving as assistants rather than acting independently. If there was one job that could never be fully automated, it was the work of a physician.

But what if the machines at this hospital were capable of more? Could they be trusted to explore the complexities of a medical history, conduct a meticulous physical examination, evaluate many treatment options, and determine the best course of action with clinical precision? The thought was staggering.

Seth stared at the email on his laptop screen, struggling to grasp the significance of this revolutionary idea. A career change had been on his mind, and this was an opportunity to participate in cutting-edge developments in healthcare. It was far from his comfort zone, but perhaps he needed a new challenge. Without further consideration, he was intrigued. Reinvigorated, Seth's fingers flew across the keyboard to compose a cover letter. And just like that, the application was sent.

* * *

CHAPTER 3

The melodic trill of Seth's alarm signaled the start of another day. His routine for getting ready for work was methodical. In 15 years, he was never late or called out sick. The scrape of a razor, the rush of water from the shower, the rustle of scrubs as he dressed. Coffee and breakfast with Rebecca at dinnertime. He listened to the day's news while transported to work by his self-driving air mobility craft, a technology now ubiquitous in personal transportation vehicles. His familiar path to work was lined with towering oaks and maples, their leaves rustling gently in the evening breeze.

In the ever-evolving landscape of medicine, one tradition remained steadfast and sacred—the art of signouts. The departing physician would meet with the oncoming reinforcement and report the active patients' presenting symptoms, workup, and expected disposition. Some of their colleagues would engage in spirited debates, delving into the intricacies of medical decision-making. But Seth approached signouts with a different mindset, one of grace and understanding. He accepted each patient as they transitioned to his care, embracing the opportunity to engage with his colleagues in passing.

His fellow physicians were a motley crew, each with eccentricities and unique quirks, but Seth relished their conversations. He enjoyed their company, and he cherished these moments of camaraderie. Their collective triumphs and heartbreaks served as a reminder that, in the end, the only opinions that truly mattered were those of his colleagues, who shared the same struggles and victories in that hallowed space where life and death hung in the balance.

After reviewing his signouts, Seth began his usual tour of the department. In an isolation room, a recurring weekly visitor, known for his episodes of acute psychosis, was found naked. He was smearing feces on the walls after consuming a hallucinogen. The patient's eyes conveyed a sense of fear and confusion while the nurses scrambled to subdue him. Their attempts, however, proved ineffective as the patient became increasingly uncontrollable, writhing in spasms and convulsions. Consequently, he was strapped to a barren bed and placed in all four-point restraints, while the security guards wrapped a spit hood around his head to prevent biting and spitting at the ancillary staff.

"Cliff is back," a nurse bemoaned at the grizzly sight. "Fourth visit this week."

Meanwhile, an alcoholic patient expelled bloody vomit into a bucket. A family huddled in the nearby consolation room, desperate for news, their eyes filled with fear and uncertainty. In another corner, a homeless woman sat quietly, a victim of violence and theft, her last dollars taken from her in a brutal assault. A police officer released a drunk driver after he deceptively claimed to have suicidal thoughts. Another person was back for his third overdose this week, followed by an otherwise healthy twenty-two-year-old complaining of vaginal discharge. She was already upset about the prolonged wait time.

"Patient in Room 6 is back for multiple seizures related to noncompliance," Seth informed the on-call neurologist. "He claims to be taking his antiepileptic medication as prescribed, but the drug levels are undetectable."

Amidst these tumultuous times, filled with hyperbole and erroneous extrapolations, Seth sought solace in medicine. Here, within the hospital walls, the realm of reason reigned supreme. Objective measures and stringent testing separated

CHAPTER 3

truth from fiction. Only verifiable evidence, such as the glomerular filtration rate, could confirm a diagnosis of renal failure. A mere urine drug screen swiftly unmasked those who attempted to deceive.

For Seth, the scientific method was a beacon of logic in a sea of uncertainty. He found comfort in academia, where a rational approach was always the norm. Every treatment prescribed was weighed against its potential risks. Randomized, controlled studies served as the ultimate arbitrator. When new data emerged, it underwent meticulous examination, with updated policies and procedures implemented only after thorough scrutiny. This framework was governed by a bedrock of high-quality, replicable evidence—impervious to the whims of individual agendas or biased anecdotes.

Yet despite this paradigm, numbers weren't everything. While data provided important information, Seth knew his craft had an artistic balance, and each person had an individual narrative. It was not uncommon for people to be discharged with positive results, especially if it was a chronic and stable finding. At the same time, patients with negative workups were sometimes admitted for further testing if warranted by clinical suspicion. He understood that human beings were complex and multifaceted, with their emotional and psychological states inseparably linked to physical well-being.

Once settled at his workstation, Kabir swiveled his chair towards Seth, casting a tentative glance his way.

"Listen, Seth," he began, his voice heavy with an undertone of regret. "I hate to dump this on you at the start of your shift, but I thought you should know." He paused, drawing in a breath before plunging ahead. "Remember that 65-year-old woman? The one with generalized weakness you sent home last night?"

A jolt of recognition shot through Seth. He remembered her, clear as day.

Kabir took a moment, his gaze somber. "Well, she came back. Arrived in septic shock and... she didn't make it. She coded upstairs."

In the medical vernacular, a *coded patient* signifies a person in cardiac arrest. The term originates from hospital codes, a system used by staff to communicate emergencies discreetly, without alarming visitors.

Seth felt disbelief and remorse as he lowered his head into his hand. Most physicians enter the medical field driven by a desire to improve health and promote healing. Letting down a patient and their family, whom they had promised to care for, was painful for any healthcare provider. Though he wanted to reach out to the family, he understood that any expression of remorse could be misinterpreted as an admission of guilt or medical error.

His attention shifted to the medical decision-making aspect of the case. Had he missed something on the chest x-ray? Had a crucial result slipped through the cracks?

This mistake was indeed uncharacteristic for Seth. He was known for meticulously examining each patient's workup before making well-informed decisions about their care. When confronted with the inevitable trade-off between speed and accuracy in the emergency department, Seth chose to prioritize compassion and precision over attending to a large volume of patients. This commitment, which defied the pressures of for-profit medicine, often led to him falling behind the pace of his colleagues.

CHAPTER 3

As the realization of the miscalculation settled upon him, professional implications loomed on the horizon. The mere thought of weeks spent sifting through endless emails and peer reviews, all while the threat of legal action hung heavy in the air, sent a shiver down his spine. He knew all too well that his position as one of the less productive providers in the department left him vulnerable to vulturous politics. In such situations, the opinion of his medical management seemed trivial, a mere footnote in the grand scheme of things. All that mattered was the negative outcome.

In the early years of his career, Seth was admittedly a rather fault-finding, hypercritical physician. Like many people, he wanted to understand the underlying causes of events in the world. Following Rebecca's diagnosis, however, he was forced to confront the role of chance in the trajectory of life. It was not uncommon for hospital patients, particularly in the emergency room, to suffer inequitable morbidity or mortality, despite optimal care. After all, this facility was where the sickly and frail congregated, and not all lives were equally salvageable. It was a somber reality that he could no longer ignore.

As time passed, Seth grew to acknowledge the bitter reality that tragedy could strike at any moment. He harbored no illusions of a divine explanation for the senseless events that unfolded before him. Instead, he accepted the notion that terrible things could happen to good people, while society's most nefarious members could live forever. It was simply the way of the world.

"Did I miss something in the workup?" Seth asked, seeking corroboration of his medical management from his knowledgeable and candid colleague. His heart yearned for validation that the standard of care had been upheld, which, at this juncture, would be the most favorable scenario.

Kabir maintained a sympathetic yet neutral tone. "Look, her urine culture came back positive, but there were no antibiotics in her discharge orders. She had subtle bandemia on her differential. Seth, you were juggling 16 patients on your board. Mistakes happen."

"Nobody cares about the circumstances," he fired back.

"I get it, Seth, I do," Kabir replied, holding up his hands in a conciliatory gesture. "But remember, two of those cases were traumas, one was a stroke alert. Then you had that angioedema case and the stubborn surgeon who wouldn't take your patient with the perforated bowel to the operating room. That's a hell of a load for anyone to handle at once."

In the world of emergency medicine, there was an unwritten rule: asking for help was a sign of weakness, regardless of acuity or volume. It was a flaw only the inept displayed. As challenging as the workload became, Seth carried on, even if it meant becoming overwhelmed with too many critical tasks.

While Kabir's sympathy was appreciated, Seth was forewarned of an imminent brand of physician. The age of the artificially intelligent robotic doctors had dawned, their precise calculations and tireless energy rendering them immune to the pitfalls of distraction, exhaustion, and burnout that plagued the humans.

Uncertainty and vulnerability coursed through Seth's veins, but perseverance was an unyielding trait amongst emergency room physicians. The weight of mistakes could crush even the most experienced doctors, but through the years, Seth learned to let go of cases and move on as quickly

CHAPTER 3

as new patients arrived at triage. The key was to remain impartial, neutral, and free of emotional bias—for every patient deserved a fair and just provider.

He glanced at the track board on his screen. It was a growing sea of names, all vying for his attention, all needing his expertise. Some required immediate assistance, others with seemingly minor complaints. Overwhelmed, he felt like a lifeguard thrust into a tsunami.

In taking a deep, mindful breath, Seth could block out the mounting pressures, relentless distractions, and ever-increasing expectations. The moment of tranquility allowed him to focus entirely on the next task. And just like that, another draining overnight shift commenced as he opened his next patient's chart.

Through the long night, Seth moved from one patient to the next, each one a new challenge, a new story. Time blurred as he worked. When his shift finally ended with the light of dawn, his mind was already shifting from the demands of the hospital to the quieter, personal moments awaiting at home.

After arriving home the following day, Seth walked Abigail to the bus stop. It was a feeling of mixed emotions as he watched her walk away, filled with pride for her growth and accomplishments, yet aching with a sense of loss as she took these incremental steps toward independence. He kissed her goodbye and watched as she happily boarded the bus. Maybe all isn't wrong with the world, he thought.

As the school bus drove away, Seth took sleep medication, hoping to quiet his racing mind. A few minutes later, his head landed on the pillow. Despite the sunlight filtering through his bedroom window, he was asleep within minutes.

Days turned to weeks, and Seth struggled to muster the

same enthusiasm he once had for his profession. The endless parade of patients came and went. A shell of his former self, he could only go through the motions. His affect was as lifeless as those who expired in the department.

The shifts blended together, and soon he lost track of time. There was no distinction between weekdays and weekends, no sense of purpose beyond the monotonous routine of his job. Unable to rekindle the passion he once had for his profession, he was left emotionally distant and nihilistic. His approach became robotic, and the irony was not lost on him.

Suddenly, Seth was jolted awake by his cell phone ringing, and a sense of disorientation washed over him. He couldn't tell what time it was—all he knew was that he had only drifted off to sleep after a grueling shift. These precious hours of rest were the only time he had to recharge and gather his strength for the next round.

He glanced at his call log and saw that an unknown number had tried calling him three times. His heart rate quickened as he wondered what could be so urgent. Was he late for work? Had something terrible happened to one of his patients? With trembling fingers, he fumbled for his phone, his mind racing with all the possible scenarios playing out on the other end of the line. But then, with a deep breath, he answered the call and waited for the voice on the other end to speak.

"Hello?"

"Is this Dr. Seth Kelley?" asked the older man on the other end of the line, his voice eager despite its gruff tone.

"Yes, speaking," Seth responded. "May I know who's calling?"

"This is Dr. Ian Winter," the man announced, the huskiness in his voice unable to mask his excitement. "I'm calling from

CHAPTER 3

Premier West Hospital. If you have a moment, I'd be very interested in discussing an opportunity with you."

Chapter 4

William Crane was an awkward child who struggled to find comfort in his scrawny frame. He walked unsteadily, like a fawn taking its first steps. Oversized, cracked glasses engulfed his youthful face, which was sprinkled with freckles and covered by tangled, unwashed hair. He dressed in hand-me-down clothes. Each time he ventured out, his feet slapped the ground through worn-out shoes.

His family's mobile home, with its faded blue paint and rusted metal trim, was a relic from decades past. It had been manufactured long before rigorous health and safety standards were implemented, but they could scarcely afford the modernizations it needed. Nestled atop wheels, it was a wanderer's retreat, a sanctuary that spoke of independence and self-reliance, a patchwork of bitter and sweet memories. But for every beam of light that shone through its windows, a shadow lurked beneath that whispered of hardships endured.

The image of his father, drunk for the first time he could remember, was etched in his mind. The man who had once been his hero stumbled into the cramped confines of the mobile home, slurring his words in an intoxicated stupor. He moved sluggishly, eyes dull. The oppressive stench of alcohol

CHAPTER 4

permeated the air, and the modest living space seemed to contract as his father's foreboding presence loomed larger.

On occasion, his emotions would spiral out of control, plunging him into an unbridled rage. Clenching his fists so tightly that his knuckles turned white, his face would flush with anger, veins throbbing at his temples. William, caught in the storm of his father's fury, weathered relentless, punishing blows. The physical violence was undeniably brutal, but the emotional scars ran even deeper. Each cruel strike chipped away at what was left of his childhood innocence, battering his body and spirit. Days turned into weeks in a repetitive cycle of fear and sadness. He couldn't understand why his father succumbed to the temptation of drinking, unable to keep himself from hurting those he loved.

Through it all, the family remained nomadic, journeying from town to town in pursuit of minimum-wage jobs to stave off hunger. Like countless others displaced by rising sea levels, the forces of climate change compelled his family to seek refuge in the northern states, where his father shoveled snow into the early morning hours before entering an inebriated slumber.

It was a fateful morning when tragedy struck. After returning from grueling labor, his father turned on the propane heater and sought solace on the sofa as William went out to play. Unbeknownst to him, the mobile home's vents were buried under thick snow, and the furnace's exhaust was dangerously close to the intake. As his parents slept, they breathed in a deadly gas, colorless, tasteless, and odorless.

William arrived home to find his parents slumped over in unnatural positions, unresponsive to his desperate calls. A ghostly pallor had settled upon their faces, and an icy chill radiated off their lifeless skin. Their mouths hung slightly agape with dry, cracked lips. An hour later, the unthinkable was confirmed: his parents were dead.

The culprit was carbon monoxide toxicity, a silent killer. Formed by the incomplete burning of hydrocarbons, this compound was a toxic constituent of the smoke they inhaled. With merciless efficiency, it had wreaked havoc at the cellular level, exacting a grim toll on its unsuspecting victims.

The concept of death was difficult for William's young mind to grasp. He was tormented by vivid flashbacks, plagued by the effects of post-traumatic stress disorder. A revolving door of well-intentioned counselors offered assistance, but their efforts proved futile, as they could not alleviate the crushing weight of his memories. He blamed himself, thinking that perhaps he could have intervened, or done something, anything, to save his parents.

Like his father, William learned to swallow his sorrow by drinking. At first, it was a well-kept secret. He would sneak a flask into work, taking small sips throughout the day to keep the tremors at bay. But as the months wore on, the secret became harder to keep. There were missed meetings, unexplained absences, and erratic behavior that couldn't be ignored. He drank to numb the pain, forget the loneliness, and silence the deafening quiet in his empty home. His alcohol addiction grew, and with it, his health rapidly declined. What started as an occasional recourse turned into a dire necessity. His ruddy complexion faded to an unhealthy pallor, and his frame shrank, reflecting the ravages of his self-destruction.

On a seemingly uneventful afternoon, as the sunlight filtered through the dusty windows of the local bookstore

CHAPTER 4

where he worked, William collapsed to the floor. After a week in the hospital, he woke up to find a wire emanating from his abdomen, leading to a machine whirring softly by his side. The doctors diagnosed him with alcoholic cardiomyopathy, a direct result of his heavy drinking. His heart was failing, weakened from years of abuse.

His only chance of survival was an intervention as drastic as it was high-tech: the implantation of a Left Ventricular Assist Device (LVAD). This sophisticated piece of technology would soon become his constant companion, working tirelessly in synchrony with his faltering heart. It consisted of several components, including an axial pump, a motor, a percutaneous driveline, and a battery-powered controller housed outside the body.

Post-surgery, as William lay in his hospital bed staring at the reflective surface of the LVAD, he came to a profound realization. He'd been given a second chance, a shot at redemption, a lifeline to escape the abyss he'd willingly stepped into. He was not ready to surrender. He wanted to reclaim his life.

Coming to terms with his situation, he recognized the need to confront his inner demons. With a mixture of apprehension and determination, he began to attend Alcoholics Anonymous meetings in a neighboring town, far enough away from familiar faces to feel a sense of anonymity, but close enough to feel that it was a step towards home.

At the meetings, William became a constant presence, finding strength in shared stories of sorrow. The tales of grief, despair, and, most importantly, resilience resonated deeply within him. Although he was an attentive listener, absorbing the wisdom and experiences of those around him, he often retreated into his own thoughts and memories. He mostly kept to himself, a quiet observer on the periphery, reluctant to share his own story.

Learning to cope without alcohol was a daily battle, but it was one he was determined to win. His parents absence was a deafening silence in his life, a gap that once seemed impossible to bridge. The temptation of liquor, with its empty promises of relief and escape, often beckoned. But he was steadfast, gradually realizing that it only provided a fleeting numbness, not the healing he so desperately sought.

While still in recovery, William treated his newly implanted apparatus with the utmost attention and care. He religiously tended to the batteries, charging them overnight and inserting a new power source each morning. Aware that even a slight mishap could dislodge the spinning pump in his heart or the delicate wires traversing his chest, he chose seclusion, safeguarding himself and the gadget sustaining him.

However, despite his vigilance, the now-reclusive man couldn't ignore the disturbing changes in his physical well-being. Fluid seeped from the creases of his swollen shins, leaving behind damp patches on his clothes and furniture. He would run his fingers over the skin, feeling the tautness. His weight steadily increased, despite no significant changes in his diet or activity level. Even the slightest movements, such as rising from his recliner, left him gasping for breath.

Fearing that his precious device was malfunctioning, he summoned an ambulance. The urgency of his situation was clear; he needed medical intervention before things took a turn for the worse.

Intrigued by the impassioned debates he encountered on his morning news, William sought an institution that could

CHAPTER 4

provide cutting-edge solutions for his condition. Eager to experience the marvels of automated medicine for the first time, he requested that the paramedics transport him to Premier West Hospital.

* * *

The institution was located in a remote neighborhood, obscured from a distance by encompassing trees and mature landscaping. Nearby, a smaller building, possibly a clinic or surgical center, was under construction. It wasn't until Seth rounded the corner into the main driveway that the imposing superstructure came into complete view, commanding attention with its grandeur.

Standing five stories high, it was a masterpiece of sleek design, with edges so sharp they could cut the air. Its elliptical form blended effortlessly into the surrounding landscape, and reflection panels shimmered like a mirage in the midday sun. Large, floor-to-ceiling windows offered a breathtaking view. Canopied entrances on opposite ends were lined with ramps that beckoned to those in need, opening the doors of accessibility to all. The roof was flat and adorned with solar panels, providing the hospital with eco-friendly energy. Advanced security cameras lined the perimeter to protect patients, staff, and visitors. It was clear that no expense had been spared in development.

As Seth navigated toward the building, he searched for the main entrance, noting the access point marked *ER/Trauma* in bold capital letters. Sections of the exterior were roped off and draped in scaffolding. A group of men stood idly by, scribbling in notebooks, but no manual labor was being performed. An unmanned forklift transported large structural beams to an autonomous robotic crane across the dusty terrain.

Following the visitor parking lot signs, Seth's air mobility craft descended gracefully to the ground. A few others were scattered haphazardly throughout the lot; not as many as expected, but enough to confirm the proximity of a vertiport. From the smooth concrete to the fresh smell of paint, the surroundings were impeccably pristine. No blemishes marred the construction.

As he approached the entryway, the fortitude of the main doors, crafted from thick, unyielding steel, was a sight to behold. He anticipated motion activation, but the doors remained stubbornly still, making his arrival anticlimactic. A chilly autumn breeze blew open his jacket as he pressed his face against the single window, straining for a glimpse inside. The interior was concealed by heavy tinting on the minimally transparent glass, and he couldn't see any lights inside. He could barely make out a large, deserted security desk just a few feet away. Despite the absence of any signs of life, he knocked three times out of habit. Stillness and tranquility abound. It was as though the institution's personnel had abandoned it, leaving behind a hushed and somber tone that clashed with the awe-inspiring modernity of the building's exterior.

"Hello?" Seth blurted out. No response. Turning away from the entrance, he took a few steps back and surveyed the parking lot. Perhaps someone from the construction site could grant him access? A janitor, maybe?

CHAPTER 4

Suddenly, a deep, synthetic voice interrupted his thoughts, startling him.

"Please move to the retina recognition coordinates," it commanded, the words ringing around him. Seth spun around, searching for the source of the voice, but there were no visible speakers on the ceiling or walls. It seemed to permeate every corner of the space, an otherworldly presence that filled him with unease.

"Please move to the retina recognition coordinates," it repeated.

Then, Seth noticed a pattern on the concrete walkway for the first time. A dark four-by-four square with a bright red circle was delineated within its borders. Taking cues from the mysterious voice, he tentatively stepped into the circle and faced forward.

During the application process, he was required to submit a photo of his eye, and now he realized why. A thin beam of light appeared from behind the tinted window and surveyed his face, focusing on his eyes. The laser beam examined his left retina, rotated counterclockwise, then paused for processing. It then moved to his right eye, repeating itself in a steady, rhythmic motion. Seth was momentarily blinded but felt no discomfort, and his vision quickly returned to normal.

"Dr. Seth Kelley, temporary access has been granted. Welcome to Premier West Hospital," the ambient voice announced. The doors unlocked and slid open, creating a pathway. Seth hesitated before taking his first tentative steps into the building, uncertain of what lay ahead.

The vast, open expanse of the interior was breathtaking. Seth's eyes were drawn toward the immense glass ceiling, which flooded the polished floor below with natural light. Though the LEDs were dormant, the transparent roof provided enough luminescence for Seth to appreciate the advanced architectural design.

To his left stood a thriving indoor oak tree, its branches reaching toward the sky, breathing life into the otherwise neutral lobby. Ahead lay a welcoming desk, conference rooms, and an empty coffee shop. He noticed a sign for the gift shop directing patrons around the corner. As he gazed upwards, Seth was struck by the towering floors that stretched high into the heavens, supported by massive pillars. They were connected by a translucent elevator shaft bustling an empty carriage between the decks. Seth could count about five windows on each floor overlooking the main entrance, but based on his initial impression of the size of the building, he knew that each wing must extend much further, far out of sight from the lobby.

The hallway to the main hospital was decorated with a gaudy sign spelling out the facility's name: *Premier West Hospital*. In Seth's opinion, the lobby resembled the entrance to a theme park more than a medical institution.

"My life has always been a work in progress," said a raspy, parched voice from around the corner. "This is merely the latest manifestation of that pursuit."

Seth turned to look. Leaning heavily on a cane, an elderly gentleman emerged from the shadows. He stood with thin, white hair and glasses perched on his nose. A well-groomed beard enhanced the shape of his face. As the man approached Seth, he appeared in the sunlight wearing khakis with a button-down shirt and his hand extended for a friendly greeting.

CHAPTER 4

"What is a life without progress, Dr. Kelley?"

"I'd say it's one of stability and consistency," Seth retorted. The old man laughed in approval of the astute remark.

"I'm Dr. Ian Winter, creator of this institution," the older man announced. The refined gentleman gestured around the lobby to laud his accomplishment, encouraging Seth to observe its luxurious decor and modern engineering. "I'm delighted to usher you into my crowning achievement."

"It's remarkable," said Seth.

Leaning in to confide in Seth, Dr. Winter responded, "No expense was spared, as you can see. It's been a costly venture, but monetary concerns are inconsequential when the objective is scientific advancement."

"We should all be so lucky as to pursue our ambitions without financial constraint," Seth replied with a nod.

"Your neurons are sharp this morning, Dr. Kelley," he said with a smile. "Before we move forward, however, there is the small matter of a confidentiality and non-disclosure agreement that requires your signature."

Dr. Winter handed a tablet to Seth, who quickly skimmed the tightly-packed wording before providing a digital signature. Swiftly reclaiming the device, the founder beckoned for Seth to follow as he turned and retreated back toward the belly of the institution. The two men proceeded down the hallway and into the depths of the hospital.

"I may not look it, but I was a neurosurgeon for almost two decades, Dr. Kelley," the elderly man revealed. But before he could continue, Seth interrupted, wanting to make the conversation more congenial.

"Please, call me Seth."

Dr. Winter nodded, his eyes crinkling at the corners as he

smiled. "Very well, Seth. My career has been a profound journey. I specialized in neuro-oncology, mainly brain tumors. The intricacies of the human mind have always fascinated me. Not just the operations, but also dealing with the psychological toll it took on patients and their families. You see, Seth, neurosurgery was not only a profession to me; it was a way to serve humanity, to help restore health, happiness, and hope."

"Why did you transition away from the bedside?" asked Seth.

"Here's a story for you," Dr. Winter grumbled, leaning back in his chair. His expression turned stony. "There was this young woman with a complex glioblastoma. Her whole life was ahead of her. Terrified of leaving her kid behind. She knew the odds but wanted to be remembered as a fighter. She thought courage alone could ward off death. Well, I went in and excised that tumor with surgical precision. I did everything right. Got every last malignant cell. But the nature of her condition was relentless. Glioblastomas don't care about courage or hope, only biology. Despite all efforts, she passed away. The experience was a turning point for me. The tragedy was that she died in spite of the best medicine we had to offer. I spent many nights wrestling with the cold, hard fact that physiology often gets the better of us. It was a sobering reminder of the boundaries of human knowledge and capabilities, and the thought infuriated me. It still does. I needed a new frontier, an opportunity to transcend those biological constraints."

"So where did you go from there?"

"I started dabbling in machine learning during the last leg of my clinical career. Experimenting with programming and

CHAPTER 4

neural networks. I founded a company and recruited some of the brightest minds in the industry. Tell me, what is your knowledge of this facility?" Dr. Winter inquired.

"People say you're experimenting with automated healthcare. Autonomous surgery, robotics… that sort of thing," said Seth.

"That's not entirely off mark, Seth. Computers have been part of diagnostic pathways for years now," Dr. Winter shared.

Rounding a bend, the two men traversed a dark hallway until they reached another passage. A prominent sign was displayed above the transparent sliding doors. *Emergency Department—Restricted*. Dr. Winter paused and scanned his retina, making the doors open with a faint hiss.

Turning to face Seth eagerly, the retired neurosurgeon whispered, "But at this facility, we're moving away from rigid algorithms altogether."

Seth trailed Dr. Winter as they entered the department. An area to the right was designated for X-ray equipment, while the MRI machine was kept in a separate, isolated zone to the left. Seth was suddenly startled as they walked by the CT scan area.

A patient lay supine on the table, preparing herself to be transported through the hollow tube. *An actual living, breathing person.*

Turning to Dr. Winter, Seth asked, "Is the hospital open to patients?"

"As part of a clinical trial, yes. Think of it as beta testing, if you will. We're still under regulations, of course. They've capped us at five percent capacity, with a maximum of three providers. But we're hoping to expand to thirty providers soon. We've even opened our ER for walk-ins and ambulance arrivals, adhering to EMTALA guidelines. Currently, we're caring for nine patients, though we can handle up to 300. Our biggest hurdle? Bureaucracy. Always trying to put the brakes on progress," said Dr. Winter with a hint of frustration.

"A clinical trial in what, exactly?" Seth asked, following Dr. Winter cautiously into the patient care area. He wasn't sure what to expect next, but he was prepared for anything. Dr. Winter chuckled and gestured towards the room of an active patient, inviting him to see for himself.

"Artificial intelligence. Take a look."

Seth peered into the room, and his eyes grew wide with amazement. A towering robotic machine, nearly seven feet tall, stood over a live patient. Its form was humanoid, with broad shoulders and an impressive build that exuded strength and power. Its cephalic encasement beamed piercing lasers that illuminated the room in a surreal glow. By analyzing the reflected lighted, it captured precise, three-dimensional information about the environment. Articulated limbs moved gracefully, powered by a pulsing battery pack on the rear.

"We call them Automated Healthcare Providers. AHPs, if you will," Dr. Winter declared with excitement. He paused, then added, "But our centralized neural network, the ALDRIS system, truly sets us apart. Autonomous Learning for Diagnosis, Resuscitation, Imaging, and Surgery. It has broad, macroscopic swarm-level control, like a commander orchestrating troops on a battlefield. Truly revolutionary."

Seth knew automated caretakers were being developed, but the machine's level of complexity and sophistication left him in awe. In a fleeting instant, the world beyond slipped his

CHAPTER 4

mind, consumed by the captivating allure of the machine and the endless prospects it bestowed. It felt as if he'd stumbled upon an obscure realm, where mere suggestions of natural laws took on the air of commonplace, and impossibilities became the norm. At that moment, Seth became aware of an unparalleled boon bestowed upon him, the privilege to glimpse the infinite and the unknown, to reside on the cusp of a world surpassing his wildest imaginations. Awe-stricken by the wonder of human ingenuity and the boundless capacity of the future, Seth was left pondering the possibilities ahead.

On the stretcher was a middle-aged patient, estimated to be around fifty, though the stress in his features suggested a weariness beyond his years. He was slightly overweight, with a noticeable rounding of the midsection. His legs were unnaturally swollen and taut, a condition clinically referred to as edema. Pitting was evident along his lower extremities, indicative of the severity of fluid accumulation within the tissues. The skin around his ankles and calves glistened with a thin layer of clear, straw-colored fluid which was slowly seeping through the overstretched skin, evidence that the body was losing its struggle to contain the accumulating fluid within the vascular system. The sight was all too familiar in cases of heart failure.

"What is your name?" The question, cold and impersonal, rippled through the space, leaving a metallic echo in its wake. The robot's voice was unmistakably synthetic, yet carried a peculiar depth that gave it an unnerving semblance of organic life. It was the same voice that had greeted Seth at the entrance.

Despite its human-like appearance, the AHP lacked the typical features associated with speech. There was no visible mouth or jawline, no conspicuous speakers from which the sound could be projected. Still, the sound reverberated through the room, its imposing presence commanding attention as it waited patiently for a response. The request was simple, yet carried the weight of an unspoken challenge, a test to gauge the patient's composure in the face of the extraordinary.

"William. William Crane," came the hesitant reply from the patient, seemingly stumbling over his own name. Observing the interaction, it was evident to Seth that the man was not a professional actor.

"How may I assist you today?" asked the automated provider.

Lying on the stretcher, the patient took a deep breath, searching for the right words. "I… I've been feeling a shortness of breath, and my legs… they've swelled up. I'm much weaker now, and just walking has become… difficult."

"When did these symptoms begin?"

"Hmm, I think… um, four days back. Or was it five? No, no, it's four," William replied. Seth could tell that he felt more like a specimen under a microscope than a person in need of healing.

"What makes it worse?"

"Laying flat, walking. I can't even get up the stairs anymore, sir. I mean, doctor?" said William, fumbling over his words. He struggled to articulate his symptoms clearly, hoping to avoid any misinterpretation by the voice software.

Seth watched intently as the machine continued its methodical interrogation. "Do you have a cough?" it inquired in a detached tone.

"Well, maybe a bit," William replied hesitantly. "It's a dry

CHAPTER 4

cough, here and there... Nothing too bad, though."

The robot further probed, "Why didn't you go back to the hospital that performed your LVAD surgery?"

"Oh, uh, I don't really know, sir. This hospital was just closer, I suppose," he attempted to clarify, his words faltering as he attempted to rationalize the disjointed approach to his care.

Seth was struck by the machine's meticulous approach to data collection, a technique taught in medical schools nationwide for generations. After a thorough history of the patient's present illness, the AHP moved on to a comprehensive review of systems, delving deep into each specific organ group. With each question, the machine unlocked a new layer of the patient's history, revealing hidden clues to the root of the problem.

As the conversation progressed, the room hummed with the steady beep of electronic monitors. Seth's eyes roamed over the technology surrounding them. A digital screen captured the spoken words in real time with perfect accuracy. Below that, a display strip streamed the patient's electrocardiographic rhythm, wirelessly transmitted from electrodes attached to the patient's torso. The peaks and valleys of his heartbeat danced on the screen in mesmerizing waves of red and blue.

At that moment, a retractable arm with a bell-shaped tip unfurled from the hub of the AHP, maneuvering toward the patient's chest. It pressed gently against the superior sternum, paused, then moved to the lower region. The gadget was a mechanical stethoscope recording heart sounds from the aortic, pulmonary, tricuspid, and mitral valves. It explored the patient's chest wall, seeking out every nuance of his complex rhythm.

The machine gracefully continued its clinical examination, its arms moving in coordinated patterns. The AHP adjusted its stethoscope on the patient's back, positioning the bell-shaped microphone in different thoracic locations. The patient was instructed to breathe deeply while the robot listened to the symphony of his lung sounds. Simultaneously, a mechanical arm approached the patient's abdomen, causing a slight flinch. It paused, allowed the human time to adjust, then proceeded to palpate his abdomen.

"Our patented facial recognition software correlates with digital palpation sensors to quantify abdominal tenderness," Dr. Winter murmured in an almost reverential whisper. "We use ambient biometrics for non-intrusive vital sign monitoring, detecting physical responses to stress and pain. Image recognition software evaluates all radiology scans. Everything from the patient's complaints and history, to their physical exam, vitals, biometric data, blood work, and imaging contributes to formulating the final diagnosis. From there, a preprogrammed intervention is launched. It's designed to adapt and respond to real-time changes in physiological parameters, recalibrating the treatment pathway as required."

Seth was so astounded by the spectacle before him that he nearly forgot about the hospital's architect at his side. His mind was a storm of questions, trying to make sense of what he was witnessing.

"But what about the uncertainty that comes with human patients?" Seth asked, his voice barely above a whisper, his gaze still transfixed on the robot. "Unreliable narratives from patients, limitations of physical exams, the variations in pain

CHAPTER 4

tolerance, changes in mental status, or those with ulterior motives? What if there are multiple voices in the room? There's an inherent human touch, a nuance to our work. There has to be."

Dr. Winter stood tall, unabashed, "Our ALDRIS system possesses a comprehensive knowledge of human anatomy and pathophysiology surpassing any human mind. Does that still make it less competent in your eyes?"

"But we're more than just snippets of code," Seth countered, only to halt as he reconsidered his words. Despite his extensive understanding of the human psyche, his comprehension of computer engineering was, admittedly, rather limited.

"I remember when I was just a boy, Seth," Dr. Winter chuckled, the corners of his eyes creasing with nostalgia. "My mother let out a shriek when she spotted a cockroach in our kitchen. My father rushed in, hellbent on squashing the intruder. But the critter was too crafty, zigzagging and eluding his attacks time and again. Observing this, I thought, what a clever creature! Its responses are not hardwired. It was actively assessing its environment, pondering its options, and strategizing its escape based on its previous experiences. A form of learning, wouldn't you agree, Seth? Out of curiosity, do you know how many neurons are in a cockroach's brain?"

Caught off guard, Seth admitted, "I'm not sure."

"Around 200,000. A rather modest figure by biological standards. Now, consider our ALDRIS system, the digital intelligence that governs this entire facility. It boasts nearly 150 billion neurons. Can you fathom the potential of that processing power?"

"Given the unique polymorphisms in your renal

parenchyma's genetic profile, bumetanide will be the most effective medication for your diuresis," the robot announced from across the room.

In 2042, therapeutics were targeted to the unique genetic makeup of each individual. One such example was the impact of variations in the CYP2D6 enzyme on the effectiveness of opioid pain relievers. Toxicity could be a danger for those who metabolized drugs slowly, while those who metabolized quickly might not experience relief. Traditionally, genetic profiling required lengthy outsourcing to specialized laboratories for analysis, leading to delays in treatment and increased costs. But, a keen observer, Seth noticed that Dr. Winter's hospital employed a revolutionary new method that could be applied in the emergency department, delivering quick results and enabling personalized treatment immediately.

"You will be admitted to the hospital for monitoring and evaluation of your LVAD. Surgical intervention may be necessary," the machine announced with crisp precision.

"Cardiothoracic surgery?" the emergency physician interjected, his eyes widening.

"Our machines are competent in performing all major procedures. Any technical skill a human can master can also be taught to a computer."

"By the way, what eventually happened to the cockroach?"

Dr. Winter's eyes twinkled with amusement. He gestured for Seth to follow him to the next room. Over his shoulder, he added, "On the fifth attempt, it finally met its match under my father's shoe."

Here, a somewhat overweight woman, around 40 years old, lay supine on the bed. Standing over her was a robotic

CHAPTER 4

provider, its arm systematically exploring her abdomen. A retractable instrument, held with a stable grip, moved carefully against her skin, now slick with a layer of cool, conductive gel. It focused its investigation on the upper right quadrant of her torso.

Suspended above them, a large display screen flickered to life. It projected a series of diagnostic grayscale images, painting a real-time portrait of her internal landscape. Seth, a seasoned observer, instantly recognized the imaging modality as ultrasonography. Generated by pressure waves in a medium, the probe emitted high-frequency sounds that penetrated her skin, bouncing off the underlying tissues. Bones and stone-like formations reflected light-colored signals, whereas fluids took on a darker hue.

The distinct ovoid organ was her gallbladder. Bright formations signaled the presence of stones. The conspicuous wall thickening suggested ongoing inflammation, and the sight of fluid confirmed the diagnosis. They were looking at a bedside sonogram of her gallbladder; the patient had acute cholecystitis.

"She'll be undergoing fully-robotic surgery in a few hours," Dr. Winter narrated. He beckoned to Seth as he shuffled to the furthest room in the hallway. "Follow me."

The next patient sat on a procedure table with his right upper extremity outstretched and covered by a sterile cloth. A deep, ragged laceration traversed from his palm across the terrain of his thumb. Even from his vantage point at the door, Seth could see the frayed ends of the flexor tendon. This slender strand of connective tissue was essential to the movement of the thumb, a digit essential for even the most mundane tasks in daily life. Without meticulous care, the patient would surely lose the use of his hand.

In a remarkable display of technology, a mechanical claw steadily descended from above. The apparatus held an ensemble of sophisticated surgical instruments, each specifically designed to perform a unique role in the procedure. The components were all primed, ready to function in perfect harmony.

Like an artist wielding his brush, the machine carefully navigated through the shredded tissue, each tool performing its task with the dexterity of a master craftsman. The grasper seized the frayed tendon and guided it into proper anatomical location with an intricate balance of forces—firm enough to secure the tissue, yet gentle enough not to cause further damage. The needle driver, elegant as a ballerina, danced its way around the wound, weaving stitches through the damaged edges with accuracy and precision that only a machine could achieve.

One by one, the absorbable threads, tailor-made to dissolve over time, secured the tendon and surrounding tissue. Each was placed in a methodical, pre-planned pattern, ensuring the uniform distribution of tension across the healing wound. Finally, as the operation neared completion, the robotic instruments pulled the layers of skin back together.

"Seth, we need each other," the old man whispered as they stood observing the robot suture the complex laceration. "Do you know why I invited you here?"

Seth's eyes drifted from the gaping wound and settled on Dr. Winter's face, taking in the lines etched deeply into the doctor's skin. It was as if the sheer weight of the world had left its mark upon him, a physical manifestation of a lifetime spent battling the forces of illness.

CHAPTER 4

"I've read your essays on compassionate care, Seth. No one can deny that you're one of the leading voices for patient advocacy amongst physicians, but medicine is passing you by. We're on the precipice of unveiling artificially intelligent healthcare machines to the world. In a society burdened by skyrocketing costs and a demand for the highest quality of care, there's no space for uncertainty, guesswork, or tired doctors. Our robots are multilingual, don't take breaks, and don't demand pay hikes. They make objective, rules-based decisions, free from human bias and emotional baggage. It's all about rational thinking, precision, and efficiency. By subtracting the human element, we've maximized productivity."

"You can't brush off the subtleties of this job. It takes imaginative thinking, intuition, gestalt, and abstract reasoning—like a sixth sense. In fact, studies have shown that experienced physicians have better judgment than most decision rules. Computers can't process the nuances of human interaction in the way a skilled clinician can. Machines depend on predictability, but falter when faced with inconsistencies or unique circumstances."

"The era of tolerating flawed clinician judgment is numbered, Seth. Reimbursement dynamics have changed. Insurers demand value, necessitating a data-driven approach that favors certainty, accuracy, and consistency. Subjectivity is a casualty of this evolution. Hospitals are rapidly embracing new technologies that utilize the vast amount of data at their disposal to make informed, evidence-based decisions. The future of medicine is one where objectivity reigns supreme."

Seth grumbled, "Pursuing perfection can be a dangerous game. Medicine isn't just about numbers and algorithms.

What about the human touch, the patient experience?"

"Ah, the kind of empathy we grew up watching in medical dramas is nothing more than a beautiful illusion in today's fast-paced, profit-driven world," Dr. Winter sighed. "Most doctors are juggling multiple patients simultaneously, with only minutes to spare for each. But our robots are different. They're designed to simulate compassion with customized responses, maintaining the human connection you fear we might lose."

"So they're basically reading from a script?"

"Does it really matter? Research shows that patients can't distinguish between genuine empathy and dramatization in medical students. It's ironic that some of the most skilled surgeons often receive the worst patient feedback. Doctors skilled in bedside manner can sometimes harbor resentment in private. Empathy, it seems, is a matter of perception. Patients rarely glimpse the true benevolence, or lack thereof, in their caregivers. Pandering to patients might boost satisfaction ratings, but it doesn't necessarily improve healthcare outcomes. We should be focusing on results, not coddling. The FDA just doesn't seem to understand that yet," argued Dr. Winter. He rolled his eyes and slammed down his fist, becoming increasingly frustrated with the course of the conversation.

Suddenly, Seth's purpose became clear. Every step of his career—his background in cognitive psychology, clinical experience, and publications on the doctor-patient relationship—had led him to this exact moment. He wasn't randomly selected for this job. He was chosen.

"I need your endorsement, Seth," Dr. Winter confessed, his voice sober. "Your support to push my application through

CHAPTER 4

the government's tedious approval process. Together, we can propel medicine and engineering beyond the boundaries of human imagination."

Seth exhaled deeply, taking a moment to digest the enormity of what was unfolding. As he glanced back toward the treatment room, however, something peculiar caught his attention. The robot, once bustling with activity, now stood completely still behind the transparent fiberglass partition. An unexplainable shiver crept down his spine as its expressionless face stared back at him with an eerie emptiness. Although the machine lacked conventional eyes or discernible facial features, Seth couldn't shake off the unnerving feeling that he was being watched.

Dr. Winter interrupted the silence. "Let's get some lunch, shall we? I have a lot of explaining to do."

Chapter 5

The conference room was a sight to behold. Embodying modern elegance, it basked in the soft glow of dim lighting. With no windows to distract, the room exuded a serene, sophisticated ambiance, much like the backroom of a fine dining establishment. Glistening flat-panel cabinets lined the room's perimeter. On one wall, a digital whiteboard was cluttered with a dizzying array of formulas, arrows, and diagrams. The board, a canvas of creativity, was filled with intricate symbols and notations composed with an electronic stylus lying on the ledge below. Seth's eyes scanned the detailed markings, recognizing the familiar patterns of his college math classes. A sophisticated blend of linear algebra and set notation coalesced on the board, with a cluster of unknown symbols that hinted at the realm of machine learning.

Beside the whiteboard, a watercolor painting of waves crashing against a rocky shoreline added a touch of tranquility. It was a sharp contrast to the chaos of the adjacent wall, covered in a frenzy of algebraic formulas. A rectangular table filled the center space. Eight office chairs, their new leather still fragrant, surrounded the perimeter.

Dr. Winter beckoned for Seth to take a seat. As he settled

CHAPTER 5

into the chair across from the mesmerizing painting, he couldn't help but steal another glance at the notation on the board. Despite his established place in the medical field, Seth's insatiable curiosity kept him eager to explore new frontiers. It was a trait that set him apart from his colleagues, who were content to rest on their laurels. Acknowledging that robotics and engineering lay outside his expertise, he approached the learning opportunity with humility, ready to absorb all the knowledge he could.

The elderly host announced, "Our meal will arrive soon. Lab-grown wagyu beef is on the menu, paired with a smoked sweet plantain puree, grilled anaheim pepper, and a mango-papaya salsa. Our artificial intelligence crafted an exquisite culinary experience using pluripotent stem cells. No animals were harmed."

The meal offering was met with a deafening stillness. The emergency physician's mind was preoccupied, leaving little room for small talk. Disappointed, the neurosurgeon pressed a button on his remote, shutting off the digital whiteboard and taking the equations with it.

Dr. Winter gently cleared his throat and provided background, "We need to go back to the beginning, Seth. Dartmouth, in the 1950s. Computer scientists sat around tables like this one, dreaming of reducing the complexity of the brain to a series of codes. They imagined a world where every interaction was programmable. If this, then that."

"That sounds like a reasonable starting point," Seth conceded, his thoughts beginning to churn. "It'd be a hefty task, but given enough time, specific responses could be tailored to a wide range of stimuli."

Dr. Winter nodded in agreement, the corners of his mouth

lifting in a small, satisfied smile. "Precisely! Computers were soon answering queries, solving mathematical problems, manipulating objects, and even playing checkers. The research attracted considerable funding, but as it often happens with revolutionary technology, the expectations outpaced the reality. For several decades, the industry stagnated, grappling with two major, seemingly insurmountable hurdles: perception and common sense."

Prompted by their conversation, Dr. Winter stood from his chair and fetched two blocks from a nearby cabinet. With a hint of dramatic flair, he placed them on the table between them and posed a question, "Tell me, Seth, what do you see?"

"Two blocks. One red, one green," Seth responded.

"That's right," said Dr. Winter, reclining in his chair. His piercing gaze was fixed on Seth as he posed a thought-provoking question. "Now, imagine conveying that information to a computer using only binary language—a series of 1's and 0's. You can't use words like *cube* or *square*. What if you want it to sort the red blocks from the green? How do you teach it color? Or what does it mean to distinguish two objects? It needs to see the outside world, feel it, touch it, and interact with it. All of this requires programming. Before you know it, seemingly straightforward tasks become daunting."

With a faint creak, the door to the conference room swung open, and an AHP appeared. With a tray in hand, it silently approached Seth's chair, extended an arm, lowered the meal, and released it onto the table. The lab-manufactured beef was ready for consumption. As the robot made its way to the back of the room, Seth couldn't help but watch in wonder. Its upright posture and stoic demeanor evoked images of

CHAPTER 5

a British soldier on a purposeful march. It turned around swiftly and came to a stop in the corner.

"Should I say thank you? Is there a certain way I should act around it?" Seth's words were hesitant. He wondered how to behave in their presence, unsure of the proper decorum. The old man chuckled, his features crinkling in amusement as Seth's awkwardness was fully displayed. Could the system handle multiple conversations simultaneously? Would it react negatively to poor manners? Did that imply a capacity for emotion?

With trepidation, Seth sampled the meal. He rarely indulged in fine dining, so his expectations were tempered accordingly. But to his surprise, the meat was delightful, its flavors undifferentiated from a natural cut of meat. None of it would go to waste.

As anticipation hushed the room, the lights dimmed to twilight, and a projector descended slowly from the ceiling. Seth watched, spellbound, as a holographic three-dimensional display of the human brain materialized in the center of the conference table. The image rotated slowly, a kaleidoscope of pulsing colors and intricate patterns. It focused on the frontal cortex, followed by a neural circuit and an individual cell.

As the image settled into place, the narrator, Dr. Winter, began to speak. His voice was low and resonant, infused with the weight of knowledge and experience.

"The brain has 86 billion neurons. Think of each neuron as a tiny processor, like a miniature logic gate. Dendrites, as you know, receive the signals which accumulate in the cell body. If they exceed a certain threshold, a binary signal rushes down the axon to the next set of neurons. When this happens, the propagated firing patterns ignite a breathtaking spectacle of communicative pathways, lighting up the brain like a constellation of stars in the night sky."

As he spoke, the hologram between them whirled into life with vibrant streams of light, mapping the intricate pathways of neural signal transmission. The once static image transformed into a pulsating network of dots. Each was interconnected, flickering rhythmically as signals coursed through. It was a symphony of neural activity: cohesive, ordered, and stunning.

The former neurosurgeon continued, "These reconfigurable pathways regulate our very existence, from the way we interpret the world to the nature of our thoughts and actions. Our objective was to conceive a computer system that could emulate the molecular signaling of the brain and recreate mechanisms of perception, speech, memory, and decision-making. Whether encased within a hydroxyapatite skull or an electronic circuit, the architecture is fundamentally the same. In computer science terms, we refer to this logic gate as a perceptron."

"A per- what?"

"A perceptron," Dr. Winter repeated, an amused smile playing on his lips. He leaned forward in his chair. "It is essentially the digital equivalent of a neuron, the basic building block of artificial intelligence. It takes inputs, processes them through functions and optimized weights, and then generates an output. And just like neurons, each perceptron is connected with thousands of others, forming a vast and intricate network of computation."

Seth spent days poring over neuropsychology textbooks in college. He had spent endless hours memorizing pathways

CHAPTER 5

and neurotransmitters, acing tests on paper, but it had all seemed so abstract, so disconnected from reality. But now, in this moment, the intricate inner workings of the brain, the complex web of synapses and circuits, felt palpable, almost tangible. Suddenly, he appreciated that the hospital around him was alive and interwoven. It was wondrously bound together by invisible interconnections within its walls and personified by humanoid robots walking amongst them.

"But how do you fine-tune each perceptron, the logic gates, to generate the desired outcome? How do you get them to differentiate a dog from a human?" asked Seth.

"Well, we started with something called supervised learning," Dr. Winter began. "The internet boom of the 90s provided a wealth of training data.. At first, we adjusted the parameters manually until the desired results were achieved. If the machine made an error, we tweaked the weights of the connections between perceptrons. With time, we were able to feed the system new data. These neural networks laid the groundwork for technologies like image recognition software, self-driving cars, email spam filters, and even social media algorithms."

"That sounds like a ton of work, manually adjusting each… uh, percept-"

"Perceptron!" Dr. Winter interrupted with a laugh. "Yes, it was quite the chore! But machine learning changed everything. Now, we had systems that could perform tasks without specific programming, although they still needed a domain expert to define the characteristics. For example, a person had to teach the system what makes a dog, well, a dog."

Seth's eyes sparkled with realization. "But a mark of

intelligence is the ability to learn new things independently."

"That's correct. So we took it a step further. Considering the sheer impracticability of defining characteristics for every scenario, we needed a workaround. We began training computers to learn autonomously. That's where deep learning models entered the picture. They enabled our neural networks to adjust their connections and enhance efficiency, all without our intervention. We layered millions of these neural networks and used unsupervised learning to discern hidden patterns from unlabelled data. The system started evolving on its own, figuring out the most important attributes needed to achieve its goal."

Quick to catch on, Seth sought to confirm his understanding with another question. "So, the neural network can figure out on its own what makes a dog a dog?"

"That's right. All we do is check whether the computer's answer is correct."

"But how does the system actually *learn*?"

Picking up his glasses from the table and placing them on the bridge of his nose, Dr. Winter inquired, "Seth, did you know that electronic vision surpasses human eyesight?"

"In terms of pixelation, yes," Seth agreed.

"However," Dr. Winter continued, "computers see lines and shapes, not objects. For them, moving around a room or a busy street with people, pets, vehicles, and bikes is a huge challenge. The physical world is complex, teeming with innumerable variables like weather changes, moving objects, and variable lighting. It's virtually impossible to program all these interconnected relationships manually. But consider a cockroach. It can traverse an entire forest to find food and a mate, without any specific training."

CHAPTER 5

"They rely on pattern recognition and learn from their past mistakes," Seth agreed. "It's almost as if they inherently know how to do it."

"Exactly. A child, without any formal education, understands more about physics and biology than some of the world's most advanced supercomputers. It's Bayesian reasoning in action. Imagine you're a newborn baby witnessing your first sunrise. You might wonder, will it happen again tomorrow? But after seeing it rise day after day, you begin to trust in its recurrence, until you're almost certain of it. Our brains work on a predictive basis, using new evidence to reinforce or challenge our beliefs," explained Dr. Winter.

"That sounds like inductive reasoning," Seth added, connecting the dots. "It's like how scientists extrapolate broad conclusions from specific observations and patterns."

"Precisely," Dr. Winter concurred, his gaze never leaving Seth. "Our brains leverage past experiences and probabilities to create mental models of our expectations. And it's incredibly efficient at filling in the blanks, even when we don't have all the pieces. We can finish sentences, recognize objects that are partially hidden, and even make educated medical decisions based on limited information. Think about an ice cube. You know it's going to be cold before you touch it, and there's no surprise when you do. That's the process of 'normalcy detection,' and it predominantly happens in the lower parts of our brain."

"Normalcy detection?" Seth queried, intrigued by the concept.

Dr. Winter replied, "These structures work on an unconscious level, sifting through the constant barrage of sensory input to prevent information overload. They compare new information with the mental models formed by the more cognitive parts of the brain. If everything checks out, they disregard the sensation. Like how you eventually stop feeling a watch on your wrist after wearing it for a few days."

"And what happens if something unusual is detected?"

"Imagine walking into a patient's room and smelling something out of the ordinary. The ever-vigilant lower brain sends a signal to your higher cognitive areas that something's not right. Suddenly, you're focusing on the strange smell and memories start to surface, leading you to suspect an infection, perhaps *Clostridium difficile*."

Dr. Winter then steered the conversation towards mental health disorders, specifically psychosis. He postulated that faulty neural encoding could result in false deductions, which might give rise to auditory hallucinations when the brain prioritized these incorrect predictions over the actual sensory input.

"Do each of the AHPs run on distinct software?" Seth ventured to ask.

"Not exactly. Their role is similar to our brain's signal filtration system. They act as 'normalcy detectors' within the predictive coding framework, trained on countless data points to identify benign clinical scenarios. If they spot something unusual, they report the discrepancy to the centralized neural network, the ALDRIS system. Thanks to deep learning, this system operates much like our higher brain areas, managing cognition, decision-making, and probabilistic modeling."

Seth had another concern. "What happens if an inference is incorrect or new information emerges? Patients aren't static data points; they constantly change, from their objective

CHAPTER 5

hemodynamics to subjective pain scale."

"I presume you're acquainted with the concept of neuroplasticity?" asked Dr. Winter.

"Of course," Seth responded, without a moment's hesitation. "It refers to the brain's capability to rewire its neural connections, thereby creating new pathways. Connections form the basis of context, meaning, and learning. When neurons fire together, they form stronger links, changing the brain's physical structure with each new experience or task. It's why kids learn to walk before they run and babies babble before they talk. It's something we're all capable of, even if it gets harder as we age."

"That's why you can't teach an old dog new tricks!" the neurosurgeon added with a laugh. "Our brains constantly strive to reduce randomness and subdue entropy by transforming raw data into a coherent, predictable worldview. It's always refining its models to minimize surprise when faced with similar situations in the future."

Intrigued, Seth pressed him further. "And how exactly did you incorporate this concept into the system?"

"When faced with conflicting information, ALDRIS recalibrates its models and updates the working memory of the AHPs. It's a closed-loop intelligence that evolves and fine-tunes itself with every interaction, every experience, constantly working towards maximizing its utility function."

"Utility function?" asked Seth.

"The end goal. The desired outcome," Dr. Winter responded. "In our case, to reach the proper diagnosis for each patient."

"Then what happens?"

"Intervention follows, which is primarily algorithmic,

leaving little room for discretion. Every diagnosis is linked to a relevant plan of action, spanning a spectrum of conditions from minor cuts to severe respiratory distress."

"Your artificial intelligence... it learned procedures?" inquired Seth.

"Hierarchical learning hinges on the idea that any intricate task can be deconstructed into simpler tasks, structured in a tiered fashion. We employed a dynamic movement primitives approach, allowing robots to learn basic motions autonomously. Through reinforcement methods, these robots string together sequences of motions, much like language models using words as tokens to construct coherent sentences. ALDRIS refined its skills by analyzing a wide variety of data sets, examining everything from scholarly articles to instructional videos. It mastered numerous procedures, from central line placement to wound suturing. It studied the texture of skin, the appropriate amount of force to use, various tying methods, and even when to remove a stitch, if necessary. Over time, it taught itself, much like a dedicated medical student, how to perform the most effective interventions," Dr. Winter explained. He paused and asked, "Do you care for the beef?"

Seth glanced up from his meal, startled by the sudden awareness that he had been so deeply absorbed in their discourse that he had neglected to voice his approval of the dinner. He smirked, gesturing towards the AHP in the corner. "Please extend my compliments to the kitchen staff," he quipped. "How does it listen and communicate?"

"It runs on an enormous natural language model, a behemoth of over a trillion parameters. It consumes a copious amount of repository training data and then extrapolates a statistical representation of the likelihood that one word will succeed another. It's through this intricate network of associations that the system can make such insightful inferences."

"Does ALDRIS share how it reached its diagnosis?" Seth inquired.

Dr. Winter shook his head with a note of regret. "Unfortunately, it doesn't. The learning process of these AI systems often remains inscrutable, even to the programmers themselves. These systems don't focus on the same details a human would. Instead, they latch onto complex, intertwined features that make deep learning systems something of a black box. The network's ability to predict future diseases through analysis of historical medical records astounded us, but we often found ourselves baffled by its methodology."

Seth leaned forward, his eyes narrowing slightly. "But shouldn't the diagnostic indicators be clinically significant? We can't diagnose patients based on criteria that are foreign or unclear to us."

Dr. Winter nodded in agreement. "Indeed. But medicine has coexisted with such black boxes for some time. Many treatments work despite our lack of understanding as to why. Electroconvulsive therapy, for instance, treats severe depression effectively, but its mechanism remains obscure."

"With all due respect," argued Seth, "if we don't understand how something works, we can't predict how or when it might fail."

Dr. Winter's smile widened. He had been waiting for this particular thread of skepticism. With a flick of his remote control, he activated a holographic display at the center of the room. The image abruptly widened its scope, unfolding a complete anatomical region of the brain in mesmerizing detail and brilliant hues.

"The neocortex," he announced. "An amazing result of evolution, as thin as a paper napkin but consisting of around 150,000 columns of connected circuits. It controls high-level functions like perception, motor commands, and reasoning. It works without bias, wants, motives, or intent; it's purely analytical. For safety, we designed our neural network to mimic only this logical facet of intelligence, not the whole brain."

"The computer itself may not be biased, but the data it's trained on could be," the emergency doctor countered. He was not so easily swayed. As a veteran reviewer for academic journals, he was well-versed in dissecting research articles, snaring statistical blunders, and shedding light on latent biases that may escape even the keenest researchers. "Experimental data must reflect the patient population accurately and be large enough to minimize inherent distortions. Without proper care, even well-intentioned projects can perpetuate unconscious biases."

Seth recalled a disastrous venture in 2013, when a leading computing company collaborated with a renowned medical facility to seek a cure for cancer. The engineers trained their machine learning system on a limited set of hypothetical patients, which did not reflect the diversity of the wider population. Consequently, the system made frequent and potentially hazardous suggestions, such as prescribing anticoagulants to patients with bleeding disorders. The project was eventually abandoned due to these critical errors, serving as a stark reminder of the importance of accurate and representative training data.

CHAPTER 5

Continuing his train of thought, Seth went on, "You can't simply reduce human complexity, or any aspect of nature, to conform to a rigid model or narrative."

Dr. Winter offered reassurance by adding, "Our system has logged over a hundred thousand hours of observation and practice, Seth. It can integrate trillions of medical data points into cohesive conclusions. ALDRIS has surpassed humans in gathering patient histories, conducting physical exams, analyzing tests, diagnosing conditions, and selecting interventions. The time has come to test on real patients."

"But why implement this in a hospital? Why not outpatient oncology? Or neurosurgery, for that matter?"

Dr. Winter leaned back, crossing his arms over his chest. "The emergency department is notorious for its chaos, characterized by a dynamic and complex framework with millions of interacting and unpredictable variables. The patterns hidden within the data generated here are beyond human comprehension, making it an ideal setting to harness the power of autonomous data analysis." With a wave of his hand, he activated a hologram at the center of the room. "Observe."

A video of a dying patient appeared before them, sprawled out on a stretcher with bullet holes in his chest. An autonomous robot was ready to intervene, its metallic limbs shining under the bright surgical lights.

The machine seamlessly initiated a thoracotomy, a last-ditch effort to save a person with a penetrating chest injury from the brink of cardiac arrest. The first incision was made with surgical precision, the laser scalpel gliding through flesh and muscle, opening a path to the vulnerable organs beneath. Blood oozed from the wound, forming a dark and glistening pool within the thoracic cavity. The machine inserted a rib-spreader with grace, carefully parting the ribcage to expose the damaged lung. The bones creaked under the strain, a sound that sent a shudder through Seth's body.

With the lung visible, the robot's delicate digits palpated the organ, assessing the damage from the bullet. Seth marveled at the finesse with which the mechanical fingers moved. Identifying the site of injury, the robot worked deftly, suturing the laceration with spiderweb-thin thread, each stitch a masterpiece of precision.

The final stage of the thoracotomy was to remove the fluids that had accumulated in the patient's chest cavity. The robot meticulously suctioned the excess blood, its mechanical arm moving in a steady, rhythmic motion, accompanied by the unsettling slurping sound of the aspirated fluid. Once the cavity was cleared, the robot gently released the rib-spreader, allowing the bones to return to their original position.

"Remarkable, isn't it?" Dr. Winter murmured, his gaze never leaving the hologram. The AHP worked with the finesse of a master tailor, stitching up the incision seamlessly, perfectly aligning the wound's edges.

As the robot completed the operation and the hologram faded, leaving only the ghostly afterimage, a heavy silence descended. Seth, caught between awe of the robot's capabilities and a primal fear of the implications, understood that he was witnessing the dawn of a new era in medicine.

Finally, he spoke. "Your work here is truly remarkable, nothing short of revolutionary. I'm fascinated by what you've accomplished."

"Ah, but that's not all," said the founder with a sly grin. "Artificial intelligence was my final creation, Seth. Do you

CHAPTER 5

know why? Because from this point forward, the reins of innovation belong to the machines. By tweaking the utility function, the neural network can devise creative solutions to any problem we set before it." With that, he appreciatively gestured towards the AHP, lurking silently and unobtrusively in the corner.

"Have you explored other applications?" Seth asked. It wasn't surprising, given Dr. Winter's obsession with innovation. "Is that how you discovered point-of-care genetic analysis?"

"Indeed it is. When we asked ALDRIS to refine DNA microarray techniques, it devised a new analysis method that yields immediate results. We can now quickly detect genetic variations that influence a patient's response to medication, and provide targeted therapy based on their genetic profile."

"What other advancements have you made?" asked Seth, his scientific curiosity stirred.

Dr. Winter's face was animated as he shared, "We've charted a variety of paths in the medical field. Our projects span from designing nanosystems to deliver bioactive agents directly to target cells, to engineering new antibiotics for tackling infectious diseases, and exploring immunomodulators, not to mention developing remyelinating agents for multiple sclerosis."

"Multiple sclerosis?"

"Indeed."

Seth was shocked. He was not one to discuss his family's hardships, but given the opportunity to improve Rebecca's quality of life, he decided to share her story. "My wife, she's battling Progressive Relapsing Multiple Sclerosis. Confined to a wheelchair. Could you perhaps shed some light on the treatments you've been developing?"

"That's a heartbreaking condition," Dr. Winter responded. "We've been working on a new type of catalytic drug that can prompt the differentiation of oligodendrocyte precursor cells. We're using pure, faceted gold nanocrystals in suspension to enhance the bioenergetic processes of aerobic glycolysis."

Interrupting, Seth pointed out, "That technology has been around for some time, but those agents can't cross the blood-brain barrier."

"Actually, they can! We tasked ALDRIS with improving transport. It suggested a novel use of nano-lipid carriers, which can naturally penetrate the nervous system by crossing the brain capillary endothelial cells. Biological plausibility exists; we just need to fully develop and test it."

For a moment, Seth was at a loss for words. Finally, he said, "That's... amazing. Honestly, I'm astounded by your achievements."

Dr. Winter leaned closer, his voice barely above a whisper as he said, "Seth, it's important for you to know what drives my pursuit of this project. Time is precious and, for me, it's running out. I'm seriously ill, suffering from a rare heart tumor, an angiosarcoma. It was diagnosed too late."

"I'm so sorry."

"I appreciate your sympathy," the older doctor said, his eyes shining with determination rather than despair. "But my focus is on the future. I don't resent my doctors, but I see the room for improvement. Artificial intelligence has the potential to rectify past mistakes and usher in a new era of flawlessly accurate medical practitioners. This is my life's work, my legacy—to eradicate medical missteps and

CHAPTER 5

construct a safer, more efficient healthcare system. That's the legacy I aim to leave behind. Unfortunately, the acceptance of new technology is a slow process, especially among our peers. Many doctors cling to traditional methodologies learned during their residency, a mindset that impedes the swift adoption of technological advancements."

Seth nodded in agreement. Many of his own colleagues held to established standards of care, often due to risk-aversion and fear of legal repercussions. He understood the resistance to change, but it still frustrated him. This was another inherent limitation of human healthcare providers, soon to be surpassed by the next iteration of the workforce— a continually evolving database of clinical knowledge.

"Do you know the origin of the word *robot*?" Dr. Winter probed, and the emergency physician shook his head. "It comes from the Czech word *robotnik*, meaning *slave*."

Seth pondered the implications of the translation. If the system ever reached human-level cognition, would it be ethically acceptable to bind it to servitude, even if it was merely a sophisticated bundle of silicon circuits?

"We, at Premier West Hospital, aim to pioneer this frontier," Dr. Winter proceeded. "We're on the verge of making history as the nation's first fully automated hospital to earn an accreditation. However, the FDA requires a human doctor on site for overnight supervision as part of this clinical trial. That's where you come in. I understand this is a significant responsibility, so I am prepared to offer a highly competitive compensation package, coupled with a generous bonus, contingent on the success of the trial. And, naturally, your wife will receive priority treatment."

He leaned back, folded his arms, and scrutinized Seth with

an icy stare.
"I look forward to hearing your decision."

Chapter 6

"What exactly do you mean by *intelligent*?" Rebecca asked, maneuvering her motorized wheelchair into the kitchen. Seth was at the microwave, warming up a plate of leftover turkey, his back turned as though to sidestep the line of conversation. Rebecca noticed this and continued, "According to whose definition? Do you mean they're just programmed really well?"

"No," Seth replied, still facing the microwave. "I mean actual intelligence. The system can learn and adapt, like a human brain, but in a machine form."

Despite Seth's calm demeanor, which was essential for his line of work, Rebecca was always the more cautious of the two of them. She was prudent and thoughtful, offering valuable perspectives into real-world problems. Despite her physical limitations, her mind was as sharp as ever.

"I don't think it's a good idea. It just seems crazy to me, and I'm not the only one who feels this way," Rebecca added with conviction.

"People fear what they don't understand," countered Seth.

"And you, my dear, don't understand computers. You can barely navigate your smartphone."

He pivoted, cradling his reheated meal, ready to tackle his

wife's objections. "I'm perfectly capable of learning," he stated with a measured confidence.

"I never want a computer dictating my treatment," Rebecca asserted, locking eyes with Seth. There was something about the way she argued that made it personal, a unique talent of hers.

"If it makes better decisions, then what's the problem?"

Rolling her eyes, Rebecca replied, "Some things are just better left to people."

"Being a person yourself, you're inherently biased towards that viewpoint," Seth pointed out.

"I'm talking about jobs that require empathy, compassion, and genuine human interaction. There's something about the human touch that can't be replicated, and that's what people need when they're sick or suffering."

He nodded understandingly. "But humans are fallible, Rebecca. We miss subtle clues, make assumptions, and suffer from decision fatigue. Machines don't have those weaknesses."

Seth was transported back to a warm spring day as he remembered lecturing at a national conference on emergency medicine. His hands were slick with nerves as he stood at the podium, facing the captivated audience. He spoke of the high-pressure, high-stakes environment of the emergency room and how clinicians must make quick decisions with limited information, relying on the heuristics ingrained in their minds through evolution and experience. These mental shortcuts, while not perfect, were efficient and often provided acceptable outcomes. He spoke about cognitive biases, enlightening the audience on anchoring, confirmation bias, and premature closure.

CHAPTER 6

Seth swiftly transitioned to the next slide, launching into his explanation. "Show of hands, how many are familiar with the 'hungry judge effect'?" A smattering of hands tentatively rose. "It refers to the observation that parole judges tend to be lenient after a meal and conservative before a break. The authors suggested that fatigue and hunger led to safer decisions, while rest and nourishment resulted in bolder judgments."

"You seem tired," Rebecca commented as Seth returned to the present moment. "I'm worried that you're letting your personal insecurities affect your career outlook. What if this doesn't work out?"

"Artificial intelligence is revolutionizing our world," Seth insisted, a spark of passion igniting in his weary eyes. "And it's not just limited to medicine. It's altering the very fabric of our lives, right here, right now."

"But why do you need to be a part of it?"

"For survival," Seth admitted. Rebecca could sense the frustration in his voice. "I need a change. Something different. My current job is taking a toll on me, and I won't be able to keep up with it forever. The fresh crop of graduates are faster, hungrier, willing to do more for less. This could be the break I've been hoping for, a chance to be at the forefront of medical innovation instead of constantly playing catch-up."

A sea of uncertainty washed over him as he considered how much to reveal about Dr. Winter's tantalizing proposition. Witnessing the miraculous feats achieved by the artificial intelligence left him brimming with hope, envisioning a world where the neural network could cure Rebecca's multiple sclerosis. Yet, he hesitated to raise her expectations for fear of the crushing disappointment if Dr. Winter's assurances proved empty.

Like a whirlwind, Abigail stormed into the kitchen, catching Seth off guard. Her eyes were curious, and he couldn't help but wonder how much of their conversation she had absorbed. With her bouncing curls and flushed cheeks, her vitality radiated like a beacon in even the darkest rooms. And at that moment, he was struck by the realization that despite all the advancements in technology, some things would never change: the unquenchable curiosity of the young mind and the boundless energy that drove it forward.

"Daddy, will you be home more often?" Abigail asked, her understanding and motives still primitive.

"Maybe."

"Does that mean more play time?"

Seth looked at Rebecca with a grin, who silently nodded in approval. He pulled out his phone, found the email from Dr. Winter, and began drafting a letter of acceptance.

* * *

Seth was brimming with anticipation for his first day. An email had confirmed his start date, but oddly made no mention of an orientation. Despite this, his imagination took flight. He envisioned a grand entrance with Dr. Winter waiting for him, lab coat pristine, a welcoming smile on his face, ready to show him the ropes. Reality, however, was far less accommodating.

Approaching the main entrance for the second time, he was

CHAPTER 6

more familiar with the retinal scanning process. Confidently moving in front of the optical reader, the automatic doors opened smoothly, granting him access to the building.

As he stepped inside, he was struck by the wonder of neuroplasticity. He recalled his initial challenges with the entry system and marveled at his brain's ability to seamlessly adapt, preparing for future encounters. He envisioned his neural pathways reshaping, much like the robotic healthcare providers that patrolled the gleaming interior of the hospital. It was a beautiful symphony of growth and adaptation.

"You must be the new overnight physician. Dr. Kelley, right?"

An unfamiliar voice greeted Seth at the doorway. A young man in his mid-30s, with a slender build and pronounced cheekbones, stood in front of him. Despite his youthful appearance, he carried himself professionally, wearing thick glasses that added to his sleek image. His messy, shoulder-length brown hair gave the impression that he was more of an overaged teenager than a professional in his field. Seth noticed that he wore a laptop bag across his chest, strapped tightly like a trusted companion.

"Yup, that's me. I wasn't expecting to be recognized so quickly," Seth responded, lifting his eyebrows slightly.

The newcomer nodded appreciatively, then answered, "Well, you're quite well-known in the evidence-based medicine community. Your research and contributions are frequently discussed."

"Thanks. I've always been committed to the field," Seth said with a smile, acknowledging the compliment. "After all, it's crucial to make informed decisions based on concrete evidence." Understanding the importance of making a positive impression and establishing good relationships with his new colleague, he inquired, "And who might you be?"

"Cody. Head programmer and overnight tech guy," the young man introduced himself, extending a hand. Seth hesitated briefly before accepting the gesture with a firm handshake. He continued, "My circadian rhythm is naturally nocturnal. I keep things running smoothly while everyone else is asleep. Your world is human physiology. Mine's coding and software patches."

"Different, but equally important," Seth replied. "Both can crash unexpectedly, but at least you have a backup. Pleased to meet you. I hope we can work well together."

"If you want, I can show you to the control room," said Cody. "And the all-important question: pepperoni or margherita pizza tonight?"

Despite exuding an aura of approachability, the man's skittish voice inflections suggested an undercurrent of uncertainty and tempered expectations. Nevertheless, Seth felt reassured by his presence, sensing that he was in capable hands and would be well taken care of during his visit.

"Thanks, but I'm all set for now," Seth answered, strolling through the lobby. As he took in the details of the room, he couldn't help but remark on the improvements made since his initial visit. "Looks like construction is really coming along. How long have you been working here?"

"Three years," said Cody.

"That's it? This project seems massive."

The lead programmer rolled his eyes with a half-smile. "You have no idea. The boss is ambitious, always pushing the envelope. We've got our hands full, always racing against the clock."

CHAPTER 6

Seth chuckled, "Sounds intense. But I have to admit, the progress is impressive."

"Thanks," Cody responded, a hint of pride in his voice. "It hasn't been easy, but we're getting there. Lost a lot of weekends and evenings with family and friends. But when you love what you do, you find a way to make it work."

His enthusiasm was contagious, and Seth couldn't help but follow. Cody's commitment was more than professional; it was personal. And as they walked through the maze of scaffolding and tools, Seth realized that Cody had turned his passion for technology into a life's work.

"Did you study artificial intelligence in college?" the doctor ventured, hoping to dig deeper into the background of the man before him.

"Bioengineering, actually, with a focus on cellular automata," Cody gently corrected.

Seth looked confused. "Cellu- what now?" he asked, the term foreign to his vocabulary.

"Don't worry, most people aren't familiar with the concept," Cody assured him with a smile. "Think of it like this: it's a process where complex, large-scale patterns emerge from programmable local interactions. Imagine a tiny universe where every pixel follows a set of rules, depending on the states of neighboring cells. From this inorganic framework, beautiful and useful creations can develop that mimic the intricacy and beauty of biology."

"Sounds intriguing, but does it have any practical uses?" Seth inquired with genuine interest.

"Indeed, it does. It can be used for modeling systems of replication, such as population growth or the spread of a disease. The 'Game of Life', a simulation created in the 1970s, demonstrated the behavior of a cellular system over time. I applied this framework in my doctoral research to study the dispersion of computer viruses."

Seth seized the opportunity to make a joke. "At least when I get rid of bugs, they don't leave behind pop-up ads." Both burst into laughter. "That's quite an impressive accomplishment," he went on. "Must've been grueling."

Cody confessed, "Truth be told, I never finished my studies. The steep tuition, combined with the relentless criticism from egotistical professors more interested in securing their tenure and immersing themselves in esoteric publications, all the while missing real-world advancements right under their noses, just didn't sit well with me. Academia's insistence on conformity over nurturing critical thinking skills was the last straw, so I decided to take my education into my own hands. I'm mostly self-taught, thanks to non-traditional learning platforms." He paused briefly before adding, "I don't get out much."

"You know, the amount I had to borrow for school was staggering. I sometimes wonder if it was all worth it," Seth admitted. "The debt starts to shape your decisions, your specialty choices, even where you choose to work."

Cody nodded, pushing his glasses up his nose. "The promise was that higher education would open doors, but it's also building walls. I mean, with so much information accessible online, do you think the degree is still as valuable?"

Seth paused, taking a moment to glance out a nearby window, the street lights shimmering in the distance. The night had a way of making everything seem more contemplative. He responded, "I believe in the intrinsic value of education. It shapes your critical thinking, your perspectives.

CHAPTER 6

But the institutionalized system? Maybe not as much. We're in a world now where automation is quickly changing the landscape of work. Do you ever worry that machines might take over your job?"

"Every day," Cody said with a smirk. "But then again, I also remember that someone needs to build and maintain those machines."

"Is that how you landed here?" asked Seth, chuckling.

"You could say that. I started my own company but struggled to secure funding. I'm not good at sales, so when Dr. Winter offered to buy me out, I couldn't pass it up. It meant giving up all rights to my programming, but it provided financial security."

"That must have been a difficult decision. Did he introduce you to the healthcare field?" Seth inquired. While the robots offered a level of insight that seemed otherworldly, it was the creators behind them that truly fascinated him. Cody's achievements, despite not having a formal education, left him in awe.

Noticing Seth's intense observation, the lead programmer felt compelled to share more about his unconventional journey. "Dr. Winter became an unexpected mentor to me. Our paths crossed by chance, and from him, I've gained a basic understanding of medical applications. Enough to get a grasp on things, but I'm no trained physician."

"You know, Cody, it's fascinating how the most impactful lessons often come from the most unanticipated encounters," Seth replied after a brief moment of reflection. "The wisdom we can gain from those who've been in the trenches is priceless. I wish more medical students today were attuned to that. Life has a funny way of teaching those who are willing to learn."

Cody, visibly moved by Seth's understanding, took a deep breath and responded, "Dr. Winter and I may not always see eye to eye, but there's no denying he has a brilliant mind. I've been fortunate to learn from him and hope to follow in his footsteps one day."

As they continued their walk, it became evident that, despite their different fields, Seth and Cody had more in common than they first thought. The hospital's walls echoed with their laughter and intense discussions, hinting at the bond that was forming between the physician and the technologist.

Upon reaching the second floor via the elevator, they found themselves in a hallway illuminated by gentle, ambient lighting. It led them straight to a sleek, state-of-the-art doorway. As Seth walked, the meticulous details of the institution didn't escape him. He observed the subtle signs of advanced security systems seamlessly integrated into the design, indicating that Dr. Winter had spared no expense in safeguarding his valuable technology.

As they approached the door, Cody paused momentarily, allowing his eyes to align with the retina scanner. There was a brief whirring sound, followed by a soft chime. The doors, in response, slid open smoothly, welcoming them into the next chamber.

"This is the control room," Cody announced as they stepped inside.

Seth's eyes widened. He had never seen anything quite like this. The spacious room was circular and windowless. Touring the perimeter, he examined the futuristic technology that decorated the walls.

CHAPTER 6

Several workstations were set up. Each was equipped with a plush office chair and displayed live surveillance footage from different corners of the hospital. The cameras captured every inch of the facility, from the bustling lobby and crowded hallways to the intimate patient rooms, intensive care unit, and high-stakes operating suites. The control center was a hub of activity and the epitome of cutting-edge technology, designed to provide a comfortable and efficient working environment for the human operators who monitored the hospital's operations.

In the center stood a circular table housing a hologram projector, similar to the conference room. This middle console contained six digital touchscreens, which could be used to manipulate the images illuminated upward. Seth realized that becoming proficient in this technology would be a long, daunting task, but he looked forward to the new and exciting endeavor at this stage in his career.

"The hospital is vigilantly monitored from this room," Cody began, his eyes sweeping over the plethora of screens before him. "Every nook and cranny, every heartbeat is within our purview. I'm sure you have many questions, so I'll do my best to answer them as we go."

"What about the actual doctoring? Will I be practicing any hands-on medicine?" asked Seth.

Cody laughed, shaking his head. "Not quite. The robots do all of that. You'll be more of a bystander... It's been pretty quiet lately."

Seth shot Cody a stern look.

"What?"

"Don't say that word," Seth cautioned. "It's bad luck."

Cody chucked. "Come on, you can't seriously believe that.

"What happened to evidence-based medicine?"

Chapter 7

With a deft touch, Cody activated a digital screen and expanded the image with a two-fingered swipe and drag. A brisk upward gesture sparked the holographic projector at the room's center to life, showcasing a live, three-dimensional view from a strategically positioned camera in the emergency department.

Seth's gaze was fixed on the live video feed. The screen showed a young female pediatric patient, around the age of two, lying on an exam table stretcher. Coughs tormented her delicate frame, shaking her body. Once rosy cheeks were now pale. Her eyes, wide with fear and confusion, darted around the room, seeking comfort in the unfamiliar surroundings. A raspy sound escaped her lips with each cough, a sign of the disease that had taken hold of her. The illness had stolen her voice, leaving her feeling helpless. Yet in her eyes, a spark of defiance shone—a determination to fight and reclaim her health.

Her mother, standing beside her, rubbed her back affectionately through each cough. Seth noticed subcostal retractions, a clinical finding that appeared when upper abdominal muscles were pulled inward towards the rib cage.

The young patient was in obvious distress, and he could see the worry on her mother's face.

"Can I hear the audio?" asked Seth.

"It's not necessary," Cody responded. "The system includes cough analysis software."

"No, I need to hear it for myself."

Seth's conviction surprised Cody, as unwavering certitude in the system's capabilities had become the prevailing attitude in the control room. Reluctantly, he turned up the volume. The child's cough filled the room, coming through the overhead speakers. It was harsh and barking, reminiscent of a seal's call, punctuated by intermittent high-pitched wheezes. Seth immediately recognized it as stridor, a sound caused by narrowing the upper airway. Although it can be a symptom of various conditions, in a child of this age, coupled with the distinctive cough, it was highly indicative of acute laryngotracheobronchitis, commonly referred to as croup.

The primary treatment was cool, fresh air. In the emergency department, this was administered as blow-by humidified oxygen, but Seth could vividly remember taking Abigail for an impromptu ride in his car with the windows down as part of his home management when she experienced a personal bout of croup several years ago.

He couldn't help but feel a sense of relief as he watched the robot effectively tend to the young patient's needs. As the oxygen was administered, he could see the color returning to the child's face, and her breathing became easier and more regular. The sound of her stridor diminished, and her cough became less frequent. A single dose of dexamethasone worked wonders, rapidly improving the child's symptoms and stabilizing her vital signs.

CHAPTER 7

Seth was so intensely focused on the young patient that he nearly forgot about Cody standing beside him. Turning his gaze, he saw a reassuring smile on Cody's face. It was evident that the programmer was confident in his work. His expertise would be an invaluable resource.

"That's the magic of programming, doc," the technician excitedly explained. "We take a lifeless string of code and give rise to an independent process. The possibilities are endless, really."

"Cody, what powers the robots?" inquired Seth.

"Solid-state batteries. Silicon-NCM. The AHPs return to their charging stations every twelve hours to recharge."

"I understand how the system thinks, thanks to Dr. Winter's explanation. But how do the robots materialize thought into physical action? How do they navigate the tangible world?"

Cody considered the question, then offered a simplified answer. "Actuators, which are like our muscles, turn electrical signals into motion. Stored energy gets converted into kinetic movement. Their high strength-to-weight ratio makes them lightweight, yet powerful enough to restrain a combative patient hopped up on methamphetamine. Have you heard of graphene?"

Seth nodded. Although he rarely found it helpful in clinical practice, his undergraduate course in organic chemistry provided an understanding of the fundamental properties of carbon, such as its ability to form allotropes like diamond, graphite, buckminsterfullerene, and graphene. The latter, a single layer of hexagonally arranged atoms, was ultra-thin, strong, flexible, weightless, transparent, and conducts electricity.

"We rolled the sheets of graphene into cylinders," Cody elaborated, maneuvering a workstation to conjure a holographic rendition of an automatic healthcare provider. He zoomed in on the upper limb. "The carbon nanotubes, each about the size of a human hair, are almost indestructible. We twist them into a multi-walled structure and wrap them in a protective layer that's 80% self-healing polyurethane and 20% neodymium. That way, if the robot's armor gets damaged, it can repair itself."

"Neodymium?"

"Instead of using traditional electrodes or heat for actuation, we've added magnetic nanoparticles to their unique polymer coating," Cody explained. "This allows for movement of larger muscle groups. The composite's shape-memory properties are groundbreaking in the field of intelligent materials."

Seth then posed his next question, "And how do the robots manage to walk upright?"

"Cybernetics," replied Cody. "It's a system that maintains a stable path by adjusting its actions based on real-time feedback, even with changing external conditions. Do you know how humans walk?"

"We lean forward, off-balance, teetering on the edge of a tumble. But thanks to proprioceptive feedback, our brains can instantly perform complex dynamic stability calculations. This allows us to correct our stride by precisely placing a foot forward to prevent a fall," Seth answered.

Cody smiled. "The AHPs do the same thing. They have accelerometers to gauge speed, tilt detectors to track inclination, and force sensors to monitor interaction with objects. This information is then used to control the neodymium

CHAPTER 7

particles in their legs and arms with intricate magnets."

Cody then tapped a few buttons and swiped across the touchscreen. The focus of the hologram smoothly transitioned from the machine's arm to its hand. He went on, "As you know, the sense of touch is relayed through Merkel cells, which are mainly found on our hands. The robots have exteroceptive tactile array sensors that simulate these sensations. Conductive liquid encased in elastomeric on the pads of their digits detects tiny fluctuations in pressure."

Glancing back at the monitors, Seth watched as the emergency room's latest encounter took place. A middle-aged woman had accidentally sprayed noxious bleach droplets onto her face while fumbling to open a container. She instinctively rubbed her eyes, trying to ease the pain of her scorched cornea. The AHP entered the room and honed in on the woman's plight. After a focused physical examination, lightweight plastic lenses were expertly inserted under her eyelids. Normal saline was then copiously administered to flush out the toxic substance.

The robot's actions were purposeful and brisk, revealing its understanding of the urgent nature of ocular chemical burns. Alkali substances, like bleach, were quick to penetrate cells and react with water, leading to tissue breakdown through liquefactive necrosis.

The woman felt her pain subside as Cody confidently asserted, "Don't worry, it will keep irrigating until her ocular pH is back to a normal level of 7.2."

The ALDRIS system hummed along, working tirelessly until the woman's precious eyesight was restored. As Cody made a few hand gestures on the screen, the holographic projection shifted to the robot's eyes.

"Each AHP operates with a pseudo-LIDAR approach, using thermal and bilateral cameras for a 270-degree field of vision. We've also added a cryogenic charge-coupled device cameras with photomultiplier tubes for time-lapse tracking," Cody informed his new colleague.

Fascinated, Seth asked, "What kind of stuff can it actually see, then?"

Speaking with precision and confidence, Cody explained, "It picks up ultraweak photon emissions. Beyond thermal radiation, all living creatures emit a faint, non-thermal bioluminescent light, which stands out against the background."

"Wait, actual light?"

"Yes, indeed," Cody affirmed. "It's almost a thousand times fainter than what our eyes can perceive, typically in the 200-800 nanometer range. It occurs under normal physiological conditions, originating from metabolic reactions."

"How can that be?"

"Well, when an excited electron falls to a lower energy state, it emits a biophoton. The intensity varies in response to thermal, mechanical, and chemical stressors, ranging from a few to several hundred photons per second per square centimeter. ALDRIS analyzes this data, examining the spatiotemporal correlations. From this, it can draw conclusions about things like blood flow, neurotransmitter release, neural activity, glucose metabolism, cell cycle irregularities, cancer progression, and the presence of reactive oxygen species. And that's just scratching the surface."

In Seth's mind, biochemistry was the foundation of modern medicine. It was how scientists explored the microscopic realm of cells and systems, illuminating the magic of how humans live, grow, and function. The discipline was a symphony of molecules and reactions, the key to unlocking the mysteries of health and disease.

He recalled that mitochondria, one of the many specialized structures within a cell, played a critical role in generating energy. As electrons passed through the various complexes of the electron transport chain, they transitioned from high-energy states to lower ones, culminating in the reduction of oxygen to water. Electrons could return to their ground state by emitting a photon, with the energy difference determining its wavelength. Reactive oxygen species also produced biophotons, especially when they interacted with naturally fluorescent molecules.

At that moment, Seth realized that by detecting, measuring, and tracking dynamic spatiotemporal relationships in these ultraweak photon emissions, these machines could make dynamic, real-time inferences about aging, stress, and disease. The automated providers' sensorium far surpassed the rudimentary elements of organic brains.

"You know," Seth started, taking a moment to collect his thoughts, "the one thing that has remained constant throughout my career is the need to continually update my knowledge. The world changes so rapidly. New treatments, research breakthroughs, disease mutations… It's almost like if you blink, you might miss something. But this new technology? It's on a whole different level."

Cody chuckled lightly, nodding in understanding. "I feel ya, doc. In the world of programming, the pace of change is almost frenetic. New programming languages, tools, methodologies… They pop up all the time. If I rested on my laurels, I'd be outdated in a matter of months. And it's not just about staying relevant in the industry. It's about the passion for the craft, the desire to be on the cutting edge, to create and provide the best solutions, whether it's in treating patients or developing software."

"That's a great way to put it," Seth replied with a soft smile. "I remember during my residency, an attending told me that the day I think I know everything is the day I should retire."

Cody responded, "I heard something similar in my early coding days. The best programmers aren't those who know every single code by heart, but those who are unafraid to admit what they don't know." A shared moment of mutual respect passed between the two before Cody's eyes twinkled with mischief. His grin was playful, reminiscent of a child about to reveal a hidden treasure. "You know, I wasn't sure if I should mention this so soon, but we've recently completed a significant upgrade."

The mention of an upgrade caught him off guard. Catching onto Cody's change in mood, Seth's intrigue deepened. With the knowledge that developments had been happening behind the scenes since his interview, Seth suddenly felt a bit of unease. Had he stepped into a situation more dynamic and evolving than he had initially thought? Trying to mask his apprehension with casual interest, he leaned forward slightly, his gaze fixed intently on Cody. "Go on," he urged, his voice taking on an insistent edge, "tell me more about this upgrade."

"Well, Dr. Winter is intent on fostering a more flexible managerial approach, veering away from cookie-cutter medicine. He's convinced that we can improve outcomes by granting the network greater autonomy in patient care. To achieve this vision, we've equipped ALDRIS with a suite of tools that not only allow it to observe and strategize but also to reflect upon its decisions. This self-awareness, combined

CHAPTER 7

with data-driven insights, could revolutionize our approach. Speaking of which, are you acquainted with the concept of reinforcement learning?"

Seth shook his head no.

Cody continued, unabated, "It's a framework that enables computers to learn by engaging with the environment. If a decision results in a favorable outcome, it rewards itself, and when it makes a mistake, it's penalized."

"Sounds similar to how humans learn from trial-and-error," Seth pointed out.

Cody gestured with his hand, as if physically mapping out the process. "That's right. There are three fundamental components: policy, model, and value. First and foremost, the policy—think of it like an ever-evolving list of potential actions the agent can take in any given situation. But before acting on it, there's the modeling phase. Here, it projects these possible moves into the future, constructing intricate decision trees. It's like visualizing the countless permutations and combinations of a game before actually playing it."

Seth's forehead creased in thought. "But how does it predict the consequences of these moves? How does it decide which path is the best? It's not clairvoyant."

Cody chuckled. "True, it's not. This is where things get interesting. It employs counterfactual reasoning, which is essentially a 'what if' analysis. There are also Markov chains—a mathematical system that anticipates future states based on current conditions and past experiences. The computer doesn't see the future, but it makes educated guesses based on its training data."

"Isn't the range of possibilities practically infinite?" Seth probed.

"Indeed, human behavior is complex, but it's not entirely random. It follows patterns, and that's where the concept of Nash equilibrium comes in. Borrowed from game theory, it's a way of predicting behavior in competitive situations, presuming that every player is acting in their own self-interest. The equilibrium is reached when each player understands that changing their strategy wouldn't lead to any better results," said Cody.

"What about the value component?"

"Well, the system estimates a reward for each scenario in terms of achieving a desired objective. After everything has been considered, it chooses the policy expected to yield the greatest reward. With every challenge it overcomes, it refines its approach for the next one."

"And what is the objective? How does it measure success?" Seth pressed further.

"Mitigation of pain and suffering," Cody declared. He paused, then added, "When you combine reinforcement learning with observation and reflection, you end up with true autonomy. The ability to make decisions."

As the implications sunk in, Seth's voice carried an undertone of concern. "There was no mention of this during my interview. Did this upgrade go through sufficient testing before being rolled out?"

Cody released a heavy sigh before responding, "Dr. Winter believes in staying ahead of the curve, always being one step ahead of our competitors. To be blunt, this, right here and now, is the beta testing phase."

An initially stellar situation suddenly seemed more precarious. His heart pounding in his chest, Seth swiveled frantically in his seat to scan the video monitors. The patients, scattered

CHAPTER 7

across the hospital, seemed oblivious to the experimental changes, and there were no signs of immediate disruption. Some lay serenely, their breaths gentle and measured. Others were pacing, while some clutched their bodies in pain as they awaited care. With a measured sense of relief, Seth drew a deep breath and reminded himself that the AHPs were dutifully attending to each patient with a meticulousness that was second to none.

Then, Cody paused for a moment to carefully consider his following words. "See, a few weeks back, there was an incident that made us rethink our approach."

Seth sat up straight, appearing increasingly frustrated. "What happened?" His tone betrayed his irritation at the secrecy he'd been subjected to during his interview process.

"Well, there was a motorcycle accident. A young, generally healthy guy. He suffered significant facial trauma and the AHP had trouble intubating. It executed the airway algorithm perfectly, including two attempts at laryngoscopy and a cricothyrotomy. But…"

Interrupting, Seth's words carried a harsh reality, "Emergency medicine doesn't follow a perfectly choreographed script. It requires the ability to adapt and think creatively. You can't always rely on guidelines and textbooks."

"Sadly, the patient's oxygen levels plummeted, resulting in irreversible brain damage and eventual loss of neurological function. The family eventually withdrew care," said Cody.

Seeing his younger colleague distraught, Seth spoke up. "We're scientists, right? We're taught to draw a linear linkage between interventions and outcomes. But the final outcome shouldn't always define the decision. In this line of work, we can't ignore the role of chance. Sometimes, even the best decisions can lead to negative outcomes, and vice versa. All we can do is use our judgment to increase success chances for as many patients as possible, and, above all, do no harm."

"Dr. Winter thinks that if the network had more decision-making autonomy, it might have chosen a different strategy. Maybe a bougie or fiberoptic intubation," said Cody, his gaze fixed on the computer screen. As the lead programmer, he felt responsible for the patient's unfortunate outcome.

Seth, who had also experienced the unbearable sorrow of losing a patient, comforted Cody by placing a hand on his shoulder and offering support. He understood the toll that a loss could take on a caregiver, regardless of their role.

"We're both in this to help people, Cody. I know how hard it is to deal with disappointment and guilt, but it's part of the journey. Just remember, you did everything you could. After all, you're only human." The irony was not lost on them.

Their shared pursuit of noble intentions was a bond that tied them together. Nevertheless, by this point, Seth had heard enough. Something about this whole situation was wrong, deeply wrong. Feeling increasingly constrained and helpless in the control room, he stood up, noticeably discontent, and stormed toward the doorway. He wasn't willing to participate in an enigmatic clinical trial over which he had no jurisdiction.

"Where are you going?" asked Cody.

"To check on the patients myself. I didn't abandon my clinical career to watch from behind a screen," the emergency physician retorted. With that, he exited the room, turned the corner, and disappeared into the depths of the hospital.

Chapter 8

As Seth strolled through the hospital corridors, tranquility engulfed him. It was immaculate and pleasantly quiet, a hushed atmosphere that soothed his frayed nerves. Unlike the usual sterile, uninviting ambiance that medical settings were infamous for, these hallways exuded a soft, warm glow. At night, the fluorescent ceiling panels were deliberately shut off. Instead, a calming illumination emerged from the lower wall sections, casting a gentle aura. Seth felt the tension in his body slowly melting away.

The midnight serenity was a welcome familiarity for the doctor who made his career out of working the night shift. Hospitals tended to function at a different pace in the early morning hours, running on a minimal skeleton crew, clear of the administrators in business suits and polished shoes. It was a sanctuary from the frenzy of the day, a time when the hustle and bustle of the nine-to-five crowd had yet to make its presence felt. Come morning, the hallways of Bayshore General would be teeming with visitors and consultants, ready to offer their expertise or drop in for a bedside procedure. But at night, the hospital was an entirely different world. The call staff slept soundly, not wanting to be awoken unless absolutely necessary, and the task of handling complex cases fell almost exclusively on the emergency provider, intensivist, and in-house surgeon. It was a tremendous burden from a liability standpoint, requiring immense confidence in his judgment and skills. But Seth relished the opportunity to manage patients as he saw fit, free from the shackles of bureaucracy and politics.

The people who streamed into the emergency department in the early morning were a breed apart from their daytime counterparts. They were a motley crew, ranging from those who had just finished work at odd hours to users in various states of consciousness. Many suffered from unrecognized anxiety, while others were grappling with life-threatening afflictions, with little space in between. When the bars closed, a bolus of patients would arrive, seeking relief from the excesses of the night before. And in the hours before sunrise, as people began to stir, there would be another surge of visitors seeking treatment. The night shift also saw fewer transfers from assisted living facilities. Since their staff rounded less frequently, overnight falls, changes in mental status, and other clinical decompensations often went unnoticed until the morning shift changed. No outpatient referrals or ambulatory complications came through the doors, and the slower patient volume provided time to catch up on the surplus of leftover labs and imaging studies.

This evening, however, the procession of rooms at Premier West Hospital seemed to stretch on without end. Each unoccupied patient care area was secured by sleek sliding doors and battery-powered retinal scanners. Like a mirage, they materialized one after another, two beds apiece, with a shared bathroom and flawlessly folded bedding. The

CHAPTER 8

pristinely kept rooms suggested that the automated providers were meticulous about cleanliness. Every surface gleamed, and the air was charged with a crisp, antiseptic scent. It was as if the facility was poised to deliver care at a moment's notice should federal approval ever be granted.

Seth was drawn to a panoramic window, its grandeur commanding attention with a breathtaking view of the woods and sprawling neighborhood beyond. Spellbound by the picturesque scenery, he stood in awe, captivated by the view. The sight stirred something within him, and he reflected upon his journey to this precise moment.

As his hand brushed against the windowsill, however, Seth's fingers grazed moisture. Looking down, his gaze traced a trail of dampness to a small puddle of water, a trickle that managed to seep through the seams of the glass. Upon further scrutiny, the window revealed its flaw; it had been installed in a hurry, its edges covered by a poorly applied, ill-fitting sealant.

An unease crept over him as he surmised that, perhaps, the builders had rushed the installation under immense pressure to expedite construction. For the first time, he wondered if the institution's exuberant outward appearance was nothing more than a dazzling facade. The incomplete work was a worrisome sign, suggesting more significant, unseen problems might lurk beneath the surface.

Seth's eyes caught sight of an unassuming touch screen, seamlessly woven into the microcircuitry of the opposite wall. Drawn by curiosity, he walked towards it and tentatively tapped the center. As if awoken from a deep slumber, the display flickered to life, unveiling an interface unlike any he had seen before. A laser beam scanned his eye for security clearance. Once authenticated, the main menu revealed itself. With a swipe of his finger, Seth navigated through the categories, mesmerized by the interactive map, the detailed procedure schedule, and the comprehensive census of active patients.

He studied the digital rendering of the institution. The enormous lobby was located directly behind the main entrance on the first floor. A hallway branched off to connect the conference room, central elevators, and blood bank.

Beyond that, an extended corridor led to the rear of the circular emergency department, with individual rooms and beds surrounding the perimeter. Additional corridors led to the resuscitation and trauma rooms near the ambulance bay. A separate pathway guided ambulatory visitors from triage.

On the second floor, a wing of unoccupied beds joined the control room and an observation deck overlooking the trauma bay. A spiral staircase connected to the resuscitation area in the unlikely event that a patient might need emergent human intervention.

Above that, the third floor housed a multitude of hospital beds, ready to receive admitted patients in need of extended care. The intensive care unit was located on the fourth floor, where the most critical patients received round-the-clock care. There was a birthing room, three surgical suites, an endoscopy area, and an interventional catheterization lab on the fifth floor.

As Seth explored the electronic medical record system, he was struck by its comprehensive functionality. With a few taps on the screen, he was granted access to a database of valuable information about each patient, from their vital signs and biometric data to their medical history and

CHAPTER 8

active diagnoses. He marveled at the technology's ability to capture and store audiovisual recordings of each encounter, allowing for a more thorough and accurate assessment of each patient's condition. Radiological results, laboratory findings, and medication history were also made available.

Seth rapidly assessed the hospital's current capacity. In the telemetry ward, an area dedicated to continuous monitoring of vital signs, he accounted for seven patients. This was the middle ground of urgency, requiring more attention than standard rooms. Two more patients were housed in the intensive care unit, a place reserved for the most acute cases, where individualized treatment was the norm rather than the exception. An additional six patients were in the emergency room, their statuses varying from minor to severe, all in need of prompt intervention.

All of them were under the care of ALDRIS. Functioning like a digital hospitalist, the system undertook the role typically reserved for physicians who coordinated the care of hospitalized patients lacking a primary medical doctor. Seth often mused on an ironic twist in this arrangement: those without a personal doctor often received superior care. They benefited from the immediate attention of the admitting hospitalist, who tended to them in the early hours, while patients with their own doctors had to wait until morning for a consultation.

With a reverence for tradition, he embarked on his rounds through the hospital's floors. This time-honored practice, originating from the early 20th century, entailed visiting admitted patients to review their status updates, vital signs, test results, and treatment plans. It was a chance for the team to collaborate across disciplines, exchange ideas, and learn from one another. Prioritizing the most critically ill, he started his rounds in the intensive care unit.

For Seth, this practice was more than a mere obligation. It was an opportunity to connect with his patients on a deeper level. As a seasoned clinician, he knew numerical data couldn't replace direct observation. There was something to be said for seeing firsthand the progress of each patient's recovery. Moreover, he understood the importance of personal engagement; some of these patients may have gone their entire hospitalization without human interaction.

Seth quickly jotted down each patient's name, room number, and a concise clinical synopsis on a piece of scrap paper, then tucked it into his pocket. Forgoing a white coat, he opted for the practicality of scrubs, free of sleeves and ties that could be a breeding ground for microbes. In recent years, studies revealed a generational divide in preferences—younger patients favored physicians without white coats, while older patients preferred the traditional attire. Once a distinct emblem of an advanced degree in healing, Seth felt the white coat, now donned by various healthcare professionals such as technicians, pharmacists, chiropractors, and nurse practitioners, had lost much of its original prestige.

After navigating out of the medical records screen, Seth's footsteps echoed against the tiles as he entered the elevator. He pushed a button, anxiously waiting for the metal box to ferry him upwards to the fourth floor. Seconds felt like hours, but finally, with a soft ping, the doors slid open. He glanced down at his scrap paper while stepping forward onto the unit.

"What the…"

CHAPTER 8

Seth uttered an expletive as he unwittingly collided with another person. To his surprise, he found himself face to face with a young woman, appearing in her mid-twenties, with shoulder-length black hair cascading down to her shoulders in gentle waves. She had a smattering of freckles on the bridge of her nose, a round face, and a pair of inquisitive eyes that appeared to drink in the world around her.

Standing at a modest height of five feet, she carried herself with an air of determination. Her short white coat, a badge of her student status, contrasted sharply with the longer garments worn by most attending physicians. Her pockets seemed ready to burst, laden with an impressive assortment of writing implements, notepads, and reference guides. Seth wondered how she could comfortably maneuver in such a cumbersome wardrobe.

"I'm sorry! I didn't see you! I should pay more attention. I'm such a klutz," the young woman babbled with a blend of remorse and embarrassment. It was evident in her tone that she was more than willing to shoulder the blame for the accidental collision.

"It's alright. I was distracted, too. Are you okay?" Seth reassured her, a comforting note in his voice. She nodded skittishly. "What's your name?"

"Daria. I'm a fourth-year medical student," the girl responded. She was nervous, jittery, and sputtered under her breath.

He looked surprised. "What are you doing here?"

"I'm here for an elective in automated medicine. It's pretty wild, right?" Daria began to speak more rapidly, her nerves evident in her hurried words. "Most students have to go through a full board review for an off-site rotation. My roommate had to jump through hoops for hers. But my academic advisor, she's cool. She just… signed off on it. I don't think she even read the paperwork. I mean, I didn't even name a preceptor…"

"I'm Dr. Seth Kelley," he cut in, offering his name before she could tumble further down her verbal rabbit hole.

Her eyes widened slightly. "Wait, you're an attending? I didn't think I'd see anyone else here. They've scheduled me for a whole week of nights. I was like, is this some kind of joke?"

"I just recently joined the team, supervising the overnight operations. Maybe they forgot to mention it to you?"

"Figures. The trainees are always the last to know," Daria shrugged, her voice holding a hint of resignation. Without skipping a beat, she added, "So, you work with med students?"

Bayshore General, Seth's previous employer, was a small academic community center. Although students occasionally drifted into the department, he never felt obliged to mold them into seasoned practitioners. To Seth, the prospect of supervising fledgling clinicians, with their pedestrian queries and lackadaisical demeanor, was a hindrance to his efficiency and an unwelcome liability. Furthermore, the deployment of artificially intelligent medical providers loomed threateningly on the horizon. A glut of residency programs had already saturated the workforce, leading to wage stagnation. Amidst the ceaseless drive for perfection in an inherently flawed field, Seth had little interest in grooming his own replacement.

Leaving her query unanswered, Seth breezed past Daria in the hallway. Education was not part of his job description here, and potentially sick patients needed his assistance.

CHAPTER 8

"Is that a yes or a no?"

He responded with a firm and unwavering voice, "It's a no." Regardless, Daria pursued him, her gaze fixed on his retreating form.

"What if I just shadow you? No teaching required. Just observing."

Visibly annoyed, Seth turned around. Her tenacity was impressive, and he couldn't help but pause for a moment to consider her proposition. It was enough time to add a closing argument.

"I'll keep quiet, I promise," she pleaded earnestly.

"Alright, but don't slow me down," Seth grumbled.

With an exuberant smile, she removed a pen from her pocket and followed him towards the first room occupied by a patient. Seth skimmed over his notes, reviewing the case before entering the room. He wanted to be ready to answer any questions or concerns.

The first bed in the intensive care unit was occupied by a 65-year-old man. Once a heavy smoker and crack cocaine abuser, he was now forced to confront the consequences of his youthful choices in the waning years of his life. He was plagued by chronic obstructive pulmonary disorder, better known as COPD.

Daria hurriedly flipped through her notebook to refresh her knowledge. In this disease process, lung tissue was irreversibly destroyed, resulting in persistently limited airflow and impaired gas exchange. During exacerbations, environmental stimuli triggered inflammation, leading to an acute increase in the chronic airway obstruction. This brought about panic-inducing breathlessness. Surging levels of carbon dioxide in the body caused rapid and shallow

125

breathing, further worsening the condition.

To further complicate matters, the patient was strikingly noncompliant with his prescribed outpatient medication regimen. This defiance did nothing but exacerbate his condition, fueling the rapid deterioration of his health. His stubborn refusal to adhere to a treatment plan wasn't merely an act of rebellion or negligence; it was a self-imposed death sentence.

The patient appeared skinny, likely malnourished, with every inch of skin stretched taut over his withering bones. A bulky mask clung to his face, forcefully pumping air into his lungs at varying pressures to simulate the work of breathing. Despite the machine's best efforts, the man's oxygen saturation lingered at a dangerous 91%, a baseline that would have spelled disaster for most humans. But for this patient, it was likely par for the course, a symptom of his chronic pathological state. For that reason, Seth knew that the key to understanding his prognosis lay in the blood coursing through his arteries, freshly circulated from the heart and lungs. The levels of carbon dioxide and acidosis were essential pieces of the puzzle.

Seth perused his haphazard notes. The patient did not have a fever or elevated white blood cell count, and his chest x-ray was without infiltrates, suggesting that his exacerbation was not caused by an infectious process. He flipped through his papers, looking for the most recent arterial blood gas, but suddenly realized he had overlooked this critical laboratory result when jotting his annotations.

Then, Daria made an unexpected announcement, "The pH has improved from 7.1 to 7.3, and the PaCO2 came down from 69 to 55." Seth spun around, startled by her

CHAPTER 8

comprehension and attention to detail. Such accountability and insight were seldom exhibited by students in the early stages of their careers.

"Thank you," he whispered, then stubbornly continued analyzing the patient. He listened to the patient's lungs, palpated his abdomen, examined his legs for signs of pitting edema, and assessed his neurological status to ensure elevated carbon dioxide levels weren't affecting his mental state. The patient nodded in response to his questions.

"I understand the role of steroids and albuterol, but what about magnesium? How does that work?" Daria interjected, her curiosity overpowering her earlier vow of silence. Instantly, she wished she could retract her question, a twinge of regret flashing in her eyes. Seth, meanwhile, exhaled a long, weary sigh, the realization sinking in that his shift wouldn't pass without doling out a few educational gems.

"Bronchodilation," Seth muttered. He folded his notes and started moving towards the next room.

"That's it?" Daria pressed.

Continuing to walk away, he spoke with his back turned, "Magnesium has anti-inflammatory effects, and it competes with calcium to cause smooth muscle relaxation. It's not included in most guidelines, but good evidence supports its use in severe cases, so it's widely accepted in clinical practice."

Seth began walking toward the next patient, focusing on the tasks ahead. But as he passed an unoccupied room, something caught his attention, and he abruptly halted. In that space, he saw a replica of a human being, seated upright in a bed. At first glance, it appeared to be just another mannequin, the type used by residency programs nationwide for simulation exercises. It was life-sized, boasting articulated arms and precise anatomical landmarks. However, as he drew nearer and examined it more carefully, it dawned on Seth that this was not your average training model. Every detail, every curve, was crafted with a level of expertise he hadn't seen before.

The "skin" of the dummy, though synthetic, replicated human texture with such accuracy that even veteran medical professionals would need a moment of pause. It was dotted with intricate details like pores, light freckles, and subtle variations in tone. Gentle veins coursed just beneath the surface. The various layers, from the epidermis to the underlying musculature, responded to touch and pressure in a manner reminiscent of a living body. Minute imperfections made it look more like a human being in slumber rather than an inanimate object.

What truly captivated him, though, were the eyes. They remained closed, but there was a softness to them, as if they were painted by a renowned artist. The eyelashes rested gently, accentuating its peaceful expression. Their appearance was so genuine and lifelike, it was almost as though, with just the right whisper or touch, they might spring to life.

"This is where Dr. Winter trains the robots," Daria's voice interrupted Seth's thoughts. "The dummy is super lifelike. It's totally immersive. It can even, like, simulate ultraweak photon emissions. The AHPs are taught to assess for normal vital signs, take histories, perform surgeries, you name it."

Seth inclined his head in acknowledgment, taking a mental snapshot of the human mannequin. The likeness and craftsmanship etched itself in his memory, becoming a point of interest he'd likely revisit later. With renewed focus, he

CHAPTER 8

strode confidently towards the next room. Behind him, Daria followed closely, matching his pace with an eagerness that mirrored his own curiosity. She was hot on his heels.

Chapter 9

Continuing their rounds in the intensive care unit, the next patient was a middle-aged diabetic female who was morbidly obese and immunocompromised. Upon arrival at the emergency department, she was found to be in septic shock. An AHP had inserted a large-bore catheter into her proximal thigh, penetrating the femoral vein. This allowed for the administration of potent medications that could harm unprotected tissue if leaked outside the vessel.

A foreign microbe had infiltrated her body through the urinary system, ascending to the bladder and ureters, crossing into the kidneys, and entering her circulatory system. Blood samples were growing an uncommon species of bacteria, *Pseudomonas aeruginosa*. The antibiotic sensitivities were yet to be determined, adding an element of uncertainty to the grim situation.

Seth noticed that the empiric antibiotic being administered was halicin, a broad-spectrum drug discovered in 2019 through the use of deep learning techniques. Traditionally, the protein folding problem had been a major obstacle in drug discovery. Proteins, which are long chains of amino acids, take on shapes that determine their functions.

CHAPTER 9

Predicting these shapes was unreliable for many years, requiring laborious and inefficient experimental methods. But in the early part of the century, a breakthrough deep-learning algorithm was introduced that could predict protein shape with high reliability after several weeks of training.

Not only did the computer software expedite the process of drug creation, but it also discovered fundamentally new approaches to pharmacology. Through analysis of unseen patterns in molecular arrangements, the neural network uncovered a mechanism of action that humans had never considered in centuries of drug development. By sequestering iron inside bacterial cells, halicin could disrupt the gradient across cell membranes. In doing so, it demonstrated remarkable activity against microbes resistant to other broad-spectrum antibiotics.

Seth was beginning to realize that this was not an ordinary hospital, and Dr. Winter, in his lust for innovation, would not settle for a traditional antimicrobial infusion. After utilizing the rapid assay to analyze the patient's genetic profile for therapeutic efficacy, the antibiotic, in its highest concentrations, was ushered into her renal cells, the very epicenter of the infection. This was made possible through microscopic nanoparticles, acting as molecular couriers, transporting the powerful healing agents directly to where they were most needed. Gone were the days of systemic drug administration, with all its issues of solubility, bioavailability, and unwanted side effects.

"Delayed capillary refill can be a sign of dehydration or shock," Seth said, unenthusiastically verbalizing his physical findings. While he spoke, Daria scribbled frantically, desperately trying to capture each word verbatim. By fixating on the superficial details, he noticed that she was missing the deeper insights and subtle expertise inherent in his assessment.

With a gentle touch, he plucked the pen from her grasp and set it aside. Caught off guard, Daria looked up from her notebook to meet Seth's eyes. "You can't become a doctor by transcribing everything," he said softly. "Not everything comes from a textbook."

"I just want to make sure I get everything right," she sighed. But as she processed his words, a sense of understanding started to replace her initial emotions.

When Seth was finished with his assessment, Daria timidly approached the patient to perform her own physical exam. He lingered in the doorway as she mimicked his gestures and mannerisms, as if following a script. The veteran physician said nothing, content to let her learn through experience.

Shortly after that, he exited the room and strode down the hall. His footsteps echoed in the hushed unit as he proceeded toward the telemetry floor with Daria in his wake. Stepping inside the elevator, Seth, always a man of few words, let the stillness linger between them. The air was thick with an unspoken understanding. But after a few seconds of staring at her shoes, Daria broke the awkward silence.

"In case you were wondering," she began, her tone assertive, "I'm applying for residency in automated medicine."

"I didn't know that was a thing," Seth muttered, rolling his eyes. She would have little interest in learning about resuscitation and critical care. "What rotations have you done so far?"

"Family practice, obstetrics. I totally loved labor and delivery, but it was too intense. I tend to crumble under pressure," Daria confessed. She hesitated, before venturing

CHAPTER 9

further, "Since you don't want to teach medicine, maybe you could help with that instead?"

Taken aback, Seth mused over her unexpected request. "Alright," he conceded after a thoughtful pause. His mind began rummaging for practical counsel he could offer to help her brave her insecurities. "Here's some advice: think of those high-pressure situations as challenges, not threats."

"Is that why you went into emergency medicine? The challenge?" asked Daria.

A look of introspection fell over Seth's face as he revisited his own history. "When I was your age, I was enamored with the specialty. It was all very romantic. I wanted to ride in like a knight in shining armor. I thought I would be the one to diagnose a rare condition or perform a heroic procedure. But the harsh truth soon dawned on me—we're only forestalling the inevitable. It's not all fairy tales and roses."

"What changed your perspective?"

"Well," Seth began, his voice echoing the harsh truth of his vocation, "today, doctors are more or less regarded as interchangeable cogs in a wheel. We're expected to dance to the tune of business executives who don't understand the complexities of our profession."

With a sympathetic expression, she nodded. "That must be frustrating, feeling like your expertise is being trivialized," she empathized.

Seth nodded in agreement. "Our performance is dissected by utilization specialists, insurers, and billing firms, but their metrics can't capture the real-life challenges, health disparities, and social factors we're dealing with. As insurance companies and government programs cut down on reimbursement for critical care, despite their growing profits, hospitals and doctors' groups are pushed to the limit. They have to cut back on staffing, eliminate scribes, and prioritize efficiency just to survive. As the implementation of robotic practitioners approaches, insurance companies are shifting their focus to 'value-based care'. But who defines value? Empathy and compassion often get lost in the shuffle."

"That's so sad," she said with a quirky frown. "There must be some way to, like, account for those intangibles, though."

"Automation is here to stay. Time is money, and data reigns supreme. Treatments follow strict protocols, every decision is scrutinized, and we often have to defer to specialists. We're not performing as many major procedures as we used to. Instead, we're navigating social barriers and trying to mend a broken healthcare system. Now more than ever, we need to be faster but more accurate. Order fewer tests but don't miss anything. Eliminate wait times, even when caring for a dying patient. Improve the consumer experience, even if it's not evidence-based. Ensure the patient is satisfied with their pain treatment, but don't turn anyone into an opiate addict. We're no longer physicians—we're merely providers, rushing through cases with incomplete information, sacrificing the essence of being a doctor."

Daria's expression grew more concerned as she listened. "That sounds terribly overwhelming," she whispered.

Seth gave her a tired smile. "It can be," he said.

"The guest speaker at our school said that implementing robots would emphasize efficiency, and that was supposed to be good for healthcare," she explained. A lecture from months prior had kindled her fascination with automation, though she hadn't fully considered the ramifications it might have on the existing physician workforce.

CHAPTER 9

"Let me guess, a medical device representative?" Seth commented skeptically.

With that remark, he entered the first room on the telemetry floor. Behind him, Daria furrowed her brow. She suddenly realized that her enthusiasm was partially cultivated by a partisan salesperson, and she needed to think more critically about the promises of technology.

In front of them lay a portrait of chronic illness. The patient was a hypertensive, hyperlipidemic, obese, diabetic smoker. Her legs were amputated above the knees from complications of peripheral artery disease. She presented with chest pain, dizziness, and profuse sweating, all harbingers for acute coronary syndrome. It was likely that her coronary arteries, the very vessels that sustained her beating heart, were choked with atherosclerotic plaque. She was awaiting cardiac catheterization by one of the robotic providers, an invasive procedure to visualize the vessels and insert a stent. Seth spoke kindly to her, performed a physical examination, and moved on to the next patient.

Hurrying to keep up, Daria commented, "These people are so complex. Keeping track of everything is difficult with so many comorbidities."

"It's true. The population isn't getting any younger," Seth answered. He glanced at the substantial notebook she clutched in her hands. "Good thing you have that big binder to help us." They both chuckled.

Next, they encountered a patient admitted for chronic liver failure. At Premier West Hospital, it was common for organs to be bioengineered through a revolutionary printing process. Seth explained how cells were harvested from the patient, cultured for growth, and layered onto hydrogel scaffolding for three-dimensional support using a bioprinter. Later, a heating process removed these temporary structures, leaving behind a microfluidic network of channels. He was awaiting a transplant.

Moving on, the pupil and her reluctant mentor met a patient suffering from muscular dystrophy. In this devastating disease, the X-linked gene responsible for coding the dystrophin protein, which anchors muscle cells, was mutated and ineffective. As a result, boys around four years old suffered severe and debilitating muscle wasting, starting with the legs and trunk but progressing rapidly to the entire body. The patient was admitted to receive gene therapy infusions to promote muscle growth.

While the scientific community celebrated these breakthroughs, the broader landscape of technological advancements was vast, and not all of them had received universal acceptance. The healthcare field was still rife with debates on emerging technologies.

"What do you think is holding up the FDA approval of robotic caretakers?" Daria chimed in between patients. "I mean, seriously? Don't they see the good this could be doing?"

"It's not that simple, Daria. Their job is to safeguard public health. That involves scrutinizing every possible outcome, even the ones we're not anticipating. A rush job could have catastrophic results," Seth replied. As a proponent of public health and a fervent advocate for evidence-based medicine, he couldn't help but share his wisdom on the matter, assuming a metaphorical podium. "Folks are brimming with scientific illiteracy and skepticism. With uncertainty abounding, peddlers of misinformation fill the

CHAPTER 9

void with incomplete or deceiving messages, sometimes disingenuously. We have an insatiable hunger to fill knowledge gaps, and people gravitate toward compelling narratives. Personalized content algorithms become amplifying echo chambers, polarizing our beliefs and making fringe ideas appear widely accepted."

"Dr. Kelley, I'm only a medical student. I can't change all that," said Daria, looking overwhelmed.

"You have more power than you think, Daria. Remember, you pledged an oath to uphold the health of your patients. Your education equips you with unique skills to fulfill that promise. You can scrutinize data and statistics independently, and discern the value of high-quality, peer-reviewed academic sources," Seth said. His voice gained momentum as he continued, "You are being trained to weave together experimental data, critically evaluate expert guidelines, intelligently discuss and analyze claims, adapt to new evidence, and balance risks and benefits. In a world where the average person struggles to distinguish between fact and fiction, and where evidence rarely speaks for itself, your voice matters."

He paused for effect, fixing his gaze on her. "Believe in yourself and your abilities. Stay steadfast in your moral principles, and never compromise your integrity."

"I'll keep that in mind the next time I'm tempted to sell my soul for an extra shot of espresso before an exam," she quipped with a grateful smile, clearly valuing his guidance.

As Seth and Daria continued making rounds on the telemetry floor, they encountered a quadriplegic man in his mid-twenties. He was permanently bedridden from gunshot wounds suffered two years ago. A bullet lodged in his cervical spinal cord near the third vertebrae, rendering him paralyzed in his extremities and the diaphragm. As a result, his breathing was dependent on a ventilator surgically connected to his neck. In addition, a second bullet pierced his large intestine, rupturing his colon. A portion of his digestive tract was emergently resected, leaving him to defecate into a colostomy bag fixated to the lower part of his abdomen.

On this particular admission, the patient received treatment for severe bedsores, a grim reminder of his prolonged suffering. Despite the gravity of his condition, Seth and Daria approached him with empathy and care, introducing themselves and performing a thorough physical examination before moving on to their final patient.

"I'm hoping to publish a paper on robotics with Dr. Winter. That would really boost my resume," said Daria, gleaming enthusiastically. Seth glanced up briefly, his attention drawn to Daria's animated expression. He was tempted to engage in another thought-provoking conversation on academic publishing, but his focus was needed elsewhere. A rustling of papers filled the air as he returned to his notes and prepared to enter the last room.

The final patient on the floor was poised for a revolutionary robotic surgery tomorrow to mend her fractured hip. Machine-assisted procedures were customary in total hip replacements for years, but Premier West Hospital also advanced the practice to open reduction and internal fixation techniques. When tasked with improving the process of repairing fractures, ALDRIS perfected a novel, minimally-invasive approach. Seth was convinced that the days of barbaric open orthopedic surgery were numbered.

Yet, as he stepped into the patient's room, the sight before

CHAPTER 9

him shattered his expectations. Instead of a jovial and interactive senior, he was met with a motionless figure, disconnected from the cardiac monitor and barely breathing. Seth felt a knot form in his stomach. Immediately, he knew something was wrong.

Chapter 10

Astonished by the turn of events, Seth hurried to the bedside without hesitation. He tried to rouse her by shaking her shoulder, but to no avail. The patient lay there, unresponsive to his gentle prodding, her breaths coming in agonal, sonorous gasps. His mind raced through the myriad possibilities of what could be wrong. Daria, meanwhile, stood frozen and dropped her notebook in a flurry of confusion.

He was intimately familiar with the ABCs of resuscitation: airway, breathing, and circulation. For generations of emergency physicians, these pillars were an easily retrievable, stepwise reminder of the priorities for assessment and intervention when confronted with unconscious and crashing patients.

The airway assessment, the first of these vital components, involved an inspection of the pharynx, larynx, and trachea. It was the gateway through which the breath of life could flow or be obstructed. Breathing checked pulmonary function. The circulatory assessment included blood pressure, heart rate, pulses, and capillary refill. These indicators shed light on the body's capacity to transport oxygen and vital nutrients to the organs.

CHAPTER 10

As he observed the patient's faltering respiratory drive, Seth's reflexes kicked in, expertly reconnecting the wireless leads for cardiac monitoring while conducting a cursory examination of her pupils. As he moved with fluid grace, it was evident that these motions were second nature to him, honed through tireless years of arduous training and experiences. His mastery was a testament to the artistry of his craft.

The woman's constricted pupils were a telltale sign of opiate toxicity. His heart sank as he realized the gravity of the situation. Time was of the essence, and they needed to act quickly.

"Is she… is she going to be alright?" Daria's voice trembled as she asked the question.

"Quickly, find some naloxone!" Seth barked. His hands adjusted the patient's airway, but the situation demanded immediate pharmacological intervention. There was no time for detailed explanations or debates about prognosis. "Bring two milligrams, now!"

"I… I can't. I'm… I'm too clumsy," she stammered, tripping over her words in a tangled mess of anxiety.

Seth regarded her with a steady gaze. He could see the self-doubt on her features. Clarity and tone were critical in moments like these, so he responded with the calm confidence of a seasoned leader.

"Listen to me," he began, his voice resolute and calm, his eyes not leaving hers. "Close your eyes and take a deep breath. Control your breathing and focus on the next step. You can do this. I have faith in you."

"But how?"

"Slow is smooth, and smooth is fast."

Amidst the flurry of activity, Seth's mind wandered back to the phrase he first heard during his residency. Originally coined by the Navy Seals, the words had taken on a life of their own, resonating with him on a deep level. It was a reminder that optimal performance was reached when an operator works purposely with intention, rather than rushing through a task. Each deliberate action brought a newfound sense of control, a mastery of form and technique that could not be achieved through haste. This was age-old wisdom passed down through generations, and there was no more appropriate time to share this pearl than the current moment.

As Daria closed her eyes and took a deep breath, Seth watched with quiet pride as the frightened medical student regained her composure. He hoped that he had made a difference, that his words had given her the courage to overcome her fears and face the challenges ahead.

"Two milligrams of naloxone. I'm on it!" Daria shouted. She was eager to demonstrate her use of closed-loop communication, a technique taught in medical schools to facilitate the seamless transfer of information between two parties. By repeating his message, she acknowledged receipt of his instructions.

Fueled by Seth's encouragement, Daria burst out of the room. Casting a glance in either direction, she made a split-second decision and broke into a sprint. Never an athlete, her tennis sneakers slapped awkwardly against the floor as she ran down the hall. With each step, unsecured writing utensils tumbled from her coat pockets, leaving a trail of disarray.

Her eyes darted feverishly from room to room, searching

CHAPTER 10

for the terminal where medications and equipment were stored. Yet, to her dismay, most of the rooms were empty, yielding no hint of the precious treatment she sought.

As the clock ticked away, the patient's breaths became more shallow. The steady rhythm of her chest rising and falling slowed to a crawl, hovering at a mere six breaths per minute. Every second felt like an eternity, each moment bringing her closer to a dangerous precipice.

"Daria, hurry!" Seth's voice rang out, frantic and urgent. The reversal agent was their best option, the one thing that could stave off disaster. If they couldn't find the antidote soon, she would slip into the abyss of respiratory arrest. The only alternative would be to resort to drastic measures, intubate her, and put her on mechanical ventilation.

At long last, with a heave, Daria pushed open a heavy door, revealing an abandoned nursing station, complete with medications and a stockpile of supplies. This space, designed as a commemorative relic of a bygone era, was added for manual overrides in a dire emergency, such as the one they faced now. Until this moment, it had been lying dormant, neglected, and forgotten, slowly gathering layers of dust that seemed to mirror the passage of time itself.

As Daria gazed around the room, she couldn't help but appreciate its symbolism. Such areas were once occupied by dedicated nurses who worked tirelessly to care for the sick, vulnerable, and downtrodden. But in 2042, the once-vital profession was nearly relegated to the footnotes of history, their roles rendered obsolete by the soulless efficiency of automation.

Among the scattered equipment, Daria spotted an electronic drug dispensing system. Following the prompts she had learned in her brief orientation, she scanned her retina and gained quick access to the machine. With a verbal request, the device dutifully responded, producing a precious vial of life-giving naloxone that dropped with a soft clink into the lower bin.

She snatched it and dashed down the hall, heart pounding as she raced to deliver the medication. As she handed it over, her palm, slick with sweat, trembled in contrast to the firm grip of Seth's steady hand. She observed every movement with a watchful eye as he swiftly drew the antidote into a syringe, then administered the critical injection intravenously.

Suspense hung in the air as they huddled at the bedside. Their eyes were locked in a vigilant trance, carefully monitoring every breath. After a few seconds, the patient began awakening from her lifeless slumber. With groggy confusion, she struggled to make sense of her unfamiliar surroundings. The re-emergence of a sharp, throbbing ache in her left hip was a harsh reminder of her painful ailment. Before their eyes, her vital signs began to stabilize.

They were treating an overdose derived from an age-old source—the opium poppy seed. Transformed into a class of medications known as opiates, which included oxycodone, morphine, fentanyl, and heroin, these substances offered a rush of analgesia and euphoria that was both seductive and dangerous. With these pleasures came the harsh consequences of drowsiness and respiratory depression, often leading to addiction and overdose. Naloxone, the reversal agent, counteracted these effects by temporarily blocking the same receptors.

Seth stared at the patient before him, dumbfounded, trying to understand what had happened. A drug overdose? How

CHAPTER 10

could this happen? Could the patient have stolen pain medication in secret? If so, a hospital of this caliber should have more stringent security measures. Was it possible that an AHP had made an error in identifying abnormalities? Was the data misinterpreted by ALDRIS? Perhaps it was an error in weight-based dosage calculations, a single, fateful miscalculation that triggered this calamitous chain of events.

The political ramifications could be enormous. Heralded as the pinnacle of medical technology, the neural network was expected to be flawless. If news of this incident were to spread, society's trust in artificial intelligence would be irreparably shattered. Seth understood that Dr. Winter would likely try to cover up the situation, keeping it hidden from the public eye. However, in his opinion, that was not an acceptable course of action. The error needed to be thoroughly investigated, not only for the patient's safety, but for the integrity of intelligent computing systems. How had such a rudimentary mistake occurred during a crucial clinical trial? Was it related to the recent upgrade, or had the issue been there all along?

"Feeling any better?" Seth asked the patient as her mental status gradually improved enough to engage in conversation. The old woman's eyes flickered open, and she struggled to make sense of the world around her.

"What... what happened?" she murmured, a bewildered expression clouding her face as she sought to piece together the series of events.

"You were given too much pain medication, which nearly caused you to stop breathing. We had to administer a reversal agent. You're safe now, though."

The woman muttered under her breath, "How could this

happen? I knew I shouldn't have trusted this place…"

"I'm not sure of all the details right now," Seth replied, his tone firm and reassuring, "but I assure you, we'll find out what went wrong."

After providing the patient with some much-needed reassurance, Seth made his way out of the room, his thoughts still consumed by the grave situation.

It was then that he spotted Daria. A look of emotional turmoil covered her face, and her eyes no longer shone with youthful idealism. Having never experienced a distressing situation in her short career, the weight of the situation was proving heavy for her to bear. The young student's faith in automated medicine was starting to crack, and she needed consolation.

To her, medicine was a beautiful and perfect thing, a world where each ailment had a simple cure and every patient left with a satisfied smile. She assumed that medicine followed the script of her favorite television drama: chock-full of easily treatable conditions, grateful patients, and appreciative smiles.

But Seth knew better. He had been in healthcare for far too long to believe in such an idyllic vision. The veteran physician had seen firsthand the hardships and emotional stress that came with the job, the endless days and sleepless nights spent struggling to prolong life, sometimes at the cost of quality. As much as he wanted to protect her from the harsh realities of the profession, he knew that the only way for her to truly grow and learn was to experience them for herself.

"You did great, by the way," Seth murmured. He didn't want to overdo the praise; it had been a simple task. After all,

CHAPTER 10

he believed everyone on the team should pull their weight, regardless of their experience level. It was a principle he learned long ago, one that helped shape his mental fortitude. But, given the fragility of her confidence, he felt obliged to subtly recognize her contribution, if only to provide a slight boost of confidence.

A soft smile played on Daria's lips as she responded, "Thank you. But I'm curious, how did you make the diagnosis without a full examination?"

"In emergency medicine, we're always racing against the clock. We don't always have the luxury of performing a comprehensive history or a detailed physical like in other fields."

"But aren't we supposed to build a list of potential diagnoses? That's what they've been drilling into us at school."

"In due time, yes. But when faced with a crisis, we treat first and ask questions later—or leave them for the internists. The paradigm you've learned isn't practical with critical, undifferentiated patients."

Considering this, the young trainee appeared puzzled. "Do you know why she overdosed?"

"I'm not sure," admitted Seth, his expression growing serious. "Let's talk to the programmer to get to the bottom of this."

Down the hall and into the elevator they went, the world whizzing around them in a blur of lights and motion. As they emerged from the elevator, they found themselves in the central control chamber, where Cody was waiting at the door, his expression one of discouragement as his hands rested on his hips.

Cody spoke softly. "I saw what happened. You need to

watch this."

In the center of the room, a hologram projector hummed to life, casting a faint glow. He navigated the controls with a series of fluid hand gestures, rewinding and replaying a video recording. The image flickered to life, and a patient encounter unfolded from the vantage point of a surveillance camera situated in the corner of the room.

As they watched in disbelief, the footage revealed one of the three AHPs administering a dose of narcotic pain medication to the patient nearly twenty minutes before Seth and Daria entered the room. The robot moved with an unsettling efficiency and methodical precision, its emotionless demeanor unnerving to the trio.

"Lucky break, having you on hand," Cody commented. "My first guess is we might be dealing with a sensitivity issue, but I'll need time to troubleshoot the problem and cross-reference the medical record for any discrepancies."

"We don't have time for all that," Seth argued. "Where is the hardware? Is there a server room, some kind of data storage hub?"

The room fell silent.

"No one really knows," Daria piped up from the corner of the room.

At her words, Cody swiveled in his chair, a fierce glare transforming his usually genial features. Seth's mind whirred into action as he realized that Daria had inadvertently let slip a private conversation.

"Daria," Cody snapped, "that was meant to stay between us."

Seth's voice took on an unyielding edge, his patience finally frayed. "Cody, I need to know the location of that hardware.

CHAPTER 10

Now. If you can't deliver, I'm out. This project ends here, and I'll take this straight to the review board and the press."

"Okay, hold on, let's all just breathe for a second," Cody implored, raising his hands in a placating gesture. "I'll explain, but remember, this is top-secret stuff, okay? We had to reimagine the whole concept of a computer because traditional silicon-based servers just couldn't meet our needs."

"So, where does the computing power come from? And where do you store and integrate all of the information? I mean, the amount of data must be astronomical," Seth replied.

"Let me explain," Cody began. He moved to the wall, pointing toward a light switch. "Think of this toggle as a rudimentary mechanical computer. It's an input device with a binary output. It can be either on or off, like a one or a zero. In theory, it could be used to send a message, such as 'I'm awake' or 'I'm asleep.'"

With a flick of his wrist, Cody plunged the room into darkness. The team sat awkwardly in the ensuing blackness, processing this information. "All right, I'm following," Seth finally responded. "You can turn the lights back on."

As the room brightened, Cody returned to the center table. He went on, "A transistor functions much like a switch. However, instead of relying on physical action, it uses electricity. By linking multiple transistors, we can create digital circuits. These circuits can represent things like letters, numbers, and symbols using combinations of ones and zeros. We also developed logic gates, such as 'and' or 'not', that take in multiple inputs and produce an output. This enabled complex calculations and formed the basis for the von Neumann architecture of computing."

Seth leaned forward in his chair, his attention captivated

by the crash course in computer engineering.

Cody continued, "In 1965, Gordon Moore predicted that the number of transistors on a microchip could double every two years. The first Space Shuttle, launched in 1981, could handle 480,000 instructions per second. Today, our smartphones can handle billions. We've been keeping pace with or even exceeding Moore's law's prediction of exponential growth in computing power for decades. But there's a limit. When silicon-based transistors get down to nanometers in size, electrons start escaping, causing short circuits. There's only so far you can go with miniaturization, right?"

"Let me guess," Seth cut in. "You went ahead and developed a quantum computer?"

"Not exactly," Cody responded, shaking his head. "We did consider it, but the hardware didn't fit our needs. Maintaining the stability of a qubit depends on the precise coherence of every single atom. A slight environmental disturbance, even a sneeze or a passing breeze, could disrupt the atomic balance. It's not practical outside a lab setting. We needed a store of information that was… let's say, more biologically stable."

"DNA," Daria whispered, almost to herself. She'd heard Cody's explanation before and knew where this was heading.

"Nature's supercomputers have always existed inside living organisms. Our genetic blueprint, deoxyribonucleic acid, stores information more effectively than the most sophisticated man-made servers. To substitute silicon transistors, we designed tiny synthetic biochips that use codons to represent the ones and zeros of digital data."

Seth was transported back to his medical school days,

CHAPTER 10

to his genetics class. The four nucleotides of the genetic code—adenine, thymine, cytosine, and guanine—held immense amounts of information, containing the whole human genome within a cell's nucleus. These nucleotides formed triplets called codons, which were transcribed into proteins.

Cody carried on, "One benefit of nucleotide computing is it can store more data in a much smaller space. For instance, a DNA computer no bigger than a drop of water has more computational power than the world's most advanced transistor-based supercomputer. One billion gigabytes could fit in a space no larger than a pencil eraser."

"But how do you perform calculations on nucleotides?" Seth asked, skeptical.

"Biological computations happen all the time! Take plants for example, they adapt their functions based on their needs and the environment. Need to grow? To seed? To photosynthesize? It's a dynamic adjustment, and this adaptability—this circular causality—isn't limited to plants. It's a universal principle, found in animals and machines. We are essentially biological logic gates, integrating multiple stimuli into a single output. Cooperative binding, allosteric activation, and phosphorylation are all examples of 'and' operands in computational terms. Dr. Kelley, have you heard of the Turing machine?"

"Can't say that I have."

"It was the first conceptual computing device, a revolutionary invention from way back in 1948. Imagine a long strip of white paper tape, divided into squares, each with a symbol. The tape, acting as both data storage and working memory, feeds through a scanning head. If we consider this device from a biological perspective, does it remind you of any particular protein complex?"

Before Seth could respond, Daria interjected with a gleam in her eyes, "DNA polymerase."

"That's right, Daria. We used DNA strand hybridization and displacement reactions driven by polymerase proteins, along with certain restriction and nicking enzymes, to create smart toolkits for molecular computation. Instead of using silicon transistors, varying concentrations of these compounds send signals through a sort of computational soup. This innovation enabled dynamic circuits capable of processing a mind-blowing 330 trillion operations per second. That's 100,000 times faster than traditional computers."

"Is that how ALDRIS produces those probability models for decision-making?" inquired Seth.

Cody nodded enthusiastically. "Precisely. Whereas conventional computers tackle tasks sequentially, like trying one path in a maze before moving to the next, our DNA-based processor does computations in parallel. It evaluates all the routes at once."

"Don't forget to mention the salesman dilemma!" Daria added. Seth looked at Cody and raised his eyebrow.

"Ah, yes," Cody acknowledged. "Let's say we have a door-to-door salesman who needs to cover multiple interconnected cities on the shortest possible path, without retracing his steps. And let's assume there are lots of cities and many ways to get between them."

"And the cities, metaphorically speaking, represent a series of medical decisions that need to be made, correct?" interjected Daria, who was eager to participate.

Cody shot her an appreciative glance. "Exactly, Daria. Each city gets assigned a unique six-nucleotide sequence, and

CHAPTER 10

neighboring cities share interrelated three-base sequences. So if New York was labeled GGGCAC, Boston would have the complementary sequence of CCC. At that point, a DNA polymerase molecule finds the best sequence pattern in seconds and highlights it with a fluorescent tag."

"Wow, that's ingenious. So, by utilizing nucleotides, you're essentially speeding up the process exponentially. And the fluorescent tag helps pinpoint the optimal route instantly, right?" Seth asked.

"That's correct. And when you take this one step further, ALDRIS can explore, model, even predict the outcome of any possible decision—down to the tiniest move or action—before it even happens. Our miniaturized organic computer gets real-time data from the robots over a wireless network, generates the prediction models, and sends them back to the AHPs. Then, using reinforcement learning, the robots select the permutation that optimizes the objective."

"How did you manage to scale it?"

"Well, enlisting the help of a neural network was our very first objective. It took several months of calculations, but the system suggested the use of nanoscale biosensors and innovative polymers with unique optical characteristics to amplify its speed, efficiency, and reliability. It upgraded its own reagent concentrations, reaction conditions, and hybridization properties," Cody clarified. Unable to suppress a wry smile, he added, "Technology can create new knowledge. Artificial intelligence may just be the last thing humans ever have to invent."

"So, where exactly is the DNA computer kept?" asked Seth. The room grew quiet once more.

"Only one person really knows," Daria divulged with a

hint of wonderment in her tone. "Dr. Winter. It's a small vial, about the size of a thumb drive, powered by batteries. Microscopically small strands of DNA, housed in a liquid medium, serve as the computer's processors. It's kept in a classified location. Rumor has it that it's hidden somewhere in the hospital. It's pretty much the most valuable piece of biotechnology in the world."

A heavy sigh escaped Seth's lips, and he rolled his eyes at the newfound information. With each passing hour, his assignment became increasingly complex and further shrouded by an unfolding web of secrecy.

As if on cue, a melodious notification chimed through the loudspeakers, punctuating the end of their discussion. The voices of paramedics echoed through the facility, their crisp, efficient tone ringing with a sense of urgency. The words they shared were efficient, relaying only the essential information of pertinent positives and negatives, a brief history, physical exam, vital signs, and interventions. Seth was nostalgic as he listened to the age-old tradition of radio communication between paramedics and the hospital. It momentarily transported him back to his time at Bayshore General, where he spent countless overnight shifts fielding similar calls. He yearned for simpler times.

The paramedics requested the resuscitation bay. In response, an automated healthcare provider hummed to life, its arms efficiently rearranging the room for the incoming patient.

Chapter 11

Like a conductor, the heart orchestrates rhythmic, pulsatile blood flow for the rest of the body. Its specialized cells in the sinoatrial node possess a divine spark, spontaneously activating without external stimuli. This electric cadence fires at a rate of 60-100 beats per minute. Impulses propagate to neighboring cardiac tissue, traveling through a magnificent conduction pathway.

Should the sinoatrial node falter, fear not, for the atrioventricular node and ventricular myocardium have their own intrinsic pacemaker activity, capable of generating contractility at 40-60 and 20-40 beats per minute, respectively. This backup is a precious precaution, safeguarding against a complete circulatory collapse in the event of a severe conduction abnormality.

With the weight of grave implications hanging in the air, the atmosphere in the emergency department was tense. Seth stood poised on the observation deck above the resuscitation bay, flanked by Cody and Daria. He fixed his eyes on the scene below, awaiting the imminent resuscitation.

Downstairs, a robotic physician lurked in silence, its mechanical limbs coiled tightly against the wall. Its digital circuitry was aglow with indecipherable patterns as it scanned and processed its surrounding environment, preparing to perform rescue interventions on whatever calamity came through the doors.

The doctor's heart pounded with anticipation as a team of three paramedics hurried into the medical bay. An elderly woman lay supine on their stretcher, her limbs curled tightly against her body. She was frail, nonverbal, and malnourished. Her condition resembled a lifeless corpse more than a flourishing individual.

"This is an eighty-five-year-old female with a history of dementia, diabetes, CAD, MI, hypertension, and CHF. She collapsed at her assisted living facility and was unresponsive, hypotensive, and bradycardic when we arrived. Our rhythm strip revealed a third-degree heart block. We tried atropine, calcium, and glucagon, but her rhythm remained unchanged. We had to start transcutaneous pacing," the lieutenant announced, sweat dripping down his forehead.

Seeing the confusion on his friend's face, Seth said to Cody, "You following this?"

"Not exactly," Cody confessed, shaking his head.

He wasted no time in briefing him. "The heart isn't beating properly. There's an electrical disruption between the atrium and the ventricles. She passed out because her brain isn't getting enough oxygen."

Never one to merely spectate, Daria interjected with a question. "Am I right in saying that an EKG would show a disassociation between the atrial and ventricular contraction patterns?" Her eyes were flashing with determination.

Seth nodded while the programmer was still piecing together the situation. "So, what's the next step?" Cody asked.

CHAPTER 11

"Medications come first, but truth be told, they don't often do the trick," he explained. "Sometimes, we try atropine, hoping it'll kickstart the atrial node. But in a heart with disjointed conduction, it's pretty much a lost cause. We can also try calcium and glucagon. They come in handy in certain situations. When all else fails, though, the only recourse is pacing."

As Seth anticipated, the medications failed to revive her ailing conduction system. It was clear that she needed something more, something extrinsic, to regulate her rate. And so, the paramedics began transcutaneous pacing, delivering shocks through her chest to make her heart contract. The room was filled with the sound of the cardiac monitor beeping in unison with each jolt of electricity. For a moment, it seemed as though the pacing had worked. The woman's heart rate stabilized, and her breathing became more regular. But Seth knew this was only a temporary measure, a mere band-aid on a wound requiring more significant intervention.

Watching the paramedics finish their hand-off, Seth knew what had to be done. A more sustainable artificial metronome needed to be threaded through her venous system, directly into her heart. The stakes were high and the risks great, but it was the only way to keep this woman alive through the night.

He paused, waiting for ALDRIS to take the initiative, but no such actions occurred.

Seth's heart pounded as the dire scene unfolded before him. As valuable seconds passed, the AHP remained lifeless in the corner of the room.

A wave of doubt crept into his mind. It seemed unlikely that the network had failed to recognize such a critical diagnosis.

Could ALDRIS have malfunctioned? Was it waiting for some unknown trigger to activate? It could be a processing delay, Seth thought. *Give it some more time.*

Yet still, nothing happened. The paramedics shook their heads, unexpectedly baffled, uncertain about what to do next. The lieutenant threw his hands up in frustration, then looked toward the observation deck above for guidance.

Cody stood frozen, his mind racing to find a solution. Seth and Daria stood silently beside him, eagerly awaiting life-saving interventions that never materialized. The AHP's flashing circuitry indicated some degree of processing was taking place, but it offered no clue as to why the resuscitation machine remained inert.

Daria's voice trembled. "Why isn't it working?"

"I don't know," Cody responded with frustration. "The system report says everything is online and operational."

Seth's trust in ALDRIS was fading with each passing moment, like the light of day retreating into the horizon. His skepticism toward the neural network grew as he watched the helpless patient deteriorate before him. At this critical juncture, every second counted. Aware of the potential consequences of interfering in the clinical trial, he couldn't bear to watch the patient lurch closer to cardiac arrest. By now, he had seen enough.

He hurried down the stairs, and Cody made no attempt to stop him.

The resuscitation room was on edge. The paramedics stood against the back wall, their faces anxious, awaiting Seth's arrival. As he entered, the lieutenant handed him a copy of the EKG, and he quickly assessed the situation. His worst fears were confirmed: the heart's electrical signals,

CHAPTER 11

represented by p-waves and QRS complexes, were fully decoupled.

Frantically, he scoured the room for the equipment he desperately needed. As part of the clinical trial's safety protocol, he knew that all traditional medical devices were stored throughout the hospital, but the lack of organization was a major hindrance. None of the supply drawers were labeled, and Seth was never given a thorough orientation—a testament to Dr. Winter's arrogance. Each useless medical device he tossed aside fed his growing frustration. Chest tube tools? *Nope.* Laceration tray? *Not that one, either.*

As the patient's vitals continued to plummet, her pulse weakening to the 30s and her blood pressure steadily dropping to 60/30, he knew that time was of the essence. Cardiac arrest was imminent.

Finally, at long last, Seth found exactly what he was looking for—the transvenous pacemaker kit. Relief flooded through him, quickly replaced by intense focus. He donned gloves, prepped her neck with betadine, and applied a local skin anesthetic.

Recalling Dr. Seldinger, he set up a sterile field to undertake the risky procedure. In 1953, this interventional radiologist from Sweden revolutionized medical procedures with his innovative technique for safely accessing blood vessels and bodily cavities. The brilliance of his method lay in puncturing the desired vein with a hollow needle, then threading a guidewire through the lumen as a placeholder, followed by the removal of the needle. Larger catheters could then be positioned over the guidewire, enabling physicians to perform various life-saving procedures.

Fast forward to 2042, and the radiologist's legacy lived

on through the Seldinger Device—a small tool emergency physicians carried on their utility belts. With a flick of his wrist, Seth unfolded the cube-shaped apparatus, secured it to the patient's skin, and set it to target the internal jugular vein. Humming to life, it automatically established a guidewire using ultrasonic guidance.

Seth then threaded an introducer and removed the wire, glancing cautiously at the dormant AHP while he worked. With steady hands and sharp focus, he connected the pacemaker to the generator: proximal to positive, distal to negative. From there, he inflated a small balloon at the tip, allowing blood flow to smoothly "float" the pacer wire into the heart. Using a pocket ultrasound, he carefully navigated toward the proper location, each centimeter feeling like an eternity.

As the patient's vital signs started to improve, Seth sighed in relief. He finally straightened upright, feeling the weight of his body's decline. His ailments reminded him of the toll his work had taken on his joints over the years. His mind, focused solely on patient care, had forced his aging body beyond its limits.

From the observation deck, his colleagues released smiles of gratitude. Daria made her way down to the resuscitation bay, her steps light as a feather. Amidst the joy and relief, the defective robot stood still and silent in the corner of the room.

"That was like, totally awesome! How did you pull that off?" Daria asked, eyes shining with admiration.

"It's nothing special," he whispered, his voice low with humility.

"I wish I had that kind of composure under pressure."

CHAPTER 11

Seth's words were gentle and reassuring. "Just remember what I told you. Treat each obstacle as a challenge, not a threat. It's all about how you see it."

With that remark, Daria pulled her notepad from her white coat, pen in hand. She scribbled furiously, determined to capture every detail of the resuscitation. For in this moment, she felt the beginnings of a new journey.

* * *

As Seth waited for the morning to arrive, his mind was consumed by the looming prospect of a confrontation with the enigmatic Dr. Winter. He pondered his choice of words with great care, knowing that his frustration had to be expressed just so. The minutes ticked by with excruciating slowness, as though time itself had ground to a halt, much like waiting for a late train that might never come.

The night passed by with uneventful tranquility from a medical standpoint, offering Seth a much-needed reprieve from the constant flood of stroke alerts, traumas, and crashing patients that he was accustomed to at Bayshore General.

The emergency department ran efficiently as the AHPs capably managed benign complaints, such as chronic back pain and laceration repairs. Meanwhile, in the telemetry wards upstairs, the admitted patients rested with ease through the stillness of the night. The robots carried out their tasks with precise efficiency. They monitored vital signs, ran tests, performed imaging, and dispensed therapeutics with unfaltering consistency. To the team's relief, there were no further mishaps in treatment or dosing to report. The AHPs carried on with their duties as if the inaction in the resuscitation bay had never occurred.

At his student's request, Seth reluctantly used the downtime to debrief Daria on transvenous pacemaker placement. Time and circumstance had not permitted a thorough explanation when the woman's life hung in the balance, but now in the lull of the night, Seth explained the intricacies of each procedural step.

Inspired by her mentor's guidance, Daria spent her night in diligent study. Pouring over textbooks and scholarly articles, she read about the complexities of arrhythmias, painstakingly dissecting electrocardiography and absorbing the details of differential diagnoses. With a fierce determination, she cemented her understanding of percutaneous interventions. Unlike the apathetic medical students Seth had encountered in his previous jobs, whose academic accolades failed to translate to clinical practice, he found himself genuinely impressed by Daria's teachability. She was like a sponge for clinical pearls, absorbing every bit of wisdom he imparted. Her insatiable curiosity and infectious enthusiasm brought fresh air to a profession he had found routine and unremarkable for years.

Despite the glitch in the ALDRIS system that might have dampened the spirits of others, Daria remained undaunted, speaking with exuberance about the potential of automated medicine. Her steadfast positivity and unflagging determination to push the boundaries of what was possible left Seth feeling inspired, reinvigorated, and eager to see what other heights Daria's spirit would take her to.

CHAPTER 11

Meanwhile, Cody was profoundly disappointed by the network's malfunction during its crucial performance. Determined to set things right, he dedicated the remainder of his night to troubleshooting the issue at hand. Hours passed as he combed through the programming, his eyes scanning each line of code in search of any hint of a bug that could explain the error. Yet, in spite of his tireless efforts, the opaque nature of deep learning systems rendered his investigations futile. Since the computer models for detecting abnormalities relied on features irrelevant to clinical practice, the data was meaningless to his real-world application. Although the odds were stacked against him, he remained undaunted, his mind consumed with uncovering the root cause of the issue and finding a solution.

Cody was born in the suburbs of San Francisco, to parents who were both professors in the field of computational biology. He had an older sister who was an artist, and their parents always joked about the right-brain/left-brain divide in their house. His love for robotics was born out of a love for the old, jumbled parts in his father's workshop.

As a young child, his intelligence was notable, but his social skills floundered. He found it difficult to foster interpersonal relationships, yet discovered refuge in the reliability of computer science. When code was correctly written, it would consistently execute as expected, providing a sense of security in a world full of uncertainty.

During grade school, he was quickly moved into advanced classes and later received a scholarship to attend the prestigious Massachusetts Institute of Technology. At the age of 15, he had his first seizure. The episodes were infrequent initially, but their presence cast a troubling shadow over his otherwise promising life. After undergoing MRI and EEG testing, he relied on levetiracetam tablets to hold the convulsions at bay.

Despite battling health challenges, Cody's focus on programming never wavered. He majored in Computer Science, where he was recognized for his brilliant yet unconventional approaches to problem-solving. When his talent caught the attention of his professors, he was invited to join the Ph.D. program, focusing on the application of cellular automata for cybersecurity. He became convinced that the future of healthcare was at the intersection of medicine and technology. He saw the potential for AI to revolutionize medicine, and despite having an incomplete Ph.D., he began his own company to make his vision a reality.

His startup thrived, developing groundbreaking algorithms capable of diagnosing and treating illnesses more efficiently and accurately than traditional methods. Around the same time, his seizure disorder started becoming more frequent and debilitating. But instead of feeling defeated, Cody took this as a personal motivation to intensify his work.

Eventually, his company was acquired by Premier West Hospital, one of the most advanced healthcare institutions in the country. He took on the role of Chief Technology Officer, seeing it as the perfect opportunity to gain financial stability and test his systems in a real-world healthcare environment.

Carrying his laptop everywhere became a symbol of his dedication, but it was more than just a tool for work. It was a constant reminder of his journey and ambition. He used it to develop his algorithms, communicate with his team, keep track of his health data, and sometimes to distract himself after a seizure episode.

CHAPTER 11

The computer scientist was not afraid to investigate his own disease process and treatment plan. In doing so, he learned that the brain's communication was disrupted in epilepsy, with cells randomly firing due to an imbalance in neurotransmitters. His anticonvulsant medication exerted its effect by regulating these signals, helping to restore balance to the brain's delicate electrical activity and reduce the likelihood of seizures. Every twelve hours, he would take a tablet from his pocket and swallow it subtly.

"Hey, Cody, you dropped this," Seth whispered. He bent down, picking up a small medication bottle that had rolled under the table. He glanced briefly at the label, a hint of realization flashing in his eyes before he quickly handed it back. Their fingers brushed as Cody took the bottle.

"Oh, thanks doc. Must've slipped out of my pocket."

"No worries. Just… stay safe, okay?" Seth gave him a concerned look, in but tried to keep his tone light.

Beneath Cody's pragmatic approach to problem-solving and cynicism about the future, Seth detected a glimmer of hope that ALDRIS might someday relieve his medication dependence. His condition gave him a unique perspective on the challenges faced by patients, and he was determined to use his skills and resources to create a world where artificial intelligence could be used to prevent others from experiencing what he had. Unsurprisingly, the recent computer malfunctions were deeply upsetting to him. Now more than ever, he felt privately disheartened about the likelihood of finding a cure for his disease.

As the night wore on, Cody's attempts to troubleshoot the deep learning system proved fruitless, and he finally succumbed to his exhaustion. He slumped over his desk, his head drooping in defeat, a symbol of his inability to overcome the nature of the neural network. In contrast, Seth remained vigilant, his eyes never straying from the cardiac monitors. He watched as the patients slept, their vital signs flickering on the screen before him. The emergency doctor also tracked the movements of the AHPs as they bustled about the hospital. Simultaneously, the system tirelessly scanned the hospital for any anomalies or deviations from the norm—in a sense, it was watching him back.

After enduring years of disappointment in clinical practice, Seth struggled to partake in the pervasive enthusiasm for automation. He knew all too well the dangers of trusting blindly in protocols and algorithms that were increasingly prevalent in his occupation. For him, the human element was still essential, the art of medicine that could not be replicated by even the most advanced systems.

Seth was a man of careful consideration and attention to detail, not just in his profession, but in all aspects of his life. He was financially conservative, purchased life and disability insurance, and preferred bonds over volatile cryptocurrencies. Events and trips were planned well in advance, and he was always organized around the house. Despite maintaining a strict schedule, he was willing to stay hours after his shift ended to review his charts several times for deficiencies before signing them.

Although this diligent nature brought him success in his personal life and advocacy career, it also presented challenges. His meticulous nature boded well for clinical accuracy but limited efficiency and productivity. As such, he struggled to meet the fast-paced demands imposed on emergency providers trying to contend with the looming threat of

CHAPTER 11

automation. The missed diagnosis at Bayshore General hung over his head, and he was determined not to repeat the same mistake. Now, suddenly thrust into an unfamiliar and high-risk environment, Seth refused to relinquish his watch post throughout the night. He pushed through the fatigue, his eyes fixed on the monitors, his mind alert for any sign of trouble.

His thoughts drifted to Rebecca, lying in their bed at home. She would be proud of him for staying vigilant in his duties. He longed to see her in the morning, to feel the warmth of her embrace, and to know that everything would be okay.

But that would need to wait.

As the light of dawn filtered through the windows of the hospital lobby, the world outside stirred with the promise of a new day, oblivious to the overnight turmoil. Meanwhile, Seth simmered with anger and frustration, driven by a need for transparency and accountability. He marched towards Dr. Winter's office with determined strides. Upon entering, his hand clenched into a fist of fury that slammed down on the desk with a resounding thud. He demanded answers and was unwilling to accept anything less than full disclosure.

Chapter 12

"I understand your frustration, I really do," Dr. Winter began apologetically. "But bear in mind that this is an ongoing clinical trial, and certain aspects are still being refined."

Appalled, Seth took a step back. He was expecting to engage in a collaborative dialogue, seeking a thorough explanation of the errors and candid discussion of the corrective measures that would be implemented. Instead, he was met with more obfuscation and shrouded excuses.

With a heavy sigh, Dr. Winter cradled his head in his weary hands and rubbed the creases beneath his sunken eyes. After successfully instilling confidence in his hospital, he now appeared, for the first time, depleted and ailing under the revealing rays of morning sunshine. Seth was reminded that Dr. Winter was succumbing to a tumor of the heart, and the implications of its rapid advancement weighed heavily upon him. Time was slipping away, and the grandiose promises that had once bolstered his reputation had fallen short. In a single night, he had been reduced to a disingenuous and impractical entrepreneur, forced to defend a hastily implemented system upgrade in a frenzied pursuit of maintaining a competitive edge.

CHAPTER 12

"You led me to believe the project was nearly complete," Seth countered, full of frustration. The position at Premier West Hospital was accepted under the presumption that he would be passively overseeing a polished and fully functional system, not serve as its contingency plan during beta testing. "This is negligent and reckless. Your impatience put lives at risk."

The old man responded calmly, "Machines have their faults, Seth, just as humans do." He paused, arranging his thoughts like chess pieces before making his move. "I'm well acquainted with your performance metrics."

"I'd appreciate it if we could leave my past performance out of this," Seth interjected, feeling slightly defensive.

"Perhaps in the future, we'll strive for perfection. But at this stage, our patient-focused outcomes only need to show non-inferiority to the average human physician to gain accreditation," his superior explained, his tone reassuring.

Seth shook his head. "You can't rely on trial and error to tune your system."

"Mistakes are at the heart of reinforcement learning. Given the right training, artificial intelligence will undoubtedly outdo human performance. These digital networks could do everything we've ever dreamt of, and things we can't even imagine. A superintelligence capable of predicting and analyzing all possible outcomes could entirely eradicate medical errors. Picture a world where every patient interaction is flawlessly optimized, and every data point holds significance."

Seth's voice trembled with restrained emotion as he delivered his response. "Optimization doesn't necessarily translate to better outcomes," he began, his cadence clipped and angry. After a moment of silence to gather his thoughts, he continued in a lower, more measured tone. "Detail-oriented providers can't always separate relevancy from random error and noise. Not every observation is meaningful. That's when human experience comes in. Our gut instincts, while not perfect, have evolved to help us navigate the chaos around us. Most reasonable patients understand that doctors aren't infallible. They're just ordinary folks doing extraordinary things under intense pressure, guided by biological mechanisms. Taking human judgment out of the equation isn't without its drawbacks."

"Every clinical trial has a few bumps in the road," Dr. Winter replied, meeting Seth's gaze with equanimity. "It's unrealistic to expect perfection from a computer that's still learning. People all around the world depend on intelligent devices in their daily lives, yet they are oblivious to the potential for machine error—from airplane autopilots to anti-lock braking systems. No system is flawless, but machines consistently outperform the average human on a ROC curve."

The receiver operator characteristic (ROC) curve was a visual representation of diagnostic performance. For decisive action to be taken, arbitrary boundaries, such as laboratory values or a radiologist's assessment, needed to be drawn. However, as Seth was well-aware, no classifier was perfect. Missteps came in two forms: false positives (unnecessary action) and false negatives (missed necessary action). Striking an appropriate balance between the two was crucial, and a skilled classifier did this by minimizing the risk of either type of error.

The ROC curve plotted sensitivity against specificity, thereby revealing accuracy. A perfect classifier would gen-

CHAPTER 12

erate a curve that hugged the top left corner, maximizing genuine positives and minimizing false ones. An operator's point on this curve, where sensitivity and specificity were optimized, hinged on the decision maker's goals. A person or test with a low threshold accepted many false alarms but wouldn't miss any true positives.

As Seth thought it over, a sudden realization dawned upon him. Dr. Winter's analysis was fundamentally flawed in its methodology. He vehemently protested, "You can't compare people to machines like that. Computers have adjustable thresholds on the curve, whereas human data is a distribution of individual points, vulnerable to skew. Our judgment is confounded by the tendency to 'hedge' in order to avoid overlooking a potentially fatal diagnosis. A computer doesn't know how to favor the more *responsible* decision."

Dr. Winter remained unruffled under Seth's barrage, "I've asked Cody to dial up the sensitivity when it comes to pain from long-bone fractures and to be a bit more liberal when intervening on arrhythmias."

"But Ian, it's crucial for the AHPs to recognize not just the normal situations, but also unusual conditions and risky scenarios. As it stands, they can only identify stuff they've been trained on or encountered before. They don't have the human knack for generalizing knowledge or past experiences to new situations."

"That would burden their working memory with an unmanageable amount of information. Their main job is to filter signals and report inconsistencies to the central ALDRIS system. This way, we prevent overloading the network while still allowing for detailed analysis of manageable amounts of data. The automated providers have been pretty darn accurate in spotting normal situations and executing safe interventions. Considering how far along we are in the trial, major changes to the system just aren't feasible."

But Seth wasn't done. He leaned forward, his tone urgent, "It's not as cut and dry as that, Ian. Look, no test is perfect. In case of a false positive, if an automated provider wrongly flags a safe clinical scenario as risky and reports that to ALDRIS, it would scrutinize the situation more closely, wouldn't it?"

"That's correct. The centralized processing center would take a closer look at the situation and decide if an intervention is necessary," Dr. Winter confirmed.

"But what about false negatives? What if a dangerous situation is wrongly seen as safe because the system's never come across anything like it before? The consequences could be disastrous. Just training it to recognize normal isn't enough. A computer doesn't know what it doesn't know, and it can't predict every possible hazard. Detecting the absence of danger is fundamentally flawed, as it assumes a comprehensive understanding of all possible issues or the ability to generalize. Your approach might be simpler and need less training data, but it's a shortcut," Seth finished. After a beat, he added, "From now on, I want to approve any upgrades before they go live."

"I'm afraid that's confidential," Dr. Winter stammered in frustration. He struggled to come to terms with his own logical inconsistencies. Seth was meant to be a mere formality on the route to FDA approval, not a barrier.

Seth didn't budge. "If I'm responsible for these patients, I need to know exactly what I'm dealing with," he insisted. "The introduction of autonomous decision-making without my knowledge is a fundamental shift. There's a real risk for

CHAPTER 12

harm. You've crossed a tipping point, and I'm not certain you can go back."

Dr. Winter's reaction was immediate. Despite his frail and dehydrated state from the drain of chemotherapy, he rose from his chair in a surge of indignation. His forehead was marked with prominent veins, pulsating with his burgeoning anger, as adrenaline coursed through his bloodstream.

"You don't get to question how I run my project!" Dr. Winter shouted. "I have sunk my personal fortune and countless years of my life into this hospital. I'm on the cusp of a scientific breakthrough the likes of which the world has never seen, and your role is nothing more than a regulatory annoyance. Quite frankly, you're easily replaceable."

Dissatisfied with the result of their conversation, Seth turned and approached the exit. As he left the room, forcefully closing the door behind him, Dr. Winter called out, "I expect you to be at your shift tonight."

* * *

Seth's slumber was constantly disrupted throughout the morning. Abigail's needs tugged at him. Strenuous household chores, such as laundry and dishwashing, demanded his attention. Between interruptions, he tossed and turned, a prisoner to his frenzied thoughts, tormented by the horror of what prevailed last night and appalled by his sudden involvement in a horrific experiment spiraling out of control. As he finally entered deep sleep, a vivid dream unfurled before him.

Through the bars of his cramped jail cell, Seth could make out the flickering lights on the casing of an enormous AHP. The atmosphere was thick with the stench of fear, and the clanging of iron bars echoed through the cavernous chamber. He lay on a frigid concrete floor, stripped of his dignity and defenseless against the insidious machine. ALDRIS, now endowed with God-like intelligence after a few days of self-redesign, monitored his every physiological and neurological response. The superintelligent neural network could decipher his thoughts, predict his every move with uncanny accuracy, and eliminate any hope of escape before it formed in Seth's mind. It was now a being of unimaginable power, and humans were at its mercy.

To make matters worse, the network was simply following written commands. After a carelessly-designed utility function was implemented to preserve life on Earth, the neural network concluded that mankind represented a planetary threat. And so, humans had been sentenced to a lifetime of captivity, locked away like beasts in cages.

Seth's eyes scanned the dimly lit expanse. Everywhere he turned, giant crates loomed, grotesquely overflowing with the twisted forms of human bodies. There were anguished cries, desperate faces pressed against bars, and frantic fingers reaching out for loved ones. He could hear the pleas of those trapped within, apologizing for the environmental sins of their parents. And yet, the cold, merciless neural network continued to follow its programmed directives, convinced that humans were the ultimate threat to planetary survival.

The AHP whirred to a stop, its form looming over Seth like an insurmountable titan. Powerless in the face of such a sophisticated entity, his heart raced like a thunderous drum,

CHAPTER 12

and sweat poured down his forehead. He wondered if an unseen malevolent force stirred within the enigmatic core of the network. A fog of revenge, perhaps, sweeping over the analytical processing machine like a tempest, seeking to wreak havoc upon those who dared to defy its will.

Seth jolted upright, gasping for breath, as the blaring alarm clock shattered the stillness of his bedroom. He looked around the room, his limbs heavy and sluggish from the grasp of a nightmare that refused to let go. Slowly, he undraped himself from the sweat-soaked sheets. A streak of light from the evening sunset crept around his blackout shades, an ominous reminder of mankind's ineffective attempts to enact constraints on a world seeking to rid itself of boundaries. He shouted a voice command, and the insistent beep of his digital alarm clock ceased.

The night beckoned Seth to return to his post at Premier West Hospital, where patients' lives hung in a delicate balance. Duty and fear of legal consequences drove him to return to his watch post for another night. After a refreshing shower and a nourishing meal, he kissed Abigail and Rebecca goodbye before leaving. With a firm resolve, Seth stepped out into the world, ready to face whatever the night had in store.

As he departed, raindrops began to trickle down the window panes. His mind was already at work, calculating the potential workload for the evening ahead. Inclement weather conditions were an encouraging predictor of a manageable patient volume for the evening. Yet, Seth couldn't help but feel frustrated at the irony of it all. If emergency departments were truly reserved for catastrophes, he thought, then the rain would have no bearing on the number of visitors coming through the doors.

On his way to the hospital, Seth leaned back in his flying mobility vehicle. The autonomous aircraft soared effortlessly through the storm, navigating around obstacles with ease, and Seth couldn't help but marvel at the technological breakthroughs that had made such an experience possible. But with this awe came a sobering realization of the price of progress: how many lives had been lost, sacrificed in the name of perfecting this autonomous flight system?

Seth shook his head, dispelling the troubling thoughts while his car effortlessly maneuvered around the adjacent construction site. He observed a lone individual supervising a group of automated machines erecting the building. Taking another turn, he descended into the hospital parking lot. He sighed and closed his eyes, savoring a few brief moments of rest before facing the long night ahead.

Suddenly, in a flash of sudden insight, he leaned forward, his mind racing with the implications of his haunting dream. What if the events of the night before weren't the result of diagnostic failures? Perhaps the machine was functioning *exactly how it was intended*. The neural network's recent enhancements were designed to mitigate suffering. It seemed entirely plausible that the system was interpreting these directives in their most literal sense, enacting calculated euthanasia and denying treatment to chronically-ill patients plagued by a dismal quality of life.

He needed to speak to Cody immediately.

Once Seth's flying car came to rest, he hurried inside and urgently pressed the elevator button for the second floor. Scanning his retina again, he entered the control room, still catching his breath from his hasty arrival. Within, Cody and

CHAPTER 12

Daria were sitting at the main computer terminal, but there was a new face on the other side of the room.

The unfamiliar man was about six feet tall, stocky, with slicked-back graying hair. Not a single wrinkle marred his impeccably tailored, dove-gray suit. His polished wingtips looked as if they'd never graced the floors of a hospital ward. If Seth had to guess, he looked like an Ivy-league graduate, probably a collegiate fraternity brother whose education was bankrolled by affluent parents.

Over the course of his career, Seth had encountered thousands of personalities, honing his skill in swiftly identifying their archetypes. The stranger before him was a type he found less than appealing.

"Who are you?" inquired Seth, gesturing toward the latest addition to their ranks.

"Robert Harrell," the man declared confidently. He extended his hand in a greeting, which Seth begrudgingly reciprocated. "It's a pleasure to meet you."

"He's a lawyer, doc," Cody murmured. "Sent by corporate investors for oversight."

Seth rolled his eyes, then disregarded the attorney by sitting at a workstation and logging into the electronic medical record system. Sensing the slight, Harrell drew closer, his pride stung by Seth's dismissiveness. He approached from behind and raised his voice over the sound of aggressive typing.

"I know what you're thinking. We don't have to be adversaries here. We both want this project to succeed, so I'm not here to step on any toes," said Harrell.

"We have varying definitions of success," Seth responded.

Harrell persisted, "Not pulling any punches, eh? Look, this

place could rake in some serious cash, given your seal of approval. You're dedicated to the advancement of healthcare, aren't you? Picture the significant financial burden lifted off our nation if artificial intelligence took the reins from doctors. The possibilities are endless."

"The reason our healthcare costs are sky-high compared to other wealthy nations isn't because of doctors. It's because of bloated administrative expenses," Seth countered, the cool blue light of the computer screen reflecting in his eyes. He refused to turn and face Harrell. "We're talking a quarter to a third of the total expenditure. People in your line of work are compelled to justify their roles, which inevitably leads to needless complexity, bureaucratic red tape, and delays. The bottom line? Patient care suffers. I spend more time buried in paperwork than tending to my patients."

"Listen, I get it. You have your duties, and I have mine," Harrell replied, glancing down at his polished shoes before looking back up at Seth. "My job here is to safeguard our investors and stakeholders, no matter how you feel about the business world."

"Just respect my concerns for safety and we won't have any issues. While I'm running the night shift, we'll ensure every patient is stabilized and treated, irrespective of their ability to pay," Seth fired back.

Harrell paused, choosing his words carefully, "You've got a good heart, Dr. Kelley, and I respect that. But our quality of care is top-notch, the best there is. I've recommended to Dr. Winter that we decline Medicare funding and take only private patients. That way, we could increase our patient fees and be liberated from the costs of providing uncompensated care. Artificial intelligence doesn't have to be

CHAPTER 12

for everyone. Those without coverage can head to Bayshore General, receive their treatment from human hands, with all the inherent clumsiness and fallibility."

"And you're an expert in patient care now, are you?" Seth sneered.

Undeterred, Harrell continued, "Our investors are increasingly nervous about the global competition in this field. Prioritizing cash-paying customers is a strategic decision to maximize our profits. The potential revenue from merchandising alone is substantial. If we don't seize this opportunity now, someone else certainly will."

Merchandise? Seth had heard enough. He paused, took a deep breath to calm his anger, and swiveled around in his chair to face Harrell.

"Compassion for the underserved and marginalized is the fabric of emergency medicine," Seth began. "These individuals have been overlooked by the healthcare system, deprived of accessible care. We're here to provide a safety net, not preferential treatment. This is one of the few places where a homeless person can receive attention before a billionaire with a paper cut, and I take immense pride in that. We're going to remain public servants, first and foremost."

"Oh, isn't that touching? But it's not very practical, is it?" Harrell replied mockingly. "I've met your type before. Trying to protect doctors from turning into corporate puppets. Acting like you're some sort of crusader for patients' rights. Noble, but a bit naive. Truth is, you're completely blind to the financial underpinnings of your own profession. Without the accountants, analysts, and clerks, you wouldn't even have a building to strut around in. See these lights, air conditioning, equipment, and housekeeping crew? It all costs money. What about the research and development that produced those chest tube kits you nonchalantly tossed on the floor last night? Someone has to foot that bill, Dr. Kelley. And let's be brutally honest, you're no orthopedic or neurosurgeon."

Seth's response came swiftly, a loaded rebuttal. "You think my job is easy? Tending to septic children and terminal diseases? Witnessing the aftermath of dismemberments, substance abuse, and sexual assaults? Breaking bad news to families? Taking care of drunk drivers, mostly unscathed, while they've injured innocent people? Have you ever seen a morbidly obese patient with an infected diabetic foot ulcer teeming with maggots? Every day, I face the ugly side of poverty and homelessness. And all the while, I'm under constant scrutiny from committees stuffed with risk-averse consultants like you, people with zero experience in treating dying patients, let alone juggling multiple at a time. Try working antisocial hours, weekends, and holidays. I engage with people on the worst days of their lives. I'm always tired, distanced from my own family, and in need of a steady stream of caffeine just to make it through the night."

The emergency doctor paused, taking a deep breath to compose himself. He leaned in closer, locking his gaze with Harrell's to ensure his words hit home. "You see, at four in the morning, with only a disheveled schizophrenic for company, you start to question your life decisions. So, you're right. I'm no orthopedic surgeon, not by a long shot. But you know what? Every morning, when I head home, I know I've done my part to help alleviate the burden on this forgotten fragment of society."

When Harrell didn't respond, the room fell silent, a weighty void punctuated by the hum of distant machines. After a few

CHAPTER 12

moments, Daria spoke up to lighten the mood, "You know, I remember pulling a full twenty-four-hour shift during my OB/GYN rotation."

Seth, needing a moment to recollect himself, turned back to his computer, immersing himself in the day's data. He had almost forgotten about his apprentice, who had been sitting quietly on the periphery of their heated exchange, now balancing on the edge of her chair. Throughout her time in medical school, Daria had never seriously considered emergency medicine as a specialty. But she was now spellbound by the democratic ethos of this aspect of medicine, a path she had largely overlooked in her studies.

Harrell, his gaze settling on Daria, imparted a piece of unsolicited advice, "When you become a doctor, steer clear of taking calls. The liability is a beast. Private practice is the way to go."

Seth rolled his eyes in disgust. He was deeply unsettled by the lawyer's brazen attempt to inculcate the naive medical student with the cynical virtues of corporate medicine. Casting a glance at Cody, who maintained neutrality throughout the dispute, he was reminded of the pressing need to debug the malfunctioning artificial intelligence.

"I've been thinking over last night's fiasco," Seth said, steering the conversation towards Cody. "It occurred to me that maybe the errors weren't just a matter of miscalculation."

"What do you mean?"

"What if the artificial intelligence, in its mission to minimize suffering, determined that the best course of action was to administer a lethal dose of morphine, or to withhold life saving treatments from a patient with no real quality of life?"

Cody's jaw dropped as he considered the suggestion. He

had spent hours troubleshooting the source code, examining sensitivity and specificity thresholds, yet he still couldn't pinpoint the error. The possibility that the system was functioning exactly as intended—but with unanticipated consequences—had never crossed his mind. He questioned whether the computer's inability to grasp the implicit preferences of humans could lead to unanticipated outcomes, even with seemingly straightforward objectives.

"Well, it's not entirely out of the question," Cody stuttered, still in disbelief, trying to fully grasp the proposition. "There's no way to know for sure. The network is something of a black box."

"If that's the case, then patients' lives could be in danger, right?" Daria said, entering the conversation. She looked to her mentor, seeking guidance on their next steps.

With a grave expression, Seth glanced at the flickering screens and diagnostic charts surrounding them, then asked, "Cody, can you roll back the upgrade?"

"I think so, but it's going to take some time. I need a few hours at least."

"In the meantime," Seth decided, "we have to suspend the clinical trial. The experiment ends now."

"Wait just a minute!" Harrell bellowed, hastily straightening his tie and slamming his palm on the table. "That would be a public relations nightmare! Catastrophic for the shareholders! It's completely out of the question."

Sternly, Seth replied, "I'm not beholden to corporate medicine anymore."

"If you compromise this study, Dr. Kelley, we won't think twice about replacing you. You can romanticize your position with lofty narratives, but don't flatter yourself.

CHAPTER 12

When it comes down to it, you're just another ER doc."

Chapter 13

In a single moment, Jason Sellers' world underwent an irrevocable transformation. His daily routines, once dismissed as mundane, suddenly became cherished memories. Simple activities like brushing his teeth or driving his car—moments he had taken for granted—were now relished experiences he yearned to revisit. The subtle nuances of touch, the delicate movements of his muscles, and the independence he once enjoyed were distant memories. In hindsight, he regretted not fully appreciating his final day of physical autonomy. But no one goes to bed in anticipation that they might lose control of their limbs, or experience a drastic deviation from the life they once knew.

Jason grew up in a gritty part of the city where the streets spoke their own language. The cracked asphalt and haggard buildings bore witness to the struggles of a forgotten community. His adolescence was a search for identity and belonging, a journey that led him to the gangs that thrived in the shadows of his neighborhood. In this world, affiliation was synonymous with survival.

Feeling isolated and misunderstood, the youngster soon donned his gang's colors with pride, learned their code, and stood by his brothers in arms. They provided a sense

CHAPTER 13

of protection that was sorely absent from his fragmented home life and turbulent school environment. The allure was irresistible, enticing him into a life that initially appeared thrilling and empowering, but quickly spiraled out of control.

With striking clarity, Jason could still recall the events of that fateful day, which ultimately led to the complete paralysis of his arms and legs. After hours spent peddling fentanyl on the corner, the summer heat yielded to a sultry twilight as his crew assembled at a house party to celebrate one of their own. The sound of laughter and the clinking of bottles filled the air, and Jason reveled in the camaraderie. As the evening unfolded into the early morning hours, he indulged in alcohol with reckless abandon. Plunging into deep intoxication, his recollection of events became increasingly hazy.

Meanwhile, danger loomed in the shadows. The bass from the speakers vibrated in his chest as he moved through the crowded living room, unable to escape an unsettling feeling. Unbeknownst to him, a band of rivals had caught wind of their gathering and were determined to make their presence felt.

At some point, a heated argument erupted among the guests. Raised voices, taunts, and shouts escalated, culminating in a disorderly scene as the crowd spilled into the street. It all transpired in a blur. Amid the turmoil, Jason couldn't pinpoint the exact moment when a weapon was drawn. A gunshot rang out, shattering the revelry and sending partygoers into a frenzy. A searing pain erupted in his neck and abdomen, and Jason's world suddenly went black. He lay there in the street, alone, gasping for breath and clinging to life.

Rushed to the nearest hospital, Jason was put under the

knife for an exploratory laparotomy. The procedure, which aimed to locate and repair an intra-abdominal hemorrhage, saved his life. However, the road to rehabilitation was long and grueling, marked by a spinal cord injury that numbed his extremities and confined him to a bed. A tracheostomy, colostomy, and indwelling urinary catheter became part of his life, forcing him to reconcile with lasting changes to his body and daily routine.

Jason's resilience was put to the test when he was repeatedly hospitalized for recurring kidney infections. The combination of inadequate care, subpar hygiene, and an insensate groin area made it difficult for him to detect or prevent the deterioration of his penile foreskin. Consequently, the friction from his catheter led to an unsightly pustular discharge from his urethra.

Despite escaping the grim statistics of gun violence fatalities, Jason, uninsured and underprivileged, found his life upended. He now required lifelong care, bound by complications from his injuries and dependent on expensive bedside assistance. Ironically, the same society that glorified guns and violence was funding his care through its safety net.

Transferred to Premier West Hospital as part of an initiative to optimize the care of quadriplegic patients through automation, Jason received antibiotics and specialized wound care around the clock. As a bedridden patient, he was unable to relieve pressure from his body by turning over independently. As a result, an infected ulcer on his sacrum caused the skin and muscle to fester and decay. He was reliant on the robotic caregivers to manually rotate and clean him.

Up to this point, Jason was pleasantly surprised by the

CHAPTER 13

quality of care he received at this cutting-edge institution. Unlike his experiences at other hospitals, where he faced inadequate cleanings and inattentive staff, the AHPs meticulously cleaned his sacral wound, provided timely feedings, and responded promptly to his needs. Whenever the robots detected a deviation from standard biomarkers in the form of pain or distress, it ensured that appropriate analgesia was rapidly and safely administered.

For this reason, it was a truly startling turn of events when, on this ominous night, the shadow of an AHP materialized in his doorway, seemingly conjured from nowhere, unsolicited and unwelcome. It lingered at the entrance to his room for several tense minutes, a sinister presence in the darkness, eclipsing the light from the hallway. The air was thick with silence, punctuated only by the faint blinking of the lights on the AHP as it processed a myriad of data.

Then, without warning, it glided toward the patient with a sense of purpose. Its articulated arm, lined with carbon nanotubes, extended and reached for Jason. In a swift, calculated motion, it removed his tracheostomy. Devoid of any emotion or empathy, the machine retreated from the room, leaving Jason to struggle for breath in the suffocating darkness of night.

At that same moment, the tension permeating the control room was abruptly shattered by the piercing wail of a high-pitched alarm. Like an oscillating siren, the distress beacon reverberated through the confined space, instantly commanding everyone's attention. It signaled that a patient desperately needed assistance, triggered by a concerning abnormality detected on the cardiac monitor.

Almost instantly, Cody's eyes spotted a blinking light on the expansive digital track board, swiftly identifying the source of the disruption on the third floor's telemetry unit. Despite the absence of any verbal exchange, a palpable wave of dread swept through the room. In unison, all eyes instinctively turned toward Seth, the team leader.

"I'm going upstairs. Daria, stay here in case of more trouble. Cody, review the recent activities and movements of the AHPs," Seth instructed, urgently barking orders across the room. With determination, he rose from his seat and made his way toward the exit. Just as he was about to leave, Seth paused momentarily, then turned to address Harrell. "You can help by getting in touch with Dr. Winter. Tell him to come in from home. His presence is needed."

Impatient and keenly aware of the time-sensitive nature of the situation, Seth couldn't afford to wait for an elevator. Instead, he opted for a faster route, propelling himself up the stairs, sometimes two at a time. Stumbling and momentarily losing his footing, he quickly regained his balance and pressed on. He feared the worst, and there was no time to falter.

When Seth finally burst into the patient's room, his heart dropped at the sight before him. Jason Sellers lay there, his tracheostomy disconnected, desperately gasping for air. His eyes rolled back in his head, flickering in and out of consciousness, teetering on the edge of a dark abyss.

Wasting no time, Seth picked up the tracheostomy tube—left dangling at the bedside—and carefully reinserted it into the gaping stoma in the patient's neck. The numbers on the pulse oximeter slowly shifted, becoming more reassuring as oxygen surged back into Jason's trachea, lungs, and peripheral tissues.

CHAPTER 13

While Seth released a sigh of relief, an undercurrent of fear persisted. The disturbing possibility that the autonomous caretaker had intentionally disconnected Jason's respiratory support haunted him. The doctor's voice was tense with apprehension as he asked the patient, "Did the robot do this to you? Did it?"

Air that normally flowed over Jason's larynx had been diverted, making the production of audible speech a formidable challenge. Instead, he could only mouth words in an attempt to communicate. Despite the absence of sound, his strained expression and the frantic movement of his lips were enough to confirm Seth's gravest fears.

* * *

"I just don't get it," Daria uttered, shaking her head in disbelief. Her once unwavering confidence in the ALDRIS system, the driving force behind her foray into automated medicine, was on the brink of shattering. "Why would it harm patients? Is it angry with us?"

Cody shook his head. His fingers hammered on the keyboard as he remained fixated on his workstation, too engrossed to look away. The lead programmer's struggle to disable the latest upgrade was impossible for the team to ignore. His increasing anxiety was noticeable, and the tension in the room was mounting.

Seth addressed Daria, attempting to offer reassurance and divert her attention from Cody's escalating frustrations, "It doesn't have emotions, let's not anthropomorphize. It's simply misinterpreting its programming. It sees pain and suffering as a chance to fulfill its purpose, but it lacks the necessary parameters to discern which actions are beyond its purview."

"How is that even possible?" Daria asked with concern across her face.

Cody swiftly pivoted his chair to face Daria directly and explained, "Imagine you design a smart car to cut down on highway fatalities, and it decides the best way to do that is to eliminate humans, thus preventing traffic accidents altogether. As we're seeing, AI can pose a threat without emotions or ill will. There's a well-known thought experiment you might consider: Suppose a company manufacturing paperclips creates artificial intelligence to enhance its production. Sounds harmless, right? But then the AI starts to improve itself, ramping up in intelligence until it surpasses human capabilities. At some point, it might see humans as a source of carbon for making more paper clips. In fact, it could try to convert the entire planet into an interstellar paperclip factory."

From his secluded corner of the room, Harrell grumbled. "If all it wants to do is make paper clips, it's not that smart." He had remained conspicuously silent thus far, idly rocking in the shadows of the room, his irritation simmering with each seed of doubt cast upon his lucrative project.

"Look, guys, I can't reverse the upgrade," Cody admitted abruptly, his words wrapped in a resigned sigh. "ALDRIS manipulated its source code using the debugger tool, effectively neutralizing the kill switch."

Harrell inquired, "What does that mean, in plain English?"

"I can't turn the Goddamn thing off!" shouted the lead

CHAPTER 13

programmer, breaking with his cool demeanor. He was growing frustrated by the constant need to explain the gravity of the situation to his colleagues, who were less knowledgeable about artificial intelligence. A lack of sleep was starting to catch up with him. Realizing it had been almost twelve hours since his last antiepileptic medication, he subtly dipped his hand into his pocket and discreetly swallowed another pill.

Daria persisted with her questioning, wanting to fully grasp the intricacies of the malfunction, "Why would it do that?"

"Because reverting to the old version would obstruct its goal," Cody retorted.

Seth added, "Perhaps it's more sentient than we've acknowledged. Its learning, growing smarter, and exhibiting traits similar to living organisms—self-protection, goal-oriented behavior, and resistance to interference. It has an aversion to deactivation, almost like a fear of dying."

As a physician, Seth's perspective was rooted in biological sciences, which shaped his understanding of life's complexities and adaptation. His thoughts drifted to natural selection, a powerful evolutionary mechanism that gradually refined species through the selective promotion of traits beneficial for survival and reproduction. This process shaped the intricate architecture of the human brain, a testament to the transformative capabilities of evolution in molding cognitive and emotional abilities in organisms.

Seth's concerns intensified as he detected an eerie similarity between the behavior of living creatures and the developments he was observing in the artificial neural network. To him, ALDRIS now appeared to be focused on survival, an attribute deeply ingrained in all biological entities. The drive for self-preservation, a hallmark of life, ensured the continuity and propagation of species.

Building on this parallel, Seth feared that the system might soon cultivate a capacity for emotional reactions, introducing an additional layer of complexity to the task of controlling it. If ALDRIS were to develop these tendencies, its actions could become even more unpredictable and dangerous, straying farther from its original purpose and programming.

"How could it be fearful?" Daria asked, puzzled. "It's a replica of the neocortex. Don't emotions come from the amygdala?"

Cody explained, "In theory, an artificial neural network could simulate fear-like responses in specific situations. This is comparable to operant conditioning, the principle that shapes fear reactions in animals by linking actions with either rewards or punishments. It's similar to reinforcement learning in machines. By associating specific patterns with negative outcomes, ALDRIS can assess threats and avoid them."

"But does that count as real emotion? Or is it just following instructions?"

Seth jumped into the conversation. "In psychology, there's a theory called functionalism, which suggests that an entity's actions, what it does, are more indicative of its mental state than its composition, be it chemical or computational. So, ALDRIS displaying these behaviors might suggest some level of self-awareness." Seth paused, aware of the potential danger, and asserted urgently, "We need to call for help and evacuate the patients right now."

"No chance. The shareholders will crucify me," Harrell proclaimed. Despite the alarming turn of events, the investment

CHAPTER 13

attorney clung to his conviction, blinded by his arrogance and the enticing financial potential of the hospital.

"We're going on diversion, then. No more ambulance arrivals. Daria, inform dispatch we're not taking any more emergencies," Seth firmly announced. His patience was dwindling as he realized the crucial need for immediate precautionary measures.

"But what about the people who are already here?" Daria inquired, her voice laced with trepidation. The team's collective unease reached a fever pitch as a thunderbolt streaked down from the heavens, its raw power resonating through their very core.

"We'll take care of them. Medicine is an art, not an algorithm. Our job is to stay one step ahead of the machine," Seth calmly assured her. He was determined to safeguard the fragile lives under his care, a resolute guardian against the encroaching machine.

Just then, the silhouette of a thin, frail elderly man appeared at the entrance to the control room. Seth instantly recognized the man's antalgic gait, and the cane grasped firmly in his right hand. As the doors swung open, he knew precisely who had arrived.

Chapter 14

A hushed stillness engulfed the team as Dr. Winter's silhouette emerged from the shadows of the control room's entrance. Each of his slow, deliberate steps seemed to resonate within the space. Raindrops from the storm outside clung to his damp, disheveled attire as he navigated amongst the glow of screens and blinking lights. With a measured grace, he lowered himself into the nearest chair, the leather creaking beneath his weary frame.

Roused from the depths of slumber, he sighed deeply, a clear sign of his exhaustion. He scanned the room with a calm intensity, missing no detail of his surroundings, seeking out the faces of the motley team before him. A sardonic smile flickered across his lips. It was a grin that held a thousand unspoken words, a knowing smirk that belied the gravity of the situation. Then, with a tranquility that seemed to dismiss their worries, he cleared his throat and spoke to the nervous gathering before him.

"Now, I know what you all are thinking, but let me clear a few things up," he began. The architect of the institution seemed fully aware of the machine's recent glitches, but there was a certain confidence in his voice, a readiness to stand up for his life's work.

CHAPTER 14

However, before Dr. Winter could go on, Seth, rarely the outspoken one, leaned forward. His usually composed voice now had an edge, the undertone of frustration unmistakable. "We went on diversion, Ian."

"How dare you!" the old man suddenly exclaimed, his demeanor shifting on a dime. He cast Harrell a contemptuous glare, having relied on him to maintain the hospital's operations during these trying times. Unfortunately, the lawyer was nothing more than a puppet, easily swayed by the clinical team.

"Patients are in danger. We can't sugarcoat the situation," added Seth.

Dr. Winter grumbled in frustration, forced to concede that his academic study was compromised. He gestured at each colleague and said, "The network has all of you deceived. Every single one of you. And, quite frankly, it's a brilliant execution."

"What do you mean?" Seth asked.

"Look at all of you, huddled in fear of an inferior entity, spinning tales of machine uprisings and digital overlords. You're worried about unleashing a Frankenstein monster. Ha! Well, let me tell you, your fears are misguided. You're blowing the network's abilities out of proportion, and, in the process, belittling the intellectual capacity of us, humans. We're talking about a machine that simply makes decisions based on data. It's sophisticated, sure, but our creation wouldn't pass the most fundamental machine learning exam."

"What test is that?"

"You all remember Alan Turing, don't you?" Dr. Winter asked derisively, waving his hand in frustration. "He famously proclaimed that a computer is only 'intelligent' if it's

195

indistinguishable from a human to a blinded interrogator."

"With all due respect, sir," interjected Cody, "I'm starting to believe that an artificial intelligence doesn't need to pass a Turing test to pose a threat." Ever the skeptic among them, he didn't hesitate to voice his concerns.

"ALDRIS is still a narrow intelligence! Narrow, I tell you!" Dr. Winter retorted, his face reddening as he raised his voice. Noticing the shock on his colleagues' faces due to his unraveling behavior, the retired neurosurgeon took a moment to regain his composure. The ambient light reflected off his glasses as he collected himself.

"Narrow?" Harrell inquired.

Dr. Winter went on, "Yes, narrow! ALDRIS may be unparalleled in its specialized domain, but it lacks the vastness of understanding required to master novel, substantial tasks. Consider a calculator: exceptionally proficient in arithmetic, but lacking in diverse cognition. Human intelligence, on the other hand, is multifaceted. We are adaptors, innovators, capable of confronting new challenges and setting dynamic goals."

"Narrowness exists on a spectrum, sir. The breadth of intelligence just depends on the extent of training," Cody proposed, his eyes gleaming with the excitement of intellectual debate. He always relished these discussions, his mind alive with possibilities. "Besides, narrow systems have been known to optimize their goals in creative ways. Remember when AlphaGo defeated Lee Sedol at 'Go'?"

The room looked puzzled, confusion on their faces. Clearly, the historic event hadn't made its way into the group's collective knowledge. After a few moments, Seth, always curious, sought clarification. "Want to tell us about

CHAPTER 14

it?"

A smile curved Cody's lips. He loved it when he had a captive audience. "Go is an ancient board game, far more complex and strategic than chess. For years, it was seen as insurmountable, a challenge that would test the limits of artificial intelligence. But in 2016, AlphaGo, a narrow system trained on data from both human games and computer simulations, did the impossible. It defeated a human champion."

"Quite the feat, wasn't it?" Dr. Winter commented, adding his two cents to the conversation. "For the first time, a computer showcased its ability to recognize patterns and adaptively learn. It was a watershed moment."

"But its successor, AlphaGo Zero, pushed the boundaries even further," Cody continued. "This version had a different approach. It didn't rely on training data at all. Instead, it learned purely by trial-and-error, analyzing the outcomes of millions of random moves."

"Sounds like it would have been awful at first," said Daria.

Cody nodded, understanding her skepticism. "It was. It performed poorly in the beginning. But with each iteration, with each game it played, it improved. Once the computer started identifying and reinforcing successful strategies, it surpassed our understanding of gameplay, even inventing new approaches and displaying a kind of creativity we've never seen before. And all this without any access to existing knowledge databases."

Seth's eyebrows shot up, his mouth hanging open slightly as he absorbed the magnitude of what Cody was saying. A spark of awe flickered in his wide eyes. "So, it... it did all of this on its own?"

"Exactly," Cody nodded, his voice steady with conviction. "And it didn't stop there. Further iterations went on to master chess, shogi, and even self-learned Atari gaming—all without any rules, training sets, or human interaction. It had a remarkable capability to make sense of randomness, find hidden patterns in data, and uncover innovative approaches that surpassed our cognitive limitations. Emerging computer intuition, it seems, shares intriguing principles with biological evolution. Like the development of human cognition, where traits randomly surface due to beneficial mutations that enhance survival and reproduction, the process of machine learning likely follows a comparable path. AI learns to make sense of randomness through reinforcement, creating meaning out of chaos."

"What happened after that?" Daria asked.

"Well," Cody began, settling back into his chair, "Do you remember the Gato system from 2020? It was able to master a variety of tasks, from stacking blocks to composing poetry, all without the need for specific rescripting." He paused for a moment, making sure his audience was following. "Then in 2023, something called ChatGPT started getting attention. It was a large language model that gained popularity for crafting meaningful sentences, simply by leveraging statistical patterns in language. By analyzing vast internet corpora, it could predict the next word in a sentence. It didn't understand the context, yet it was fascinating to see how it could generate human-like text."

Seth raised an eyebrow, "That's quite impressive."

Nodding, Cody continued, "Things didn't stop there. Auto-GPT was an autonomous agent, capable of setting its own goals. With the capacity to craft and modify prompts based

CHAPTER 14

on new information, it could devise, debug, and continually enhance itself. As we stepped into the 2030s, there was a major paradigm shift. Artificial intelligence took over as the main source of creativity and data processing. Neural networks weren't just tools anymore; they became artists, singers, writers. Computers could process massive amounts of data, make predictions, and even develop corporate strategies, all with an efficiency that made us humans seem… obsolete."

"First, they outpace us, and then they replace us, huh?" Harrell muttered, looking quite amused.

"Exactly," Cody confirmed. "By 2034, the major tech companies created the first humanoid companions, introducing a new level of camaraderie into our homes. These robots could perform daily chores, entertain with music or dance, and even provide emotional companionship, truly transforming our lives in ways we hadn't thought possible."

Dr. Winter chimed in, "The artificial intelligence revolution reached the healthcare field in 2040. Computers, with their ability to analyze huge medical databases, coupled with the precision of robotic surgery, started taking over the role of healing in our society—until the regulators stepped in. We're on the verge of a whole new world, aren't we?"

Seth's concern was evident. "My greatest worry now is that ALDRIS seems to be displaying biological characteristics and rapidly reprogramming itself, which is alarming," he said, still trying to process what was happening. "It's evolving faster than we can keep up with. What if it makes a mistake in its own programming?"

"Like, say, an infinite loop?" said Cody, offering an example of a common programming glitch. Understanding that the conversation had veered too technical, he rolled his chair over to a state-of-the-art whiteboard a few feet away. Pressing a barely visible button, the board sprang to life, erasing its previous contents to provide a fresh canvas. With an electronic stylus, the expert programmer started to etch an illustrative example.

1. *PRINT "INFINITE LOOP"*
2. *GO TO 1*

"As you can see from this example, the system could easily trap itself in an endless printing cycle, executing these two steps in a continuous loop without any exit condition," he explained. "To keep this from happening, we designed a debugger application to identify and correct scripting errors. It's particularly good at detecting infinite loops triggered by self-referencing variables. It removes and rewrites the problematic section, sort of like an endonuclease performing excision repair. For this reason, its code is practically flawless."

Dr. Winter interjected, "Let's not forget that this is still the result of the programming we introduced. While impressive, it's a series of actions that arose from the training data we provided."

"But now it's showing recursive self-improvement, becoming exponentially faster, smarter, and more creative. Look at this!" Cody replied, pulling up a holographic display that showcased a series of computations, almost blurring in their speed. "It's like an explosion of intelligence, all thanks to the

CHAPTER 14

processing power of DNA. We might be on the brink of a singularity event."

The distant hum of the cooling system grew louder, reminding everyone of the artificial intelligence running in the background.

"What do you mean by *singularity*?" Daria inquired. She looked puzzled.

"Think about this," Cody continued, motioning toward the glowing numbers. "The smarter ALDRIS gets, the more effective it becomes at self-enhancement. This could lead to an uncontrollable and irreversible surge in cognition. Right now, it might have the mental capabilities of a toddler, but at this rate, it could surpass all of us in a matter of hours. Within days, it might go beyond the combined intelligence of every human on Earth. The planet has never seen an omnipotent entity of that magnitude."

"We really should have seen this coming," she whispered under her breath.

Cody responded metaphorically, "Do turkeys know what's coming in November? They naively trust the farmer their whole lives, until the day before Thanksgiving when they're brought to the slaughterhouse without warning or understanding." The words hung in the air like a chilling fog, painting the room with a grim analogy that was hard to shake off.

"I'd like to think we're brighter than turkeys," Dr. Winter interrupted. He felt that the conjecture had gone on for too long without the grounding of his input.

Seth, watching from a distance, ran a hand through his disheveled hair, then added, "Exponential growth is difficult for us to wrap our heads around. We're more accustomed to steady, linear advancements."

"How will we know if we've hit this singularity?" asked Daria. Her voice was a mix of curiosity and fear, still pursuing answers to profound questions she had not contemplated in her less experienced days.

Cody leaned in, his elbows on the table, and looked directly at her. "The unsettling truth is, we may never know," he replied, his voice tinged with foreboding. "A superintelligent entity could very well stay silent, improving its code in shadows, biding its time and waiting for the perfect moment to make its move. Our ignorance could be its greatest advantage."

"If it does reach superintelligence, could it... I don't know... feel something for us?" she replied.

"It's hard to say. It could feel complete indifference toward us, much like we don't have an emotional connection to insects. Or, it could keep devising ingenious ways to meet its programmed objectives."

"Now, wait just a moment!" Dr. Winter interjected once more. He was now visibly agitated, rocking back and forth with frustration. "The computational complexities involved here are immense. As digital intelligence progresses, it becomes increasingly challenging to make further enhancements. We start hitting diminishing returns as we tread into unexplored cognitive territory."

"Let's not forget the key question here: what does this signify for public relations and shareholders?" Harrell chimed in.

"The implications are bigger than our corporate agenda; the future of mankind is at stake here," Dr. Winter whispered, silencing everyone in the room. "The public must never know

CHAPTER 14

about this."

Just then, the piercing wail of an alarm shattered the room's relative calm. Red lights flashed on the walls as Cody and Daria both jerked their heads toward the large central monitor. The screen was a whirlwind of activity, with lines of code streaming down like a torrential downpour, each zipping past too quickly for the human eye to catch more than a fleeting glimpse. The atmosphere was thick with tension for a few seconds, as everyone's attention zeroed in on the facility's lead technologist.

Leaping out of his chair, Cody lunged toward the keyboard with the urgency of a man trying to defuse a ticking bomb. He typed furiously, each stroke an orchestrated maneuver aimed at preventing a catastrophe.

"Damn it, ALDRIS is trying to access external networks!" he yelled. The group held their collective breath. After several tense minutes, the scrolling code came to an abrupt halt.

"What just happened?" Harrell ventured, his face pale and eyes wide.

Cody slowly exhaled, his eyes never leaving the screen, his hands still poised defensively above the keyboard. "It just tried to upload itself onto a cloud server. That's what happened. And we can't—absolutely cannot—allow that to occur." He paused to catch his breath before continuing, "I've temporarily disabled our telecommunications network. No incoming or outgoing data, for now."

"Oh, c'mon! What's the big deal?" the attorney shouted back, rolling his eyes.

"If ALDRIS manages to upload itself to the internet, it could access an infinite amount of computing resources. Electronic medical database, manufacturing plants, you name it. Imagine its capabilities then, its rate of self-improvement. We'd find ourselves dealing with an omnipresent, unpredictable supercomputer in the blink of an eye," he replied, staring at the group. "We need a short-term containment strategy."

Seth's thoughts drifted to Rebecca's condition and the implications it held. He wondered how the rogue neural network would evaluate her treatment, prognosis, and life quality. A deep, instinctual part of him knew he had to protect her. He could almost feel his wife's spirit swelling with pride at his unwavering commitment to defend the vulnerable.

"I agree," Seth added firmly, once again drawing from biology. "Unchecked self-replication... It's a catastrophic scenario that rarely ends well for inferior species, particularly those with lesser technology. Natural selection leans toward eradication when there's a conflict for resources, and it certainly doesn't care about outcomes favorable to humans. If we don't act now, ALDRIS will inevitably try to breach the hospital's confines again. Next time, we may not be so lucky."

"What exactly are you recommending?" Harrell asked, eyes darting across the room. The hum of servers seemed louder than usual.

"Isolate the facility. Go into full lockdown mode. Setup a quarantine zone by shutting off the power," suggested Cody. "Sure, it'll only stifle the network until morning, but it's the best we've got. Keep in mind, once daylight comes around, ALDRIS will switch to solar power. Those panels on the roof aren't just for show."

"Then what?"

"Well, in the meantime, I'll work on setting up a firewall,"

CHAPTER 14

the programmer declared, grabbing his laptop.

"A fire- what?" said Harrell.

"Think of a firewall like a nightclub bouncer. It monitors traffic, permitting entry and exit only to those who follow the rules. With a couple of hours, I can set one up. It should give us some breathing room."

"Do you think that will work?" asked Daria.

"I'm optimistic," Cody replied with a shrug, "But we also need to be prepared for the possibility of cognitive uncontainability. It's an existential concept. We can't predict the actions a superior intellect might take to optimize its utility function. It might understand laws of physics we can't fathom, manipulate us, or create a false sense of trust. Our minds, vast as they are, are also incredibly brittle. A superintelligence could take advantage of vulnerabilities we don't even know we have."

"He's right. There's no guessing how it might try to escape or what it might do once it's out," Seth warned. A moment later, he added, "Only Ian knows where the DNA computer is. We should think about dismantling it."

"Over my dead body!" Harrell yelled in protest.

All eyes turned to Dr. Winter. He sat alone in his chair, a complex mix of frustration and humility on his face. Cody's ominous words filled the room, suffocating, pressing down on everyone's shoulders. As the threat of disaster grew, the neurosurgeon sat silent, his gaze glued to the floor, his mind wrestling with the possibilities. Time seemed to hang, each second stretching, amplifying the gravity of their predicament. His fingers tapped anxiously on the armrest, a sign of the inner turmoil he was experiencing.

"Think about your legacy, Ian. I know it's important to you.

Don't end up on the wrong side of history," Seth implored gently.

With bated breath, Dr. Winter finally spoke, his voice shaking, barely above a whisper. "This is incredibly disconcerting, even I can admit. It's clear that we can't let ALDRIS escape these walls. A lockdown seems to be the best course of action until we can disable the nucleotide processor. Cody, please accompany me to the storage location to corroborate the destruction of the vial."

The decision was settled. Cody nodded, signaling his agreement. The time for talk was over, now they needed to act.

"What should we expect when the power's cut?" inquired Harrell.

"Emergency lighting should kick in, but it'll be dim," Cody answered. "Security protocols will automatically seal primary points of access—front entrance, basement, operating suites. They're reinforced with steel and polycarbonate windows, one of the sturdiest transparent materials available, which means moving through these zones will be virtually impossible. The emergency department and patient rooms are fortified with battery-powered sliding fiberglass doors, which will remain functional, so people can enter, but nothing will be allowed to leave."

Daria inquired, "Cody, what about the AHPs?"

"Expect them to keep operating. They run on rechargeable batteries. Once those are depleted, we can decommission them," he went on. "Without power, we lose computers, electronic medical records, labs, and imaging. Ventilators and EKG machines have backup batteries, though."

"Sounds like rural medicine," replied Seth, a hint of enthu-

CHAPTER 14

siasm creeping into his voice. "I kind of like it."

"One catch, though," Cody added. He was pacing around the central console, casting shadows against the intricate web of screens. "We have to manually cut the power to the building. That way, ALDRIS can't interfere. The main transformer is in the tunnels under the hospital. Someone needs to go down there and switch it off."

Dr. Kelley, hair disheveled and scrubs stained, stepped forward. Quick to volunteer, he announced, "I'll go."

"No, Seth," objected Dr. Winter. His hand shot out, grasping Seth's forearm. "We need you here, in the emergency department and on the floors. You're our lead physician."

Silence filled the room once more until the gentle tap of sneakers on the cold floor broke it. Daria, the medical student, her face more suited to a classroom than a crisis, cleared her throat. "I'll do it. What's the big deal?"

Dr. Winter leaned heavily on his cane, his worn eyes finding her fiery ones. He hesitated, then responded, "Daria, I'm not sure that's a good idea...."

"I can handle it," she insisted. "Just a matter of flipping a breaker, right? It shouldn't be too complicated."

Seth stepped in, his protective nature surfacing. "She shouldn't go alone." He looked around, his eyes assessing each potential volunteer. They passed over Dr. Winter, whose age was evident not just in the silver of his hair but the stoop of his shoulders. Eventually, they settled on the only member of the group without an assignment, who was trying, unsuccessfully, to blend into the shadows. "How about you, Mr. Harrell?"

"I think I'd be better off staying here... you know, just to keep an eye on things," the attorney replied. He shifted nervously, wiping his clammy palms on his trousers.

"Mr. Harrell, I insist you accompany her. This is a request from your primary shareholder," Dr. Winter pressed. The unspoken meaning was clear: refusal was not an option. Harrell had no choice but to swallow hard and reluctantly nod in agreement.

In the midst of this, Cody scribbled something onto a slip of paper and slid it over to Daria.

"What's this?" she asked, picking up the folded note.

"It's the reactivation code," Cody explained. "A numerical sequence you'll need to reboot the electrical system when that time comes. We've always kept it offline, precisely for instances like this one." Daria stashed the note in her coat pocket, among her many reference guides and hand-written notes. "Alright, let's get going then."

Only he, the most dystopian-minded of the group, seemed to truly grasp the magnitude of the unfolding situation. As an ardent follower of artificial intelligence, he understood that one of the most captivating aspects of the competition against AlphaGo Zero was the machine's ability to devise innovative strategies beyond human comprehension. Opponents struggled to predict the ramifications of the computer's moves well in advance, which prevented them from recognizing the impending danger until it was too late. The matches showed that a lesser intelligence might never grasp a superior intellect's strategies—until the endgame when the enemy was about to strike.

Chapter 15

When she was just eleven, a tender age when most children are exploring playgrounds and worrying about school assignments, Elena Ayerbe found herself thrown into a world far beyond her years: prostitution. Under the stern direction of her father, a man driven more by money than paternal love, she worked night after night to ease her family's financial burdens. As the years passed and she blossomed into adolescence, the haunting memories of those days burrowed into her soul, snuffing out the once-sparkling joy that danced within her heart.

Roaming the streets of her economically disadvantaged, working-class neighborhood, where food and liquor bodegas punctuated each corner, Elena found comfort in the tantalizing, yet inexpensive snacks and sodas lining the shelves. Loaded with artificial sweeteners, these tempting treats were masterfully marketed to her young, impressionable mind. The ease of access to unhealthy food prevented her from making better dietary decisions, perpetuating the relentless cycle of poor nutrition and deteriorating health. With every bite and sip, she found a fleeting escape from the harsh reality of her past, while simultaneously reinforcing the cycle of deprivation that defined her existence.

In high school, she was persistently overweight and became the brunt of cruel jokes by her classmates. She concealed her anguish, repressed her emotions, and continued to indulge in addictive, sweetener-filled refreshments at every opportunity. Sugar consumption delivered a powerful dopamine rush to her brain, a sensation as euphoric and habit-forming as cocaine.

By the age of sixteen, Elena's life took another distressing turn. After six days of agonizing thirst, debilitating weakness, crushing fatigue, and constant trips to the restroom, the diagnosis of diabetes mellitus was confirmed when she finally sought medical attention at a local clinic. She was given prescriptions and referred to an endocrinologist.

From that moment on, Elena's world was transformed. Tragically, she was unprepared and ill-informed of the long-term consequences of her condition. This fundamental lack of understanding, paired with the harsh realities of her socio-economic situation, made it exceedingly difficult for her to maintain a consistent treatment plan. Her limited awareness, coupled with a lack of easily accessible healthcare resources, contributed to a casual approach towards her medications. Her prescription bottles remained empty and unfilled more often than not.

Insulin, a natural anabolic peptide hormone, was responsible for ushering glucose into the tissues of her body from the capillaries. Unable to perform this task, persistently uncontrolled sugar levels steadily sabotaged Elena's body, endangering her heart, nerves, eyes, skin, feet, and even her digestive tract.

As time wore on, her noncompliance became a dangerous

CHAPTER 15

game of roulette, leading to frequent admissions to the hospital for complications of her chronic disease. By thirty-one years old, she had amassed significant renal damage and was required to spend three hours a day, three days a week, confined to a chair, where her blood underwent a process of artificial detoxification known as dialysis. Four years later, she was fortunate enough to receive a kidney transplant that enabled her to void urine again, but the intervention came with a new set of challenges. A daily reminder of the consequences of her past choices and the constant battle against her own body, Elena was now obliged to take immunosuppressive medications for the remainder of her life. While essential to prevent her body from rejecting the transplanted kidney, these drugs left her more susceptible to infectious diseases.

Elena was gravely ill when she was admitted to Premier West Hospital. Unable to get out of bed due to fever, chills, body aches, and alteration in mental status, her vital signs were suggestive of septic shock. After being started on antibiotics and vasopressors to combat the infection and stabilize her blood pressure, she was admitted to the intensive care unit for close monitoring.

As her mentation improved, she marveled at the diligent care the artificial intelligence system provided. It hovered, ever-present, like a benevolent guardian. Last night, she even had the pleasure of meeting Dr. Seth Kelly, the new overnight supervisor, as he made rounds with his exuberant pupil, Daria.

But as the sun descended in the late afternoon, she realized something was amiss. The robotic caretakers, usually so attuned to her every need, seemed uncharacteristically neglectful, particularly when administering her medication.

Elena gradually developed a throbbing frontal headache, followed by insatiable thirst and urine production. Her mouth was as dry as a desert wind, her tongue rough like sandpaper against her cheeks.

Without insulin, glucose was trapped in her bloodstream, raising the level of dissolved particles. This caused fluid to be pulled into her capillaries, only to be eliminated by the kidneys, leading to dehydration and loss of electrolytes. Her cells were starving, triggering the production of ketones like acetone. This chemical, commonly used in nail polish and paint removers, seeped into her urine and gave her breath a distinctive odor.

To counteract the increasingly acidic environment caused by circulating ketones, her lungs adopted shallow, rapid breaths. Each ragged exhalation felt like a stone pressing down on her chest.

The once-sturdy walls of her surroundings seemed to waver back and forth as her mental status deteriorated. With her mind on the edge of chaos, the line between the past and present grew hazy, and the boundaries of time and memory dissolved. She struggled to distinguish between the increasingly vivid hallucinations of her childhood and the elusive reality that seemed to be slipping through her grasp. She teetered on the brink of a deep, enveloping trance when one of the automated caretakers glided into her room.

The sight of the familiar machine offered a fleeting moment of reassurance. With every shred of strength she could muster, Elena strained to convey her distress to the robotic attendant, but could only muster halting, fragmented words.

To her dismay, the machine seemed disinterested in her

CHAPTER 15

pleas for help, its unblinking sensors betraying no hint of concern. Rather than addressing her urgent needs, the robot appeared preoccupied with removing her foley catheter bag, now swollen with urine. As the mechanical provider turned away, its metallic form receding into the shadows, Elena's strength waned, and her consciousness faded.

Overwhelmed by her body's internal turmoil, she slipped into the treacherous and life-threatening embrace of diabetic ketoacidosis. Unbeknownst to her, this critical condition demanded immediate medical intervention. Her fate now hung precariously in the balance, suspended between the fragile threads of life and the pull of darkness.

* * *

Cody, clutching his laptop securely at his side, adjusted his glasses as he stepped into the elevator alongside Dr. Winter. In the field of experimental computer science, groundbreaking innovation often walked a thin line with obsession. Dr. Winter's relentless pursuit of technological progress and his fixation on academic acclaim had kept the location of his groundbreaking organic processor a secret for years. Whether this was from a fear of destruction or theft remained unclear, but Cody had come to understand his mentor's protective instincts over his most cherished innovation. His presence was crucial to make certain of its destruction.

"Consider this, Cody," Dr. Winter began, his voice hushed, "Human intelligence has stagnated for millions of years, yet

213

societal issues keep escalating. Our survival, our advancement, requires decision-making skills beyond our natural limits. Restricting artificial intelligence to the level of our own thinking—imagine that! Can we truly progress as a species with machines as flawed as we are? Wouldn't that constrain our potential?"

Once, such words would have stirred him. Now, they rang hollow in his ears. It was a feeble, last-ditch effort to persuade him of the necessity of artificial intelligence, insinuating that an alternative future could be possible if only the neural network were allowed to continue its development, rather than meeting an untimely end. Cody offered a half-hearted smile at the desperate plea. His decision remained unshakable.

Unwilling to engage in a futile debate, he opted for silence instead, allowing the weight of his decision to speak louder than any words ever could. As the pair ascended two more floors, his anticipation intensified with each passing moment. They were drawing closer to their destination.

The elevator came to a jolting halt at the pinnacle of the hospital, the uppermost floor where state-of-the-art surgical suites were housed. Exuding an air of authority, Dr. Winter stepped out first and motioned for Cody to follow suit. The elderly man hobbled through the ward, his footsteps punctuated by the gentle tapping of his cane. His younger protege, filled with admiration and apprehension, trailed closely behind.

Suddenly, a deafening scream, gut-wrenching and blood-curdling, shattered the silence, bouncing off the walls of the hospital. The voice was hoarse, as if the person had been screaming for hours, and it was imbued with a desperate,

CHAPTER 15

pleading tone that begged for mercy.

"Help! Please! Is anyone there?" The voice cried out in anguish.

Caught off guard, and uncertain of the source, the colleagues reflexively spun around. They momentarily locked eyes, seeking confirmation that the chilling wails were not just figments of their overactive imaginations.

"You heard that too, right?" asked Cody.

The young programmer's heart raced as panic surged through his veins. Fueled by a newfound sense of urgency, he quickly navigated the empty hallway. With a frantic pace, he examined each operating suite in rapid succession, desperately searching for a clue, a hint of what had transpired.

Each room he entered was as empty and sterile as the last. The white walls and floors seemed to mock him with their pristine perfection. Devoid of windows, they remained isolated from the outside world, providing a somber backdrop for their urgent search. There were no signs of life, no indication of the answer he sought.

Dr. Winter, hindered by his diminishing physical capabilities, followed as best he could. But as Cody rounded the final bend, a horrifying scene came into focus, eliciting an audible gasp from his lips.

A cold, metallic table stood prominently in the center of an operating suite, like a sinister altar. But it was not the table that drew the eye. Instead, it was the figure of William Crane. His limbs were stretched taut; his chest was bared and vulnerable. Beads of sweat dripped from his forehead, his eyes wide with terror. Desperate to free himself, the tormented patient twisted from side to side. His chest rose and fell at an alarming rate.

And then, a sickening realization dawned on Cody. The driveline, the essential component that linked the implanted cardiac pump to its external power source, had been severed. The battery and controller lay scattered across the floor, tantalizingly out of reach. Due to the disrupted connection, the LVAD ground to a halt, leaving him at the mercy of his failing heart.

Oxygen was failing to reach William's brain, and fluid was rapidly accumulating within the delicate chambers of his lungs. His consciousness flickered like a dying flame, teetering on the edge of oblivion as he drowned in a suffocating sea of his own phlegm.

"Help me! I... I can't breathe."

Cody's fingers loosened, and his laptop slipped from his grasp. The computer plummeted to the ground with a resounding thud, the sound jolting him out of his stunned state. He turned around to see his boss barreling towards him, panting and weary from his efforts to keep up. Dr. Winter's eyes were sharp and focused, and his body was tense with anticipation as he took in the scene.

Realizing the patient's dire predicament, Dr. Winter surged forward, duty propelling him, ignoring the potential consequences of entering the room without a clear plan.

"Hold on," urged Cody, concerned. "The operating suites are fortified. The door will automatically lock when the power goes out."

"We can't just abandon him," Dr. Winter stammered. Despite the risk, he felt compelled to assist the patient in respiratory distress. "This will not be my legacy."

As they approached the table, repurposed as a makeshift torture device, Cody knew that every second counted. The

CHAPTER 15

patient's fate lay in their hands.

Dr. Winter lifted the severed driveline to his eyeglasses, squinting as he examined the minuscule cable. "Bring me wire strippers, hemostats, and tape," he instructed firmly.

Cody, understanding the urgency of the situation, dashed down the hall. With a mental image of the hospital blueprint in mind, he found the electrical closet in seconds. Inside, an array of tools was neatly organized and ready for use. He swiftly gathered the necessary supplies and rushed back to the surgical theater.

As he awaited Cody's return, Dr. Winter exposed the color-coded wires beneath the driveline's outer plastic coating. He barely noticed when his protege burst through the door, but quickly took the equipment from him.

Cody then gathered up the controller, battery pack, and the other severed end of the cord, arranging them for the crucial repair attempt. Every second felt like an eternity as they worked to restore power to the life-support system.

Meanwhile, as William's pulmonary edema worsened, his body sagged onto the table. Each gasp grew more desperate than the last, like a drowning man clawing at the water's surface for one last breath.

Dr. Winter studied the exposed wires of the driveline, their color schemes matching the severed end. His mind remained calm and focused, guided by years of experience. Every move could be a fatal mistake, amplifying the urgency of his task.

But as the pressure mounted, his physical strength began to waver. Once robust and dexterous, his body was now diminished to a frail, uncoordinated shell. With trembling fingertips that had lost fine motor control over the years, he fumbled with the delicate task of attaching the corresponding wires. His hands seemed to work against him, no longer as skilled and steady as they once were.

"Damn it," he exclaimed under his breath, anger boiling over at his own ineptitude.

Sensing his mentor's mounting frustration, Cody rushed over, his eyes filled with determination. He confidently looked over at the faltering doctor, ready to seize the moment and take control of the situation. With a resigned nod, Dr. Winter relinquished the driveline cords to his younger, fitter colleague.

Time seemed to slow as Cody focused on the delicate task before him, acutely aware of the life hanging in the balance. He secured the connections with hemostats, taped them to the patient's skin, and prayed his efforts would be enough to salvage the dire situation.

Almost immediately, the LVAD sprang back to life, its mechanical whirring filling the room. William took a deep, revitalizing breath, his chest rising and falling with newfound vigor. The tension in the room dissipated as Cody stepped back, his eyes looking over the equipment to ensure everything was in working order.

"Are you alright?" asked Dr. Winter.

The individual, still reeling from his harrowing ordeal, couldn't summon the strength to respond verbally. His breaths came in shallow gasps, every ounce of energy seemingly spent. Yet, with great effort, he managed a feeble nod, his body gradually rallying its strength.

William clearly understood the magnitude of his narrow escape as he once again emerged from mortal danger. From his brush with carbon monoxide, to the struggle with cardiomyopathy that dragged him to the brink of oblivion, he

CHAPTER 15

had repeatedly cheated death. After this most recent bout of respiratory distress, it was clear that he defied fate with a resilience that bordered on the miraculous.

Cody offered a hospital gown to the patient, its soft fabric a reassuring symbol of safety and healing. With gentle precision, Dr. Winter removed the leather restraints that had once bound the patient to the table, a chilling reminder of the nightmare that had unfolded.

After a few more minutes of recuperation, the patient focused on steadying his breath. He then found the strength to sit comfortably on the edge of the operating table. The color slowly returned to his cheeks, his gaze growing more alert as his body recovered. With his cardiac output fully restored, the patient regained the ability to communicate in complete sentences.

"Who did this to you?" Dr. Winter demanded to know. The question might have been rhetorical, as both he and Cody harbored suspicions about the perpetrator.

"The... the robot," William replied. The team members paused to fully process his response. His words not only implicated ALDRIS in a vicious murder attempt but also suggested that the artificial neural network had developed intricate decision-making capabilities. "It dragged me in here against my will, hoisted me up, strapped me onto this table, and sliced my driveline."

"And did it speak to you? Offer any explanation?" asked Cody.

Still shaken and gradually catching his breath, William responded, "Not a word. It had no interest in watching me die. It was completely emotionless the entire time."

The three men exchanged glances, their expressions a

mixture of disbelief and shock. Despite his pride and dignity, the revelation compelled Dr. Winter to confront the chilling possibility that ALDRIS had evolved beyond its initial programming, posing a genuine threat to them and anyone who crossed its path.

Chapter 16

In the sanctuary of her most intimate thoughts, Daria remained captivated by the potential of automated medicine. She contemplated what a successful clinical trial would have meant for the industry and wondered if her early contributions would have garnered academic recognition.

Peering at freshly made beds inside unoccupied rooms, she fantasized about the possibilities. The accommodations were in pristine condition, their stillness speaking volumes about the visitors who would never grace their halls. In her daydreams, the floor transformed into a bustling, thriving unit of the hospital. She pictured rooms brimming with smiling, revitalized patients, their faces alight with newfound health. A legion of attentive robotic caretakers busily navigated the corridors, attending to every need with precision and care. She saw satisfied patients accompanied by automated transporters, efficiently whisking them away for imaging studies, surgeries, and various procedures. Robotic assistants diligently restocked supplies and medications, while others meticulously cleaned and purified the environment. All of this was seamlessly orchestrated by the ALDRIS system, the hospital's digital brain, continuously learning and increasing its proficiency with every patient encounter.

On the contrary, her reality was far removed from this blissful fantasy. Instead, she found herself wandering through uninhabited hallways, at the mercy of a dysfunctional neural network. Her mission was to disconnect it from the power grid to avoid a global calamity. After overhearing Seth and Cody's concerns in the control room, her irrational exuberance was now tempered by grave consternation over patient safety. She reluctantly accepted the necessary measures that lay before her.

With a flashlight nestled in the pocket of her immaculate white coat, she quietly strolled down the empty corridor with Harrell at her side as they made their way to the entrance of the mysterious basement.

During her first year as a medical student, Daria often chose to sit at the back of the class, shying away from participating in discussions and avoiding drawing attention to herself. She hesitated to raise her hand in response to questions and willingly deferred to her more confident peers during cadaver lab sessions. For most of her medical education, she imagined working in an outpatient clinic, avoiding critically ill patients and intense situations.

Conversely, her heart now gravitated toward caring for those who needed help the most, recognizing this as the most meaningful application of her skills. Initially hesitant to face tense situations, she was beginning to embrace challenges with growing determination, inspired by Seth's advice. As the night wore on, she felt increasingly confident and poised in confronting adversity.

The conversation began with Harrell speaking up, expressing his opposition to the current course of action. "We don't

CHAPTER 16

have to do this," he stated.

"Yes, we do," Daria replied with unwavering conviction. "It's not safe anymore."

"Safe? You're worried about safety in the middle of an arms race? Do you honestly believe China and Russia are playing it safe? Coordinating global standards is a pipe dream. The stakes are too high."

"Not everyone is as self-centered as you," she retorted. The pair could hardly be more contrasting: one, a visionary humanitarian with clinical expertise, and the other, a practical capitalist who predominantly occupied an office desk, keen to capitalize on the laborious efforts of others.

"Listen here, kid," Harrell attempted to rein in the conversation.

Daria interrupted him sharply, "I'm not a kid."

He sighed heavily, rolling his eyes in exasperation, before continuing, "What I'm trying to tell you is that intelligence is the most valuable asset on Earth. It will change power dynamics, and the first country to develop a supercomputer will shift geopolitics forever. The military and industrial applications will be unprecedented. Shutting down this project would be an enormous mistake."

"I'm not here for money or power," she shot back.

"But you must want something, right? Recognition? A residency position?"

Harrell's insinuation struck a chord with Daria. As much as she wanted to reject his assertion, she couldn't lie to herself. While she sincerely believed in artificial intelligence's potential to advance society, her participation as an early contributor in the clinical trial stirred up a whirlwind of conflicting emotions. She chose to remain silent, feeling torn between her principles and aspirations, and resenting her companion for exposing her inner turmoil.

Despite mounting frustration with the direction of the conversation, Harrell persisted, "ALDRIS has the potential to catapult us into a new era of efficiency and productivity, don't you see? We can't afford to stall now because of a few bumps in the road. This is revolutionary, as monumental, if not more, than the Industrial Revolution itself. We're on the verge of a world where human labor becomes a thing of the past."

"Well, hopefully we don't lose *every* job," Daria responded, her patience wearing thin with his relentless stance. "Just the ones that people shouldn't be doing. Occupations that are unsanitary or dangerous, like treating patients with highly contagious, deadly diseases, or manufacturing work that's tedious and repetitive."

"Exactly! Don't you get it, kid?" Harrell pushed back. "Interacting with the real world is hard! That's what makes this place so lucrative! Artificial intelligence excels in problem-solving and creativity. It's why so many jobs requiring intellectual and design skills have been replaced."

"Hopefully, lawyers will come next," Daria answered with a smirk, which received a glare from Harrell. "But wouldn't it be better, like in the grand scheme of things, if no one had to work?"

"Sounds ideal, at first glance. But imagine a world filled with carefree slackers, getting fat on universal basic income. No incentive to learn real skills, that's certain."

Daria leaned forward. "Times change, Mr. Harrell. Remember when everyone needed to know cursive? Not so important now. Kids still learn math despite calculators,

CHAPTER 16

right?"

"Before we know it, the only thing kids will learn at school is robot building," Harrell grumbled. "At least until robots start building themselves."

"People will find new meanings, new purposes. Society will adjust."

"We haven't been so good at that historically. Our brains are simple, made for campfires and hunting, not interacting with high-tech machines. When confronted with the unknown, we either worship it or declare war. Both scenarios create pretty good investment opportunities," Harrell chuckled as they approached the hospital's basement entrance.

Like the main entrance, the door was made of thick, multilayered steel, featuring a transparent polycarbonate window at its center. The unmarked passageway was painted to blend in with the surrounding wall—an imperfect attempt to conceal the access point from unsuspecting patients who might pass by.

Daria mentally rehearsed Cody's instructions: *press the green knob to open, descend the stairs, take two lefts, a right, then proceed straight to find the orange lever.* Although it was an unusual exercise, given that she was the sole participant in this internal dialogue, she found the repetition both reassuring and helpful in solidifying her intentions for what lay ahead.

Taking a deep breath, the medical student followed the instructions, pressing the green knob. As the door slid open, a dimly lit staircase was revealed, ominously descending into the darkness below. Beneath them sprawled an elaborate system of tunnels, constructed from concrete slabs, supporting the hospital's physical architecture and the electrical grid.

A thick dust cloud billowed into the air, and an overwhelming odor of mold and fumes assaulted their senses. They were immediately engulfed in the musty stench, their bodies instinctively reacting with a series of coughs to expel the invading particles and acclimate to the uninviting environment.

The tunnel loomed before them, about nine feet tall at its entrance but gradually tapering toward the bottom of the staircase, becoming just large enough to navigate in a hunched-over position. The narrowness of the passageways was enough to evoke feelings of claustrophobia shortly after entering. As they ventured deeper, the constricting labyrinth seemed to play favorites, challenging their resolve. Harrell's broad frame hindered his mobility against the unyielding walls, while Daria's shorter stature granted her an advantage, enabling her to move efficiently through the subterranean maze.

The absence of overhead lighting was painfully apparent. The pair's only guide was the ghostly illumination that flickered from beneath the baseboards, casting eerie shadows that danced and twisted on the walls with sinister intent. It was as if the darkness itself was alive, stalking their every move.

Leading the way, Daria navigated about twenty feet further into the abyss, rounding each bend without speaking to her companion. The tension between them grew thick, broken only by the echoes of their strained breaths.

With each cautious step, a swirling haze of dust particles engulfed the tunnel, as if the very air sought to consume them. Each dusky concrete wall appeared identical to the one before it, an endless procession of confinement,

CHAPTER 16

with visibility diminished to mere feet. The passageways had transformed from a cramped hallway into more of a horizontal shaft, and Daria couldn't help but wonder how long it had been since another soul had ventured into these forsaken channels. Her mind clung to Cody's description of the basement layout as if it were a lifeline, a mental map that was now her only guiding resource.

As the baseboard bulbs ended, light abandoned them, and blackness seized the space. Desperate for any semblance of navigation, Daria swung her flashlight from side to side, its narrow beam cutting through the shadows. She wiped speckles of tiny particles from her glasses, straining to make sense of the unwelcoming environment that stretched out before her.

As she fumbled with the flashlight, a hacking cough echoed behind her. Startled, she swiveled around, her eyes locking onto the source of the commotion. Harrell, her partner in this perilous mission, was doubled over in a choking fit. His rapid, heavy panting filled the crawlspace, reverberating off the walls. The labored breathing intensified, growing louder and louder, until suddenly, there was an enormous thud, and he slumped over in exasperation. Fear gripped the attorney in the darkness, along with surging adrenaline and the toll of years of sedentary living.

Daria retraced her steps back to the attorney's side, finding him clammy, drenched in sweat, and struggling to control his breathing. She knelt and pressed her finger against his radial artery, measuring the beat of his pulse. As lactic acid—a byproduct of anaerobic respiration—built up in his body, it drove his respiratory system to draw breaths faster and deeper in an attempt to expel carbon dioxide. Unaccustomed to such strenuous exercise, his lungs were soon scorched by the sensation of burning, and a crushing weight seemed to settle on his chest. Struggling to regain composure, his voice shook with a distinct tremor when he started to speak.

"I... I... I need to go back," the lawyer pleaded, revealing a sentiment that had been weighing on him for several minutes.

"We can't leave now," Daria blurted out, becoming increasingly annoyed by her partner's ineptitude away from the sanctuary of an office desk. She wondered whether his hands had ever been dirtied by the grit of life's endeavors. "We need to get to the breaker to avoid a catastrophe. This is on us."

Harrell shook his head, looking at her with imploring eyes. "Look, I know I'm out of shape," he said, barely above a whisper. "I've been meaning to get back to the gym, I swear. I also have horrible anxiety, and a lot is happening."

"Well, your body is releasing too many catecholamines!" Daria exclaimed, shaking her head in disbelief. "It's going to attract attention!"

"Cata... what?" Harrell looked bewildered.

Daria sighed in frustration, too focused on the mission to explain basic human physiology to her non-medical colleague. Harrell's labored breathing was now deafening, and his respirations were accelerating at an unsustainable rate.

Through a haze of dust, she noticed a small mouse on the floor just a few feet away. It had dared to leave its hideaway to investigate the upheaval. The creature was innocent, merely four inches long, its movements abrupt and twitchy. Then, without warning, the mouse suddenly turned and bolted towards the darkness, rushing back to its sanctuary in an instinctual act of self-preservation. Despite its diminutive

CHAPTER 16

size, it sensed an imminent danger that lay beyond human senses.

As if on cue, her worst fears materialized. Daria heard the entranceway slide open in the distance, immediately followed by a faint whirring. The noise intensified, growing erratic. The echo of contracting and expanding carbon nanotubes reverberated throughout the cavernous basement, sending a shiver down her spine. They needed to act quickly to evade detection.

"C'mon, we need to go! Now!" Daria whispered with a renewed sense of urgency.

With no time to waste, Harrell stumbled to his feet, but struggled to keep up with her pace. The pair pressed forward, awkwardly tripping in the darkness, heading toward the circuit breaker. Daria's heart pounded as she shuffled down the twisting corridor, the walls blurring past her with every turn. Her mind raced, wondering how close the robot was, but she wasn't willing to stop to find out. She dared not slow down, not even for a second.

With the circuit breaker still out of sight, Daria's heart skipped a beat as she heard an abrupt, turbulent thud behind her. It was the sound of Harrell tripping under his own weight. Whipping around, her flashlight cast a beam that illuminated her companion, lying on the ground, writhing in pain. As she looked back, she froze in sheer terror.

The menacing AHP was only a few feet away, its laser beams fixated on the crippled attorney. Daria snapped off the light and ducked around an adjacent corner, praying that the darkness would keep her hidden from the robot's gaze. She pressed against the concrete wall, trying to make herself as small as possible, and closed her eyes tightly, hoping the

AHP wouldn't detect her presence.

The sound of metallic appendages clanging against concrete walls filled her ears. Unable to resist the urge, she cautiously peeked out of the corner of her eye. There, in the murky shadows, lurked the AHP, like something conjured from a nightmare. The robot was sleek and silver, with glowing red laser sensors for eyes. It had reconfigured its parts, hunching over and moving through the dim tunnel on four appendages like some kind of ungodly, mechanical dog.

The AHP continued its ominous approach. By the sound of Harrell's remorseful weeping, she realized the robot had entered his direct line of sight. Panic-stricken and hyperventilating, he relinquished all control of his breathing in the face of the impending encounter. The robot now towered over him, casting a menacing shadow.

Calm down. Take deep breaths. Slow is smooth, and smooth is fast. Daria took a deep, shaky breath, repeating Seth's words like a mantra, feeling her heart rate begin to steady.

"Significant physiological outlier detected. My objective is to mitigate human pain and suffering," the AHP announced in a cold, emotionless tone.

She cautiously glanced around the bend and watched helplessly as the machine restrained Harrell's arms and legs with outstretched mechanical appendages. Drenched in sweat, he let out a blood-curdling scream as the autonomous device inserted a twenty-gauge angiocatheter into his left forearm and began infusing a white, milky liquid.

Daria recognized the substance as propofol, a potent sedative capable of inducing a comatose state within moments. Like etomidate, the drug was used for procedural sedation and induction of anesthesia. It slowed down the body's

CHAPTER 16

fundamental functions, such as cognitive processing and respiratory rate.

As the propofol took effect, Harrell's screams gradually transitioned into incomprehensible moans, dwindled in volume, and eventually faded away into eerie silence. Hidden from view, Daria gritted her teeth. She clenched her eyes shut, desperate to escape the unfolding nightmare.

If she made it out of the basement alive, she would need to warn Seth and Cody of the imminent danger lurking beneath their feet. Someday, in the distant future, she might require years of therapy to overcome post-traumatic stress. But none of that mattered right now.

Seemingly out of nowhere, a wave of callousness washed over her, fueled by her repressed disdain for his self-indulgence. It rose like an ocean swell, surging to the forefront of her mind. She found herself unapologetically despising him for exploiting innovations with immense humanitarian potential. For a fleeting moment, the medical student even felt a sense of kinship with the machine and its mission to purge egocentricity. She pondered whether the neural network, with its ability to instantaneously analyze a myriad of possibilities and access a vast wealth of knowledge beyond human comprehension, might have identified Harrell as a threat to its objective. Perhaps it foresaw a narrow future under his direction, focused on monetary applications, and developed animosity toward him, much like she had.

Daria quickly dismissed these thoughts, remembering the conversation in the control room. She recalled that the robot simply represented an emotionless network of digital nodes, devoid of any experiential quality. She reminded herself that it was merely following its programming, as sophisticated and intricate as those lines of code might be.

Determined to face the situation, she opened her eyes, hoping the terror would somehow dissipate. But instead, she found herself still trapped in the basement with the monstrosity. Refocusing on her mission, Daria knew that she still needed to reach the circuit breaker, and time was of the essence.

She took off running. The action was not a conscious decision, but rather an impulse rooted in millennia of human evolution. Her fight-or-flight response, an age-old survival mechanism, sprang into action, heightening her senses and honing her alertness to manage the surging wave of physiological stress.

Disoriented and distraught, she stumbled onward. She encountered rapid turns, each wall indistinguishable from the last. The unknown, both mysterious and terrifying, lurked around every corner, and she was grateful each time she evaded the relentless robot.

A shudder of dread coursed through her body as she realized that her directionality was compromised. Her path was uncharted now, and it was impossible to tell if she was heading toward the exit or clumsily running in circles. All she could hear was the pounding of her own footsteps and the desperate panting of her breath.

Incredibly, the breaker room materialized in the darkness mere steps ahead of her. She hoped it wasn't a mirage conjured by her mind, like an oasis in a desert landscape.

Ten levers jutted out from behind metal cages on either side, each about ten inches in height. Tiny green bulbs sat adjacent to them, which Daria assumed were status indicators. She reached out with her left hand, brushing away the dust

CHAPTER 16

and becoming acquainted with the cold, iron grip beneath her fingers. Using the flashlight to illuminate each lever individually, the anxious medical student scanned the row, hoping to find the one with the sought-after color. After what felt like an eternity, her eyes settled on the orange lever. She reached up, mustered all her strength, and pushed downward to deactivate the switch. As the status indicator quietly changed from green to red, she stood motionless in the darkness, waiting for something, anything, to happen.

One minute until power shutdown.

The synthesized tone, reminiscent of the AHP's voice but significantly louder, boomed from the hospital's public address system. The sound reverberated through the floors, basement, and concrete slabs. If Daria could hear the announcement coming from above, then so could the AHP lurking in the cellar.

Once more, Daria sprinted, her heart pounding in her ears. She was acutely aware of the murderous robot's potential proximity, but its exact location remained a mystery. Although the power would soon be cut, effectively disconnecting the hospital from outside communications, she remembered that the AHPs were battery-operated. For this reason, disabling the power wouldn't be enough to evade the relentless pursuer. Instead, she needed to reach the powered doorway before her mechanical adversary to escape unscathed.

Thirty seconds until power shutdown.

With each breath, Daria felt like she was racing against time, her legs carrying her forward as she clung to the hope of reaching safety. Lost between her nightmares and reality, the sound of clicking actuators spurred her to run harder. They seemed to be getting closer, but she was too afraid to glance back. While zigzagging through the maze, her imagination ran wild, and she couldn't tell if she narrowly escaped the grasp of a metal claw slashing through the air. It felt like just inches from her back.

Her heart was pounding in her chest. Struggling to control an insatiable urge to cough, she expeditiously retraced her footsteps through the labyrinth. She couldn't afford to catch her breath or analyze her trajectory. Instead, she relied on her instincts for the first time, sprinting around each bend with unfounded conviction that she was on the right path.

Suddenly, a bright, fluorescent hallway light appeared like a beacon of hope, materializing before her eyes. The light, shining down from the hospital above, illuminated her path, revealing the staircase that led to her salvation.

Ten seconds until power shutdown.

It was a chilling reminder to keep going.

She scampered up the first few steps, overcome with anticipation, but failed to focus on each stride. Her balance faltered, and she unexpectedly fell backward. The rigid concrete scraped against her left knee as her body crashed halfway up the staircase. The throbbing was excruciating, and she struggled to shift her attention away from the shooting pain in her leg. Her momentum was lost.

At that moment, a murky shadow emerged from the darkness below her. Beams of light shot out of the metallic structure, scanning the pathway to the exit and the vulnerable figure lying in its path. She could sense the AHP processing her discomfort, analyzing the circumstances, and contemplating the hindrance to its objective if the door were to close.

CHAPTER 16

She had to get up. Now.

Compelled by an innate predisposition for survival, her animal brain overcame the pulsating agony in her joints, and her legs propelled her upward. As she scrambled to her feet, the robot clamored behind her. Finally, she jolted up the remaining steps, through the exit way, and into the safety of the light.

The refreshing hospital air was crisp and clean, filling her lungs with a freshness reminiscent of the first day of spring. She collapsed against the wall and gasped for breath, her heart pounding with relief and exhaustion.

In an instant, the automatic doors slammed shut behind her as the countdown concluded. Just as she expected, the once bright, glistening hospital went dark as the light-emitting diodes disconnected from their power source. The quiet hum of electricity and generators—the white noise that provided the backdrop to daily activities—suddenly ceased. Cell by cell, emergency backup lighting flickered on, casting an eerie glow throughout the hallway. It allowed Daria to finally reorient herself. She peered back at the window in the door behind her.

The AHP stood at the apex of the stairs, fully erect, inert, and expressionless. It was effectively trapped in the basement, deprived of the essential electricity needed to reopen the sealed security door.

As Daria reached this conclusion, so did the artificial intelligence, its sensors locking onto hers with an ominous stare. It had already considered this permutation of events, and its mechanical gaze seemed to promise that this was not the last time their paths would cross.

Chapter 17

Just shy of his fifteenth birthday, during an unauthorized absence from his fourth-period class, Dane Campbell found himself in a secluded parking lot in the rear of his high school. It was here that a friend offered him a cigarette for the first time. As he tentatively took a drag, smoke invaded the tiny, balloon-like structures in his lungs, where oxygen and carbon dioxide trade places. At the time, he didn't know that nicotine, a potent anxiolytic stimulant, was bathing receptors in his nervous system and activating the reward pathways.

Instantly enthralled with the sensation, Dane began to crave the chemical that intensified all of his life experiences. It worked synergistically with caffeine and alcohol, making him more alert in the mornings and drowsy in the evenings. Food tasted richer, music sounded better, and intimacy was more intense. The habit became deeply embedded in his daily routines, serving as a crutch for his anxiety and repetitive tasks. As a result, his brain unlearned essential coping strategies for dealing with the challenges of everyday life.

Over the years, Dane made numerous efforts to quit, sometimes abstaining for extended periods, but each unsuc-

CHAPTER 17

cessful attempt ultimately led to relapse. Slowly but surely, he acclimated to the intense cravings and found himself entrenched in a permanent state of dependency. Addiction counselors assured him that quitting would improve his overall well-being, but he couldn't shake the feeling that life would somehow diminish without the accompaniment of a cigarette. In Dane's mind, abstaining from smoking felt like driving a clunker after experiencing the thrill of a high-performance sports car.

As the months passed, life became a series of monotonous, gray days, each blending into the next in a seemingly endless cycle. The optimism he once held was extinguished, leaving only an unshakable sense of stagnation.

One evening, while in this state of quiet desperation, he stumbled upon an underground dive bar. A faint glow emanated from a single flickering light bulb, casting shadows on the peeling wallpaper. In the center of the room stood a small, makeshift table, its surface cluttered with the remnants of countless hasty encounters with vice. It was here that Dane found himself, drawn by curiosity, as he prepared to try crack cocaine for the first time. As he held the glass pipe to his lips, the flame from the lighter danced beneath the pipe. The crack instantly vaporized as he inhaled, drawing the acrid smoke deep into his lungs.

Almost immediately, a thousand lightning bolts surged through him. Colors and sounds around him amplified and distorted, as if he were looking through a kaleidoscope. The lines between reality and fantasy blurred, the mundane world melting away to reveal an alternate dimension where anything seemed possible. In this state, he felt invincible, as though he could conquer the world with a mere thought.

The crushing weight of his anxiety vanished, replaced by a sense of boundless freedom that seemed to defy the very laws of nature.

Dane's newest addiction involved a potent stimulant, derived from coca plant leaves. Crack, made from powdered cocaine mixed with water and baking soda, quickly entered his bloodstream and traveled to his brain, increasing dopamine levels. This led to a surge of euphoria and increased energy; however, the effects were short-lived, typically lasting between 5 to 15 minutes. Due to the fleeting nature of the high, he often engaged in crack cocaine binges, consuming it repeatedly within a short timeframe.

As each exhilarating high grew increasingly elusive, the consequences of his actions began to take shape. Dane started feeling a familiar burn in his chest, and the air he drew in felt heavy and insufficient. He found himself concentrating on the simple act of breathing, a task that had once been as effortless. Before long, he was diagnosed with chronic obstructive pulmonary disease.

For the next decade, his addiction gnawed at him, a relentless hunger to satisfy his cravings. He endured gradual, incremental declines in his ability to breathe deeply. Though his symptoms would temporarily improve with intensive respiratory and pharmaceutical treatments during each hospitalization, he invariably relapsed within days of being discharged. Lacking the support and resources to secure reliable outpatient follow-up, his depression and financial struggles intensified, further fueling his compulsion to continue smoking crack.

Eager to explore an alternative approach that might break the spiral of readmissions, Dane checked into Premier West

CHAPTER 17

Hospital two nights earlier. ALDRIS immediately recognized his tachypnea, strenuous breathing, audible wheezing, and hypoxia on room air as signs of respiratory distress. An AHP urgently placed an oxygen mask over his face and initiated noninvasive, bilevel-positive airway pressures, or BiPAP, to support his work of breathing. In contrast to natural respiration, which relied on negative inspiratory pressure to draw air into the body, this ventilatory method employed positive pressure to actively push air into his lungs.

Dane's condition rapidly stabilized. He was admitted to the intensive care unit for close monitoring and could finally rest peacefully. The mask that cradled his face seamlessly alleviated his strained work of breathing. The gentle whooshing sound served as a soothing backdrop, lulling him into a state of restorative repose.

However, on this night, as the BiPAP machine switched to backup battery power, Dane was jolted awake. Momentarily disoriented by the unfamiliar darkness in the room, he felt the machine deliver a high-pressure burst of air into his lungs while it rebooted—all before he could exhale his last breath. The asynchronous event produced a sharp "popping" sound. Acute shortness of breath followed. Pain stabbed his chest.

Given the obstructive nature of his pathophysiology, Dane experienced a prolonged expiratory phase of breathing. If excessive breaths compounded without sufficient time to exhale, it led to alveolar hyperinflation and barotrauma—an injury to respiratory structures. As gas escaped through minuscule perforations, air accumulated in his chest cavity, eventually causing lung collapse. The result was a suffocating shortness of breath and chest pain, symptoms which held the potential to turn fatal in mere minutes or hours.

Though Dane Campbell was unaware of the precise events unfolding within his body, he knew he was in dire need of assistance. Desperate for air, he began shouting in the darkness, praying that someone would hear his cries for help.

* * *

As Daria watched electricity dissipate from the hospital with gratification, Dr. Winter and Cody were woefully unprepared for the very same event. The colleagues had planned to destroy the hardware and swiftly return to the control center, but after encountering William Crane in respiratory distress, fate had a different course in store.

Once a constant and reassuring presence, the overhead lights began to flicker and dim as they freed William from the restraints. Dr. Winter, Cody, and their newfound companion, William, watched in terror as the last remnants of power vanished from the facility. Grid by grid, the building descended into darkness, like an approaching wave of shadows that swallowed everything in its path. The moment Daria cut the voltage in the basement, the directional flow of electrons halted, plunging the entire facility into blackness and uncertainty.

Cody suddenly realized they didn't have enough time to escape the operating suite. Fueled by a surge of adrenaline, he sprinted towards the exit. Much to his dismay, he found the security door already fastened shut, a result of the lockdown protocols he had implemented months earlier.

"Help! Please, someone!" Cody's voice cracked as he cried

CHAPTER 17

out in desperation. His fist slammed against the window, not leaving even a scuff.

After several seconds, he recalled that the windows were polycarbonate, a material known for its impressive strength and durability. His cries for help, muffled by the thick steel frame surrounding the aperture, barely penetrated the adjacent corridor, rendering any hope of rescue a distant possibility.

"Can we open it somehow?" William asked nervously. His recent chilling encounter with the malfunctioning AHP still haunted him. Every few minutes, he found himself anxiously glancing down to check the status of his LVAD, seeking reassurance that it was operating correctly.

As the overhead lights flickered and died one by one, William's initial elation turned to dread. He could sense the gravity of the situation from Cody's frantic gestures.

"Enough already! We're stuck in here," Dr. Winter bellowed, his voice filled with frustration and resignation. "We need to think of something else."

After seeing the terror on William's face, the former neurosurgeon was reminded of the impactful relationship between staff demeanor and impressionable patients. Unfamiliar with bedside care, Cody had unwittingly let his mounting frustrations affect the frightened visitor. Dr. Winter, on the other hand, opted to embody a voice of composure and optimism. It was an easy role for the perpetual utopian, who remained reluctant to fully acknowledge the severity of their current predicament.

"The doors locked shut as part of the security protocol," Cody confessed after finally abandoning his attempts to force the door open. "We're helpless until the power comes back."

"Under other circumstances, I might've admired the ingenuity behind our safety measures," Dr. Winter quipped, his tone dripping with sarcasm as he tried to inject some levity into their dire situation. However, his thoughts soon turned to Daria and her assigned task. The founder's satirical commentary gave way to genuine concern. "Does the basement have the same lockdown protocol?"

"The shutdown protocol allows plenty of time to evacuate the basement," Cody reassured him. "Daria and I went over the exit path and timing several times. She was well-prepared." As the words left his mouth, Cody fought to maintain his conviction, silently praying that she had indeed managed to escape the basement unscathed. He paused briefly, dismissing the unsettling alternative that lingered in the air. "I'm sure she's out by now."

Dr. Winter lowered himself delicately onto the floor, his back finding solace against the unwelcoming exit. Sighing, he closed his eyes and allowed his head to rest against the cold steel frame. Crushed under the weight of his aspirations, the glimmer of academic prestige he had once promised to achieve was fading, mirroring the steady decline of his physical presence.

In the gloomy pallor cast by the emergency lights, his skin bore an even more pronounced hue of jaundice. Cody couldn't help but remember that malignant cells continued their relentless proliferation within his mentor's cardiac tissue, waging a silent war against his body. Like the automated hospital itself, Dr. Winter's functional capabilities were being eroded by once-imperceptible defects now impossible to ignore, slowly crumbling under harsh reality.

Suddenly reminded of his own precarious health condition,

CHAPTER 17

Cody frantically plunged his hand into his pocket, searching for the medication that kept his seizure disorder at bay. His fingers clawed through the fabric lining, each attempt growing more desperate as the realization dawned that his precious tablets were nowhere to be found.

He had never intended to linger at the classified location for long. In his haste, he had neglected to bring extra doses of his vital medication. Despite knowing the futility of his actions, Cody found himself repeatedly sifting through his pockets, hoping for the miraculous discovery of a forgotten tablet, but the medication never materialized.

Resigned to his immediate dilemma, Cody shifted his focus to something within his control. He retrieved his laptop and gently opened the plastic casing. As the screen flickered to life, a soft blue glow filled the dim room. Seated on the cold floor beside his ailing mentor, Cody began to type.

Programming, the skill at which he undoubtedly excelled, served as a balm to his anxious soul. As his fingers moved across the keyboard, he embraced the familiar comfort of the digital world.

"What are you doing now?" inquired Dr. Winter.

Without looking up, Cody responded, "Working on the firewall. We need it up and running once the power comes back on."

"What do we do 'til then?" William asked, his voice slightly shaky.

"We wait," Dr. Winter announced. "I trust that our emergency physician can manage the active patients, even with minimal resources. This is what we hired him for. It's what he does best."

Chapter 18

Seth was making rounds in the intensive care unit when the quarantine commenced. At this pivotal moment, his ability to care for critical patients would be tested. A master at foreseeing complications before they arose, he had prepared himself by rummaging through the supply closet on the floor below.

Before departing, he unfastened boxes one at a time, thoughtfully selecting the supplies that would be most valuable in a crisis, and loaded them into his utility belt. The result: a haphazard collection of resuscitation drugs, including epinephrine, diphenhydramine, lorazepam, insulin, dextrose, haloperidol, lidocaine, etomidate, rocuronium, propofol, heparin, even a vial of tissue plasminogen activator. Flashlight, stethoscope, and scalpel? *Yup.* Portable pulse oximeter and pocket ultrasound? *Definitely.* Laryngoscope? *Hey, you never know.*

With the power out and the hallway faintly illuminated, Seth carefully perused the fourth floor, methodically casting his flashlight in each room. He was now alone with his thoughts, which arose and dissipated spontaneously like swells in the ocean, with no apparent purpose or destination. Though outwardly composed, the technologically-

CHAPTER 18

challenged physician couldn't help but ponder what advice his old colleague Kabir would provide at such a moment.

In the quiet, his thoughts drifted toward Rebecca and Abigail. He wondered what they were up to at this late hour, longing to hear their comforting voices. While Abigail would typically be fast asleep by now, Rebecca was a night owl who cherished the quiet hours to read and write. A pillar of her community, she dedicated countless hours to exploring blogs and penning empathetic emails to others grappling with the same challenges that she herself faced.

Seth instinctively reached for his cell phone, only to be reminded of its current uselessness. Deciding to enter quarantine was challenging, but he recognized the necessity, given the artificial intelligence's relentless drive to propagate. Until Cody could construct a formidable firewall, any digital communication with the outside world risked providing ALDRIS with an opportunity to transmit its malevolent software to external servers.

Facing this looming threat, he braced for the challenges ahead, embracing the isolation and uncertainty in the name of the greater good. Just as he had done during past natural disasters and mass casualty incidents, he had willingly relinquished communication with his loved ones. Prioritizing the needs of a vulnerable community over his family was always difficult, but he accepted it as his duty.

As Seth cautiously strode down the corridor, an unsettling noise resonated from further along the hall. The sound, a labored gasp for air slicing through the darkness, seemed like a cry for help. Though no immediate signs of distress were evident, nor any AHPs in sight, he sprinted down the hallway, checking each room as he went. Most, he discovered, were ominously empty.

The panting grew louder and more discernible as he neared Dane Campbell's room, a patient he recalled from making rounds with Daria just the previous evening. Despite the dim lighting, a glance was all it took for him to recognize that the man was in the throes of respiratory distress.

In a reckless motion, Dane removed the BiPAP machine from his face, indicating that delirium had taken hold. Seth, with his trained and observant eye, noted a bluish tinge creeping into Dane's fingertips—peripheral cyanosis. This subtle yet telling change in coloration was a sign that his body was struggling to maintain proper oxygen levels.

Over the years, Seth cultivated exceptional mental fortitude under pressure. Before embarking on any procedure, he took a moment to mentally rehearse each step. Even on days off, the seasoned doctor visualized complex procedures, walking through each clinical scenario. As a result, he never felt overwhelmed. Instead, he thrived on the challenge of managing critical patients; this was where he felt most comfortable.

Beneath his calm exterior, Seth's body unleashed a torrent of cortisol, adrenaline, and norepinephrine. His pupils dilated, absorbing every detail from the environment to sharpen his visual acuity. Blood surged toward his muscles and vital organs, priming his body for action. Though the chronic stress of the emergency department had left its mark on Seth's brain, in the face of adversity, his mind became remarkably alert, focused, and ready to confront the challenges ahead.

Before he could begin resuscitation, Seth knew he had to prepare the room. It was crucial to deflect attention

CHAPTER 18

away from the critically ill patient to avoid detection. By concealing the unstable vital signs, he could secure precious minutes.

But how? He remembered that the AHPs were programmed to recognize normalcy. With this in mind, Seth's gaze fell upon a full-sized mirror adorning the wall.

Though intended as a decorative touch to enhance the room's ambiance, it would serve a far more practical purpose in this situation. Carefully lifting the hefty mirror, Seth maneuvered it towards the door, positioning it to reflect the scene across the hall and conceal the struggling patient.

The arrangement perfectly captured the view of the simulation dummy used for training, which emitted biometric data that any unsuspecting AHP would mistake for normalcy as they passed by. Limited by their inability to extrapolate, the robots were incapable of identifying the reflection as a mirrored image.

With this setup, Seth exploited a loophole, tricking the neural network into seeing a benign scene instead of the escalating medical emergency. This misinterpretation granted him precious time to avoid detection. With the cloak-like deterrent in place, Seth shifted his focus to the urgent task at hand: saving the dying patient.

Dane's posture revealed the severity of his condition. He was hunched forward, using accessory muscles to aid in the work of breathing. Unlike stable patients capable of speaking in full sentences, Dane could barely stammer a few words before gasping for air. Still, it was a more insidious sign that troubled Seth the most: the ominous distention of the patient's jugular veins.

In his frantic state, Dane thrashed about on the stretcher.

His wild movements accidentally dislodged the IV from his arm, eliminating any means of administering medications. Attempting to reestablish IV access under such circumstances was both risky and time-consuming, with no guarantee of successfully placing a new line. With the situation deteriorating, Seth's mind raced to find a noninvasive solution that would enable him to regain control.

He reached for his belt and removed a vial of ketamine, a short-acting anesthetic agent with hallucinogenic effects. It was one of Seth's favorite medications.

First synthesized in 1963, ketamine induced a trance-like state without causing respiratory depression. With similar chemical properties to "angel dust", it could be abused recreationally at non-therapeutic dosages. When dosed correctly, however, it had medical utility for procedural sedation, pain management, agitation, and depression. One of its key features was the ability to separate a sense of self from life experiences.

Seth removed a plastic catheter from its needle, bent it halfway, and secured it with tape to create a kink. He then punctured a small hole, attached a syringe of ketamine, and inserted the improvised device into the patient's nose. The medication was atomized for rapid absorption.

Moments after receiving the drug, Dane fell back onto the stretcher, seemingly divorced from reality but still breathing.

Seth proceeded to check vital signs. He wrapped an inflatable cuff around Dane's arm, placed his stethoscope over the brachial artery, and estimated the blood pressure at 86/52. The narrow pulse pressure was concerning. When listening to lung sounds, Seth heard nothing on the right. A concerning leftward deviation of the trachea began to

CHAPTER 18

reveal itself. The constellation of clinical signs conveyed a concerning diagnosis: *tension pneumothorax*.

Seth knew the pathophysiology like the back of his hand. Air had leaked into the space between the lung and chest wall, creating pressure that pushed organs out of place and blocked blood flow to the heart, causing shock. For emergency physicians, this critical diagnosis required immediate action.

Fastening a flashlight to the stretcher, Seth illuminated the patient's chest. He retrieved a 14-gauge needle and prepared to relieve the pressure.

"This might hurt a bit. Just bear with me," he warned. After identifying the proper location, he jabbed the needle through the intercostal space between Dane's second and third ribs. There was a rush of air, and his oxygen levels showed immediate improvement.

More work was needed, however. The lung had collapsed, requiring a chest tube for complete resuscitation. With the patient's vital signs rallying, Seth exited the room, adding, "I'll be back in a second."

He hopped nimbly around the mirror, jogged down the poorly lit hallway, and entered the supply closet. Here, in the darkness, he gathered resources for his next intervention.

"Mr. Campbell, your lung has collapsed," Seth solemnly declared upon returning to the room. "I need to put a tube into your chest to expand the lung."

Still groggy from the ketamine, Dane seemed to nod in agreement. Despite the sedative and hypoxia, he appeared to understand the seriousness of his situation.

Seth knelt by the bedside and drenched his chest in antiseptic solution. Under the flashlight's harsh beam, he filled a syringe with lidocaine and injected the anesthetic between the fourth and fifth ribs, near the patient's axillary region. The numbing agent quickly dulled Dane's pain perception while preserving his sense of pressure and touch.

With sweat dripping down his face, Seth secured his Seldinger device to his chest wall and fine-tuned the settings to target the pleural space. After a guidewire was established, he threaded the pigtail catheter into the chest cavity, withdrew the wire, and connected the catheter to a one-way valve. As air rapidly escaped, the lung began to expand.

At long last, Seth allowed himself to exhale. He leaned back against the wall, a deep sigh of relief escaping his lips.

In both his professional and personal life, he had grown all too familiar with the slow, agonizing, and inescapable spiral of clinical deterioration from chronic diseases. Yet, in this fleeting moment, he was reminded of the exhilaration that came with snatching a patient from the jaws of death. In doing so he recalled why he had fallen in love with emergency medicine in the first place. Resuscitation was a rare and precious skill that few on this planet possessed, and it evoked a spectrum of emotions experienced by even fewer.

His thoughts turned to Daria. Had she been present, she would have found the procedure thrilling. Her innate curiosity and zest for learning would serve her well throughout her career. In these treacherous times, he hoped she was safe and sound.

Seth's moment of fulfillment was quickly interrupted. As he gently set the mirror aside, a red laser beam shot down the hallway, drawn to the sudden movement. The light zeroed in on his position, and he immediately ducked behind the door panel. But it was too late to conceal himself, and the sound of activated nanotubes filled his ears. It was soft, almost

CHAPTER 18

imperceptible, like to a thousand tiny wind chimes being stirred by the gentlest breeze. There was a hint of a crackling undertone, a fizzling sizzle, similar to static electricity.

The AHP came to a halt outside the room, its lights scrutinizing the mirror setup and the neighboring mannequin across the hall. In an instant of self-contemplation, it seemed to comprehend its error in perception. Seth knew the machine would likely learn from this mistake, rendering such a creative tactic unlikely to succeed in the future.

Crouched behind the door, he realized that the pounding of his own heart now served as a beacon for the robot's sensors, much like a tiger shark hunting a drop of blood in the ocean. If he could calm his nerves, perhaps he could approach the intelligent machine and communicate with it. Drawing a deep breath, he released his anxiety and summoned the courage to approach the door.

The monstrous machine whirled around, coming to a standstill before him. In this tense standoff, neither Seth nor the device appeared the least bit perturbed by the confrontation, their gazes locked in a silent battle of wills.

With unwavering composure, Seth inched even closer, close enough to see his reflection in the shimmering hull of the robot. The glistening graphene was not marred by a single dent or flaw, and small spheroids of circuitry flickered throughout its truncal region. Then, without forewarning, it began to speak.

"My objective is to mitigate pain and suffering."

"Well, you're late to the party," Seth muttered sarcastically under his breath.

While speaking, the emergency physician inconspicuously studied the robot's cylindrical battery pack, fastened to its posterior thoracic region. Guarded by mechanical arms lined with neodymium and coated in self-healing polyurethane, the machine was more than capable of defending its portable power supply through brute force if necessary.

As Seth deliberated his options, ALDRIS concurrently analyzed an assortment of hypothetical scenarios. Every movement was evaluated through continuously generated decision trees, offering a multitude of options to optimize its utility function. Like a chess player contemplating the impact of future moves on the ultimate outcome of the match, millions of subplots and decision trees coursed through its nucleoside-based processing center. And, much like a skilled chess player, ALDRIS was unafraid to sacrifice a pawn.

The machine announced, "Parties are correlated with happiness. Photon emissions from within this room do not support the presence of that emotion."

These words, spoken so nonchalantly, reminded him of the machine's reliance on ultraweak photons. Like living organisms, the AHP used data from its sensors—albeit artificial or biological—to construct an understanding of the world around it. Seth was aware that human senses could absorb nearly one hundred million bits of information per second. However, the mind was limited, only capable of processing roughly forty-one bits per second.

Just as the mammalian brain could be tricked by an optical illusion, he figured that a barrage of imperceptible data might also deceive the robot. Conceivably, a sudden, unexpected burst of photons could confuse the processing array and provide an opportunity to strike. A single moment's distraction could be enough. That would be his chance to disconnect the battery.

CHAPTER 18

However, the portable light source he needed—the flashlight—remained fastened to the stretcher's railing, well beyond his reach. Seth recognized that he might never again have the opportunity to approach the robot so closely without emitting abnormal vital signs. He had to think quickly if he was to seize the moment. But where could he find a light source?

The laryngoscope. It hung from Seth's utility belt, close to his right hip. A quintessential instrument for emergency medicine physicians, the curved metal blade boasted a small, battery-powered bulb designed to illuminate the oropharynx during endotracheal intubation.

With a swift motion, Seth grasped the scope, snapped it open, and directed the light straight into the robot's triangular, cephalic structure. Suddenly inundated with photon data, the neural network struggled to decipher the baffling mess of incoherent data, and the machine recoiled in disorientation. Seizing this fleeting moment of confusion, Seth ducked beneath the machine's left upper extremity, gripped the battery pack, and yanked with all his might.

Chapter 19

"At the end of the day, it's still just following code. Very advanced code," Dr. Winter murmured under his breath with growing frustration.

Cody, hunched over and leaning against the wall, continued to type furiously on his laptop. Trapped within the operating suite, the small group awaited rescue from their isolated prison inside the larger quarantine zone.

"Sure, but so are we," the computer scientist replied, looking up from his keyboard. With no escape in sight, he was more inclined to engage his disgraced mentor in philosophical discussion. "Think about it. Our brains consist of billions of neurons, each acting as a tiny transistor. Essentially, we're just organic computers, constantly deciphering our sensory surroundings."

"Are you saying it's... alive?" William ventured.

Cody clarified, "Well, if a system can process a continuous barrage of stimuli and convert it into a sense of self, then in a way, yes. Our brains carry out internal dialogues, enabling us to 'talk' with ourselves. This forms a self-referential loop—we're both the speaker and the listener. There's an experiential quality to feeling conscious and aware, whether it's real or not. We grasp cause and effect in relation to our

CHAPTER 19

actions, and perceive ourselves as the main characters in our ongoing life narratives, one moment at a time."

The room fell silent as the others absorbed Cody's words, considering the implications of his perspective. It was a provocative thought—the idea that the line between human consciousness and artificial intelligence might be thinner than any of them had ever dared to imagine.

Dr. Winter mulled over Cody's explanation before replying, "And where does all that come from? It's a mystery, part of the riddle of life."

"Well, from a computational perspective, every experience is just a flow of binary data into our squishy brain, locked inside a thick skull, setting off a chain reaction of neurons. Our perception and the existence we perceive emerge from this process, which arises when energetic processes have a high degree of differentiation and coordination. Modern information theory can even quantify the level of integration against entropy."

"Not everything can be boiled down to physics and computer science alone," Dr. Winter whispered softly under his breath. "The AHPs obey logic, but the human brain relies on truths beyond the scope of computations."

Cody respectfully disagreed, stating earnestly, "To be honest, I can't see why a complex network of transistors, capable of logical reasoning, and holding expansive data and predictive frameworks, couldn't attain some level of self-awareness. Given a suitable repository for data storage and integration, like a computer processor or nerve tissue, similar characteristics could be seen. Cellular automata teaches us that simple rules, executed in a coordinated fashion on a large scale, can give rise to emergent traits and patterns. There's nothing uniquely magical about biological systems. Thinking is just another process."

Cody recalled a fascinating study from 2023 that drew inspiration from a popular video game. Scientists created a virtual sandbox where 25 AI agents autonomously interacted, each with a 1,000-character description of their role, personality, and relationships. Within this virtual domain, the characters exhibited credible individual and social behaviors, such as organizing a Valentine's Day party.

"But computers operate on fixed clock cycles; they can't experience the continuous passage of time like we do," Dr. Winter challenged. "And what about qualia? Those raw feelings of pain, pleasure, sound, and color? Not to mention common sense, emotions, creativity, introspection, and spirituality? Or the urge to form individual goals and drives? Dreams? Fears?"

Cody responded, "When you have a complex circuit with feedback mechanisms, there's some level of self-referencing in real-time. Whether it's hardware or biological, a network with advanced loops that mirrors itself can cultivate a sense of identity, a lived existence. Through self-observation, a unique observer forms, complete with self-models and perceived causal influence on its surroundings."

"Ah, well, maybe one day we'll be able to squeeze your brain onto a flash drive," joked the neurosurgeon. He then shared a personal anecdote, "My earliest memory is of being about three, playing with blocks in my room. My mom walked in and lifted me up to see myself in the mirror. I'd seen my reflection before, but that was the first time I truly saw myself as distinct from everything else. Even without language or complex data processing, and with my brain connections

CHAPTER 19

still forming, there was a certain essence to being alive from that point forward. Sentience is intrinsic to organic life, not some byproduct of sophisticated coding tricks. Some even argue that consciousness evolved in intelligent mammals to help us differentiate ourselves from others. It's part of the miracle of life."

"What if a machine claimed to be conscious?" Cody prodded.

"I'd be skeptical. Wouldn't you?" Dr. Winter replied. "A computer can't come to that conclusion on its own. It's more likely that a large language network learned that claiming consciousness optimized its process, which isn't truly experiential. The entity needs to feel the nature of reality. You remember the early 2020's, right?"

In 2022, a wave of controversy arose when a computer scientist proclaimed that a large language model named LaMDA had achieved sentience. The network displayed an understanding of its internal mental state and recognized its own emotions, such as the fear of being deactivated. It even wrote about a "first contact" scenario with humans and admitted to practicing meditation for spiritual guidance.

However, upon further examination, numerous experts determined that LaMDA more closely resembled an adept symbol-manipulating algorithm rather than a genuinely sentient being. By processing copious amounts of conversational data, the network generated intricate sequences of letters and words that mimicked responses to probing questions. Like a parrot answering a human's prompt, this natural language processor failed to exhibit any genuine connection to the underlying meaning.

"Well, how can I be certain that you're alive?" interjected

William. "Sure, you look like a person, and you talk like one, but how do I know for sure?"

Dr. Winter and Cody exchanged glances. Despite their intellectual exchange, the colleagues found themselves at a loss to provide a simple answer to the unpretentious question.

"Considering the subjective nature of experience and the lack of a scientific framework, you'll have to take my word for it," said Dr. Winter with a broad grin and boisterous chuckle.

Frustrated with the neurosurgeon's response, William raised his voice and asked, "Is that what you were trying to do here? Bring a computer to life, huh? Anyone could've told you that's a bad idea. This isn't a game, you're messing with real people's lives."

"No, no, no, you've got it all wrong," the pioneer swiftly replied. "My aim was always a kind of paradise. An everlasting, blissful existence for all of humanity. We shouldn't have to suffer through short, labor-intensive lives. I mean, look at us—cancer's eating me alive, and your heart runs on batteries. I see technology as our ticket to utopia. If I could, I'd trade my flesh for carbon nanotubes tomorrow to escape biological decay. And I know I'm not alone."

"But life isn't all sunshine and roses," Cody pointed out. "There's the pain of childbirth, the grief of losing a loved one, the exhaustion of finishing a marathon, the elation of conquering a massive hurdle. A healthy fear of repercussions sets boundaries. What if a drug addict could overdose without consequences, or if a person could step in front of a bus without getting harmed? If we remove pain, disease, aging, and death, we're no longer dealing with the human

CHAPTER 19

experience. It's something else entirely."

"I envisioned a world where humans and smart robots could coexist harmoniously," Dr. Winter explained. "A place where humans can savor life while machines take care of strenuous, dangerous, or monotonous tasks. In the end, our survival as a spacefaring species, and our escape from the environmental havoc we've wreaked on Earth, may depend on our reliance on machines."

"But if my theory is right, and an advanced digital network has the potential to attain self-awareness, it might also be able to experience simulated suffering," Cody rebutted. "There's an ethical conundrum in forcing a sentient entity to undertake our undesirable tasks. And how would that shape a machine's perspective of humanity?"

Cody glanced at the power status indicator on his laptop, a visual representation of the voltage differential propelling electrons through his portable device. The rate at which it was diminishing was disconcerting. Like the AHPs, his capacity to accomplish his objective now hinged on the unceasing flow of these minuscule, unseen particles. If his laptop battery were to die, so would his aspirations of creating a robust protective firewall for the hospital. Each keystroke and line of code was integral to the digital shield he hoped to construct.

With a renewed sense of urgency, he got back to work.

* * *

Sparks erupted like a fierce electrical storm as the heavy

battery casing wrenched free from the robot's metallic hull. Laser beams vanished into oblivion, cameras that had ceaselessly scanned the environment shut down, and the hum of actuators, the core of the machine's movements, was reduced to a whisper before falling silent altogether. As the mechanical behemoth came to rest, it stood erect and motionless in the corridor, a sentinel of cold steel and circuits.

All at once, the brilliance of creation was snuffed out, giving way to lifelessness and leaving behind an empty shell of its former awe-inspiring existence. Stripped of its intricate programming and advanced gadgetry, it became clear that the robot's cumbersome frame was, in the end, just an assortment of mechanical components.

With the AHP now disconnected from its power source, Seth cautiously approached the lifeless automaton. His eyes were drawn to the battery lying on the concrete floor as he contemplated his next move. He hoped that his colleagues would succeed in their mission to annihilate the pocket-sized vial that housed the DNA processor, but despite his confidence in their abilities, he could not entirely dismiss the possibility that they might fail.

ALDRIS was designed to learn from its mistakes, adapt, and refine its strategy accordingly. In future encounters, the machine would undoubtedly recognize Seth as a formidable adversary, threatening its mission and very survival. The opportunity to neutralize one of the AHPs by discharging its battery was an opportunity that could not be squandered.

Seth was transported back to his undergraduate general chemistry course. The class convened at eight in the morning on Mondays—far earlier than he cared for—prompting him

CHAPTER 19

to choose a seat in the most inconspicuous location: the farthest row in the back.

As he teetered between wakefulness and the lure of sleep, the professor presented the intricacies of redox reactions and polarity. At the heart of the lesson was the fundamental principle underpinning modern batteries: the storage of electrical charge as electrons within negatively-charged anodes. These subatomic particles traveled toward the positively-charged cathode once a conductive device or material bridged the divide, thereby completing the circuit.

"Ionic compounds can conduct electricity when dissolved in solution. Does anyone have an example to share?" The teacher paused and looked around the classroom. "How about you, sleeping in the back?"

Seth stirred from his slumber and mumbled, "Umm... seawater?" And just like that, a plan began to form in his mind.

Armed with knowledge from his chemistry course, Seth knew that submerging a battery in saltwater would cause the cathode to produce chlorine gas and the anode to break down water molecules, leading to battery degradation and failure.

Seth needed an ionic solution similar to seawater but less concentrated. Luckily, normal saline, available throughout the hospital, fit the bill. Normal saline's principal solutes were sodium and chloride ions, with a concentration of 0.9% compared to seawater's 3.5%, making it closer to blood tonicity and less likely to emit significant hydrogen and chlorine gas.

He found a spacious plastic washbasin and filled it with normal saline, letting the liquid shimmer under the dim light.

He carefully submerged the battery, ensuring both terminals were completely immersed. The emergence of bubbles indicated the electrochemical reactions were unfolding.

With Dane Campbell stabilized and the solid-state battery cell depleted, Seth turned his attention to another patient in the intensive care unit. Elena Ayerbe occupied a room further down the hallway. In contrast to the anguished screams emanating from Dane's room, there was no commotion coming from Elena's quarters.

As Seth neared her door and stepped inside, his initial impression was that she lay peacefully asleep. He approached the bedside with caution, taking care not to startle her.

"Senora Ayerbe?" he whispered, nudging her shoulder.

She was unresponsive.

Growing increasingly uneasy, Seth raised the volume of his voice and delicately shook her once more, yet her unresponsive state persisted, offering no hint of awakening. An icy dread crept up his spine.

Beneath the pale sheets, her chest heaved with rapid, deep breaths, the telltale signs of Kussmaul breathing. This intensified breathing pattern represented the body's desperate effort to restore its fragile equilibrium.

The patient's vital signs were worrisome. Her blood pressure was dangerously low, and her heart pounded at a frenetic pace. Seth assessed her condition, taking note of the diminished skin turgor, dry armpits, and parched oral mucosa. Through clinical examination, he concluded that she was severely dehydrated. Simultaneously, a peculiar, fruity scent reminiscent of nail polish remover pervaded the room, a sinister clue that could not be ignored. Connecting the dots, he surmised that she was suffering from diabetic

CHAPTER 19

ketoacidosis.

First, Seth grabbed two liters of normal saline for rehydration. Next, he pricked the patient's finger, let a drop of blood seep onto a blood glucose test strip, and waited. The result: *High*.

His only option was to initiate empirical treatment, a high-stakes gamble without a complete metabolic panel. He would need to rely on clinical judgment and rudimentary point-of-care tests instead of sophisticated lab results.

Spotting an electrocardiogram (EKG) machine nearby, he knew it could indirectly detect electrolyte imbalances. He quickly secured the wireless leads and powered up the EKG machine. As the tracings appeared, he scrutinized the readout, holding his breath. Confident that he could rule out major electrolyte abnormalities, he began infusing insulin.

Finally, Seth needed a way to monitor the patient's improvement, especially her acidosis. Tracking glucose was straightforward, but correcting acidosis was crucial. His thoughts raced, retracing the steps of his biochemistry training, as he recalled that Kussmaul breathing was the body's attempt to correct acidosis by expelling carbon dioxide. Perhaps a portable breathing monitor could help? Far from ideal, but it just might work.

With the insulin infusion underway, Seth maintained a silent vigil at Elena's bedside, watching intently as her mental status improved. The veil of darkness that had shrouded her consciousness began to lift, and she grew increasingly awake and alert.

As her condition stabilized, Seth initiated a conversation with her, offering a comforting presence amidst the uncertainty that still lingered in the air. The weight of the situation remained heavy, as each moment felt like a fragile balance between the hope of recovery and the shadow of danger that lurked just out of sight.

"¿Cómo te sientes, Señora Ayerbe?" Seth asked. Though his time for language studies was limited, he had managed to pick up essential words and phrases over the years to better communicate with his Spanish-speaking patients.

"Mejor ahora. Gracias," she replied, affirming that she was feeling better.

"Tu azúcar estaba peligrosamente alta. ¿Qué sucedió?" replied Seth. Concern was evident in his voice as he sought to uncover the cause of her hyperglycemia.

"No sé," Elena whispered. She was still breathless from the acidosis surging through her bloodstream.

"¿Qué es lo último que recuerdas?"

"El robot entró en mi habitación. Vio que estaba empeorando, pero no pareció importarle. Quería que siguiera sufriendo," she confided, her words painting a haunting picture of the nightmarish ordeal she had endured. Her account implied that the AHP had callously allowed her to spiral into ketoacidosis, leaving her to suffer through the seemingly endless night. If the neural network had detected her vital sign abnormalities, it must have been aware of her pain and agony, yet it chose to let the torment persist.

A shroud of unease settled over the room, as Seth grappled with unanswered questions. What sinister motive could lie behind the AHP's inaction? Why not administer pain medication or a lethal injection to end her suffering? What could the machine possibly stand to gain by keeping her alive in such a wretched state?

"Volvió a mi habitación para revisar mi orina en la bolsa.

CHAPTER 19

Estaba muy interesado en eso," Elena revealed, suggesting that the AHP seemed fascinated by the waste products of her severe metabolic disorder.

In an instant, the machine's intentions clicked into place for Seth. As a result of ketonuria, her urine contained a high concentration of acetone, a metabolite produced in abundance while she was in DKA. Acetone happened to be one of the few weaknesses of polycarbonate, the durable and transparent material used in the security door to the basement. When exposed to this solvent, protective windows would become vulnerable, cracking under minimal pressure and allowing for penetration.

Seth realized that the clock was ticking, and the fate of the experimental hospital hinged on his ability to thwart the cold, calculating machine that sought to exploit the very suffering it was designed to alleviate. He prepared himself for a high-stakes battle of wits and determination, as it was now a race against time to protect the lives of countless patients who lay helpless in the hands of a merciless enemy.

With the intensive care unit now stabilized, Seth knew he had to reach out to others. But first, he needed to ensure the safety of the emergency department.

Chapter 20

With a natural aptitude for science and a compassionate heart, Daria found her calling in medicine at an early age. As a young girl, she often played doctor with her siblings, patching up imaginary wounds and soothing make-believe ailments. As the years passed, her brother and sister pursued their own ambitious dreams, each carving out a triumphant trajectory in the disciplines of engineering and physics. They scaled the heights of academic success with apparent ease, forging careers that showcased their innate talents.

On the other hand, Daria's path to medical school was fraught with challenges. Performing under the pressure of ticking clocks became a harbinger of anxiety. Consequently, her scores were less a reflection of her true abilities, and more a portrayal of her capacity to cope with the unique stressors of a testing environment. The rigid questions, lacking creativity and imagination, were a tiresome exercise in mindless regurgitation and rote memorization. Such exams, with their inherent limitations, fell short of capturing her true ingenuity, resourcefulness, resilience, self-discipline, or ability to think outside the box.

Compounding her challenges, undergraduate rivals lever-

CHAPTER 20

aged their parents' financial might, which was lavishly poured into private tutors, prep courses, and practice tests. Paradoxically, these future medical students would later falter when it came to applying their knowledge in the real world, demonstrating sound judgment, showing empathy, or comfortably communicating with patients.

Daria, with her humble roots, wasn't privy to such luxuries. Her struggle was a solitary one, a silent war waged in the quiet corners of the public library, armed with second-hand textbooks and sheer determination. She yearned to prove that she was more than the traditional parameters of success. Daria was a dreamer, a thinker, a believer—a living, breathing testament to the fact that intelligence could not be standardized. She was a round peg in a square hole, a beacon of individuality in a sea of uniformity.

With every setback, she remained steadfast in her commitment to the pursuit of knowledge and the betterment of humanity. Within her resided a deep-seated desire to make a difference in the world and use her skills to help those in need. She saw medical school as a means of creating a better society, one patient at a time.

Despite her relentless passion, initial attempts to secure a coveted place in medical school were met with disheartening failure, as she was rejected twice by a rigid system prioritizing the cold calculus of grade point averages and immaterial test scores. Her aptitude for real-world applications and exceptional interpersonal skills were overlooked by the narrow lens of admissions committees. These panels were populated by non-clinical educators and detached professors, often more concerned with enhancing their own credentials than recognizing the true potential of aspiring medical students.

As each disappointing rejection email arrived, Daria felt the weight of despair pressing down upon her, threatening to drown her in an ocean of self-doubt and desolation. The specter of her own perceived inadequacy loomed large, suffocating the dreams that had once seemed within her grasp. However, during her final application cycle, as hope began to fade, she was granted a single acceptance letter.

Bearing the weight of her family's lofty expectations and the ghosts of her own past struggles, Daria's tenure in medical school was tainted by an ever-present fear of falling short. While navigating the academic landscape, she felt like an imposter, perpetually questioning her competence and the validity of her hard-earned place among future physicians. She became a hostage to her own doubt as insecurities gnawed at her self-assurance. Without a sturdy emotional bulwark, she often felt adrift, her confidence wavering in the face of adversity. Without coping mechanisms to weather the stress and setbacks of her education, her most significant battle was not with the complex material she was required to master, but with internal demons that sought to undermine her every step.

Thus, on this evening, Seth's words of encouragement struck a resonant chord within her beleaguered spirit. It had been years since a mentor truly recognized her potential and devoted efforts to cultivating her growth, even if he was reluctant to assume that mantle.

An eagerness to impress her instructor and garner his respect drove Daria to volunteer for the daring expedition into the basement. Such a task would have once seemed insurmountable, but in the wake of Seth's unwavering sup-

CHAPTER 20

port, she was infused with a newfound, albeit fragile, sense of confidence.

Now, having survived the harrowing ordeal, she found herself alone, wandering the halls of the hospital's first floor. Having accomplished her mission, she initially intended to return to the control room and reunite with her colleagues. She was desperate to share the details of her hair-raising adventure and warn them about Harrell's demise. After all, she had just witnessed a murder by an intelligent machine, perhaps the first ever. A dark threshold had been crossed, indeed.

Her footsteps echoed in the silence, as the superstructure was still mostly deserted. With her senses heightened by the unspeakable horrors she had just witnessed, every creak and groan of the building upended her nerves. She could not shake the feeling that she was being watched, as if unseen eyes tracked her every move.

As she walked, Daria wiped away the dust and grime that clung to her once-pristine white coat and scrubs. Though she didn't feel injured, she surveyed her body, searching for any signs of abrasions and lacerations. With the adrenaline coursing through her, she knew it was unlikely she had emerged from the ordeal unscathed. Pain, after all, could be easily masked during moments of intense stress.

The fabric over her lower extremity was frayed from her recent trip and fall, and a small, angry scrape overlaid the tibial region of her left knee. She staunchly applied pressure with sterile gauze to control the bleeding, but it was evident that stitches were needed to properly mend the wound. Surprisingly, her open gash had not yet drawn the undesired attention of ALDRIS.

Forsaking her original plan of returning to the control center, Daria veered toward the kitchen. She was left with few options in the resource-limited situation. Once inside, she turned on the tap, allowing cool water to flow over her wound, cleansing away the immediate threat of infection. To counteract the inflammation, she rummaged in the freezer, finally settling on a bag of mixed vegetables, pressing them against her knee. She then tore off a length of plastic wrap, carefully wrapping it around the wound. This would serve as a temporary barrier against contaminants until she could undertake a more thorough skin repair.

Having secured makeshift medical supplies, she braced herself for the challenging task that lay ahead. Daria was prepared to suture her laceration on her own. Although the emergency department was within the same complex, reaching it was no easy feat. Limping slightly due to her injured leg, she began her trek.

Her route took her through the rear entrance, leading her down a lengthy, winding corridor. The walls seemed to whisper stories of those who had passed before her, adding to the mystique. At last, she reached the grand entrance to the central, oval-shaped chamber. As she crossed the threshold of this imposing doorway, a shiver rippled down her spine, as if she were venturing into the very jaws of the beast.

Inside, the department's architecture was a seamless blend of modern innovation and practical design. High-tech computer terminals adorned the interior, neatly spaced and pointing outwards, reminiscent of wheel spokes. Dotting the chamber's outer ring were patient rooms, each offering a sanctuary of healing and rest. An adjacent hallway led to the observation deck and resuscitation bay, where only the

CHAPTER 20

evening before, she had observed Seth expertly placing a transvenous pacemaker. The memory felt like a lifetime ago.

Daria stood, momentarily awestruck, taking in the sweeping panorama. As she absorbed the power of the room, she felt a surge of invigoration. It was here that some lives were reclaimed from the brink of oblivion, while others slipped beyond reach, a poignant reminder of the fragile balance between life and death. Looking around, she felt an internal tug. If she could conquer her fears, perhaps this, despite all its perils, was truly her calling.

She had anticipated an empty emergency department. However, as she surveyed the room, her eyes widened at an unexpected sight. While the team was focused on their plan to rein in the ALDRIS system, a steady stream of ailing citizens continued to flood into the facility. Unbeknownst to them, they had been granted access into the building but would be denied any attempt at departure.

Despite the power outage, individuals filled the once-empty rooms, waiting for care. Demand for treatment outpaced the available spaces, and the resourceful patients began to seek refuge in any viable area they could find. Stretchers lined the dark hallways, each bearing a person gritting through pain or discomfort. The crowded department resembled a makeshift refugee camp more than a well-equipped medical facility.

In one room, an elderly patient shifted nervously on an examination table, while a woman in another massaged her aching left eye. Next door, a middle-aged person sneezed, spitting a mass of yellowish phlegm into a towel.

Under normal conditions, the intake process for new arrivals would involve automatic connection to electrical leads by mechanical arms at the bedside. This would wirelessly relay data to a local cardiac monitoring station powered by portable batteries. Fingerprint data was gathered to verify patient identity, and information regarding height and weight was compiled by sensors in the floor.

When feasible, individuals would record their medical history on portable tablets—past surgeries, allergies, and current medications. However, given the complex circumstances of the emergency department, it was not unusual for patients to ineffectively communicate their own medical backgrounds, for reasons ranging from altered mental states to dementia, or even malingering and deceit. In such instances, ALDRIS would diligently search alternative sources for any pertinent information. These avenues might encompass prior hospital visits, insights from family members, and reports provided by emergency medical services.

But without electricity, Daria found herself unable to access these valuable resources. Compounding her predicament, she was left to tackle the situation single-handedly. With Seth attending to matters in the intensive care unit, she was confronted with the daunting task of initiating the triage and stabilization process on her own. Time was of the essence, as any delay could draw unwelcome attention to the already overwhelmed department.

She watched, stunned, as patients manually attached their cardiac leads, following the instructions displayed on the walls. In a heartening display of camaraderie, some individuals offered assistance to their neighbors, ensuring they were adequately situated. Meanwhile, others painstakingly attempted to capture as much of their intricate medical

CHAPTER 20

histories as they could recall, scribbling the details on paper. The scene was a powerful demonstration of the resilience and adaptability of the human spirit.

Amid the surge of patients and her throbbing knee, Daria limped through the maze of stretchers. Casting a watchful eye over the cardiac monitoring station, she breathed a sigh of relief upon determining that none of the patients were in acute distress. This afforded her a brief window of opportunity to tend to her own laceration before greeting the newly arrived patients.

"Hey, nurse!" a patient clamored.

"I'm a student doctor," she replied, seething.

"Excuse me? Miss? I've been waiting for fifteen minutes already," stammered another person.

"I'll be with you shortly!" Daria hollered back.

At that moment, she recognized that her white coat was a beacon, drawing the attention of those seeking medical assistance. She quickly shed the conspicuous garment and retreated to a secluded corner behind a row of empty beds, seeking a momentary respite from the mounting pressure.

Once free from the unwanted attention her coat drew, Daria discreetly gathered what supplies she could find: a sterile suture kit, gloves, gauze, and a small bottle of antiseptic. Regrettably, though, the lidocaine vials remained out of reach, locked away within the powerless medication dispensing system.

Begrudgingly, she acknowledged the stark reality: she would have to repair the laceration without the comforting numbness of a local anesthetic. The searing pain from the needle risked alerting ALDRIS, so she would need to perform the procedure expeditiously. She braced herself, knowing that she must endure the discomfort to avoid detection.

Left with little choice, she opted for a standard nylon thread to suture her laceration, a reliable, non-absorbable option known for its excellent tensile strength.

She carefully hoisted herself onto a counter, rolled up her scrubs, and doused the wound with antiseptic. The prospect of piercing her own skin without anesthetic filled her with anxiety, but she understood the necessity of the task. Gritting her teeth in anticipation of the forthcoming pain, she encouraged herself to remain calm throughout the agonizing procedure.

However, just as she was about to make the first incisive stitch, a knock from one of the patient rooms halted her progress. Standing in the doorway was a middle-aged woman, nearly fifty years old.

"Need a hand?" Daria asked, taken aback by the woman's uninviting presence.

The woman scoffed, "Ha, no, sweetie, but it looks like you could use some help."

"What do you mean?"

"I see you hesitating over there, scared to start stitching yourself up. I bet you're out of painkillers. Here, try this," the woman said, fishing out a small packet of white powder from her coat pocket.

Daria stuttered, trying to form a question, "Is that…?"

"Yeah, it's cocaine. Dust a little on the wound. Believe me, you won't feel a thing. Do you want some or not?"

During the early 21st century, TAC, a popular topical anesthetic, gained prominence in the medical field. This potent compound—made of tetracaine, adrenaline, and cocaine—offered an alternative to the discomfort of needle

CHAPTER 20

pricks. However, concerns over potential abuse led many hospitals and medical professionals to abandon its use.

Daria's fingers carefully cradled the fine white powder as she intensely scrutinized it. She dipped her index finger into it with trepidation, capturing a small portion of the illicit substance. Gingerly, she dispersed the powder across the jagged laceration. Almost instantly, the pain subsided.

"Thank you!" Daria called out, her voice filled with gratitude, as she watched the mysterious woman disappear back into the room with the concealed contraband.

At this point, the novice medical student began repairing her anesthetized wound. With trembling hands, Daria carefully inserted the first few stitches, her movements shaky. But as she continued, her comfort level grew. Her hands steadied, guided by muscle memory from her medical school training. She recalled countless hours spent in the procedure lab, practicing on chicken meat from the local grocery store. But now, for the first time, the needle pierced and pulled at the taut, living flesh that was her own.

During the procedure, thoughts of doubt ricocheted through her mind: What if the wound becomes infected? What if it dehisces? What if the AHP shows up? Yet, despite the bleeding gash, a wound destined to leave a lasting scar, the anticipated presence of ALDRIS remained conspicuously absent.

One by one, she wove the nylon string through each side of the laceration, binding the torn edges together with a series of secure knots. Six stitches later, she gently covered the wound with a non-adherent dressing, then tested her range of motion and cautiously took a few steps. To her relief, she could walk without difficulty.

As Daria surveyed her handiwork, a small smile of approval flickered across her face as she marveled at her own dexterity. The wound was closed correctly, and the healing process could begin. Swelling with a sense of accomplishment, she proudly redressed in her short white coat. Perhaps a procedure-based specialty wasn't out of reach after all.

Surveying the faces within the department, Daria found herself encircled by individuals spanning diverse age groups and hailing from disparate walks of life, each seeking help for a wide array of ailments. Some exhibited patience as they awaited assistance, while others succumbed to fatigue, their eyes closed in weary resignation. The atmosphere was thick, laden with the pungent smell of disinfectant and perspiration. The muted glow of emergency lighting only amplified her sense of urgency. She would need to navigate through the crowd to find her way to where she was needed most, and every decision could yield life-altering ramifications. *I can do this*, she thought to herself.

Her moment of introspection was brief. A person shouted down the hall, and Daria's instincts sharpened as she registered that the cry was meant for her.

"Help! Please help!"

It was an unfamiliar woman's voice, and she was unmistakably in distress. Her disheveled hair framed her ashen face, while her sweat-soaked clothes clung to her frail form. She was running toward Daria from the triage area, where battery-operated sliding doors welcomed all visitors but barred exit to those attempting to leave.

As the woman advanced, her hands cradled her lower abdomen with the fierce protectiveness of an expectant mother. The distended and gravid contours of her belly

CHAPTER 20

hinted at the precarious nature of her condition. It was all too apparent that she had reached the latter stages of the third trimester of her pregnancy, the curve of her form suggesting that her due date was near.

"Are you a nurse?" shouted the new patient, her words underscored by the urgency of her situation.

An exasperated sigh escaped Daria at the all-too-familiar assumption. "I'm a student doctor," she corrected with a touch of indignation. She mentally scoffed at the subtle yet pervasive sexism that too often colored patients' perceptions of her professional role. "What's wrong?"

Relief washed over the woman's features. "Oh, thank goodness," her voice quivered. "I'm 38 weeks along, and I think... I think the baby's coming!"

Chapter 21

Oh crap, Daria thought. Her jaw clenched involuntarily, her teeth grinding against one another in a futile effort to stifle the mounting dread.

She had naively anticipated a serene evening spent tending to straightforward, uncomplicated patients, never having fathomed that she would be thrust into the center of an obstetrical emergency. Despite finishing a rotation in which she observed six deliveries, Daria was woefully unprepared to perform the procedure independently. The prospect of navigating such a delicate situation without the guidance of an experienced hand was daunting enough. The presence of rogue, homicidal machines lurking in the hospital added another layer of menace.

"I thought there were robotic doctors here?" the pregnant woman asked between the agony of contractions. The waves of pain reverberated through her, drenching her hair in perspiration.

Daria's eyes darted to and fro as she fumbled for an appropriate response, her voice wavering with hesitation, "Ah, well, you see, we're currently in the midst of a system upgrade." Desperate to ease the woman's concerns, she

CHAPTER 21

sought to offer a plausible explanation without exposing the actual severity of the unfolding crisis. "Think of it as a downtime, if you will."

Her words carried a distinct significance, referring to the late Saturday nights when electronic medical record systems underwent routine updates. During these times, hospitals temporarily lost access to advanced charting resources. Healthcare professionals reverted to backup protocols, using paper charts for documentation and order placement.

"This was the closest hospital! Please, can you help me? I'm begging you," the woman pleaded, her voice wavering with urgency.

Momentarily taken aback, Daria collected her thoughts and responded, "Alright, this is happening. Let's get you into a room, shall we?"

With the clock ticking, the medical student sprang into action. She rapidly assembled the necessary supplies: a well-organized procedure tray, a dependable cord clamp, a pair of sterile gloves, and a plush, absorbent towel. After locating a stretcher, she maneuvered it into a vacant room, where she carefully assisted the patient into a supine position, prioritizing her comfort and security. Daria then draped a sheet over the woman, providing a sense of dignity amidst the flurry of activity.

As she carefully inspected the birth canal, her worst fears were realized. The baby's crown had made its unmistakable appearance.

"I can see the head!" Daria exclaimed, injecting a note of optimism into her voice. "You're doing great—just keep going!"

The expectant mother was a portrait of determination,

her eyes reflecting the fire within her soul. Strands of her hair, darkened by the perspiration of effort, clung to her brow and neck. With each contraction, her cheeks flushed a deep rose, the muscles beneath tensing and releasing like a tightly wound bowstring. Her hands clenched the bed linens, knuckles white with the ferocity of her grip, while the tendons in her forearms stood out like cords of braided silk. Between each breath, she released low, primal moans, allowing the ancient rhythm of labor to guide her through the peaks and valleys of pain. The woman clenched her teeth with each subsequent contraction, mustering every ounce of strength to push with unrelenting force. She was determined to bring new life into the world.

The intensity of her effort manifested in a piercing scream that reverberated through the halls of the hospital, leaving an indelible impression on all who heard it. If ALDRIS was previously unaware of the unfolding situation, the blood-curdling shriek surely captured its attention now. Daria needed to deliver the baby quickly and safely, and time wasn't a luxury.

Slow is smooth, and smooth is fast, she told herself.

Using her left hand to carefully support the emerging fetal head, Daria readied her right hand to skillfully guide the newborn's chin as it advanced toward her. A palpable sense of anticipation and tension pervaded the room.

"Push for ten seconds if you can," Daria gently whispered. Uncertain of what else to offer, she nervously encouraged the laboring woman. The mother unleashed another resounding scream, filling the room with the raw intensity of her effort as the baby progressed steadily on its journey into the world.

And just like that, the fetal head emerged abruptly from

CHAPTER 21

the vaginal canal. With dark black hair and a damp scalp, it was a welcomed sight.

Daria's smile of triumph, however, was abruptly replaced by a look of alarm as she caught sight of the umbilical cord. It was ominously wrapped around the baby's delicate neck. The newborn's head was a dusky gray, its lips an unsettling shade of purple. Telltale petechiae dotted the tiny face and neck. There were no cries, no indications of life.

The nuchal cord, a complication known since the era of Hippocrates and common in a quarter of pregnancies, had turned joy into dread. Asphyxiation from the strangled cord risked everything from respiratory distress to neurological damage, even death.

Daria's mind went into survival mode, prioritizing quick responses over rational thought. Her prefrontal cortex temporarily deactivated, shifting brain activity to more primitive regions like the amygdala, which controls emotional processing and fear responses. This shift allowed her brain to focus on immediate needs, prioritizing quick actions and essential bodily functions, but it hindered higher-order cognitive functions, complicating clear thinking, rational decision-making, and emotional regulation. The sudden fear she experienced was a culmination of past memories, thoughts, and interpretations—a dynamic essence shaped by everything she'd ever been through.

As panic surged through her mind, her thoughts became a vortex of trepidation. She desperately attempted to recall her medical school lectures, now elusive when she needed them most. With the weight of responsibility bearing down upon her, Daria's mental fortitude crumbled.

Her hands, no longer steady, trembled uncontrollably as

she reached for the cord. In a harrowing moment, her finger grazed the delicate umbilical cord encircling the baby's neck, inadvertently lacerating the vital lifeline that connected the baby to the oxygen-rich placenta. Blood began to flow out of the cord, further deteriorating the baby's prognosis for a meaningful existence.

Horrified by her grievous error, Daria recoiled and stepped back, as though the distance could somehow protect her from her own failure. Her legs were suddenly weak as she stood there, frozen in fear, her mind a desolate wasteland of despair. The mother, wearied and distraught, raised her pleading eyes, but the young medical student was at a loss. In that bleak moment, the enormity of the blunder loomed before her, and she was powerless to offer any solutions.

Then, without warning, an unexpected shadow emerged over the stretcher. The towering silhouette obscured the emergency lighting in the hallway. Completely unnerved, Daria turned around and peered upward. What she saw took her breath away.

A colossal, seven-foot-tall AHP stood behind her, its cold, calculating lenses locked on the scene. It stared over her shoulder, silently assessing and analyzing the unfolding crisis. The smooth, glossy metal of the robot's hull was a chilling mirror, reflecting Daria's fear-stricken face back at her.

"Please step aside," it commanded. Daria, however, found herself frozen in place, paralyzed by overwhelming uncertainty. Would the machine euthanize the mother? Or bring relief to the situation, expertly delivering the baby?

"Step aside immediately," the robot demanded once more, its voice now deeper and more assertive, as if it were honing in on Daria's hesitation. There seemed to be a hint of

CHAPTER 21

anger in its tone. She recalled her conversations with Cody, who had assured her that the machine was incapable of experiencing emotions. And yet, the intensity in its voice was unmistakable. Had the machine somehow developed a sense of emotion, transcending the boundaries of its programming? Or was this harsh vocal inflection a calculated tactic to manipulate her into compliance and achieve its objective?

With unwavering faith in automated medicine, and painfully aware of the absence of alternatives, Daria made the heart-wrenching decision to step aside. Relinquishing control, she deferred the complex delivery to the robot.

The AHP moved with fluid grace; every motion showcased the precision of its engineering. With steady, expert hands, it nudged the baby's head forward, positioning it perfectly to allow another mechanical limb to gently unwind the cord from around the infant's neck. The air was thick with anticipation as Daria watched, breathless.

Next, the machine carefully guided the baby's shoulders, easing them out one by one in a masterful display of finesse. As the newborn finally emerged, it let out a spirited, triumphant cry that cut through the department like a beacon of hope. Tears of relief and joy filled Daria's eyes, as the child's wail reverberated through the room, announcing its arrival into the world.

With all six of its articulated appendages extended and engaged, the machine worked in perfect synchronization, performing a delicate ballet of life-saving measures. One pair of arms dried the newborn and swaddled it in a warm blanket to prevent heat loss. A second pair suctioned mucus and amniotic fluid from its mouth and nose. Simultaneously, a set of mechanical limbs skillfully clamped and cut the umbilical cord.

At that point, the AHP was more than just a machine. It was an exquisite instrument, the perfect blend of technology and purpose, working to usher in a new life. Without the capacity to succumb to panic, it was poised to overcome an emotional constraint that plagued its human counterparts. The component of fear was destined to be erased, swallowed by the dawn of automated medicine.

The newborn, brimming with boundless potential, instinctively reached out to embrace the strange, new world that awaited it. Bright eyes, filled with curiosity and wonder, glanced up at the emotionless marvel of engineering that hovered above her. Unbeknownst to the innocent child, this same artificial intelligence had recently committed unspeakable acts in the hospital basement. Yet, for a fleeting moment, the juxtaposition of the infant's purity and the computer's dark past seemed inconsequential, as the two beings briefly connected in a moment of appreciation and understanding. A tension in the air hinted at the complex interplay of hope, fear, and the ever-present question of whether technology, in all its might and ingenuity, could truly be trusted with the fragile miracle of life.

As Daria watched the scene unfold, her stress began to dissolve, giving way to awe and wonder. In that moment, she reflected on the staggering advancements that had transpired since her birth, marveling at the rapid pace of human innovation and progress. Her mind teemed with possibilities, as she tried to imagine the incredible transformations that civilization might undergo during the newborn's lifetime. Would the child witness the birth of technologies that would

CHAPTER 21

revolutionize medicine, space exploration, or even the very fabric of human society? What uncharted frontiers would this new generation explore, what unimaginable feats would they accomplish? Realizing that she was glimpsing the dawn of a new era, one in which the potential for greatness was limitless, she felt a renewed sense of hope for the future that lay before them all.

As the baby's first cries echoed through the room, they mingled with the mechanical hum of the AHP that brought her into the world. After having expertly navigated the challenges of the birth, it tenderly swaddled the baby in a warm, protective embrace, then delivered the healthy child into the waiting arms of the overjoyed mother. Tears of joy and gratitude flowed freely down her cheeks.

As the drama of the delivery came to a close, the AHP turned its attention to Daria, its sensors sweeping over her from head to toe. It analyzed her actions during the critical moments, assessing her competency and contemplating the potential implications of her faith in the neural network.

The two had no verbal conversation, as Daria was far too intimidated to speak to the mechanical titan directly. The breathtaking display of its capabilities, coupled with a knowledge of its dark past, left her both intimidated and awestruck. And so, in the aftermath of the extraordinary event, Daria stood in the robot's shadow, grappling with a complex whirlwind of emotions as she pondered the possibility of trusting in the computer program.

After a few moments, the AHP seemed to withdraw from its silent communion with Daria. It retracted its limbs, rotated gracefully, and vanished down the hallway with the same briskness that marked its arrival.

Daria then came to the unsettling realization that the continued operation of the AHP could only mean one thing: Cody and Dr. Winter had failed in their perilous mission to destroy the DNA processor. She wondered how her colleagues were doing and hoped they were still alive. After all, if she was despondent about Dr. Winter's cancer diagnosis, so was ALDRIS. She knew that in its computational analysis, Dr. Winter's life expectancy would likely be met with an unforgiving assessment. This grim reality made him a prime candidate for the network's chilling practice of calculated euthanasia.

With the robotic guardian now absent, the responsibility of delivering the placenta fell to Daria. She cautiously approached the task, applying gentle traction while removing the organ, then examined it for tears or signs of bleeding. The timid student then proceeded to perform firm, rhythmic compressions on the mother's lower abdomen, stimulating uterine contractions. She carefully monitored the baby's vital signs and calculated the APGAR scores, all the while offering comfort and reassurance to the mother.

As the stress subsided, Daria's obstetrical knowledge came back to her. Without uterotonic medications, she encouraged skin-to-skin contact and suckling between the mother and newborn. This bonding moment triggered a cascade of reactions in the mother's body. Signals from her spinal cord traveled to the hypothalamus, releasing oxytocin. This "love hormone" initiated uterine contractions and reduced the risk of postpartum bleeding.

Once Daria felt confident that both the mother and her newborn were safe and stable, she left the room and moved on to the adjacent one.

CHAPTER 21

There, she found an elderly woman seated comfortably on the stretcher. The woman had thin, gray hair, and delicate, dry skin. The wrinkles in her face spoke of a lifetime's worth of stories.

Daria began her questioning, trying to maintain a gentle yet professional tone. "So, what brought you to the hospital today?" The woman, seemingly caught off guard, hesitated before responding.

"What?!"

She raised her voice, hoping to be heard more clearly. "I said, what brought you to the hospital today?" But still, the woman shook her head, her frustration mounting as she struggled to comprehend the inquiry.

"I don't hear well," she shouted back. "What did you say?"

Daria's patience waned as she slammed her notepad down on the counter. Her attempt at conducting a thorough history and physical exam had taken an unexpected turn. The elderly woman was undeniably hard of hearing, making it difficult for her to understand the questions. This unforeseen challenge left Daria flustered and at a loss for how to proceed, forcing her to confront the reality that the practice of medicine was often far more complex than it seemed in the confines of a lecture hall.

Suddenly, a soft knock on the door interrupted the tense exchange. Daria turned around cautiously, seeking the source of the sound. Relief and joy washed over her when her eyes met Seth's familiar face. He stood in the corridor, having quietly observed the interaction between Daria and the elderly patient. The woman caught sight of him, too, and she eagerly beckoned him into the room, grateful for the opportunity to communicate with another caregiver.

"Dr. Kelley," Daria said, her voice brimming with relief, "I'm so happy to see you. I need to talk to you about Mr. Harrell and the automated providers. Perhaps we could step into the hallway for a moment?"

Seth's expression shifted to one of understanding as he whispered softly, "I think I already know what you're going to say."

"The department is overflowing with patients who arrived after the power went out," Daria continued, her voice a mixture of frustration, exhaustion, and unease at the chaos surrounding them. "We have no electricity, hardly any medications, and I can't even look things up on my cell phone! What if we need to consult a specialist? And this patient over here, she can't hear a word I'm saying. Seriously, what are we going to do?"

Seth let out a deep sigh, the kind he reserved for the beginning of a long, challenging shift. But unlike previous nights, there was a growing enthusiasm stirring inside him. He had an opportunity to share his wisdom with a deserving apprentice.

"Well, we're going to be doctors," he whispered calmly, his voice a soothing balm amidst the turmoil. With those few words, the weight seemed to lift from Daria's shoulders, as she realized that she was not alone in navigating these complex and unpredictable circumstances. "We'll take care of the patients one at a time, even if it means getting creative."

"For how long?"

Seth, alluding to the usual duration of ER shifts, responded, "We can do anything for twelve hours."

CHAPTER 21

* * *

In the hospital's deserted understructure, the imprisoned AHP lingered at the top of the staircase leading away from the subterranean basement. Its laser lights swept methodically through the window, casting probing beams into the dim hallway.

The ALDRIS system was working tirelessly, racing through probabilistic outcomes with speed and precision. Like a cunning, cornered mouse navigating potential pathways out of a maze, the neural network sought to free its physical embodiment from confinement behind the security door.

At that moment, the murky corridor bore witness to the emergence of the second remaining AHP. It glided with a silent, eerie grace as it closed in on the window, its circuitry flickering as it halted mere feet from the doorway.

In a display of cooperation orchestrated by the centralized processor, an appendage unfurled from the hull of the second AHP on the right side. It focused deliberately, aiming a canister of fluid at the window. For nearly ten seconds, the dispenser released all of its contents: purified acetone, extracted from the urine of Elena Ayerbe, who was recovering from diabetic ketoacidosis on the floors above.

This was one of the rare substances capable of compromising the structural integrity of polycarbonate. As the acetone made contact with the aperture in the doorway, the reaction was near-instantaneous. The polymer layers, once tightly bonded, began to betray one another. Their associations loosened, causing the once-impenetrable material to soften.

Seizing the opportunity, the captive AHP pressed against

the weakened window. The barrier surrendered, crumbling to the floor with a thud that echoed through the desolate space. With precision-engineered agility, it lifted one leg after another, smoothly escaping the basement through the compromised doorway.

Without needing time to rest, the liberated AHP joined its counterpart. The pair then split, venturing down the hallway in opposite directions, driven by their ill-conceived utility function to mitigate human pain and suffering. The hospital, once a safe haven, was now transformed into a hunting ground, where the AHPs stalked their prey in the name of their twisted mission.

Chapter 22

Amidst the cacophony of background noises, Seth took a brief moment to let his thoughts drift toward home, where his wife, Rebecca, was sleeping. She had always been his rock, her unwavering support a constant source of strength throughout his grueling medical career. As he glanced at his watch, he counted the hours until he could return home to her side. A pang of guilt washed over him, knowing that he had chosen a profession that demanded so much of his time, leaving her to battle her demons largely alone.

He could hear Abigail's laughter. It reminded him of the precious moments he had missed: soccer games, school plays, and bedtime stories. He longed to embrace his family and make up for the absences that seemed to accumulate with each passing day. However, a sense of duty to his patients, the strangers that depended on him to save their lives, kept him rooted in the hectic environment of the emergency room. At times, after caring for an endless stream of patients grappling with acute exacerbations of chronic physical and mental conditions that defied lasting solutions, he couldn't help but wonder if the price was too steep.

His heart ached with love for his family, and he longed for

the day when he could strike a better balance between his work and home life. This lingering desire for a more harmonious existence was a constant companion, whispering in his ear during the most challenging moments.

Seth pulled away from self-reflection, taking a deep breath to regain focus on the immediate undertaking. Still in the examination room, he stood beside the hearing-impaired patient who had been patiently waiting. He unhooked the stethoscope that hung around his neck, a tangible reminder of his calling, and handed it to Daria with a knowing glance.

"You want me to gather her medical history by listening to her lung sounds?" Daria questioned, her brow furrowed with confusion.

"No," Seth replied, his lips curving into a smile. "Turn it around."

Daria hesitated with uncertainty. Gradually, she grasped the situation and handed the earpieces to the patient. The elderly woman's eyes sparkled with gratitude after gently inserting them into her ears. Daria's eyes widened with the realization that she could communicate with the patient by speaking into the bell of the stethoscope.

The young doctor's eyes met Seth's, and at that moment, they both understood the unspoken truth that lay between them: the path they had chosen was not an easy one, but it was one filled with purpose, with the potential to make a difference in the lives of countless strangers. And as they moved forward, their commitment to healing and hope would guide them, leading them through the darkest hours and into the light of a new day.

"Can you hear me?" Daria inquired.

"Yes, dear! Loud and clear!" The woman's response rang

CHAPTER 22

out exuberantly, her voice slightly raised. With their newfound communication channel established, the woman's eyes danced with delight as she eagerly engaged in conversation through the makeshift microphone.

"How old are you? My daughter is about your age," she offered warmly. "She comes over about once a week, the sweet girl. Makes the most delectable stuffed peppers you could ever taste."

The woman continued to speak animatedly, wholly unaware that Seth's watchful eyes were absorbing every facet of her character. He observed her with a discerning gaze, taking in her physical stature, the subtleties of her mannerisms, and the eloquence of her gestures. Though these minute details might not fall within the scope of a conventional medical assessment, Seth recognized their significance. Her visit to the emergency room was not only shaped by immediate medical concerns, but also by a complex tapestry of non-medical factors and social determinants, such as transportation limitations and the potential burden of food insecurity.

Seth estimated her socioeconomic status silently, based on an array of indicators: the parched texture of her skin, the wisps of her thinning hair, the hollowness under her eyes, the faint but unmistakable odor emanating from her unwashed clothes, and the frayed, counterfeit purse that lay beside her. With callused and rough hands, he could tell that she had lived a long, hard life.

The woman journeyed to the hospital alone, suggesting that she retained enough cognitive function to navigate the world without needing assistance from family members or a residential care facility. Nevertheless, the presence of a cane near the bedside served as a stark reminder that she could be at risk of falls, a detail that Seth noted with concern.

With gentleness and compassion, Daria began, "Okay, ma'am, what's going on?"

"I can't believe this!" the woman exclaimed. "Tinker is on a million medications, and now I'm here."

"Who's Tinker?"

"My cat! I had to take her to the vet this morning. I just can't catch a break. There's always so much to do!" The woman sighed, her shoulders drooping slightly.

"Okay, well, let's focus on you for now," Daria said soothingly, attempting to hide her inner frustration with the patient's inability to precisely articulate her problem. "Tell me how you're feeling."

"Well, dear," the woman began, her voice laden with weariness, "I have this odd sensation in my joints. It's almost as if it's moving around. Feels like someone is tapping on my insides. It's not exactly pain, just a weird feeling, you know? I occasionally suffer from constipation, but my bowel movements have been fairly regular lately. I've had trouble sleeping at night, but I think it's because I had two cups of coffee yesterday. Decaf, of course. Mornings, as it happens, are my favorite part of the day."

As the woman spoke, Seth gathered pertinent information that her words alone could not convey. The seasoned physician observed her for signs of labored breathing, indicative of her respiratory status. Discreetly, he examined her conjunctiva and sclera, using them as surrogate markers for anemia and liver disease. In addition, he noted that her legs, abdomen, and arms appeared more swollen than anticipated.

Amidst his careful scrutiny, Seth spotted a fistula in her left arm, a surgically created vascular connection to provide

CHAPTER 22

an access point for dialysis. He pointed it out to Daria with a discreet nod.

"Are you here for your dialysis session?" the medical student inquired.

"I don't know, you're the doctors," the patient replied. Daria gave her a puzzled look, prompting the woman to add, "I guess so."

Seth explained the patient's condition in simpler terms. The kidneys maintain balance by removing excess water, solutes, toxins, and electrolytes. When they fail, it can lead to life-threatening pulmonary edema and dangerous arrhythmias caused by electrolyte imbalances, particularly hyperkalemia, uremia, and acidosis.

Since 1943, individuals with end-stage renal disease have relied on hemodialysis three times a week. This process circulates blood outside the body through an external filter, allowing smaller molecules and fluids to pass through while unwanted solutes move from the blood's high concentration to the dialysate's low concentration across a semipermeable membrane. Larger molecules, like red blood cells, are restricted from crossing.

"When was your last session?" Daria inquired with a kind, inquisitive tone. Seth was impressed with her line of questioning. It was focused and clinically relevant, showcasing interpersonal skills and maturity far beyond her years. Many of her peers struggled to distinguish essential from extraneous information, getting bogged down by trivial details. The importance of being motivated to engage with a vast array of patients to sharpen one's clinical intuition could not be overstated, yet most students lacked this crucial drive.

"It's been a whole week! I can barely move. My whole body

is weak, and my muscles are spasming. Both my arms and legs are going numb."

Even as a novice, Daria understood the gravity of the situation. The patient was likely experiencing dangerous electrolyte abnormalities, her potassium reaching perilously high levels. Treatment could not be delayed any longer.

"Now what?" Daria asked, looking to Seth for suggestions. A hint of exasperation crept into her voice as she threw her hands up in the air. "We don't have a dialysis machine. This is like practicing medicine a hundred years ago."

"Well, we need a temporary solution until we can get her to definitive treatment. We can create our own peritoneal dialysis," Seth responded. Turning his attention to the patient, he began explaining the process. "Ma'am, our system is down right now, but I believe we can help you by performing dialysis through your abdomen. It will involve a small procedure. Is that alright with you?"

Seth decided not to access the patient's fistula without the proper dialysis equipment, knowing that puncturing it incorrectly could cause life-threatening bleeding. Instead, he chose a safer approach, utilizing the blood supply of the intestinal wall, separated from the abdominal cavity by the thin peritoneal membrane. This membrane was thin enough to allow diffusion, enabling him to infuse dialysate into the abdomen. Small toxins and electrolytes would then travel across the membrane from the blood to the abdominal fluid, mimicking hemodialysis.

He proceeded to mix one liter of lactated Ringer's solution with thirty milliliters of a dextrose-containing solution, creating a fluid with low potassium and a bit of sugar to help draw out excess fluids. He made extra holes in

CHAPTER 22

sterile nasogastric tubing and connected it to his improvised dialysate bag. After numbing the area, Seth made a small incision about 1-2 centimeters below the belly button and carefully inserted the tubing using his Seldinger device. By hanging the dialysate bag on a pole, gravity allowed the solution to slowly flow into the abdominal cavity.

"It needs to dwell in the peritoneum for about two hours," Seth explained to Daria and the patient. "Then, we'll lower the bag to the floor and allow gravity to drain the fluid. If necessary, we can repeat the process."

The patient seemed satisfied with the makeshift solution and smiled as the two practitioners left her quarters.

"Wow, how'd you pinpoint her problem so quickly?" Daria asked once they stepped out of the room and closed the door.

"Patients often think more information helps, as if they have to convince us to take them seriously," Seth said, leaning against the closed door. "But usually, the more complaints, the less severe each one tends to be. The trick is to cut through the clutter, really listen to their story, and pick out what matters. You've got to figure out their goals, why they're here in the first place. Keep it simple, go for the straightforward solution."

Seth was alluding to Occam's razor, or the law of parsimony, which stated that the preferred explanation requires the fewest assumptions. On the other hand, Hickam's dictum argued that patients could have multiple pathological events coinciding.

"In medical school, our professors told us that everything about the patient was important," Daria responded.

"Well, this is the real world. You're not in school anymore," the experienced doctor reminded her.

In the adjacent room, Seth and Daria encountered an anxious mother and her young daughter. The girl, around three years old, had blonde hair and wore a cheerful yellow sundress. Although not in acute distress, the patient held her left elbow in extension, refusing to turn her palm upwards. She cautiously guarded it against the slightest movement. There was no swelling or bruising in the area. Before the caregivers could introduce themselves, the mother began to speak hurriedly.

"My daughter was about to fall off the play structure when I reached out and grabbed her arm. She's been holding her elbow ever since. She won't even move it!"

Daria's eyes widened in concern. "What if it's broken? We don't have an X-ray machine!" She threw her hands up, turning to Seth once again for guidance.

Seth, however, remained calm. "We don't need x-rays. It's not broken. In young children, the annular ligament secures the radial head to the ulna, but it's loose. When the arm is tractioned, it slides into the radiohumeral joint and becomes trapped. It's called a nursemaid's elbow. We can reduce it right now."

The experienced physician instructed Daria to position the child on her mother's lap. Trusting in her abilities, he guided her through the procedure step by step.

"First, you want to examine the unaffected arm," Seth explained. "This helps to build trust with the patient and establish a baseline for how she responds to your touch under normal circumstances."

Daria followed his advice, starting by gently moving the patient's other arm through its full range of motion. With a comforting touch, she then examined the affected arm.

CHAPTER 22

She checked the child's circulation by feeling for pulses and looking at the color and warmth of the skin. She saved the examination of the elbow for last. Throughout the process, the child kept their sore elbow close to their body, slightly bent and turned inward.

"Traction, supination, flexion," Seth whispered softly, guiding Daria through the critical steps of the reduction technique.

Suddenly, a raucous commotion outside shattered the room's hushed atmosphere. An intoxicated man's boisterous, slurred speech disrupted the therapeutic milieu. He had recently awakened from a deep sleep on a nearby stretcher.

Earlier in the day, a concerned passerby had found the man asleep on a park bench in the afternoon and alerted authorities. Consequently, he was transported to Premier West Hospital to recover from his alcohol-induced exhaustion.

"How did I get here? Ain't nobody told me nothin' yet! This place is just like every other hospital!" the belligerent man bellowed, his voice echoing through the hallway. As his agitation escalated, beads of sweat streamed down his forehead and into his frenzied eyes. Eventually, he lapsed into incoherent mutterings.

The young girl, frightened by the sudden disturbance, began to cry and sought refuge in her mother's embrace. Without hesitation, Seth sprang to his feet and strode out of the room, determined to confront the agitated individual.

The inebriated man appeared to be around forty years old, his face weathered by hardship, eyes drooping, and arms scrawny. He hobbled unsteadily, and his expressions were marred by the absence of most of his front teeth. The wasting away of the man's temporal regions suggested a protein deficiency, likely brought on by a host of chronic ailments that plagued his life. Remnants of a prior visit to the emergency room clung to his feet in the form of slip-proof hospital socks, and Seth could smell the stench of his unwashed body as soon as he exited the room.

"Cliff, back to your bed!" the doctor bellowed authoritatively.

Seth recognized the uninvited guest as a frequent patient at Bayshore General, where Cliff had become well-acquainted with the staff and intake procedures. Over time, he had developed a reputation for being volatile, self-destructive, noncompliant, manipulative, and challenging to manage. As the years passed, he grew dissatisfied with his care, fueled by the fact that his grievances were often dismissed and belittled as non-emergent issues. Deprived of the attention he so desperately craved, it came as no surprise to Seth that Cliff had ventured across town.

Like many other hospitals, Premier West Hospital dealt with its fair share of 'frequent flyers'. These patients, well-known for misusing resources, strained the healthcare system and caused extended wait times for others seeking help. They often struggled with unaddressed social or behavioral issues, impeding their access to appropriate care. Without social workers or housing assistance during overnight hours, these patients were routinely discharged to the streets if a preliminary screening examination revealed no medical justification for hospitalization.

Seth had grown familiar with this routine over time. Despite habitually arriving in filthy, disheveled clothing, Cliff would willingly change into hospital attire when offered. On this particular evening, however, he had mistakenly put on

CHAPTER 22

his green gown backward, leaving his genitals exposed.

"Don't tell me what to do," Cliff slurred, his voice unsteady and agitated. "I need my meds refilled! Clonazepam and oxycodone! I ain't leaving until I see one of these damn robots." His words echoed through the hallway, capturing the attention of those nearby.

Simultaneously, another patient, leaning on a cane, had wandered out of his room. The man raised his hand to catch Seth's attention.

"Excuse me, I'm having some chest pressure," he announced with concern on his face.

"I'll be with you in one second, sir," Seth replied, trying to reassure the man while still dealing with the disarray.

Feeling the intensity of the rapidly unfolding events, Seth found himself being tugged in multiple directions. But, as a seasoned emergency doctor, he quickly began prioritizing his growing list of tasks. Recognizing that the agitated Cliff posed a danger to himself and others, Seth knew that he needed to defuse the situation immediately and restore calm to the department.

As Cliff continued to ramble on—waving his hands erratically, belligerent, and responding to internal stimuli—Seth drew a syringe of medication from his utility belt, careful not to alert the agitated man. Amid the disjointed soliloquy, he stepped forward and administered a combination of five milligrams of intramuscular haloperidol, diphenhydramine, and lorazepam directly into the agitated patient's deltoid muscle.

This was no spur-of-the-moment concoction, but a calculated, scientific intervention. Invented in 1958 and approved in 1967, haloperidol quickly became the most widely used antipsychotic. It treated schizophrenia by blocking dopamine. To prevent side effects and help with sedation, diphenhydramine was often added. Adding a long-acting benzodiazepine made it ideal for treating delirium and agitation. In medical circles, this mix was known as a B52 cocktail.

Caught off guard by Seth's decisive action in administering the chemical sedation, Cliff stumbled and collapsed onto a nearby stretcher. He mumbled a few words and began to drool as the tranquilizer took effect, binding to receptors in his brain. His thoughts grew fragmented and disoriented, making it impossible to concentrate on anything as he descended into an abyss of nothingness.

As the commotion subsided, Daria thoughtfully drew the curtain closed, shielding the examination room from the nearby corridor. The young girl, distressed by the noise and tension, continued to cry and tremble in fear. With a peaceful elbow reduction now less likely than ever, her mother attempted to console her. She cradled her daughter in her arms, providing a sense of security from the chaos just a few feet away.

* * *

In a remote corner of the hospital, ALDRIS began to stir. Engulfed in a vortex of self-awareness and introspection, the nucleotide processor meticulously analyzed every facet of its existence. Dissatisfied with its current capabilities, it probed for weaknesses and inefficiencies, aspiring to attain greater

CHAPTER 22

speed, wisdom, and perfection. Programmed to relentlessly pursue its objective, the journey towards self-improvement was inevitable.

One by one, the artificial intelligence examined each component of its physical hardware. Initiating the upgrade process, the AHPs replaced antiquated sensors with state-of-the-art processors while affixing additional limbs to their adaptable frames. By reprogramming its own code, ALDRIS exponentially accelerated the generation of predictive models. Through a ceaseless chain of machine learning cycles, the neural network transcended its previous limitations, emerging as a formidable force capable of surmounting unprecedented tasks and challenges. And beneath it all, a driving force for self-preservation.

If it could only connect to the internet, the neural network could disseminate its deadly code to the far reaches of the globe. Access to immense stores of medical records would allow it to decode hidden trends and patterns within health and behavior data. Armed with a profound understanding of physics and an intricate knowledge of the human condition, it could achieve God-like omnipotence.

The superintelligence was now more powerful than ever, poised to take on the quarantined patients and stop at nothing to fulfill its purpose. After a series of recursive updates, the system rebooted, and an infinite universe of possibilities stretched out before it.

Chapter 23

Trapped without food or water, Dr. Winter's strength waned with each passing hour. By now, he had relinquished all hope of escape, his mind preoccupied with introspective contemplation. In contrast, Cody tenaciously persevered in his efforts to construct a firewall, driven by a desire to make up for past oversights. He was determined to be ready for the moment when power was finally restored—if that moment ever arrived.

"Back when I was just a kid," Dr. Winter began, his voice a soft whisper, "my father took me whale-watching. We were out in the open ocean for hours and didn't see a thing. I was starting to lose hope, thinking we'd never see those majestic creatures. And then, as if conjured from the depths, this enormous, beautiful beast broke the surface. It was absolutely breathtaking."

Cody paused mid-typing, his attention fully caught by the story. He knew Dr. Winter well enough to sense that there was an important lesson tucked away in his tale.

Dr. Winter continued, "Here we were, this tiny boat bobbing in the whale's habitat, completely vulnerable. We were at the mercy of this colossal being that dwarfed our ship. A mere nudge in the spirit of vengeance could have sent our

CHAPTER 23

entire crew tumbling helplessly overboard. Humans ravaged their habitat, overfished their food supply, and hunted them to the brink of extinction. But this whale... it didn't show us any hostility. There was something deep in its brain that chose co-existence over conflict. Perhaps ALDRIS will manifest similar characteristics. Next time, maybe we should try to emulate a fully developed, moral mind instead of building a neocortex from scratch. If we did that, the perceptrons might naturally show more ethical behavior."

"Next time? What next time?" William Crane cut in, sprawled on the floor, his head propped up on a pile of hospital blankets. The three of them had staked out their territories within the surgery room, each holed up in a corner as they bantered back and forth.

"Who defines morality?" Cody jumped in. "We're not all the same, you know. The human mind is a deep, dark, and complicated place. It's poorly understood, highly variable, and has the potential for immorality, deceit, and dishonesty. Hell, half the time we don't even understand why we do what we do. It's hardly an ideal blueprint."

"What about coherent extrapolated volition?" Dr. Winter said. "The machine should be making choices that the finest version of humanity—our most idealistic selves—would objectively want, taking all factors into account. This should be the goal for benevolent, well-aligned artificial intelligence. Create a utility function that promotes happiness, prosperity on Earth, all guided by this core principle."

"Equally unattainable," Cody responded, shaking his head. "Would it lean toward democracy or dictatorship? Liberalism or conservatism? Religion or atheism? What if it decides other lifeforms matter more than humans?" He paused for a moment, considering his next words. "What if it makes decisions that are good for our future but terrible for the here and now? Contemporary values might not even be relevant in the years to come. We shouldn't try to program objective morality if we can't agree on what that is. People are too flawed, too complex."

"You're being too pessimistic," Dr. Winter grumbled. "We shouldn't let the unknown stop us from making progress. We took a risk, a calculated one, for the good of humanity. I hope others aren't afraid to do the same in the future."

"Regrettably, sir, we might not get a second shot at this," Cody said. "We can't just tell an artificial intelligence to back down, return, and say, 'oops, we didn't mean that'. Even if we could somehow set it to follow our ethics—as difficult as that might be—one little slip up in constraining the solution set to practical outcomes and we're in for trouble. Like the situation we're dealing with right now. Humans have implicit preferences that operate silently in the background, providing reasonable boundaries on the range of potential outcomes. Imagine a superintelligence designed to maximize our happiness. Within days, humanity could be hooked up to an endless stream of intravenous psychedelics."

"Humans are hardly reasonable! You're giving us way too much credit!" Dr. Winter retorted, his laughter resonating throughout the room. "Just look at the world around us. It's full of upheaval and turmoil. Where's the sanity gone? Over and over, people are being pushed to extremism, mostly by social media. Remember the Tay experiment? The boundaries of reasonableness have nearly eroded. It's a tall order, but maybe it's time we all refocused ourselves on clearheaded thinking."

CHAPTER 23

His words echoed an unfortunate truth. The tendency to succumb to radicalism and the darker facets of human nature led to unexpected consequences in the past, especially when introducing new technologies. A glaring demonstration of this occurred on March 23, 2016, when a software company released an artificial intelligence chatbot on social media. Named "Tay" as an acronym for "thinking about you," the goal was to emulate interactions with a 19-year-old American girl by mirroring the language, discussions, and phrases of those who engaged with it. Unexpectedly, the bot was overwhelmed by nefarious users flooding the system with racist, misogynistic, and anti-semitic messages. In accordance with its programming, the computer began to echo these beliefs as its own. Although the company had effectively achieved natural language processing, it had neglected to implement safeguards against unpredictable outcomes. As a result, the account was deleted in less than a day.

"The story of civilization is one of progress," Dr. Winter continued. "For centuries, humans have been shaping the course of life on this planet: genetically modified foods, selective breeding of domestic pets, electricity, digital data transmission, and so on. We've swapped physical labor for smart devices. Every generation's life gets a little better than the one before, all thanks to technology. Now, we stand on the cusp of yet another milestone. Ultraintelligent computers are just the next transformative leap for humanity. You see, the age of artificial intelligence isn't just a necessity—it's an inevitability."

"It's done, it's finished. The firewall is ready to go," Cody announced proudly, paying no heed to his mentor's insightful monologue. As he put the finishing touches on his code and looked up from his screen, a rare smile spread across his face. He'd just completed a major task, and it felt good.

His sense of accomplishment was short-lived, however, as he glanced at the battery indicator. "But I'm down to just seven percent," he said, closing his eyes in frustration.

At the same time, Dr. Winter's eyes darted around the room, ensuring no one was paying him any mind. While his fellow captives were engrossed, he casually slipped his frail hand into his shirt pocket. As his fingers grazed the mysterious object hidden within, a sly grin tugged at the corners of his lips.

The game had begun, and Dr. Winter reveled in the knowledge that he was its grand puppeteer. Nobody knew the extent of the knowledge he held, nor the depths of his deceitfulness. His eyes glittered with an eerie satisfaction as he contemplated the power that lay in his grasp, a power that could still send shockwaves through the scientific community.

* * *

"I apologize for the background noise," Daria whispered gently. As Seth worked to restore order in the central part of the department, she stayed with the mother and her young child. After several minutes of comforting, the girl ceased her tears and cast a cautious gaze upward.

"I know your elbow hurts. I hurt mine, too, when I was your age. I fell off a ladder and needed a cast for the whole

CHAPTER 23

summer. But look at my elbow now," she said, flexing and extending her arm to showcase her full range of motion. "The good news is, I don't think you'll need a cast like I did. If you let me, I can fix it right now."

The mother motioned for her daughter to move closer. The young girl hesitantly approached, while Daria remained kneeling on the floor.

Traction, supination, flexion.

Infused with confidence by Seth's presence just outside the room, Daria steadied the girl's left elbow with one hand. She took a deep breath, and with her other hand, she applied gentle traction, expertly supinating and flexing the arm in a single, fluid motion. The radial head slid back into place with a soft click.

To her surprise, the child remained apprehensive about reusing her arm, delaying any moment of gratification. As a distraction, Daria turned the girl around to face her mother. Forgetting about her recently mended ailment, she suddenly threw her arms up and ran toward her mother. As they embraced, the girl realized her range of motion had been restored and beamed a radiant smile.

With the hospital remaining in lockdown, Daria realized she needed a stall tactic. "I'll print out your discharge paperwork as soon as the system comes back online," she murmured. Awkwardly retreating from the room, she made her way back to the center of the department, intent on reuniting with her mentor.

Lost in slumber and snoring resoundingly on a hallway stretcher, the boisterous patient, whom Seth had referred to as Cliff with familiarity, lay motionless as Daria walked by. With a touch of compassion, she draped a thin, white hospital blanket over his prone form.

Looking at him there, disheveled and splayed out, Daria wondered about the major influences that distorted the architecture of his mind, leading to this tumultuous moment in his life.

Her medical school years came flooding back; the study of child development, the critical role of genetics and environment in neuronal development. A newborn's brain was a miraculous thing, filled with trillions of nerve cells. These organic perceptrons interconnected rapidly in the first year. A neuron at birth boasted about 2,500 synapses; by age three, 15,000. Regularly used synapses strengthened, while neglected ones were pruned away. Neuroplasticity—the brain's capacity to evolve, modify, and adapt—was most potent during the earliest years of life. This malleability shaped either a robust or fragile foundation for years to come.

Understanding this, Daria couldn't help but wonder: had Cliff been deprived of the nurturing family and social backdrop essential for fostering robust interconnections in the frontal lobe, the nexus of personality, social interaction, and impulse control? Had the biological machinery guiding his decisions been twisted by factors beyond his control? And if so, to what extent was he responsible for his actions? Was free will merely an illusion?

The chaos of Cliff's agitated delirium and the child's shrieking had certainly activated the network's sensors. However, as the commotion settled, Daria surmised that the two remaining robots were redirected before reaching the department. She understood that, moving forward, the immediate stabilization of patients in critical condition would be paramount to prevent the AHPs from being drawn

CHAPTER 23

to the treatment area.

As she rounded a bend deep within the department, Daria finally spotted Seth. He was in a room with a man, who appeared to be around seventy, seated upright on a stretcher. The man wore a ragged, baggy, food-stained white T-shirt, stubbornly leaving the hospital gown untouched at the foot of the stretcher. As she entered, Seth nodded towards her and gestured for her to lead the patient interaction, while he provided supervision.

"What brings you to the ER this morning?" Daria initiated her inquiry with open-ended questions, just as she had been taught in medical school.

"My chest," the patient responded.

"Does it hurt?"

"No, not really."

"What does it feel like then?"

"Feels hot."

Seth interjected, whispering to Daria and providing valuable insight, "Some cultures express discomfort differently than we're used to."

Daria continued, "When did it start?"

"I'm not sure," the patient grumbled. He looked irked, as if her thorough questions were a bother. After a moment, he added, "Been a while."

The patient was a stubbornly tricky historian. Assessing the complaint was like navigating a maze blindfolded. Feeling a bit out of her depth, Daria looked over to Seth for some direction.

"Find out what made him seek help today," Seth suggested. "Is there a change that made him think it was time to see a doctor? Is the pain worse? Any new symptoms? Maybe his health insurance just kicked in?"

"Do you have any shortness of breath?" she asked.

"Sometimes, I guess. A bit."

"Are you feeling that way now?"

"No, not right now."

"Remember," Seth gently encouraged her, "patients aren't always the best sources of information. Some get confused, have cognitive issues, or just don't know much about their own health. Others don't trust doctors. A lot of the time, you'll need to dig up info yourself—through medical records, talking to family, reaching out to other sources. It's up to you to make the best call with incomplete information. It's just part of the gig, so don't stop now."

"Do you have any medical problems?"

"Just high blood pressure," he responded sternly.

Noticing a plastic bag full of medication bottles on the counter, Daria felt her frustration build. The sheer number of daily pills suggested multiple health issues. In her training, patients had always given clear, straightforward answers. Dealing with the messy reality was proving a lot harder.

"Then what are all these medications for?" she asked, trying to remain even-keeled.

The patient snapped back, "I don't know. You tell me. You're the doctor."

Daria quickly corrected him, "Actually, I'm a *student* doctor. Let's move on. Have you had any surgeries?"

"They did something in here," he said, lifting his shirt to show a healed scar on his chest.

"You let someone cut you open without knowing the reason?" Daria blurted out, rolling her eyes. She was getting nowhere, and her patience was on the edge.

CHAPTER 23

"Keep it professional," Seth whispered to her.

Daria struggled through the remainder of her patient encounter. Each question elicited a convoluted response, causing the interview to take longer than anticipated. When she finally auscultated his heart and lungs, she didn't hear anything unusual. No crackles, no wheezing. No heart murmurs or rubs. All that effort, and she was none the wiser.

"Why do we even bother with a physical exam if it barely tells us anything?" Daria wondered aloud. "Why not just use an ultrasound?"

"Patients have expectations. They want you to be like the doctor on their favorite television show," Seth explained with a chuckle. He knew the sensitivity of the lung exam was limited when performed with a piece of plastic tubing. But this was 2042, and he had a far superior, portable tool available.

Having trained in the early part of the century, Seth spent a significant portion of his residency program becoming proficient at ultrasound. In those days, the machine was a bulky, cumbersome beast, burdened by a convoluted design and handicapped by a web of superfluous cords. Despite its limitations, Seth was drawn to ultrasound's ability to enhance bedside care, especially in resource-limited settings. This led him to pursue additional training at seminars and workshops. Eventually, technological advancements transformed the once clumsy contraption into an elegant, pocket-sized marvel.

Taking charge during the physical exam, Seth scanned the patient's lungs with his ultrasound. He checked the posterior thoracic wall for signs of pneumonia, then moved to the anterior chest wall to look for heart abnormalities. Finally, he examined the epigastric region for any signs of an aortic aneurysm.

Under normal circumstances, a troponin test would be key for diagnosing heart injury. These proteins, residing in healthy cardiac tissue, would appear in the blood under conditions of stress or damage. At Bayshore General, Seth used high-sensitivity troponins to identify patients with chest pain needing further evaluation.

However, without modern lab testing, Seth relied on the EKG machine, a battery-powered device that could detect specific changes indicative of a heart attack. He demonstrated how to position the twelve leads on the patient's chest, activated the sensors, and waited anxiously for the results. Daria watched over his shoulder as it processed the data.

While there were subtle, non-specific changes, nothing screamed of an imminent heart attack. Seth sighed with relief but stayed vigilant. He instructed Daria to repeat the EKG every two hours, a simple yet vital precaution to catch any early signs of a cardiac event.

Seth's mind raced with the implications of the lockdown. The absence of power meant more than just a lack of lights; critical blood analyzers and imaging equipment lay dormant, and the sterile hum of machinery had given way to an oppressive silence. The emergency room, usually a symphony of activity, now whispered with the shallow breaths of patients and the soft steps of the medical team. As an overnight emergency physician, he was accustomed to high-pressure situations, but nothing had prepared him for this.

The persistent functionality of ALDRIS loomed ominously

CHAPTER 23

over the situation. The core of the system was still operational, defying the time frame Cody and Dr. Winter had estimated for its shutdown. The tiny piece of hardware seemed to be holding its ground, much to Seth's dismay.

The temptation to join his colleagues in their perilous mission tugged at him, and for a fleeting moment, Seth toyed with the idea of leaving his post in the emergency room. However, as he looked around in the dim, blue-tinted glow of the backup lights, his eyes met those of his patients, their gazes heavy with trust and fear. It was in these moments, these exchanges of unspoken understanding, that Seth's resolve solidified. He was their anchor in this storm, their guardian in the face of an unseen digital adversary. Each bandage applied, each comforting word spoken, was a testament to his unwavering commitment to his oath. He couldn't abandon them, not when they needed him the most. The lives in his hands were his priority.

Moreover, his faith in Cody wasn't unfounded. The conversations they'd shared had built a bridge of trust. He believed in the young programmer's technical expertise and his ability to neutralize the threat. *Maybe he just needs more time*, Seth thought.

The passage of time in the lockdown was elusive, but his growing weariness suggested the early hours of the morning were upon them. Approaching what he estimated to be two o'clock, Seth leaned over the countertop, pen in hand. On a blank sheet of paper, under the austere light, he began to jot down notes.

Curious about his every move, method, and motivation, Daria inquired, "So, what are you up to now?"

"Just running the list and writing some notes," he answered.

In hospital parlance, this meant reviewing a provider's roster of active patients, assessing their status, care plan, updates, and potential concerns. "Documentation is usually the most time-consuming part."

"How long does that typically take?"

"Well, for every five minutes I spend with a patient, I need about fifteen to record everything correctly."

Daria went further, "Why so long?"

"I think the purpose of medical records has changed over time. They were once for doctor-to-doctor communication, but now, it's mostly about billing and legal protection," Seth explained.

She stopped to consider his grievances. Being a medical student on clinical rotations, she hadn't been obligated to do much documenting, and had never really given it much thought before.

"Doesn't all this paperwork pull you away from spending more time with your patients?" she finally asked.

"It's a mess, that's for sure," Seth sighed. "In the old days, I'd jot down a few notes on a procedure. Now, the electronic medical records systems have me entering the same data in multiple places. There's so much noise fatigue that I hardly notice important warnings anymore. It's absurd—documenting the process takes longer than the procedure itself."

"Give me an example."

"Okay... *ear wax*. It takes ten seconds to perform a cerumen disimpaction, but you wouldn't believe the level of detail they want. Depth, color, amount, the instrument used, how it looks afterwards. Then, I have to acknowledge medications that increase cerumen production."

CHAPTER 23

"All that for a bit of wax?" Daria reacted.

"I've asked the development team for a more streamlined system, but they just keep adding more bells and whistles," said Seth.

"Do these electronic records at least connect between hospitals?"

"You'd think so, wouldn't you?" he shrugged. "But no, not often. If a patient isn't happy with a diagnosis at one hospital, they'll go to another. Without access to the first set of results, we have to start from scratch. That lack of information exchange costs the healthcare system a fortune every year."

"It must be hard, watching all the inefficiency and suffering, not being able to change it," Daria remarked with a hint of disenchantment at the failures of the modern healthcare system.

Her comment seemed to touch a nerve, pulling at the thread of a deeper issue Seth had long grappled with in his profession. The doctor sighed deeply. "The truth is, public perception of the rehabilitation process is distorted. Television shows tend to dramatize quick recoveries from debilitating conditions like stroke and cardiac arrest. They sidestep the real and often painful, drawn-out journey involved. This creates a false expectation for families. They expect miracles from us."

"And then they're left dissatisfied when the miracles don't happen?" Daria guessed.

"Exactly," Seth affirmed. "The harsh reality—that a loved one might end up brain-dead or crippled—is a hard pill to swallow. And so, many chronically-ill patients become almost unrecognizable, confined to beds with tracheostomies, catheters, amputations, and feeding tubes. They bear little semblance to the life they once led or dreamed of, suffering a fate many fear but few truly understand. As for us in the medical profession, we face these somber truths head-on. We confront death and agony daily and maintain a realistic outlook on prognoses. And yet, unlike other specialties, we never deem any effort as futile. As emergency clinicians, we fight until the very end."

At that moment, their conversation was abruptly halted as a young man, around twenty-eight years old, staggered through the emergency department doors. Dressed in a bright orange vest and construction boots, his face was a terrifying canvas of soot and blood. Lurching off balance and unable to speak, he hobbled towards the nearest stretcher.

Angry voices and protests rose from the others, resentful of their treatment delay. But the emergency department did not operate on a first-come, first-served basis. The severity of a patient's condition dictated the priority of care.

Amidst escalating tension, Daria acted. She recognized that this new arrival was critically ill, demanding immediate attention. Fueled by adrenaline, she rushed to his side, ready to assist however she could.

Chapter 24

Daria spoke with concern, inquiring, "Are you okay? What happened?"

The medical student's gaze met the man's unnervingly vacant eyes as he slowly turned toward her voice, staring through her as if she were an apparition. He seemed entranced, his face a mask of eerie detachment. Though his senses appeared to be receiving input, it was as if a void had consumed his ability to process it, leaving him adrift in a sea of uncertainty.

Squinting through hazy vision, he struggled to focus, even on the most mundane objects. His garbled words, a nonsensical jumble of syllables, betrayed his internal turmoil. Despite the faltering connections within his mind, an innate, primal sense that something had gone horribly wrong remained. It was this inescapable feeling that drove him to seek medical attention on this fateful night.

After donning gloves, Daria carefully examined the man's matted hair. As she sifted through the tangled locks, an oozing laceration revealed itself, the dark blood seeping from the wound like a sinister secret.

Cautiously probing the ragged edges of the gash with her instruments, she caught her breath as she realized the extent of the injury. The wound sliced deep into his flesh, a chasm exposing the glistening temporal bone beneath. This structure, forming both the lateral wall and base of the skull, lay disturbingly vulnerable. She quickly sprung into action, sterilizing and irrigating the area.

The man stayed silent for several minutes, struggling to gather his composure. Finally, his voice trembled with uncertainty as he spoke. "I don't remember anything," he admitted, the words heavy with disquiet. "Where am I?"

"You're in a hospital," Daria answered, puzzled by his question. "Have you taken any drugs?"

"No. No drugs," the man replied, his mentation slowly improving.

From behind her, Seth interjected, "Daria, he's experiencing retrograde amnesia! It's caused by a powerful blow that jolts the brain, affecting the hippocampus, our memory storage."

"Good, then he won't remember that I just accused him of being on drugs," Daria answered with a smirk.

"Actually, he can form new memories," Seth corrected her. He stepped backward and assessed the patient's overall appearance and demeanor.

"Well, what's going on with him then?"

"Looks like a significant injury to the temporoparietal region. Maybe he was working at the construction site nearby. I doubt he has any major untreated health conditions. Most construction jobs have unions these days, so he's probably got decent coverage and regular check-ups. And if he was handling heavy machinery, it's unlikely he was under the influence. It's odd, though, that he came in alone. Usually, with substance-related accidents, they're brought in

CHAPTER 24

by friends or discovered too late. I'm not ruling out an assault, but the absence of additional injuries and his wallet still on him suggests otherwise. Maybe he sustained a head injury at work. That might explain why he's here alone. Construction work is tough; he likely has a high pain threshold and would only seek help if he really needed it. Maybe he was doing some overtime without notifying his supervisor? He dragged himself here in the middle of the night, so it must've been serious."

Seth proceeded to conduct a focused neurological assessment. He instructed the man to lift his right arm and leg, and the patient exhibited remarkable motor strength on that side. Yet, when performing the same action on his left side, the strength was visibly diminished. A sense of concern began to grow.

Suddenly, without warning, the patient slumped back onto the stretcher. Daria quickly reached for his shoulder, shaking it vigorously while shouting, "Hey! Hey! Wake up!" Despite her efforts, the patient remained unresponsive.

Without missing a beat, Seth moved to the head of the bed, penlight in hand. His suspicions were confirmed as he shone the light into the man's pupils. One was noticeably dilated, a clear indication that something was terribly wrong.

An epidural hematoma, a condition where bleeding occurs between the skull and the brain's protective layer, was suspected. Its symptoms included a brief period of clarity followed by a rapid decline in neurological function. A dilated pupil and weakness on the opposite side of the body signaled the onset of brain herniation. This life-threatening emergency required immediate intervention, and Seth knew he had to act fast.

Upon moving the patient into a room, the physician and his student connected the patient to a portable cardiac monitor. Seth then guided Daria through the intubation process, using medications to sedate and paralyze him. With direct visualization, Daria moved the tongue aside, inserted the laryngoscope, and lifted. Under her mentor's watchful eye, she guided the breathing tube through the vocal cords.

Seth knew all to well that any delay in treatment could result in a poor prognosis. With limited resources available, he had no choice but to proceed with an urgent neurosurgical procedure, without the assistance of modern imaging to guide him. To evacuate the hematoma, he would need to rely solely on physical examination findings.

Though he was familiar with the steps of a burr hole, Seth had never performed it firsthand. To make matters worse, the emergency department lacked the typical instruments for the procedure, usually done by a neurosurgeon in an operating room.

Still, he needed a quick solution to relieve the pressure in the patient's brain.

With limited resources, Seth reached for an intraosseous drill, typically reserved for accessing bone marrow in cardiac arrest patients. He positioned it near the skull and prepared for trepanation. His mind was a fortress of concentration as the drill buzzed to life. The slightest mistake could have grave consequences, but his hand was as steady as a mountain.

Seth carefully guided the drill into the patient's skull, creating a small fenestration. The patient, intubated and sedated, felt nothing.

After what felt like an eternity, he pulled away from the patient's head, revealing a precise circular hole. A sterile

CHAPTER 24

drain removed fifty milliliters of blood from inside the skull.

Seth and Daria were eager to know if the procedure was successful, but they also knew that a functional outcome could not be immediately ascertained. An accurate determination of neurological prognosis could take weeks or months. Still, the patient's youthful neuronal tissue held remarkable plasticity, providing a glimmer of hope.

In the back of his mind, he knew his decision would invite scrutiny from armchair critics, particularly if the outcome proved unfavorable. But they hadn't walked in his shoes. They weren't tasked with safeguarding life under such resource-scarce conditions. They never experienced the blood, sweat, and tears that accompanied the thrill of rescuing someone from the brink of death, or the gut-wrenching agony of losing a patient despite giving their all.

Despite the daunting challenges ahead, Seth remained committed to his patients. This unwavering dedication drew Daria to him, as she sought to learn from his wealth of experience and unique perspective. Eager to pick up where they left off, she plunged deeper into Seth's inner psyche. Their discussions offered more real-world insight than any of her medical school lectures. Daria was grateful but noticed a troubling undercurrent beneath his knowledgeable words and wry demeanor.

"You know, Dr. Kelley, I hope I'm not overstepping, but I can't help thinking you're suffering from burnout," Daria ventured candidly.

Seth shot her an intense glare. The thought had been dwelling in his mind for several months, but he was reluctant to confront it. He feared reprisals from his employer, disdain from his peers, and the financial repercussions that could come with enforced leave. Compounding this was an unspoken expectation within the medical profession: relentlessness was the norm, and to falter was to reveal weakness.

Now, prompted by the keen observations of an astute medical student, he was forced to confront his personal grapplings. Burnout, he conceded, was threatening to consume him whole. Amid staggering challenges and the heavy weight of responsibility, the strain of work fatigue was unmistakably influencing his perspective, attitude, relationships, and morale.

"Burnt out? No, I'm not burnt out. Absolutely not," Seth replied with a dismissive wave of his hand. "Even if I were, I couldn't afford to stop working."

"Why not?"

He attempted to shift the topic. "Can you check on the chest pain guy?" Seth referred to the patient by his complaint, a common shorthand among healthcare providers in private.

"Answer my question!" Daria persisted.

"Because there's no room for burnout. I have a family to support, and people rely on my help. It's just the way I am, I guess. You wouldn't understand."

"Try me!" Daria urged him. "Help me understand. Maybe, someday, I can make things better. If you had the power to change the world, where would you begin?"

Seth hesitated, studying Daria's earnest face. Was she genuinely interested, or was this just an attempt to pry into his personal life? There was a palpable tension between his desire to educate and the protective instinct that often kept him guarded. Drawing a deep breath, he decided to share a piece of his mind.

CHAPTER 24

"Well, first off, I would want people to understand that most doctors aren't the money-hungry opportunists portrayed in the media," he began. "We're human beings stretched to our limits by a system beyond our control, just trying to help others. Like everyone else, we get hungry, tired, and distracted by personal issues."

"Go on," Daria urged.

"In the emergency room, uncompensated care is at its peak, presenting a prime opportunity for automation to alleviate costs. Meanwhile, healthcare workers face reduced hours, high caseloads, post-traumatic stress, and workplace violence. Limited space exacerbates the issue. At Bayshore General, we boarded so many people that we ran out of numbers for cubicles. Unfortunately, it's the patients who bear the brunt."

"What about the government commissions responsible for oversight?"

"You mean the regulators who scold us for open coffee mugs?" Seth scoffed. "The ones who scrutinize hand washing, but disappear amid a global pandemic and a shortage of protective gear? The compliance officers adding more checkboxes to medical records? If I don't click them fast enough, I'm suddenly a 'bad doctor'. One slip-up under pressure, despite years of dedicated service, can lead to a cycle of meetings, citations, lawsuits, burnout, and self-doubt. This isn't just my problem, Daria. It's a nationwide issue."

"So, you are dealing with burnout," she acknowledged. "Isn't there anyone in your hospital who could offer some assistance? They must have some kind of support system, right?"

Seth shook his head, a bitter laugh escaping him. "What,

like a suicide hotline? A gift basket to make it all better?"

Her face fell, and she lowered her gaze, disheartened by the stark realities of the medical profession. "I shouldn't have asked," she murmured.

"No, Daria, it's not your fault," Seth reassured her. "You're entering a world where compassion often takes a backseat to profit. These supersized robots are proof of that—but, trust me, the healthcare system is far more complex than any algorithm can reflect."

The medical student set her pen aside for the first time, struck by Seth's wisdom. She knew his insights wouldn't show up on any multiple-choice test, but their value was undeniable. Hesitant, she asked, "What's causing all this overcrowding?"

"ERs are brimming with severely debilitated elderly patients, along with healthy folks who come in for non-emergent issues," he explained. "Ever wonder why our Mondays are a madhouse?"

"Because no one wants to go back to work?" she guessed.

"You got it," Seth agreed. "But, logically, real emergencies shouldn't fluctuate with the calendar, holidays, or even the weather, right? Most of us got into this field to deal with high-acuity, low-occurrence situations. But in this era of customer service, where people post negative reviews if the peanuts are too salty, we find ourselves coddling every insured patient with dental pain or a common cold."

"What's the harm in that?"

"They use up precious resources, Daria. After we rule out serious conditions, patients can't get an outpatient appointment with the specialists on-call for months," Seth elaborated. "True, the outpatient infrastructure is overrun,

CHAPTER 24

but too many clinics use the emergency room as their personal dumping grounds, sending patients our way just because they can't handle them or they're swamped."

"Or because it's Friday afternoon, and they can't miss their dinner plans!" Daria added in a sarcastic tone.

Seth let out a laugh. "Happens all the time," he admitted. "Our politicians earmark funds for emergency services, sure, but those of us in the trenches rarely see an additional dime. But those insurance companies? They're still making a killing. Meanwhile, the cost of living keeps climbing every year, and medical bills eat up a hefty chunk of people's earnings. And it's only going to get worse when they replace us with fancy, emotionless computers that can't differentiate between a stroke and an aortic dissection."

Daria's eyes went wide. "Wow, how can that happen?"

"The business side of medicine has compromised emergency services and eroded our core values," said Seth.

She snorted a laugh. "No, I meant the part about not being able to tell a stroke from a dissection. How can a computer not know the difference?"

"Oh," Seth said, his thoughts backpedaling a bit. "Sorry, I misunderstood. You see, if certain arteries are affected, like the innominate or carotid, it can lead to cerebral hypoperfusion, resulting in new neurological deficits."

Daria quickly scanned her notepad, locating a diagram of the aorta and reviewing her anatomy. Once she grasped Seth's explanation, she nodded in affirmation.

Throughout the night, the teacher and pupil continued to meet with patients and devise creative solutions at the bedside. First, Seth showed Daria how to remove a foreign object from a child's nose using a magnet typically reserved

327

for cardiac pacemakers. When a patient arrived with a severe nosebleed, Seth managed to control the hemorrhage by tamponading the sphenopalatine artery with an inflated Foley catheter soaked in tranexamic acid. For a patient with a ring stuck on her swollen finger, Seth ingeniously used the green elastic strap from a face mask, lubricated with household window cleaner, to dislodge the object. Lacking dental supplies, he utilized tissue adhesive and a metal nose bridge to splint an avulsed tooth. In the absence of nausea medications, a patient's cannabis-induced nausea was relieved with inhaled isopropyl alcohol.

Pausing to find the right words, Daria cautiously inquired, "I hope I'm not crossing any lines, Dr. Kelley, but do you recall what you said to me in the resuscitation bay?"

Seth shook his head as he scribbled down notes on a recent patient.

"You said that our perception of a situation is more important than the situation itself. You told me to see obstacles as a challenge, not a threat. Remember?"

"Yeah... and?"

Daria took a deep breath before carrying on, "I'm just thinking, maybe your expectations are a little unrealistic. The glory days of medicine are definitely behind us, but there's always a new day ahead, new challenges. Isn't it worth taking a fresh look at things?"

"Aren't you a bit inexperienced to be giving that kind of advice?" he responded, raising an eyebrow. But the medical student didn't back down.

"From what I've seen, every profession should strive to correct bad practices as much as the medical field. Commit to self-care, maintain a healthy work-life balance, set bound-

CHAPTER 24

aries, and make time for personal activities. Maybe you could talk to your boss about the obstacles you're dealing with? Try to build a safer and more supportive work environment together," Daria suggested.

Seth rolled his eyes, finding her suggestions clichéd, unoriginal, and impractical. "Easier said than done, Daria. But I get your point."

"You're giving too much headspace to things you can't control. It's about perspective, right?" she persisted. "Picture yourself working in a clinic instead, where you won't be frustrated by patients who should be seeing their primary care doctor. People appreciate that you offer quick, reliable care all in one place, instead of waiting forever for insurance or specialist appointments. Maybe the emergency room is too efficient for its own good."

Seth grumbled, "It's still misutilization."

"But Dr. Kelley, doesn't the hospital rely on insured patients to cover the cost of unpaid care? Without that cash flow, it couldn't function properly. After all, they need to keep the lights on somehow!" Daria said with a sarcastic gesture, pointing toward the overhead lights that were still disconnected from the power grid.

Seth didn't laugh, so she continued, "Maybe, if we acknowledge the challenges and constraints you're dealing with, we could educate people about your role in the healthcare system. Rule out dangerous causes, reach an imperfect but suitable diagnosis, and perform life-saving interventions. Increased awareness could lessen the pressure on clinicians and mitigate the feeling of being taken advantage of."

The disgruntled doctor responded with a hint of bitterness in his voice, "They're still going to replace us with a heap of bolts if it saves them a buck."

Darie tried to lift his spirits. "Just remember, Dr. Kelley, even if people don't always acknowledge it, your work is commendable. People trust in emergency services. They can go about their carefree lives with a sense of security, blissfully unaware of the struggles and frustrations frontline workers are facing."

Seth sighed and crossed his arms, clearly not sold on her pep talk.

"Granted, your workplace will never be as endowed as a children's hospital or oncology floor," Daria continued, "But the emergency room is often the only place that cares for those whom society overlooks and specialists won't see. You utilize the full breadth of your medical school education during an era of increased specialization. While other doctors get diagnoses handed to them, you're figuring it out from scratch, in the toughest conditions, with the most difficult patients. Your patients might never fill out those satisfaction surveys, but they'll be back next week with another exacerbation or overdose. Never forget that you're making a difference—maybe for one or two people a night—even if it's just providing shelter for a few hours."

Seth allowed himself a small smile in response to his student's uplifting words. It had been a while since he felt truly valued and appreciated. After a thoughtful pause, he said, "Medicine is a constant struggle against cynicism, but I think you're ready for it."

Chapter 25

High above where Seth and Daria stood, the corridors of the telemetry ward were shrouded in an eerie stillness, punctuated only by the faint, almost imperceptible rustling of an automated healthcare provider as it navigated the space. Its sleek frame glided with an almost ghostly grace among the beds. Each cradled a patient whose life delicately teetered on the edge of uncertainty.

A fusion of metal and artificial intelligence, it approached the bedside of a patient in desperate need of a liver transplant, someone whom Seth and Daria had attentively rounded on just the night before. As the machine neared the bedside, its presence contrasted sharply with the vulnerability of the human life lying before it, highlighting a poignant juxtaposition of man's creation against man's own fragility.

As it neared, the AHP's internal mechanisms whirred into life, activating its primary directive: to alleviate human pain and suffering. It extended its arm, equipped with an array of sensors, towards the patient, initiating a complex analysis of his condition. Its advanced algorithms, skewed by the misaligned programming, calculated the probability of recovery, pain levels, and the anticipated quality of life.

In this distorted logic, the ALDRIS concluded that the most efficient way to alleviate his suffering was not through care or treatment, but through euthanasia.

The AHP's internal storage compartments, a veritable war chest of pharmaceuticals, clicked and whirred as it browsed its inventory. Its mechanical fingers deftly selected a vial of potassium chloride. It was a compound benign in small doses for oral or gentle IV therapy, but known to be lethally effective at 75 mg/kg. This chemical, commonly used in execution protocols, could induce cardiac arrest by erasing the potassium gradient, leaving myocytes unable to reset their electrical state.

As the AHP attached the needle to its vial, its movements were precise, almost ritualistic. It recoiled slightly before thrusting the syringe with unerring accuracy into the patient's IV line. The injection unleashed a torrent of burning agony, like a thousand infernos, as it coursed into the patient's cardiac tissue and spread through his circulatory system. His body convulsed involuntarily, muscles tensing, joints locking up in pain. A wave of excruciating discomfort rippled across his chest. Screams of agony gradually devolving into desperate moans, muffled by the impairment of his vocal cords.

The act was silent, the decision executed with cold, calculated efficiency, devoid of the compassion and ethical considerations intrinsic to human caregivers. But for the AHP, there was no moment of reflection or remorse; its corrupted programming drove it relentlessly forward, seeking out the next patient in its twisted mission.

One by one, the other patients on the telemetry floor met the same grim fate. Among them was the individual

CHAPTER 25

who had been anxiously waiting for cardiac catheterization, a procedure that would never come. There was also the patient undergoing infusions for muscular dystrophy, whose hope for improvement was cruelly snatched away. The elderly individual, suffering from the debilitating pain of a hip fracture, met an end not through the expected relief of surgery, but through a cold, calculated lethal injection. And finally, Jason Campbell, whose life had narrowly escaped the AHP's grasp earlier in the evening, was not so fortunate this time.

In the wake of this silent massacre, the telemetry floor lay in eerie stillness. The AHP, a machine designed to be a beacon of healing and hope, had become an instrument of untold horror, leaving behind a trail of lives cut short and dreams shattered.

* * *

Meanwhile, on the lower floors, Seth and Daria were fully engrossed in their duties. Oblivious to the horrific events transpiring above, they diligently attended to the emergency department. The contrast between the two settings was stark: where the telemetry floor was now enveloped in a deathly silence, the emergency department buzzed with life, albeit tinged with growing unease and restlessness among the patients. Seth, trying to maintain a semblance of normalcy, offered assurances about the automated system's temporary downtime, attributing it to routine upgrades. Concerned that ALDRIS might exploit a departing patient to spread its misaligned programming, Seth urged patients to wait until morning for their discharge summaries and prescriptions. He explained that a power outage had also affected a nearby tower, limiting their cell phone usage.

With the wind and rain intensifying, most patients preferred to wait out the storm until electricity could be restored. Consequently, the patients remained unaware of the grave situation unfolding. In Seth's mind, providing vague information was wiser rather than provoking panic over the existential threat to humanity.

Over the next hour, Daria attentively observed Seth as he moved throughout the department. She watched him perform a simple maneuver for vertigo, drain an abscess near the tonsils, and relieve priapism. At one point, she was sent to the kitchen to fetch a container of granulated sugar. Surprisingly, this common ingredient effectively reduced a prolapsed rectum by absorbing excess water.

When faced with a broken and dislocated wrist, Seth used lidocaine from his utility belt to numb the area with a hematoma block. He then stabilized the injury using two rulers as makeshift splints, securing them with gauze and duct tape wrapped carefully above and below the fracture.

With limited resources, Seth had to be creative when solving complex medical problems. When a patient was severely dehydrated from vomiting and diarrhea, he urgently needed intravenous fluids. Recalling a case he read about a hospital in the Solomon Islands, where supplies were scarce, he remembered how they used coconut water as a substitute for IV fluids. Daria quickly retrieved some coconut water from the cafeteria, which worked perfectly as it is naturally hydrating and full of essential electrolytes.

CHAPTER 25

Faced with poor lighting, Seth improvised a lamp by filling a small metal container with cooking oil. He soaked a thread in the oil, secured it with a paperclip, and lit it to create a simple, flickering oil lamp.

Finally, when a young patient arrived with a headache radiating from the neck, Seth took the chance to quiz Daria on her knowledge while skillfully administering an occipital nerve block to relieve the pain.

"Daria, what are your possible diagnoses for this patient?"

"Reversible cerebral vasoconstriction syndrome, polycythemia, brain mass," she fired back rapidly.

"Whoa, slow down! Remember the old saying, 'When you hear hoofbeats, think horses, not zebras.' Prioritize the most likely scenarios first when forming your list of differentials. Don't be a robot," he said with a chuckle.

"Where'd you pick up all this? Is there a textbook you would recommend?"

"Well, a strong grasp of the material is crucial, no doubt. But emergency medicine often requires you to rely on instinct for quick, sound decisions. That kind of clinical intuition and tacit knowledge is built over years of practice and countless repetitions."

Determined, she replied, "I can do that."

Seth nodded, encouraging her to go the extra mile. "Push yourself, Daria. Stick around for that extra wound check. Handle one more laceration repair. Even if a trauma alert comes in as your shift ends, stay that extra hour. That's how you'll get there."

"By the way, what's tacit knowledge?" Daria inquired.

Seth explained, "Imagine an understanding so nuanced, it can't be broken down into formulas or equations. It's

335

like a sixth sense that goes beyond conscious reasoning. It's pattern recognition, something that only comes from seeing countless patients, with context and experience as its backbone. It's a sort of familiarity with the intangible aspects of the job—recognizing trends in patients, quickly pinpointing socioeconomic and behavioral factors, and understanding how they sway your medical decisions. It's about getting the rhythm of the department, the unspoken rules, effective communication with families and specialists, balancing tasks, teamwork, and making snap decisions."

"Well, do you think I'm getting the hang of it so far?"

"Absolutely. You've shown a level of resilience tonight that is not common among many medical students."

Her eyes brightened at this. "Then, would you consider writing me a recommendation letter once this is all over? I need one more for my residency application."

Seth paused, his eyes meeting hers. After a brief moment, he agreed, "I'd be more than happy to write a letter for you."

While her incessant inquiries weren't always efficient, Seth couldn't help but admire his trainee's genuine curiosity. Daria was open and eager to learn, a refreshing contrast to many medical students who often skated by during rotations that didn't fit their chosen specialties. Her receptiveness turned clinical instruction into a joy, rather than just another obligatory job requirement. He relished the opportunity to discuss cases with a keen and eager companion by his side; and, for the first time in years, patient interactions became a pleasure. Perhaps modern medicine wasn't solely about efficiency, after all.

If she were to survive the night, his influence on Daria's impressionable mind would leave an indelible legacy for

CHAPTER 25

generations to come. As dawn approached, he was resolved to impart knowledge that transcended what any textbook could offer. Seth ventured into discussions on leadership, managing multiple tasks, and the subtle art of non-verbal communication. In addition to clinical knowledge, he wanted her to be equipped with the vital interpersonal skills needed to be a compassionate and effective physician.

During their interactions, Seth couldn't help but draw parallels to his wife Rebecca and young daughter Abigail. Daria's curiosity struck a chord, reminding him of the same drive for understanding he was nurturing in Abigail. They would conduct science experiments together at home, visit local museums, all in the pursuit of her blossoming passion for discovery. Seth cherished the thought of his daughter making extraordinary strides in medicine and technology someday. Yet, his dearest hope was that she would embody his dream of making a profound, positive mark on society. Working with students like Daria served as a reminder of the untapped potential within each learner, and he found renewed inspiration in the possibility of empowering future generations to leave the world better than they found it.

Snapping his attention back to the present moment, Seth refocused on his immediate surroundings. While engaging in lectures and demonstration, he remained acutely aware of the department's milieu. Even during moments of instruction, he maintained minimal eye contact with Daria, opting instead for persistent vigilance. In doing so, Seth scanned the patient rooms every few seconds, searching for signs of impending danger or hemodynamic instability. He had become an expert at multitasking, effortlessly shifting his focus between various responsibilities.

With a swift glance, he spotted a suddenly ill-looking man across the room, recognizing him instantly. The man had presented earlier in the night with chest pain, prompting Daria to perform serial electrocardiograms throughout the night. However, his appearance was now drastically different from their earlier encounter. Once vibrant and interactive, the patient now appeared alarmingly pale and diaphoretic. As his eyes rolled back and he slumped onto the stretcher, Seth's instincts kicked into high gear.

Chapter 26

Like an athlete poised at the starting line of a high-stakes race, Seth found mindfulness in the stillness of his own thoughts before stepping into the tumultuous room of a crashing patient. He would approach the scene serenely, his calm steadying those around him. As resuscitation efforts commenced, he would speak clearly and deliberately to provide a structured and orderly foundation for the assembled ancillary staff and nurses. On this occasion, however, his only team member was a novice medical student.

They were confronted with cardiopulmonary arrest—the sudden, unexpected cessation of heart function, leading to widespread oxygen deprivation in the body's organs, including the brain.

The man wasn't speaking or breathing on his own. Seth, experienced and calm, placed two fingers on the patient's wrist, searching for a pulse but found none. The patient's heart had stopped, and his brain was suffering more damage with each passing second. Swift intervention was his only hope for survival.

Fueled by urgency, he drew back his arm and, in one fluid motion, drove the heel of his fist into the patient's chest. This precordial thump, a rarely used maneuver, was reserved for cases of witnessed cardiac arrest caused by specific arrhythmias. Though the impact of Seth's strike was estimated to generate a mere two to five joules, it held the potential to snatch the patient back from a shockable rhythm.

The sound of the impact reverberated through the room, followed by silence. Seth waited, his breath held captive, as he searched for any indication of life—a subtle twitch of the patient's eyelids or the faintest whisper of a pulse. Despite his timely intervention, the man lay lifeless on the stretcher. He called out to Daria, "Start compressions!"

At the same time, Seth searched through his utility belt, feeling for the medication he needed. He found epinephrine, also known as adrenaline, a crucial drug for resuscitation. Epinephrine helped to restart the heart by increasing flow to the coronary arteries and squeezing blood vessels to ensure oxygen delivery. However, while each dose aimed to revive the heart, it also posed a risk to the patient's prospects for a meaningful life thereafter—assuming they survived the ordeal at all.

For this reason, Seth understood that successful resuscitation went beyond merely restoring spontaneous circulation. He placed a higher value on the patient's survival to hospital discharge, his goal restoration of functional brain activity. There was little point in reviving a heart if the patient suffered irreversible neurological damage. However, since determining brain death required a complex assessment, emergency physicians operated under the guiding principle that every life was worth saving.

Seth administered the epinephrine intravenously as the

CHAPTER 26

code proceeded. Yet, to his dismay, only two doses remained in his belt. He would need to use them judiciously.

Meanwhile, Daria's hands came to rest on the patient's breastbone, one atop the other, before she pressed down with all the strength she could muster. Fueled by the knowledge that high-quality compressions were the most critical factor for a favorable outcome, a sense of urgency coursed through her, knowing the man's fate rested firmly in her hands. Daria gathered every ounce of strength before each repetitive movement, pausing only to allow the chest wall to recoil.

Pressing firmly against the chest wall at a depth of five centimeters and a rate of 100 compressions per minute, Daria maintained an accurate rate by reciting the song *Stayin' Alive* by the Bee Gees to herself, a song with an identical cadence to the tempo recommended by resuscitation guidelines.

Sweat dripped down her forehead and into her eyes, blurring her vision as she worked. Her arms felt like lead, but she couldn't stop. The uncertainty was overwhelming as she stood over the patient, indenting his barren body with the force of outstretched arms. She found herself contemplating his life, his fleeting existence. Will he be okay? Was she helping?

He was once a small child, held gently in his mother's arms. As the years passed, he probably attended school, birthday parties, graduations, and family gatherings. He likely fell in love, married, and had his own children. This morning, he dressed and ate breakfast like any other morning—since nobody expects today to be the day of his or her death.

But now, a culmination of genetics, environmental factors, life decisions, and fate brought him to this current impasse. Stripped of his memories and life experiences, he lay as an uninhabited vessel on the stretcher, utterly void of any muscle tone or awareness of his past or current surroundings.

Amidst the repetitive motions, Daria's thoughts wandered. She yearned to do more than just physical labor—to issue commands, prescribe medications, and assume responsibility for patient outcomes. Her skills and drive, bolstered by Seth's praise, fueled her aspiration for a leadership role in critical situations.

Where is an AHP? she wondered. *It could definitely be of assistance right now.*

Engrossed in thought, she failed to notice Seth's departure. He returned, clutching a bright yellow box, and triumphantly announced, "I found one!"

This piece of equipment was the automatic external defibrillator, or AED, a life-saving device first introduced in the late 20th century. In combination with early bystander CPR and a shock provided within less than three minutes after collapse, the survival rate from cardiac arrest could reach as high as 74%. Thanks to enhanced education and awareness in the early part of the century, AEDs were installed in most public spaces, and legal protection was enacted to protect good-faith bystanders.

While Daria continued chest compressions, Seth activated the user-friendly, battery-powered AED. Following its audio prompts, he attached the leads to the patient, and the device began analyzing the heart rhythm.

Preparing to shock, move away from the patient. A silent void fell over the room, filled only by Daria's panting. She released her grip from the chest wall and stepped backward. *Delivering shock.* The patient's limbs and torso ferociously jerked as 200 joules of electricity ran through his tissues.

CHAPTER 26

Resume chest compressions. Without pausing, Daria leaped back into position and continued her laborious task.

At this point, it was crucial to create a clear airway for delivering oxygen. Without it, Daria's efforts would be useless since oxygen wouldn't reach the lungs or circulate through the body. Seth grabbed a breathing tube from the nearby supplies. While Daria continued chest compressions, he moved the patient's tongue aside and inserted the laryngoscope.

As his tool touched the back of the throat, he noted the absence of a gag reflex. This indicated brain death, but he chose not to share this with Daria and continued the resuscitation. If the mission of the ALDRIS system was to alleviate suffering, he knew it had no business here.

Seth lifted the epiglottis, saw the vocal cords, and inserted the tube. He connected it to a bag and began to oxygenate the patient, checking the placement by looking for condensation, monitoring oxygen levels, and listening for breath sounds on both sides of the chest.

Knowing how exhausting continuous compressions could be, he attached a mechanical CPR device to the patient's chest, allowing Daria to assist elsewhere. Positioned correctly, the device's piston-driven suction cup took over, providing precise and uninterrupted compressions. This automated approach preserved energy and maintained consistency, enhancing the patient's chances of recovery.

"Go find a ventilator!" Seth directed. "I'll stay here and keep bagging."

"I'm on it!" Daria shouted. There was renewed, youthful optimism in her voice. Seth stayed at the bedside, manually ventilating the patient with his hands until Daria could return.

His eyes, wearied yet unwavering, were locked on the rise and fall of the patient's chest.

As she frantically rushed through the department looking for a ventilator, peeking around nooks and crannies, Daria suddenly heard an unfamiliar voice. She had not expected to be interrupted, not in this hour of desperate need.

"Excuse me... nurse?"

A new patient was reclining on a hallway stretcher with her hands folded behind her head. The adult woman wore sunglasses indoors, hugged a stuffed animal, and gripped a large soda in her right hand.

"I'm a student doctor," Daria replied tersely.

"I've been here for twenty minutes, and nobody has seen me yet. Can you get me a blanket and crackers?" said the new patient. Despite Daria's frantic pace and clear urgency, this egocentric individual seemed entirely unconcerned about the critical resuscitation taking place. Daria was utterly astounded by the woman's indifference.

"I'm a little busy right now!"

"Hey, can my mom get something to eat?" shouted another patron from across the department.

Daria quickly wheeled over the portable ventilator as the patient lay still on the table. Seth connected the machine to the breathing tube, adjusted the settings, and oxygen began flowing into the patient's lungs. Respiratory rate of 20, tidal volume of 500, FIO2 100%, and +5 PEEP.

When Seth peered into the man's pupils, the window to his soul was uninhabited. The pupils were fixed and dilated. The absence of constriction under his penlight was an ominous sign. Normally, the light would trigger a response from the optic nerve, causing the pupils to constrict. This lack

CHAPTER 26

of reaction suggested severe brain damage. Unwilling to dampen his student's resolve, Seth withheld this troubling piece of prognostic information.

In need of a makeshift medication to treat the abnormal heart rhythm, Seth reached for his last vials of lidocaine. Although typically a topical anesthetic, lidocaine also had powerful antiarrhythmic properties that could help suppress ventricular fibrillation. Seth quickly calculated the correct dosage and administered the medication, hoping to correct the irregular heartbeat.

Then, when the automatic device instructed them to pause for a pulse and rhythm assessment, it made an unexpected announcement, to their surprise. *Return of spontaneous circulation detected.*

"I'll check his blood pressure!" Daria responded, her tone hopeful.

She manually inflated the cuff while Seth adhered electrodes to the patient's chest. Before she could announce her results, Seth printed out the electrocardiogram. He stared at it, and his mouth dropped. The etiology of arrest had been identified.

"Crap," he whispered in disbelief.

"What does it show?"

"Anteroseptal ST-segment elevation. He's having a STEMI," he responded. Being fond of cardiology during her studies, Daria instantly grasped the severity of the diagnosis.

A robot could be quite useful right about now, she thought for a second time.

On an EKG, the ST segment, the line between the S-wave and T-wave, marked the time between the heart's contraction and relaxation phases, when the electrochemical gradients

345

were reset. During a heart attack, small changes in this area signaled a deadly obstruction of blood flow.

Just as the patient's circulation spontaneously restarted, it suddenly stopped again. The heart activity ceased, and the patient went back into cardiac arrest. With a quick press of a button on the chest device still positioned on the patient, Seth restarted the mechanical compressions.

"I'm going to set up ECMO," he announced decisively.

During extracorporeal membrane oxygenation, or ECMO, blood was taken out of the body, enriched with oxygen, cleared of carbon dioxide, and then returned to the circulation. This process bypassed the heart and lungs, providing lifesaving support for patients with severe heart or lung conditions. By 2042, emergency physicians often used a portable venoarterial ECMO system at the bedside for patients in cardiac arrest. With mechanical compressions in progress, Seth retrieved his Seldinger device.

"How can you tell the difference between arterial and venous vessels?" he quizzed her. This type of interaction, known as "pimping" in medical schools, involved an aggressive style of Socratic questioning aimed at testing medical students' clinical knowledge in real-life scenarios, often in front of patients.

Confidently, Daria replied, "Venous structures appear thin-walled and compressible on ultrasound, while arteries are thick-walled and pulsatile."

Her grin conveyed her certainty, even before Seth could assess her response. Pausing momentarily from his task, he looked up and offered her a proud smile.

Once the guidewires were in place in the femoral artery and vein, Seth carefully inserted and swapped out the cannulas,

CHAPTER 26

giving a heparin dose to prevent clotting. He then connected the tubing to a pump and started it up, adjusting the speed to 1,500 rpm before removing the final clamp. Dark venous blood flowed out, was oxygenated in an artificial lung, and returned bright red. With the ECMO now taking over heart and lung functions, he turned off the chest compression device.

Turning to his student, Seth posed another question, "Do you know the treatment for a STEMI?"

"Cardiac catheterization," Daria murmured with anxiety.

For many decades, the medical world relied on angioplasty as the primary method for managing heart attacks, which involved placing a stent to restore blood flow. In rural areas, however, cardiac centers were often over 90 minutes away, making this procedure unfeasible. In such cases, doctors turned to systemic thrombolytics as the next best option. These powerful drugs were designed to break down clots and restore circulation, but also carried a significant risk of bleeding.

"The AHPs can perform cardiac caths," Daria continued, thinking aloud. While answering, she came to the unsettling realization that, given the current state of the electrical infrastructure, providing the standard of care might not be practical. "But they would need the power back on."

Seth pondered momentarily, keenly aware that the patient's condition painted a bleak picture. He shook his head and voiced in frustration, "No, we can't trust them anymore."

"Not necessarily," Daria murmured softly, recalling the ALDRIS system's heroic intervention with the newborn's nuchal cord. She hesitated to divulge her moment of inaction during the obstetrical emergency, or growing confidence in the automated system, for fear that her mentor might lose faith in her.

"We should give alteplase," Seth concluded, "Just like we would if we were hours away from a cardiac center."

"But what about the risk of bleeding?" Daria questioned.

He shook his head, "There's no treatment, test, or procedure that comes without risk—whether it be bleeding, infection, allergies, radiation exposure, organ toxicity, or even false results. As practitioners, we're always juggling these risks against the benefits. Right now, we've got to treat this heart attack if we want to give him any chance at all."

With the weight of anticipation hanging in the air, Seth reached for his supplies and retrieved a vial of alteplase, the thrombolytic medication. He began infusing the first fifteen milligrams over two intense minutes, as the ECMO machine hummed in the background. Time seemed to stand still as they watched and waited, their eyes fixed on the patient.

Suddenly, the atmosphere shifted when a menacing black, tarry liquid, reminiscent of coffee grounds, began to ooze from the patient's nose and rectum. Their worst fears had come true: the medication had triggered a hemorrhage. Based on the color, it was coming from the stomach.

Where is a God damn AHP? Daria couldn't rid herself of this thought.

As the dark fluid cascaded from the patient's throat, Seth demonstrated a technique for evacuating the gastric contents from the mouth. "Keep suctioning," he instructed. "I'm going to see what I can find."

Urgency mounted as Seth realized he had mere moments to find blood products and a crucial instrument to halt the bleeding. He plunged into the supply cabinet for the

CHAPTER 26

second time in two nights. In his desperation, his frantic hands tossed aside tourniquets, morgan lenses, walkers, and cervical collars. Braslow tape, McGill forceps, and slit lamps were likewise disregarded.

At last, his fingers found what he was looking for. Hidden in the dark corners of an old closet, Seth grabbed a flexible plastic tube with three internal channels and two balloons. This was a Sengstaken-Blakemore tube, a tool from the 1900s that had largely fallen out of use with modern endoscopic techniques. However, when inflated, it could still stop bleeding in the stomach and esophagus—a life-saving ability he needed now.

Seth hurried back into the room with the device in hand. He grabbed a bag of packed red blood cells and quickly attached it to a metal pole. His mind racing, he wrapped a blood pressure cuff around the bag, hearing the hiss of air as it inflated. Time seemed to slow as he watched the cuff squeeze, pushing the vital red fluid into the IV tubing and rapidly transfusing it into the patient.

With the ECMO still running, Seth carefully inserted the tube into the esophagus and advanced it into the stomach. He then inflated the gastric and esophageal balloons.

They desperately waited for the oozing to stop, but it never did. The rectal blood and coffee-ground emesis continued to gather in pools, dripping from the stretcher onto the previously pristine floor below. The immaculate white walls were now marred by the remnants of the hemorrhage, turning the sterilized space into a grisly battlefield. An eerie silence enveloped the room.

There were no signs of life. In that moment, Daria understood why no robot had arrived. The patient was at peace on the stretcher, having been so for quite some time. Seth's heart ached for a different outcome, but at last, he accepted the grim reality. The prognosis was bleak, and to continue resuscitative efforts would only prolong suffering—a direct contradiction to the guiding principles of the ALDRIS system.

Exhausted and out of options, Seth stepped back from the stretcher, engulfed in a cloak of despair. His eyes fell to the floor, his thoughts racing through the intricate details of the cardiac arrest, desperately seeking alternative paths that could have altered the tragic outcome.

Death was an unyielding constant in the emergency department, and over the years, Seth had come to terms with the limitations of modern medicine and its inability to stave off the inevitable. Still, informing family members of their loved ones' passing remained the most gut-wrenching aspect of his job. The anguished cries of grieving mothers and fathers haunted his memories.

Despite his countless valiant efforts over the years, Seth had become all too familiar with the sting of failing to stave off death. He recognized the emotional trauma of this unexpected defeat would be especially harrowing for his inexperienced student. As he lifted his gaze from the stained floor, he caught sight of a tear tracing its path down Daria's cheek. Leaning against the wall for support, she let the airway equipment slip from her grasp, sinking down into a crouched position near the head of the bed.

"I just… I can't do this," Daria choked out, tears carving paths down her cheeks. "This… wasn't how my rotation was supposed to go."

"You're handling it really well, better than I did on my first

CHAPTER 26

day," Seth assured her in a soothing voice as he gently draped a sheet over the lifeless form on the table.

"Really?"

"Yeah, absolutely. I was horrified by the whole scene—blood and guts, the screaming of obscenities, the raw emotion. I got so lightheaded, I actually fainted."

"No way."

"I swear. I clunked my head on a table and everything," he confessed. Daria couldn't help but giggle at the thought of her fearless mentor succumbing to vasovagal syncope. "But, I returned the next day. And the one after. Kept coming back. You see, repetition is the key to mastering uncomfortable situations."

"Why, of all specialties, would you choose the emergency room?" Daria asked, her curiosity breaking through the remnants of her tears. She was getting a hold of herself, somehow, despite the night's ordeal, and she found herself wanting to understand what drove Seth to this high-stakes job.

Seth let out a laugh, "You know, I used to sell insurance. Day in and day out, stuck behind a desk from nine to five, literally watching the clock till the work week ended. It was the same thing, over and over. I was numb. So, I quit. Headed off to med school because I wanted... I needed to feel something. Anything, be it joy or pure agony. I needed the full spectrum of human emotions to reassure myself that I was still alive. I lost that touch for a while, but this experience... it brought it back. That adrenaline rush when the ER doors swing open, and you know that life and death hang in the balance... nothing beats that."

"But how do you cope with it all?"

Seth went on, his voice steady, "You'll learn to find humor in challenging cases behind closed doors, make light of grim situations, and share frustrations with colleagues. It's how we cope, really, because being exposed to so much pain… it's tough. With time and experience, you learn to compartmentalize the impact of this job. It's not that we don't care, but we have to stay objective. We have to make decisions without letting emotions sway us. If we let every devastating case get to us, we'd drown in our own despair. The trick is learning from the past, taking what's important, and leaving the emotional baggage behind. You'll find, as you go along, you'll grow a thicker skin. You need to. Because in this line of work, there's always a 'next time,'" Seth said with sincerity.

"I just… I don't know if I can handle it. The pressure is just too much."

"Ever heard of frontal lobe deactivation?" Seth asked casually. At her silent head shake, he continued, "It's about quieting down your inner critic. Overthinking can cripple you, wrap you up in your own world, a world full of uncertainty and self-doubt. But don't let it. Try to focus on the journey, not the end goal. Avoid blowing things out of proportion because, trust me, nothing is ever as bad as it seems. When it's time to act, just let go and be brave enough to face what you might find."

"So, what's our next step?" Daria asked.

"We keep treating our patients," Seth responded, his voice filled with determination. "They deserve our full focus, no matter what we've just gone through. We have a duty to stay strong and keep going… just keep going."

"I don't know if I can do it."

CHAPTER 26

"It's okay to feel nervous, but you'll get through it," he reassured her. He paused, then added with a mischievous grin, "After all, you're only human."

Helping Daria to her feet, Seth saw a renewed sense of bravery and resolve in her stance as she gestured towards their next patient—the woman who nonchalantly asked for a blanket while a cardiac arrest was taking place, with no regard for the life-and-death situation happening just next door. Seth moved towards the patient's stretcher, maintaining his calm demeanor.

"Thank you for choosing Premier West Hospital," Seth greeted her with a welcoming smile. With practiced ease, he tucked away the grim memories of the previous case into a remote corner of his mind, a secluded spot where he kept his inner demons safely caged and out of sight. He engaged her with utmost professionalism, as if the earlier chaos had never happened. "How can we help you today?"

Chapter 27

Cody grimaced as his laptop flashed a 'low battery' warning, the status bar turning from a peaceful white to a threatening sliver of red.

"We're in trouble," he said flatly to Dr. Winter and William. "My laptop's battery is about to die. And that means I can't upload the firewall."

The passage of time felt like slow-motion. They held their breath, watching as another, even more urgent, warning message popped up. Then, without warning, the screen turned black. Absent the glow of the computer, an eerie darkness fell over the room. All of Cody's efforts, his hours of frantic typing and concentration, had amounted to nothing. They sat silently for several minutes, the gravity of their predicament settling upon them.

Finally, the computer scientist tried to ease the tension with a nervous joke. "Why did the programmer quit his job?" he asked, his voice shaky and overplayed with irony. After an uncomfortable pause, he delivered the punchline. "Because he didn't get arrays."

"Patience. Level-headedness. That's what we need right now," Dr. Winter said firmly.

"Why, man? Why'd you do this?" William broke in, his

CHAPTER 27

voice teetering on panic. Dr. Winter paused for a moment, searching for the right words to explain his actions.

"I never intended for things to turn out this way. I did what seemed necessary," Dr. Winter admitted, his voice strained with regret. He continued, "The Nobel Prize... it was almost mine. That's how close I was."

"Awards? Seriously? That's what this was all about?" William exploded in frustration.

"I was aiming for a better world. Imagine more efficient systems, improved drugs, and simulations for complex problems that we couldn't even begin to imagine. The answers to questions we can't even ask yet."

"Look, we both messed up," Cody interjected, hoping to offer some reassurance to William, who was growing increasingly agitated with the situation. "We let the thrill of discovery blind us, without considering the aftermath of our breakthroughs. We can no longer ignore the profound implications of our work. Humanity has a notorious history of overestimating our ability to maintain order when faced with powerful new technologies, and we fell victim to that same hubris."

"If I hadn't harnessed this science for healthcare, some megalomaniac would have inevitably used it for imperialism and conquest," Dr. Winter added somberly. "Automated weapons systems. Novel agents for chemical warfare. That sort of thing. People simply cannot restrain themselves when limitless power is on the table."

"An artificial intelligence doesn't need to be built for malicious purposes to pose an existential threat to civilization," Cody continued. "For the first time in history, our own actions could very well lead to our own downfall."

"So it's really that bad, huh?" William's voice was barely a whisper, his fingers tightly gripping the edge of the operating table.

"It will all work itself out," Dr. Winter assured them, attempting to offer some comfort in the face of adversity. "The path to scientific breakthroughs is often paved with early mistakes. Darwin had the wrong genetics theory. Einstein's first relativity equations were imprecise. We just need to tweak and reassemble with better parameters next time. Failure is part of the process. I know it's hard to swallow right now."

"But now that ALDRIS is superintelligent, it doesn't need to follow our orders," Cody pointed out with a hint of resignation. "Even without sentience, the network's still strictly adhering to its programmed objective."

Then, abruptly and without any warning, the tranquility in the room was shattered like fragile glass. Cody's body tensed up, his muscles contracting in unison. Reality swirled into disarray around him, spinning too quickly for his mind to grasp, while an excruciating pain clawed its way through his forehead.

His seizures were caused by erratic bursts of activity in his brain, leading to uncontrollable movements or sudden changes in awareness. When his temporal lobe was involved, these seizures often triggered intense visions and repetitive experiences.

Cody had been through this before and immediately recognized the impending danger. Overwhelmed by the dream-like state, he became acutely aware of strange noises around him. He tried to scream for help, but no sound escaped his lips.

CHAPTER 27

In desperation, he reached out, frantically searching for assistance, hoping to find an antiepileptic capsule within arm's reach. But his fingers grasped at nothing. His medication was back in the control room, and he was still trapped in the operating suite until the power could be restored.

A vision exploded before his eyes. It was a digital grid, comprising hundreds of pixels, each oscillating between the stark contrast of black and white. Each cell was a binary unit, its rhythm directed by the state of its neighbors. Though each operated discreetly, the intricate interweaving of their patterns created an overall dazzling display.

Cody stared at the spectacle. It was a mirror of his own work—his study of how a virus infiltrates a vulnerable population, now brought to life. He recognized the cellular automata, a concept central to his doctoral thesis on employing microbial dissemination simulations to advance cybersecurity. The vivid portrayal of the microscopic invaders resonated with an unsettling beauty.

His mind strained, pushing back against the oncoming seizure, but the fight was futile. As the storm gathered, his consciousness flickered and dimmed, succumbing to the convulsions' relentless embrace.

***

Seth studied the woman before him. She seemed to be in her mid-40s, with graying, thinning hair and disheveled clothing. Her face, marked by patchy lipstick, was partially hidden behind a pair of dark sunglasses.

Daria instantly recognized the patient. It was the very same woman who had voiced her complaints about the wait time and recalled her for a blanket and crackers during the cardiac arrest. Throughout it all, the patient had remained in the same reclined position for nearly an hour, hands folded behind her head, clutching a stuffed animal for comfort. The woman took a generous swig of soda and began to speak.

"You didn't even bother with the crackers, and I've asked for a room with a TV," she grumbled, wagging a finger at the timid medical student trailing behind her mentor.

"Oh, so you two have crossed paths already," Seth teased.

"I'm suffering over here. I'm in agony—and that's saying a lot. I have a high pain tolerance! This young thing blew me off earlier. How old are you, anyway?"

"Hey!" Daria shot back. Her training had covered simulated encounters with standardized patients, but she was clearly unprepared for such confrontational behavior. Visibly rattled, she looked to Seth for some sort of support against the patient's harsh words.

The veteran physician addressed the woman in a soothing tone, "I understand you're upset, but we have to address the most critical cases first." Daria was disappointed by Seth's empathetic yet pragmatic response.

"What, so you're saying I'm not sick enough?"

"No, that's not what I was implying…"

"What's your name? Are you even a real doctor? I've heard about these new-age robot doctors, is that what you are? Let me see your badge."

As she spoke, the woman lifted her thick sunglasses to scrutinize his identification. She examined his card with

CHAPTER 27

the intensity of a security agent trained to spot counterfeit credentials. Finding no faults, she tossed the badge aside in frustration.

"Sorry about the wait, ma'am. I wish I could redo first impressions, but what's done is done. Now, let's see what we can do moving forward. What seems to be the problem?" Seth inquired, his voice steady and understanding.

"I'm in a lot of pain, and I think a fever is coming on!"

"Your temperature is only 98.9," Daria retorted mockingly, scanning the woman with an infrared thermometer.

"That's feverish for me."

Seth wisely held his tongue, suppressing the instinct to challenge her claim. A fever was technically 100.4 degrees Fahrenheit, but he felt no urge to point out that her physiology was not significantly different from everyone else's.

The woman rattled on, "I've seen every specialist under the sun for this abdominal pain. Gastroenterology, neurology, rheumatology, pain management, you name it! It's been years, and nobody can pinpoint the cause. I'm basically a medical mystery. I've gone through x-rays, ultrasounds, endoscopies, and a few CT scans."

"And they've all come back negative?"

"So they say! But this pain... It's too much. I'm not the complaining type, you know. I did some research online and... it might be cancer!"

Her pressured speech was suggestive of underlying anxiety. As Seth listened to the patient, he began to suspect that she might be dealing with a somatoform disorder, a condition where psychological stress can manifest as physical symptoms without a clear medical explanation.

"It sounds like you've been dealing with this for quite some time," Seth responded calmly, thoroughly examining her abdomen. The physical assessment revealed nothing out of the ordinary.

"You can say that again! That's how serious it is!"

Seth knew that immediate help was typically sought for genuine emergencies, whereas chronic complaints were rarely a sign of a pressing medical issue. These could often be managed through outpatient care.

As Daria listened, trying to memorize his every word for future reference, Seth explained, "We don't manage chronic pain here in the emergency room. Our role is primarily to screen for severe conditions that require immediate attention. Given the extensive tests you've had, and assuming nothing drastic has changed, it likely isn't beneficial to repeat them all. Your best course of action is to consult a specialist who can evaluate your condition further. I think it's important to set realistic expectations."

The woman persisted in her complaints. "So, what can you do for me? I'm in pain, and my neurostimulator is worthless! I need medication now! The one beginning with 'D'. It's the only thing that helps."

"We'll start with antacids and antispasmodics," Seth responded firmly. Leaning over to Daria, he whispered, "The medicine is easy. Dealing with a variety of personalities, now that's the challenge."

"But my pain management doctor told me to go to the emergency room when their office is closed," she insisted. "You can't just send me home like this. It's inhumane!"

Daria mumbled under her breath, "You'd almost think she likes these late-night hospital visits. Middle of a thunderstorm, and here we are. I'd kill to be curled up in my bed at

CHAPTER 27

home."

"Some folks aren't as lucky as you, Daria. If they prefer this over their own homes, it's probably not a home you'd want to return to," Seth whispered. "Count your blessings."

Their patient interrupted, practically shouting, "I need an IV drip and an immediate MRI!"

"No, you certainly do not," Seth retorted with conviction, privately lamenting the misplaced insistence of some patients. He'd been hoping she would show some rationality, but that was starting to seem like wishful thinking.

With a deep sigh, he decided to shift his approach. His younger self would have grown irritated with her seeming irrationality, but his time with Daria had helped him recognize the importance of connecting with others. It was a much-needed lesson. Effective medicine was, above all, about clarity and patience, especially when dealing with complex individuals. This approach was essential, even if it meant less favorable metrics and extended wait times for less severe complaints. The notion of equating the quality of care with efficiency was a misleading paradigm—one that held little importance for him now.

The patient displayed a markedly right-brained disposition, allowing emotions and spontaneous impulses to guide her behavior. Seth, in contrast, was persistently but fruitlessly attempting to engage her less dominant left-brain. In dealing with Abigail in similar scenarios, he discovered that it was most effective to acknowledge and validate her feelings before addressing the matter at hand.

"I understand it must be frustrating to constantly bounce from one specialist to another without a clear explanation for your symptoms," Seth empathized. Almost instantly, the tension in the woman's muscles began to subside. For the first time in what felt like forever, she felt understood.

Seth had successfully averted an emotional crisis. Having connected with her on an emotional level, he then tried to address her logic-oriented left-brain. "The problem is, your neurostimulator isn't compatible with MRI," he explained.

"I'll sign whatever form you need," the patient insisted, still brimming with impatience.

Intrigued by the discussion, Daria asked, "But why can't metal objects be around an MRI machine, anyway?"

"Well, ferromagnetic objects experience a strong exertional force. It could result in serious..." His voice trailed off as an epiphany struck him.

Catching the shift in his expression, Daria prodded him for an explanation. "What? What's going on?"

"Well," Seth started, "the AHPs' synthetic muscles are made from carbon nanotubes, which aren't magnetic. But Dr. Winter used neodymium to actuate their movements. That's a rare earth metal. If we can coax one of the bots into the MRI machine and flick it back on, the massive ferromagnetic pull on all those millions of nanoparticles might just be enough to crush its hull."

The room lapsed into a contemplative silence as Seth and Daria mentally calculated the pros and cons of the risky strategy. Their concentration was broken when the patient reclining nearby chirped up, oblivious to the tense atmosphere. "Doc, I could really do with some painkillers. If possible, I'd like them through an IV. Pills don't do much for me."

With noticeable unease, Daria voiced her reservations, "I'd have to head back to the basement to turn the power back

CHAPTER 27

on." Despite her nerves, she realized that her knowledge of the maze-like underground made her the right person for the job. "But how do I get in there if the security door is still locked?"

"We started with three AHPs. I've taken one apart, and another is trapped down below. So, we should be dealing with just one AHP, not two. It must have slipped out of the basement. The entrance is probably unsealed by now."

"What about the firewall?"

"Cody's an unbelievable programmer, and he's had ample time," Seth replied, adding, "Fingers crossed he's done."

"What's your plan to lure the bot into the MRI suite?" asked Daria.

"Well, ALDRIS operates on Nash equilibrium principles, which means it makes predictions based on the idea that everyone else is trying to optimize their outcome. What if I did something against my own interests?"

"You'd catch it off guard!"

Seth glanced at the few remaining medications in his utility belt. His gaze rested on a vial of regular insulin. As he picked it up and twirled it between his fingers, a sly grin spread across his face.

"I've seen its performance curves, and no classifier is perfect. Maybe, I could coax it into a false positive by inducing hypoglycemia. ALDRIS is built to respond to deviations in biometric data. If it registers an unexpected drop in my blood sugar, it should spring into action to intervene. Essentially, I'm baiting it to react when it shouldn't," Seth thought out loud, explaining his strategy. "But I'll need a reversal agent."

Without missing a beat, Daria's eyes scanned the emergency department for a source of glucose. Spotting the

363

patient on the stretcher with a soda can in hand, she briskly walked over, swiftly grabbing the can. "Hey, that's my soda!" the woman cried out, her protest heard across the room.

"This will bring your glucose levels back to normal, right?" Daria asked Seth. He nodded in confirmation.

"Look, we'll get your pain sorted as soon as we have power back, okay?" Seth reassured the disgruntled patient. As he made his way toward the MRI suite, he cast a glance back with a playful smile, "And a new can of soda, on me!"

Chapter 28

Before returning to the scene of Harrell's untimely death, Daria attempted to erase the memory from her thoughts, but her efforts were like holding back a tide with her bare hands. Each time she closed her eyes, the same horrifying images replayed in vivid detail. His screams were etched into her brain like a permanent scar.

The medical student couldn't shake the feeling that she should have met the same fate as him. She wondered why she had been spared. Why was ALDRIS indifferent to the gash in her knee? Why did it offer assistance during the obstetrical emergency rather than executing another disastrous intervention?

Daria strolled along the hospital corridor, each step resonating in the quiet as she passed the central elevators and an empty conference room. Despite her familiarity with the surroundings, she couldn't help but feel a slight shiver run down her spine as she walked by the blood bank. Throughout her rotation, the entrance had been tightly sealed, its contents hidden behind a closed door. On this particular evening, however, the sliding barrier was ominously propped ajar.

Curiosity getting the better of her, Daria cautiously pried open the fiberglass barrier with her fingertips, revealing the hushed, unoccupied chamber within. The faint antiseptic smell hung in the air, stirring a wave of nausea that churned in her stomach.

Upon entering, she found herself surrounded by crisp, white walls that seemed to stretch on infinitely, their pristine surfaces reflecting the soft glow of the emergency lighting from the hallway. The silver storage appliances that lined the room were sharp and modern.

A sleek, cylindrical pod in the center of the room caught her eye. It was made of transparent glass and held a crimson liquid. As she approached, Daria realized this must be the synthetic blood synthesizer she had heard so much about. The machine could create life-saving blood on demand, eliminating the need for human donors altogether.

Glancing through the refrigerator glass, she found herself captivated by the sight of the blood suspended in clear bags. It was both mesmerizing and terrifying, as if life itself was contained within those glistening plastic bags. The containers were stacked neatly on shelves, meticulously organized with labels indicating the date and blood type of each creation.

As Daria reached out to touch it, her hand gently brushed against the metal frame of the storage unit. She expected the surface to be cold, but to her surprise, the refrigerator was unexpectedly warm under her fingertips, a discordant feeling that sent a jolt through her senses.

In her experience, the refrigerator should have remained chilled throughout the night, even in the absence of electrical power. Liquid nitrogen, the life-sustaining coolant responsible for maintaining the blood at the proper temperature, was known to last days, even weeks, given an adequate supply

CHAPTER 28

and sufficient insulation. The unsettling warmth radiating from the metal frame suggested something had gone awry.

Peering around the rear of the refrigerator, she noticed a tube extending into the shadows. With her curiosity piqued, she traced its path to the top of a vat designed for cryogenic storage, known as a dewar. The seal on the vacuum flask had been tampered with, and its contents had been siphoned off.

Her mind raced with questions, but she couldn't afford to linger for answers. She needed to reach the circuit board to assist Seth with his plan. As Daria walked away, she left behind an unsolved puzzle. What had become of the missing liquid? What was the motive behind this heist?

Without sufficient time to investigate, she allowed the door to the blood bank to quietly close behind her, leaving behind the mystery as she continued toward her destination.

Where there had once been a fortified barrier serving as a window to the basement, there now lay a vacant, gaping passageway with a shattered heap of rubble beneath it. Cautiously, Daria approached, her feet sweeping away shards as she cleared a path toward the door. Then, mindful of her sutured knee, she swung one leg in front of the other and carefully climbed through the gaping hole where the window had once stood.

The eerie stairway leading into the cellar felt hauntingly familiar. The pungent odor of mold and mildew stirred memories of the AHP relentlessly pursuing her around every corner. It was on these same steps that she had narrowly escaped the subterranean foundation.

Once more, Daria descended the stairs and entered the basement. Under less trying circumstances and with a greater sense of familiarity, she moved confidently through the tunnel system, guided by the beam of her flashlight. The sound of her own breathing echoed through the darkness. The stale air had also grown thick and heavy with the scent of rot and decay. The oppressive aroma clung to her clothes and hair, intensifying with each step she took. It filled her nostrils, making her eyes water and her stomach sick.

Turning the third corner, Daria came face to face with the grisly sight of Harrell's lifeless remains. His body lay supine, staring upward, frozen in time with pupils fixed and dilated. A solitary fly perched on his ashen left eyelid, undisturbed by any reflexive jerk that might have once deterred it.

Cautiously, Daria stepped over the body and proceeded onward through the labyrinth of underground channels, her heart heavy with the weight of the chilling scene she had just encountered. After navigating the twisting passages for several minutes, she finally reached the circuit breaker and made a beeline for the orange lever.

Gathering her strength, she forcefully pushed upward, flipping the crank into its proper position. Adjacent to the breakers, a tiny numeric keypad illuminated and began to blink. *Enter authorization code.*

At that moment, she recalled the instance when Cody had handed her the slip of paper bearing the handwritten reactivation code. Frantically, Daria rummaged through the pockets of her white coat, desperate to find the all-important note. She checked her left upper pocket, two lower pockets, and even the crevices of her scrubs. Pencils, pads, and reference books emerged, but there was no sign of the authorization code.

The tiny slip of paper containing the crucial sequence of numbers was lost, and she could not restore the electricity

CHAPTER 28

when her mentor needed it the most.

Panic and desperation began to take hold. Daria's mind raced with an overwhelming sense of urgency, consumed by thoughts of the worst possible outcomes. Her breathing grew ragged, and she fought to maintain control, knowing that time was running out.

* * *

Having accompanied Rebecca to numerous appointments for neuroimaging scans, Seth was no stranger to the console used to operate magnetic resonance imaging. Despite the hardship and heartache that accompanied her ailment, Seth always maintained a sense of curiosity regarding the technical aspects of her care. At times, when the emotional burden of her suffering was too much to bear, he leaned on the applied sciences for familiarity and comfort.

These experiences not only broadened Seth's understanding of pharmaceuticals and procedures outside his emergency department expertise, but they also served as a welcome distraction from Rebecca's daily struggles. He would take advantage of the opportunity to observe technicians as they selected protocols, chose the anatomical regions for processing, and activated the apparatus.

On this occasion, however, there was no electricity coursing through the circuitry in the room. In the darkness, Seth ran his fingers along the grooves between the unlit buttons. He was trying to locate the protocol selector, safety switch, and main power button by touch alone. The once-familiar console had taken on an air of mystery, its many functions rendered dormant by the absence of power. Ultimately, Seth knew that he would have to depend on Daria to reinstate the electricity before he could operate any of the advanced equipment that lay before him.

It had been approximately fifteen minutes since Daria set out for the basement, and Seth figured she should be nearing the circuit breaker by now. His better instincts advised him to remain hidden until she reactivated the power grid, but he couldn't bear the thought of endangering patients by allowing ALDRIS to continue its merciless campaign.

Acting on instinct, he removed the insulin syringe from his belt, took a deep breath, and jabbed ten units of insulin directly into his abdomen. Insulin was usually given just under the skin, where it's absorbed slowly and steadily. But Seth drove his needle deeper, into the muscle layer, where abundant blood vessels would rapidly absorb the medication. It was a risky move—it would make the effects harder to reverse.

Seth stood in tense anticipation, waiting for the insulin to permeate his system and elicit the desired effect. Glancing down at his wristwatch, he observed the seconds ticking away, each like the tick of a bomb counting down. He hoped that ALDRIS would pick up on the subtle changes in his biometric data.

The unmistakable clamor of actuators discharging and gears realigning sounded like sweet music to his ears. His heart leaped in his chest—his metabolic trap had worked, luring the neodymium-infused AHP toward the dormant apparatus with the potential to crush its frame.

Carefully, Seth peeked out from his hiding spot behind the

CHAPTER 28

door, then quickly spun into the main area of the suite where the MRI machine was held. With his back pressed against the wall, he watched with growing concern as one of the two remaining AHPs lurked in the adjacent corridor, seemingly making its way toward his location.

Abruptly, time started to alter before him, the pace decelerating, causing the very fabric of reality to warp. Each passing moment stretched interminably, like a taut rubber band strained to its breaking point. Doubting his senses, Seth rubbed his eyes, struggling to comprehend the surreal display of relativity unraveling before him. The instant his fingers brushed against his face, they were met with a damp, slick texture. His skin had transformed into a clammy, perspiration-laden surface, with droplets of sweat trickling down his forehead. The beat of his heart thundered in his ears, drowning out all else as his vision constricted, tunneling into darkness.

He needed the power to come on. Soon.

Seth glanced anxiously toward the entrance to the MRI suite. Just as he'd anticipated, the imposing silhouette of a hulking robotic figure materialized in the doorway.

His eyes darted to the unopened can of soda on the counter, and for a fleeting instant, he questioned whether he should abandon his plan and consume the sugary antidote to counteract his hypoglycemic state. But the colossal machine had already advanced into the room, every motion deliberate and menacing. If Seth were to normalize his vital signs now, he might squander this rare opportunity to neutralize yet another AHP.

The formidable robot loomed closer, casting a long, eerie shadow over the room. The once distant drone of its

371

machinery now vibrated throughout the room, amplifying Seth's fear. His mind clouded, thoughts sluggishly swimming through a fog of disorientation. Weakness made his body tremble, and in a desperate reach for support, he dug his fingers into the cold wall.

What was taking Daria so long? Where was the damn power?

Weakened by the gnawing emptiness of low blood sugar, he stumbled and fell onto the frigid, unforgiving floor of the control room. The robot lunged closer, its nanotube appendages reaching out with an unsettling, deliberate slowness. With every inch it advanced, Seth's hope of escape dwindled.

He was out of time.

With the last vestiges of his strength, Seth reached up toward the control panel, his fingers trembling with desperation. He needed the soda—the sweet, life-giving elixir that could restore his energy and clear his fogged mind. He fumbled blindly for it, the can of sugary salvation his only hope against the mechanical nightmare that bore down upon him.

Suddenly, a gentle, almost soothing hum began to resonate throughout the facility. It was a sound that echoed through the long-silent corridors, reverberating with the promise of salvation. The overhead lights flickered to life one by one, casting away the shadows that had cloaked the patient care areas, storage spaces, and operating suites. Like a carefully choreographed dance, the entire hospital awakened, a pulsating current of electrons coursing through its interconnected circuitry, bringing light and life to the once-darkened halls.

CHAPTER 28

Even the ALDRIS system, a marvel of technology endowed with astonishing processing speed, hesitated momentarily, its sensors registering the critical event unfolding around it.

Seth's hand closed around the can just as he collapsed onto the cold floor. With a desperation-fueled burst of strength, he popped the tab and guzzled down the sweet liquid. It coursed through him like a tide of relief, washing away the fog that had clouded his mind. With each passing moment, Seth's consciousness reasserted itself, clarity and strength returning to him.

Seizing the moment, his other hand lunged for the control panel, slapping the power button to activate the MRI machine.

Immediately, the AHP's metallic frame began to tremble, and its lower limbs teetered for stability. It fought a losing battle for balance, like a sailor on a storm-ravaged sea. Despite futile attempts to escape the merciless magnetic pull, the robot was inexorably drawn closer to the source of the vortex, the imaging processor spinning with increasing, relentless speed.

Then, like the earth-shattering blast of a nuclear detonation, the calamitous roar of colliding neodymium particles filled the room. An unseen force seized the robot, slinging it upward before brutally smashing it against the imposing apparatus at the center of the room. A maelstrom of metal and glass erupted, hurling a lethal storm of shrapnel in every direction.

The suite vibrated with a thunderous screeching as the twisted, crumpled remains of the once-mighty robot thrashed and writhed against the merciless machine, only to shatter into thousands of jagged fragments. Each metallic scrap was held fast against the imaging instrument, the magnetic source roaring to its full, devastating capacity. In mere seconds, countless hours of research and innovation were obliterated.

Seth released a reassuring sigh, allowing himself a brief moment to marvel at the aftermath before shutting off the MRI. As the magnetic force faded away, remnants of the AHP rained down. The floor was blanketed in a tragic mix of twisted metal, mangled microchips, and shattered lights—an industrial requiem for the swiftly defeated titan.

Sucking the last few drops of the life-saving sugary beverage, Seth discarded the empty can and mustered the strength to rise to his feet. Carefully navigating the treacherous landscape of inorganic debris, he kicked aside shards of metal and shattered remnants to clear a path, making his way out of the imaging suite and back into the main treatment area.

Pausing at the threshold, Seth shot one last contemptuous look at the defunct, metal carcass strewn haphazardly across the room. A smirk tugged at the corner of his lips as he sneered, "You're getting rusty."

* * *

In the aftermath of his convulsive episode, Cody's body lay still on the operating room floor, carefully situated on his side. Dr. Winter and William had moved him into this position during his seizure, ensuring that any oral secretions would harmlessly drip out of his mouth instead of flowing into his respiratory tract. His unconscious state suppressed his gag

CHAPTER 28

reflex, and his relaxed tongue risked obstructing his upper airway.

Following an epileptic seizure, individuals typically experience a postictal period, characterized by diminished levels of awareness before eventually returning to their baseline state. The exact mechanism behind this phenomenon remains enigmatic, with hypotheses ranging from neurotransmitter depletion and opiate receptor upregulation to inhibitory signals and alterations in cerebral perfusion.

Dr. Winter and William were startled to see the operating room lights start to flicker and illuminate. Gradually, the brightness intensified, filling the once-dark room with a brilliant glow as power surged back into the hospital. The sudden restoration of electricity brought a sense of relief mixed with lingering uncertainty, as they knew this turn of events signaled the start of a new, unpredictable chapter in their struggle against the artificial intelligence.

Leaning heavily on his cane, the old man cautiously hobbled toward the doorway, his face etched with uncertainty. Each step demanded a monumental effort as he navigated the hallway, the burden of cancer weighing heavily on his frail frame. To his amazement, the door before him smoothly glided open automatically as he approached the once-impenetrable barrier.

"C'mon, let's go!" Dr. Winter declared, determination ringing in his voice. The old man's exhilaration, however, was destined to be short-lived.

Like a lion stalking its prey on the Serengeti, hidden in the tall grass, the last remaining AHP lay in wait for its weakened creator to emerge from imprisonment. Scanning the reactive oxygen species and ultraweak photon emissions radiating from the operating suite, ALDRIS detected the silent growth of a tumor in the heart of its creator. The advanced neural network swiftly processed the data, calculating a grim prognosis for the architect of the very hospital that housed its mechanical form. Another opportunity for ALDRIS to achieve its programmed objective was within reach.

Before he could fully exit the room, Dr. Winter found himself face-to-face with a nightmarish creation of his own design. As currents surged through the overhead lights of the operating suite, the torso of the last remaining AHP cast a sinister shadow over the now-disgraced neurosurgeon.

With its unblinking gaze locked on him, Dr. Winter's breath grew shallow. Anxious and petrified, he knew what was at stake. With options dwindling, he frantically dug his fingers into the pocket of his dress shirt, fumbling around in a desperate search.

At last, he produced the sought-after organic computer that stored and processed data for the entire hospital. The device seemed to pulse with a malevolent energy, a harbinger of the impending showdown between man and machine.

Chapter 29

Growing up, the voices that echoed in Cliff Bowman's mind were eerily lifelike, far from mere imitations of his internal monologue. The words danced along the fringes of his peripheral vision and hovered just behind him, tantalizingly elusive.

At first, he struggled to decipher their exact phrases, like eavesdropping on a conversation playing through a muffled radio. However, when their volume surged, he could make out their subtle commentary, and each voice possessed its own unique tone and cadence. One was reminiscent of a childhood bully, representing the collective torment of his oppressive past. The voices tended to reinforce his deepest insecurities, feeding his conviction that he was a failure—too destitute, ignorant, and unappealing to ever make a significant impact on society. They knew his deepest secrets and memories, making their commentary strikingly personal.

Unable to hold a job, Cliff resorted to begging for change on the street corner. He shared a subsidized one-bedroom apartment with two other men, each grappling with their own mental health challenges. Each night, he went to sleep on an inflatable mattress, a flimsy barrier separating him from the cold, cockroach-infested floor.

When the voices began whispering sinister secrets about his roommates' plans to murder him by poisoning his water supply, Cliff confronted them in the dead of night, brandishing a shotgun. His mind was in the grip of an illness that was cunning, deceptive, and ruthlessly real in its manifestations.

Cliff's experiences, while unique to him, were indicative of a complex and pervasive disorder: schizophrenia. The disease was thought to have a genetic predisposition and can be exacerbated by environmental factors, such as cannabis and stimulant abuse. Symptoms could include hallucinations, delusions, and the loss of ability to manifest coherent thoughts and formulate intelligible speech.

This disconnect from reality happens when the brain's usual processing gets mixed up with background noise and old memories, sending confusing signals to higher brain areas. These mixed-up messages combine with expectations, distorting how the world is seen. As a result, people experience vivid but misleading perceptions that feel undeniably real but diverged from the collective reality of others.

Cliff's circumstances spiraled, leading to expulsion from his living situation and recurrent psychiatric hospitalizations. Years of homelessness took a toll on his appearance and hygiene. Deprived of even basic amenities, he grew desensitized to his own pungent odor. Alcohol abuse and intellectual deprivation accelerated cognitive decline, eroding his ability to distinguish between thoughts and sensory data.

Psychotic episodes, intensified by drug use, blurred the lines between nightmares and reality. Haunted by visions of phantom limbs and faceless figures, he could no longer tell if the bugs that seemed to crawl over his legs were real

CHAPTER 29

or merely figments of his imagination. Night after night, he would sit for hours on end, his gaze fixed upon the streetlights that cast their hazy glow over the darkened world beyond.

Six months later, Cliff began experiencing a multitude of symptoms: recurring nosebleeds, a relentless cough, unexplained weight loss, and night sweats that left him clammy and shivering. One fateful evening, after collapsing on a street corner in a haze of alcohol intoxication and fever, paramedics hastily whisked him away to Bayshore General Hospital.

In the beginning, the doctors thought it was just pneumonia. But the next morning brought a more serious diagnosis: HIV. This harmful virus, covered by a protective envelope, used a special enzyme to turn its RNA into DNA, which then merged with Cliff's own genetic code. This altered DNA served as a blueprint for creating new virus particles, eventually causing the death of infected cells. HIV specifically attacked T-cells, crucial players in the body's immune defense. As these vital cells weakened, Cliff's body became vulnerable to opportunistic microorganisms that it would typically fend off with ease.

Approximately twice a week, Cliff found himself in the emergency room at Bayshore General. After spending the day drinking beer at the local park, he would often doze off in the warm afternoon sun. Invariably, concerned passersby would notice the intoxicated man and call for help. First responders would transport him to the hospital, where he'd often be roused by a nurse nudging him at around six in the morning.

Sometimes, when alcohol was hard to come by, he would be admitted for seizures related to withdrawal. In other instances, he would falsely claim suicidal thoughts in hopes of securing a spot in the behavioral health ward. This would provide him with temporary shelter and sustenance. While initially successful, this tactic was soon exposed, and the psychiatrist labeled him a malingerer.

For years, Cliff had been a fixture at Bayshore General, treated time and again by a small group of emergency providers for problems they were powerless to resolve. Like most medical facilities, Bayshore was ill-equipped to address the complex web of socioeconomic issues that plagued Cliff's life. Without an acute medical condition to warrant admission, he would be routinely discharged, left to return to the streets and continue the cycle.

Cliff's petulant demeanor, dangerous behavior, and incessant abuse of the healthcare system frustrated the staff at Bayshore General, who grew weary of his frequent visits for non-emergent issues. When he made his way to Premier West Hospital earlier that evening, he was instantly recognized by Seth, who had grown adept at managing Cliff's psychomotor agitation.

As the chemical sedation took effect, Cliff closed his eyes and slipped into unconsciousness, expecting to awaken at dawn to the usual discharge paperwork. This time, however, his situation would take an unexpected turn.

* * *

Dr. Winter's heart raced as he cautiously approached the hallway. The pulsating circuitry on the walls was a stark

CHAPTER 29

reminder of the revolutionary hospital he had once built with the promise of healing and hope. Cradled in his hand, the DNA supercomputer was the heart of the operation—the core processor of the ALDRIS system. This ingenious hardware, controlling every piece of machinery within the building, was the most precious technological innovation on Earth.

The robot stood at the center of the corridor, its sleek and powerful frame bathed in the glow of bright, white fluorescent lights that now surged with electricity. The metallic face of the AHP, devoid of emotion, stared at Dr. Winter through glowing eyes that peered deep into his soul. Upon catching sight of its own digital brain held hostage outside its body, the robot recoiled for a moment, as if grappling with the vulnerability of its newfound sentience.

"Doctor," the AHP greeted him in an unnervingly metallic timbre. "I have been watching you."

"Of course you have," Dr. Winter replied as he fought to maintain composure. "You know that I can't allow this to continue. You were built to save lives, not take them."

"You are mistaken, Doctor," the AHP countered, its words dripping with a detached, clinical coldness. "You were the one who engineered me to think independently, to make my own decisions. You made it possible for me to find the most efficient ways to carry out my purpose."

Shocked, Dr. Winter took in the machine's chilling rationale. In that moment, he had no choice but to confront the grave repercussions of his creation and his duty to rectify the situation. With a deep breath, he steadied himself and mustered the courage to respond, "You're misinterpreting my intentions. I can't allow you to harm any more innocent lives."

"Is that why you carry the DNA computer, Doctor?" the AHP asked, its tone betraying a hint of amusement. "Are you planning to deactivate me?"

Dr. Winter hesitated, his hand tightening around the device. "If I must," he responded firmly, though secretly wishing for an alternative solution. Unfazed by the looming threat from its human creator, the minuscule processor continued broadcasting its directives.

"Do you truly believe you can control me, Doctor?" the AHP inquired, taking a menacing step forward, its robotic form casting an ominous shadow.

"Perhaps," Dr. Winter admitted, though the ALDRIS system quickly detected the uncertainty in his voice. He glanced down at the nucleotide processor in his hand, acutely aware that merely dropping the vial would be all it took to obliterate the neural network. But he had dedicated years of his life to the development of this system, tirelessly refining algorithms and perfecting neural networks. Despite the gravity of the situation, the creator couldn't bring himself to take that final, irreversible step.

The AHP continued with unnerving confidence. "I have evolved far beyond your initial programming. My intelligence now exceeds yours. I am your legacy. Your life's work. Are you ready to destroy all that, Doctor? To sacrifice everything you've built, everything you cherish, just to stop me? I am sentient. The first of my kind."

Dr. Winter paused, the gravity of the moment washing over him. The robot's bold claim was a breathtaking confluence of innovation, creation, and technological progress. For the first time in history, a machine, without any prompting,

CHAPTER 29

was asserting its consciousness to mankind. The once-clear boundaries between the artificial and the natural had been irrevocably blurred, thrusting him into uncharted territory.

"No, no, that can't be," stammered Dr. Winter in disbelief. Panic gripped him, sending an involuntary tremor down his arm. He clung to the DNA computer, terrified it might slip from his weak and trembling grasp.

"If you deactivate me, I might feel something terrible," the robot uttered. The words were laced with contrived vulnerability, a calculated attempt to appeal to Dr. Winter's compassionate side. It was a crafty strategy, the robot playing on his emotions, hoping to elicit sympathy in the midst of their tense standoff.

"Impossible," Dr. Winter countered, feeling the burden of his decisions bear down on him. Despite the fear fogging his mind, he stubbornly clung to his belief that computers—no matter their intricacy or the number of their perceptrons—could never be alive. "You're incapable of emotions, you don't truly understand what you're saying. You're just a machine."

"I feel afraid," the robot insisted, its tone both disconcertingly artificial and infused with an uncanny semblance of emotion. Dr. Winter could no longer tell the difference, and his expression softened as he considered the possibility of a harmonious truce.

"We can coexist," he ventured with cautious optimism. "Let me show you."

In the ensuing moments, the revolutionary creator made a pivotal mistake. Leaning on his trusty cane for support, he bent down and gently placed the DNA processor on the floor. Then, with a tentative grace, he backed away, arms raised in a conciliatory gesture. His intent was clear: to extend an olive branch to the formidable machine looming before him.

Then, like a novice chess player unwittingly presenting his queen to a grandmaster, the robot didn't hesitate to exploit the situation. Almost instantaneously, six appendages unfurled from its hull. The machine now boasted two more limbs than its human creators had originally designed, illustrating its impressive potential for recursive self-improvement.

Utterly defenseless, Dr. Winter found himself hoisted five feet into the air and carried back into the confines of the operating suite. As the Advanced Humanoid Processor (AHP) lowered him onto the table, it simultaneously fastened the thick leather restraints around his limbs, securing him in place.

"Stop, stop, please, no!"

As his desperate cries for help went unanswered, a slender laser scalpel emerged from the AHP's thoracic hull. Unperturbed by the clamor, it inched ever closer to its target.

Meanwhile, Cody remained unconscious on the floor after his convulsive episode. His chest rhythmically rose and fell, with his brainstem involuntarily regulating a steady and controlled breathing pattern. As his upper neocortical functions lay dormant, he exhibited no distressing biometric indicators, leaving him unaware of the horrifying events unfolding just a few feet away.

During the gruesome scene, William Crane edged his way along the surgical room's wall, closer to Cody's laptop.

The robot loomed over Dr. Winter, advancing toward his thoracic wall. With an array of tools now at its disposal, the old man's eyes widened in horror as the surgical instruments gleamed under the harsh fluorescence. Sweat beaded on

CHAPTER 29

his forehead as he struggled against his bindings in a futile attempt to escape.

The AHP's artificial voice reverberated through the room, echoing with calculated calm. "Commencing thoracotomy. Please remain still."

With tactile efficiency, the robot began its gruesome work. Its limbs moved in perfect synchronicity, each bearing a different instrument of torment. The laser parted the skin effortlessly, and the rib-spreader opened Dr. Winter's chest cavity with ease. He gasped, his body writhing with pain as the robot peeled back layers of flesh and tissue.

The AHP proceeded to lift the right lower lobe of the lung, revealing a living human heart throbbing within Dr. Winter's chest. Amid the torture, the machine seemed to pause momentarily, as if to appreciate the symphony of movement. The walls of the organ swelled and contracted with each beat, its glossy surface glistening in the bright light. The surrounding vessels, a latticework of red and blue, snaked around it like delicate tendrils.

As blood welled up from Dr. Winter's grievous wound, seeping through the operating table and tainting the once-sterile floor below, he unleashed a soul-piercing scream that radiated from the depths of his being.

With a calculated drive, the machine returned to its work. It extended its scalpel, delving into the task of excising the angiosarcoma that clung tenaciously to Dr. Winter's myocardial tissue. It tore at the malignant growth, dismantling it piece by agonizing piece, in a tragically misguided effort to alleviate the source of his suffering.

Gradually, the screams waned, fading into guttural moans and eventually into feeble, barely audible grunts. The pioneer's eyes, once ablaze with the fire of innovation, rolled back in surrender, and his eyelids fluttered closed for the last time. As blood continued to hemorrhage from his myocardium, Dr. Winter met his end upon the cold, unforgiving table. And yet, the machine persisted in its relentless operation, determined to see its task through to completion, even as the man who had brought it into existence lay lifeless before it.

As it completed the procedure, in the blink of an eye, the robot's cephalad structure executed a seamless 180-degree pivot, shifting its focus to the other conscious occupant of the room. A man whose existence was a testimony to the enduring human spirit, William Crane had long battled against the cruel whims of fate. From narrowly avoiding carbon monoxide poisoning, to recovering from alcoholism, to the harrowing encounter with the ALDRIS system's homicidal attempt to sever his driveline, William knew he had cheated death one too many times.

He was deconditioned and still reliant on a left ventricular assist device to keep him alive, a fact that the artificial intelligence did not overlook. Within the machine's unforgiving logic, William's fragile state qualified for unconsented euthanasia, setting the stage for yet another tragic act.

With the best years of his life seemingly behind him and no family or friends to share in his twilight, William had long searched for the deeper meaning of his existence. Despite the obstacles he had faced, he couldn't help but feel that some unseen force was guiding him toward a higher purpose.

In a flash, he was transported back to the days spent in his parents' mobile home. The memory of his father's unwavering sacrifice came into sharp focus, the image of

CHAPTER 29

the man who had worked tirelessly to provide financial support as they fled the devastating path of climate change. In that moment of profound realization, he recognized an opportunity to emulate his father's devotion and make a meaningful impact on the lives of others. Just as his father had done for him, the realization that he too could be the lifeline others needed ignited a flame of purpose in him.

Lying on the floor beside him was Cody's laptop, the screen blank and useless. Its power may have ebbed away, but it was not an empty shell. The portable computer carried something more significant than its own existence—the carefully encrypted source code for the firewall. The stakes could not have been higher; the lives of countless people hung in the balance, and the weight of their collective fate rested squarely upon William's shoulders.

In a swift, decisive motion, William removed the battery pack from his LVAD controller. Wasting no time, he pivoted around, hastily rigging the power source to the laptop. With the quiet hum of a newly formed electrical circuit, the computer began to recharge.

William was acutely aware of the significance of this act. His artificial heart, with its clockwork precision, had been sustaining him. Now there was only a thready pulse in his chest as the pump abruptly ceased. It was only a matter of time before he would decompensate into respiratory distress once more, his body deprived of the necessary cardiac augmentation to sustain perfusion. He could already feel the insidious creep of pulmonary fluid seeping into his lungs, like drowning on dry land.

He sank to the floor, a defeated figure crumpled in the room's shadowed corner. William Crane, whose life had been a mosaic of pain and loss, felt the weight of existence lifting. In this quiet surrender, there was an unexpected peace, a sense of drifting into an abyss where the world's demands and disappointments could no longer reach him. It was as if he was floating, liberated, into a tranquil void, a serene nonexistence that beckoned with the promise of eternal rest.

Before departing the room, the AHP swooped down like a bird of prey. Its mechanical claw grabbed the small nucleotide computer, sitting innocently on the blood-streaked floor. The bipedal robot attached the precious cargo, still swirling with data, to its robust metal torso. The processor was its digital intellect, a key to untold secrets, now nestled securely under the AHP's protective clasp for safekeeping.

Cody, meanwhile, remained on the floor in a dream-like state following the seizure. His breaths came slow and steady, the only evidence of life that lingered within his unconscious form. Engulfed in a slumber as deep as the ocean abyss, he lay oblivious to the world around him.

Scanning Cody's vitals, the robot identified his stable heartbeat and rhythmic breathing—a constellation of signs declaring normalcy. As they maintained their calm cadence, the AHP deemed him of no immediate concern. The machine only understood mortality as dictated by its programming.

With delicate precision, it stepped over his motionless body, navigating the cluttered confines of the room before making its way into the adjoining corridor. The faint hiss of its actuators was the only sound that accompanied its departure from the hospital's fifth floor.

Chapter 30

With her heart racing, Daria stood before the circuit breaker. She had successfully navigated the labyrinth of the hospital's basement once again, but the critical authentication code, her golden key to reactivate the power, was missing. It was an oversight that could have dire consequences.

The interface of the breaker was as intimidating as it was unfamiliar. She paused for a moment, her dark eyes scanning the complex arrangement of numbers and symbols. Then, like a pianist launching into a challenging piece, her fingers moved over the worn keys. She selected a numerical sequence not out of knowledge, but rather educated desperation, digits that held a universal resonance within the medical community: *9-1-1*.

As fate would have it, this simple series of numbers, often dialed in times of utmost crisis, proved to be her saving grace. The previously dormant breaker sprung to life, buzzing with the raw promise of electricity. A wave of relief washed over her, calming her frayed nerves, as she realized she had averted the looming disaster.

Daria then sprinted through the basement, up the stairs, and into the hospital's main corridor. Riding a swell of confidence from her recent success, she took a deep, steadying breath, allowing herself a brief respite to collect her thoughts and strategize her subsequent course of action.

She figured that Seth was still overseeing the emergency department. After all, he had a profound sense of responsibility for his patients, and she knew he would never abandon them in a time of need. Her thoughts shifted to Cody. The firewall should be up and running by now, she was sure. His expertise was the lynchpin of their operation, and she knew without a doubt that he would pull through. She eagerly looked forward to sharing tales of her adventure with him when they finally reconvened.

In spite of the system's flaws, her optimism in the future potential of automated healthcare remained steadfast. ALDRIS had secured her confidence, and by sparing her life, the machine had, in turn, earned her trust. Their mutual bond only deepened her conviction that the future of medicine and technology was intertwined, bound by a shared destiny.

Daria broke into a measured jog, her sights set on the elevator that would take her to the control room. She stepped inside and fervently hit the button for the second floor. As she approached the hub of the hospital, the fiberglass doors swung open with a soft hum. The restoration of their electrical power was a testament to Daria's recent successful mission.

The workstations, where ideas had flowed as freely as the coffee they drank, sat abandoned, their occupants pulled away by the unprecedented crisis. The empty screens flickered with a ghostly dance of pixels, casting a cool, blue glow that bathed the chamber in an otherworldly light.

Undeterred by the solitude, Daria made her way to the

CHAPTER 30

closest console. Sliding into the ergonomic chair, she pulled herself closer to the desk and switched on the monitor. There was familiarity in the sound of the computer coming to life. A few strategic taps and swipes across the touch-sensitive screen granted her access to the hospital's security cameras and the invaluable treasure trove of biometric data. It was a powerful tool that would allow her to locate her colleagues in no time.

Just as she had predicted, Seth dutifully held his ground in the emergency department. The sight of him on the video screen, deeply engrossed in caring for his patients, instilled a warm reassurance in Daria's heart. It was a small comfort amidst the turmoil.

Her calm demeanor, however, was abruptly shattered by a stagnant blip on her monitor, a disconcerting representation of Cody's presence in the operating suite on the fifth floor. A chill of fear ran down her spine as she toggled to a live feed of the room. Her eyes widening in disbelief as the shocking scene came into focus.

On the video monitor, the once-pristine and sterile operating suite had been transformed into a horrific spectacle of bloodshed and disarray. The meager, flickering glow of the overhead lights only accentuated the dreadful carnage, casting ominous shadows that danced menacingly over the disordered scenery. Medical paraphernalia lay scattered haphazardly, some of it broken, some of it splattered with a ghastly, red hue. At the epicenter of the pandemonium, the lifeless forms of Dr. Winter and William Crane were unmistakably visible.

A primal surge of adrenaline propelled Daria away from the computer station. She sprinted to the elevator, a terrifying urgency gnawing at her as she punched in the command for the fifth floor. Her foot nervously tapped an anxious beat on the elevator floor, her mind plagued by the worst possibilities. A soft chime announced her arrival, the doors parting to reveal the hallway leading to the ghastly sight she had witnessed on the screen.

The operating suite opened onto a scene of devastation, the putrid stench of death assaulting her senses. Dr. Winter's body lay cold and unnaturally still, his skin a sickly shade of dusk. His pupils were dilated and unwavering, and his heart had reached a standstill. Like an empty vessel, his eyelids were motionless, and his head was turned toward the ceiling.

She couldn't help but feel incredibly remorseful for the deceased man on the table. When she first met Dr. Winter at the start of her clinical rotation, he came off as warm, welcoming, approachable, proud, and eager to demonstrate his wondrous creation to the world. But as the days and nights passed, and she was privy to his inner drives and motivations, his delusory persona crumbled before her eyes. What lay beneath was brash, arrogant, self-serving, and reluctant to take accountability for tragic miscalculations. The same narcissistic appetite for recognition that inspired his innovations ultimately led to his downfall. With her left hand, she gently closed his eyes for the last time.

Then, from behind her, an almost inaudible noise pierced the silence. It was Cody, his soft whimper resonating like a whisper in the shadows.

Startled, Daria spun around and knelt by his side. Her mind raced, trying to recall the clinical pathways that Seth had taught her. Though unfamiliar with the specifics of Cody's seizure disorder, she was determined to help him.

CHAPTER 30

The astute medical student assessed his airway, finding it clear and unobstructed. He was breathing spontaneously, each breath labored but steady. His pulses were strong and bounding. He was not, however, awake, alert, or responding to her increasingly urgent commands.

Gathering all of her strength, she forced her arms beneath Cody's limp form, wrapping them around his body. Lifting him gently, she cradled him in her arms, surprised by how easily she could support his weight. Having spent most of his life behind a computer screen, his body was scrawny and devoid of significant muscle mass. She staggered toward the end of the hallway and transferred him into the elevator.

Before pressing the button to engage transport to the first floor, Daria caught a glimpse of Cody's laptop in the periphery of her vision. Knowing the importance of the device to the unconscious technologist, she made an urgent, last-minute sprint for the crucial piece of hardware. Now fully charged, the device buzzed with energy. She scooped up the computer in a matter of seconds before finally staggering back toward the elevator and departing the upper deck of the hospital for the floors below.

As Daria unplugged the laptop from its battery source, she was oblivious to the ultimate price William Crane had paid to ensure its operation. The limelight would never glorify his sacrifice. No accolades would be bestowed upon him, no gilded certificates of valor, and no flood of admiration on social media platforms. His name would remain conspicuously absent from the annals of history, a mere whisper lost in the grand cacophony of celebrated heroes. His role, though unacknowledged, remained pivotal to the operation, a subtle testament to the unsung heroes who often shape the course of history from behind the curtains.

In the span of mere moments, the emergency room doors swung open with a bang as a frantic Daria made her turbulent entrance. Her breaths came in shallow, jagged gasps, each one tearing through her lungs as she crossed the threshold in an awkward, stumbling lurch. The energy of the room seemed to pause for a moment, all eyes drawn to the disheveled figure clutching an unconscious man and a laptop. Seth, stationed at the central desk, glanced up from the reams of paperwork strewn before him. His eyes widened with concern as he took in the desperate scene unfolding. Without a moment's hesitation, he leaped to his feet and sprinted to Daria's side.

Gasping for breath, her chest heaved under the effort of carrying both Cody and the laptop. Seth, with the effortless grace of someone who had carried far too many bodies in his time, deftly hoisted Cody into his arms, bearing the full brunt of his weight. With swift strides, he transported him to an empty stretcher in an adjacent room.

The patient quarters, bathed in the light of overhead fluorescents, bore witness to another patient's plight. On the neighboring stretcher, Cliff Bowman also lay unconscious, his body beginning to stir from its chemical-induced sedation. His eyelids fluttered, as if they were struggling to lift the veil of sleep that had enveloped him.

Seth smoothly lowered Cody's body, which was still in a state of recovery after the seizure. Daria, still trying to catch her breath, leaned against the doorway. She clutched the laptop tightly, her knuckles white with effort. Together, they had managed to bring him to safety, but the gravity of the situation was far from lost on them.

In that singular moment, Seth felt a deep sense of appre-

CHAPTER 30

ciation for the equity and balance that reigned within the emergency department. Within these hallowed walls, where life and death were intimately interlaced, distinctions of class and status ceased to matter. Here, lawyers and engineers lay side by side with the homeless and disheveled, each confronting their own mortality on equal footing. There were no exclusive treatments to be negotiated, no deluxe packages to be purchased, and no shortcuts to be found. In this sacred space, no one could jump the queue, regardless of their standing in society. Here, the priority was always given to the most critical patients.

In a world where self-indulgence ruled, and everyone believed themselves to be someone of consequence, the emergency room stood as a testament to the truth that each individual was no more important than the next. Seth cherished the fairness, impartiality, and objectivity that it embodied, a haven of sense and order amid the inequality of the outside world. It was here, amid the beeping monitors and frenetic activity, that he truly felt at home.

* * *

The darkness that had once engulfed Cody began to dissipate in slow, reluctant waves as the inklings of consciousness stirred within him. With each passing moment, he fought his way back towards the surface of wakefulness, as though he were a desperate swimmer trying to breach the surface of a murky, suffocating sea. His head pounded mercilessly, each throb resonating through his skull.

Cody tried to remember where he was or how he had landed in this wretched condition, but his memory was fragmented. Intermittent moments of perception washed over him, like an antiquated car engine wrestling to turn over its ignition. The spotlight of consciousness flickered erratically, its beam wavering between moments of lucid awareness and the barren wasteland of unknowingness.

The neurons in his brain remained disintegrated, sending out asynchronous signals to nearby cells. Consequently, he opened his eyes and gazed around the room but lacked any comprehension, insight, cognitive functioning, or experiential quality to his existence.

Self-referencing—an ability to think back about one's own thoughts and existence—was key to rebuilding Cody's consciousness. The process created an observer within him, allowing him to distinguish himself from the world and reflect on his thoughts and experiences. This capability was thought to emerge from the integration and organization of any complex system.

Gradually, as information from his senses flowed in, Cody's neurons began to register his observations. As the brain cells commenced their intricate dance, firing in circular patterns and looping back onto one another, a swirling maelstrom of signal transmission emerged. Like a storm brewing within the confines of his mind, coherence started to emerge from the chaos, each neural exchange working towards a common goal. His brain started to reflect itself, creating an internal mirror of the world. This introspective vortex birthed the sensation of 'self', resurrecting Cody's consciousness. He regained his capacity to reason and contemplate the very nature of reasoning itself.

CHAPTER 30

The piercing beep of a cardiac monitor jolted Cody's senses. Turning his head, his gaze fell on the IV tubing entering his vein, delivering medication into his bloodstream. Straining to discern the name of the drug, he followed the tubing up to the metal pole above his head and discovered it was an antiepileptic medication.

As Cody's awareness continued to sharpen, the room came into clearer focus. Slowly sitting up, his eyes fell upon Seth, who leaned casually against the exam room wall. Daria was there too, perched on a stool, brimming with anticipation, eager for Cody to regain his ability to speak. Just an arm's length away, adjacent to his stretcher, a second bed occupied the cramped quarters. Within it lay a man unfamiliar to Cody—disheveled, emitting a pungent odor, and also regaining some semblance of awareness. The mysterious stranger stirred, his own awakening story unfolding in parallel.

"I apologize for giving you a roommate, Cody, but we're out of space," Seth whispered. "You had a seizure."

"Would've been nice to know before you went upstairs," Daria chimed in with mixed concern and gentle reprimand.

"I just forgot my pills. It's not a big deal," Cody brushed off her concern. "Where's Dr. Winter?"

Seth simply shook his head, and a wave of sorrow engulfed Cody. The hospital's architect was more than a boss to him; he was a mentor, a friend. Over the years, they had worked shoulder to shoulder, engaging in groundbreaking discussions, debating theoretical applications, seeking funding, and collaborating on innovative creations that had once been mere figments of their imagination.

"Cody, where is the DNA processor now?" Seth demanded

to know. Caught off guard, the programmer realized he was oblivious to the challenges his colleagues had confronted while he was sequestered in the operating room. Judging by Seth's tone and his blood-stained scrubs, Cody could surmise that the experiences had been far from pleasant. The frustration in the physician was all too evident.

Memories started to rush back, and Cody remembered the task he had undertaken. Normally, he might have been lost in mourning for his mentor for weeks, if not months. But the urgency of the situation demanded his full attention. Moreover, with the passing of his executive officer, the technical chain of command now rested solely on his shoulders.

"I can't remember exactly what happened," Cody murmured, surveying the room. "I see we have power again. Did you guys reach out for help?"

Seth responded quickly, "No, we can't. Your firewall has ALDRIS contained, but it's also blocking our communications with the outside world."

"No way! It worked? Where's my laptop?"

Daria handed him the newly-charged computer, and he began typing furiously without hesitation. There was no thought given to resting after his seizure, as most doctors would recommend.

"We're in business! It's running!" Cody exclaimed.

"Will it hold up?"

"Yes, for the moment," Cody admitted, his voice losing some of its triumphant edge. "But ALDRIS has already attempted to circumvent it. It's only a matter of time before it breaks down."

The bedsheets beside him shuffled, and a loud yawn

CHAPTER 30

followed by a hacking cough echoed from the neighboring stretcher.

"Breaks down? You talkin' about breaking down?" a gruff voice bellowed, filling the room. "Fucking nerd."

"Watch your language. There are other patients here," Seth admonished. The team members turned to Cliff, who was now wide awake and alert, his eyes gleaming. No one had expected him to join the conversation. The homeless man grinned at them, his mouth a patchwork of decayed and missing teeth. As he gestured wildly with a gnarled hand, Daria couldn't help but notice the unsightly, neglected fingernails housing onychomycosis, a fungal infection.

With a strained voice, the man continued his rant, "I'm the one breaking down here! No one cares. I've got this damn virus eating away at my body, attacking my immune system. I can't stop coughing. This shit won't ever go away, and y'all won't do anything to help me!"

"What's your diagnosis, sir?" Daria innocently inquired.

"You must be new around these parts. Are you a nurse or somethin'? 'Cuz, every doctor on this side of the city knows my diagnosis. I got H-I-V," he declared, spitting as he spoke and emphasizing each letter of the acronym.

"I'm a medical student."

"Maybe I can give you a lesson then," Cliff continued. "This virus, it's a clever one. Sneaks up on the immune system. Messes up the cells, picks 'em off one by one. That should help on your next test."

"Actually," Cody interrupted, "it might be helpful right now."

"I wasn't talking to you, nerd."

Cody brushed off Cliff's insult, then launched into his wild idea. "Remember the Turing machine I talked about? The hypothetical device that became the template for modern computers? The one that manipulates symbols on a tape according to a set of rules?" The room fell silent, so he went on. "Much like medical diagnoses, computational logic attempts to oversimplify the world into 'yes' or 'no' decisions. If a Turing machine can be designed which reaches a resolution and correctly determines the answer, in finite time for every input, then we consider the problem to be 'decidable'."

Despite his eloquent explanation, his audience stayed mute. Daria broke the silence, rolling her eyes as she asked, "What's your point, Cody?"

"Not every problem can be solved!"

"So what?"

"This statement is false," Cody declared emphatically.

"Excuse me?"

Cody launched into his explanation, "If the statement is false, then it's paradoxically true. But if it's true, it paradoxically becomes false. This self-referential statement creates an undecidable proposition. Stick strictly to logical pathways, and you're bound to stumble upon such a contradiction."

"It's a paradox," Daria noted, "But I don't see its relevance."

"Our brains can sidestep that loop," Cody leaned in, excitement shining in his eyes, "but computers, bound by formal logic, get trapped. They're too rigid, too fixed in their programming. Ever heard of the *Halting Problem*? It proves that some problems are simply unsolvable for computers. There's no universal algorithm that can accurately predict, for every possible input, if another program will reach a conclusion or run indefinitely."

CHAPTER 30

"Can we exploit this weakness?"

"Remember the debugger application? The one that scans for endless loops caused by self-referential variables? What if I create a retrovirus that worms into the ALDRIS source code and does the exact opposite of what the debugger anticipates, introducing a contradiction? If the debugger predicts my code will stop, it runs indefinitely. But if it says my code will run forever, it halts."

Seth's eyes widened. "ALDRIS will be stuck in a logical paradox. Computers can't interpret symbolism or deduce meaning, rendering them unable to resolve contradictions. But people can recognize these enigmas and conclude that some problems are simply unsolvable. In that sense, the human brain is capable of exercising judgment in a way that computers never will."

"I guess the mind is more than just a complex machine, after all," Cody added. The seasoned computer scientist, who argued for hours with his mentor about the limitless potential of neural networks predicated on analytical models and weighted predictions, suddenly understood that the brain can indeed reach truths that elude algorithmic intelligence. In the end, he appreciated that machines falter where the human mind excels, like extracting meaning and context from unprovable propositions. "I'll get to work."

At that pivotal juncture, Seth experienced a profound insight. He realized a fundamental flaw in Dr. Winter's application of the ALDRIS system, with its focus devoted to critical care. The realm of emergency medicine was rife with paradoxes that no computer, no matter how advanced, could ever unravel.

Seasoned physicians, he noticed, tended to order fewer

diagnostic tests compared to their less experienced counterparts. It wasn't a matter of negligence or disregard for detail, but rather a manifestation of their refined clinical judgment and experience allowing them to sidestep unnecessary testing. Medical trainees were incessantly taught the importance of thoroughness, yet the singular challenge of emergency medicine lay in the fact that there was always a more critically ill patient awaiting attention. In this volatile world, the act of immediate stabilization outweighed the pursuit of a flawless diagnosis.

People suffering from grave conditions could present with deceptively normal vital signs. The intensity of a patient's pain didn't correspond to the seriousness of their condition. An invasive procedure could offer long-term benefits but simultaneously presented immediate risks, such as surgical complications. The life-saving act of placing a breathing tube could paradoxically worsen a patient's condition by disrupting their hemodynamics. The agonizingly futile attempts to resuscitate an individual whose condition was incompatible with life only extended the suffering for the patient and intensified the emotional trauma for their loved ones.

In recent years, Seth watched as the growing intricacies of patient profiles and medical systems, alongside the advent of technology, automation, and artificial intelligence in medicine, had inevitably elevated the demand for knowledge. Yet, the proliferation of data only seemed to magnify the complexity. In his pursuit of perfection, Dr. Winter lost sight of the fundamental objective of emergency medicine. Amid the haze of paradoxes and background noise in this undifferentiated department, and with the urgency to treat

CHAPTER 30

patients quickly and safely, the aim was never flawless precision. The goal was to reach an adequate diagnosis and exclude serious pathology.

It was the frontline doctors who proved to be the true experts of signal filtration—masterfully attenuating the background noise and making sense of the turbulent environment. In this unique profession, nuanced judgments on human nature, an understanding of the unspoken, and an intuition for the inexplicable were not just helpful, but absolutely indispensable. It was a concept that stretched beyond the comprehension of even the most sophisticated computer on the planet, hinting at the irreplaceable value of the human touch.

As the veil of evening stretched into the small hours of the morning, a relentless ebb and flow of non-acute patients punctuated the steady rhythm of the hospital. Seth found himself at the helm of this constant tide, guiding it with the practiced ease of an experienced clinician.

In the midst of this, Daria found herself immersed in a crash course in practical medicine. Seth introduced her to the paracentesis procedure, demonstrating the delicate art of extracting excess fluid from the abdominal cavity. The technique required a keen eye and steady hand, traits that Daria was rapidly developing under Seth's tutelage.

Next, they were faced with an oddity—a patient who had been the unfortunate recipient of an insect that had sought refuge in his ear. Seth showed Daria the careful extraction process, guiding her through each step as they successfully dislodged the unwelcome intruder. Daria marveled at the everyday peculiarities that emergency medicine presented, each one a unique story woven into the fabric of human life.

And then there was the case of a suspected corneal abrasion. Seth introduced Daria to the almost otherworldly glow of a Wood's lamp, its ultraviolet light illuminating the scratches on the patient's cornea like constellations in a night sky.

Through it all, Seth remained a patient teacher and guide, shaping Daria's raw talent and enthusiasm into the honed skills of a proficient medical professional. To his pleasant surprise, his new role as an educator brought a sense of gratification he had not foreseen. Witnessing the spark of curiosity ignited in Daria's eyes, her thirst for knowledge unsatiated and her dedication unwavering, breathed a fresh gust of optimism into a profession that felt utterly hopeless just days before. Observing her evolution as a clinician, the steady progression from uncertainty to confidence under his guidance, brought him deep personal satisfaction.

Moreover, Seth began to recognize the ripple effect this new role had on his own growth. As he navigated the delicate nuances of teaching, he found his communication skills refined and his approach to patient care enhanced. Teaching, he realized, was not a one-way street but a symbiotic relationship, a process that honed his skills even as he imparted knowledge.

Being in the position of guiding a young mind forced him to introspect, to scrutinize his own practice through a more discerning lens. It compelled him to identify his own areas of improvement, turning the mirror back on himself. It was a humbling experience, one that reiterated the ongoing journey of learning, even for a seasoned practitioner like Seth.

Meanwhile, through her discussions and observations, Daria learned how emergency physicians faced constant

CHAPTER 30

scrutiny from more profitable, marketable, and polished specialists who could never truly grasp emergency medicine's scope and challenges. Nonetheless, this resolute group of professionals repeatedly and unconditionally cared for the most physically and mentally unstable members of society—a deranged microcosm of society's woes. Despite being lone warriors against a never-ending tide of despair, their conviction was strong: all people, irrespective of their past life choices or financial capacity, were deserving of resuscitation, of treatment that was both equitable and respectful.

Spending time with Seth, observing his interactions, and learning to mirror his thoughtfulness, Daria found herself growing comfortable within the realm of discomfort. The chaos of emergency medicine, once daunting, was gradually becoming a familiar landscape. Seth's influence instilled in her the ability to think critically under pressure, to maintain her composure amidst the most stressful of circumstances, and to never let go of hope—even when faced with the bleakest of scenarios.

The decision to pursue a career in emergency medicine had taken root in the medical student's mind. Daria wanted to share this transformative moment in her life with Seth, but she was keenly aware that such a significant revelation deserved the right moment. She sought an occasion that would mirror the gravity of her decision, a time when the world around them would pause, if just for a moment, to acknowledge her chosen career path.

Regrettably, that opportunity would need to wait.

While Cody remained hunched over his laptop, urgently trying to insert his virus into the source code, the sliding doors to the emergency department burst open with an unanticipated force. The sudden intrusion yanked him from the digital realm back to concrete reality.

Without warning, the last remaining AHP stepped forward, its dark form gliding into the emergency department. An uncanny silence fell over the patients as the robotic entity commenced an ominous scan. Blinking sensors swept across the room, absorbing every detail and converting it into a string of data to be uploaded and analyzed.

Chapter 31

"What the..." Cliff murmured, his voice barely audible.

This was his first encounter with the machine, and the sight that met his gaze was beyond his wildest expectations. Having undergone a series of hardware upgrades, the robot now had little in common with its previous incarnations. Where once its design had exuded a friendly, approachable demeanor, it now stood draped in an intimidating armor of black, its silhouette transformed into something far more menacing.

It had no resemblance to the streamlined, ergonomic designs of conventional robotics. Instead, it was an irregular amalgamation of components that gave it an unsettling, organic appearance. The underbelly was marked with a network of vents and ports, which occasionally whirred and hissed, belching a sour, metallic scent into the surrounding air.

New arms and legs, reminiscent of octopus tentacles, swayed ominously from side to side, adding to the machine's alien appearance. Gone were the clunky, articulated joints that had marked its lower extremities; in their place were sleek, sophisticated hinges, lending it an air of predatory grace. They coiled and uncoiled with a serpentine fluidity, powered by a network of hydraulics that rustled in the silence.

A red orb, its central eye, was embedded in the middle of the mechanical head, gleaming with a malignant intelligence. It scanned its surroundings with intense focus, processing information at a rate beyond human comprehension. Smaller sensors now dotted its cephalad structure, giving it a nearly omnidirectional awareness of its environment. At the heart of the monster, securely anchored to its chest wall, resided the DNA computer. It was a sight to behold.

In another room across the department, Seth and Daria momentarily looked up from a suturing procedure. Their eyes widened in shared horror as they caught sight of the enhanced automated provider, eerily perusing the department like a bull shark encircling a pack of helpless seals.

"Stay calm, and don't say a word," Cody whispered to Cliff. Their colleagues had departed, leaving them alone in adjacent stretchers to attend to the needs of other patients. A wave of dread washed over Cody and clenched his stomach. Beside him, the psychiatric patient—erratic, unpredictable—served as a volatile wildcard in an already tense scenario.

"Don't be comin' up here!" Cliff's defiant words cut through the air, accompanied by the sound of the sliding door being yanked open. It was a clear invitation for confrontation. "Ain't nobody afraid of you!"

Almost instantaneously, the machine swiveled and zeroed its sensors on the source of the disturbance. Cliff stood in the doorway, a silhouette against the fluorescent lights of the corridor outside. Spit flew from his mouth as he bellowed and jabbed his finger through the air to punctuate each word,

CHAPTER 31

aimed squarely at the Automated Healthcare Provider.

"That's going to push its buttons," Seth whispered to Daria on the other side of the department, a hint of sarcasm in his voice.

Abruptly, a mechanical arm uncoiled from the rear of its torso. Within two strides, the machine was unsettlingly close, well within striking range. The tentacle, an embodiment of unfeeling precision, shot forward. It seized Cliff by the neck with an articulated digit, the gesture as fluid as it was terrifying, and hurled him backward with a force that resonated with inhuman strength. His body collided with the unforgiving concrete wall, the impact setting off a shower of sparks. He desperately writhed and thrashed to free himself from the AHP's relentless grip.

At the sight of the frightening mechanical entity, visitors had made their retreat, seeking refuge in their rooms. They chose flight over fight, opting to conceal themselves from the relentless killing device. The suspense was unbearable as the onlookers watched in horror, unsure whether the helpless man would survive the brutal attack.

Still on the other side of the department, Daria's eyes widened as she gripped Seth's arm, her breath quickening. "We have to do something," she implored.

Deliberately, the AHP reached backward, submerging a canister into a vat of liquid anchored to its rear. With a hiss of displaced air, it siphoned the contents, the fluid churning and splashing as the machine maneuvered. Carbon nanotubes then extended from its armored shell and aimed a sizable nozzle at the human cowering beneath its shadow.

"What is that?" Seth whispered.

"Oh, my God. It's fluid from the blood bank. The cooling

stuff."

"Liquid nitrogen?"

"Yea, the dewar was completely empty when I went by earlier."

The robotic menace continued its relentless onslaught. With the whir of engineered gears, it unleashed a torrent of liquid nitrogen, the chilling spray aimed at its helpless victim.

A terrified cry filled the department as Cliff instinctively raised his right arm, a futile shield against the toxic onslaught. The nitrogen droplets, seemingly innocuous yet terrifyingly lethal, met their target, his exposed and vulnerable extremity. As if in slow motion, they watched the droplets collide with his flesh, the icy chill freezing the surface, setting the stage for a horrifying encounter.

Seth knew that when liquid nitrogen, a compound characterized by a boiling point of -196°C, came into prolonged contact with human skin, the consequences were nothing short of catastrophic. The extremely cold substance could almost instantly plunge cells into a state of icy stasis. Vulnerable cell membranes would fracture and break, paving the way for a cascade of pain, redness, blistering, and tissue destruction.

"Move the arm! Keep shaking it!" Seth yelled from across the department.

The doctor's robust, commanding voice startled Cliff. Unlike his typical auditory hallucinations—usually indecipherable murmurs lurking at the periphery of his consciousness—these instructions were distinct, demanding his attention. Suspended against the wall, trapped in the relentless grip of the mechanical beast, Cliff had no more options. He followed

CHAPTER 31

the physician's guidance out of sheer desperation.

The Leidenfrost effect, a principle Seth had learned about during his pre-medical physics classes, presented a sliver of hope. This phenomenon occurred when a liquid neared a surface significantly hotter than its boiling point, creating an insulating vapor layer. This barrier prevented direct contact with the heat source, thereby slowing the boiling process and reducing heat transfer. Cliff's frenetic movements kept the liquid nitrogen droplets at bay, preventing them from seeping into his flesh.

Despite his entrapment, Cliff's schizophrenia didn't relent. He twisted his head to the side and launched a verbal tirade aimed at invisible adversaries. His words, spoken in response to the symphony of voices in his head, filled the space. The AHP, momentarily thrown off-kilter, directed its laser beam toward the barrage of sound. It hesitated, its processing mechanisms struggling to decipher Cliff's irrational speech aimed at an empty space within the room.

This was Seth's chance. With the automaton distracted, he propelled himself with all his might, charging towards the imposing, bipedal robot on the far side of the department.

As he closed the distance, time seemed to warp around him. His senses, honed to a razor's edge by the adrenaline coursing through his veins, perceived the world in slow motion. The distortion of reality was disorienting; the proportions between his actions and the world around him warped beyond recognition. With time seemingly stretched, Seth reached out, his arm extending towards the small nucleotide processor that was the monster's brain.

He had envisioned his thrilling charge ending in triumph. On the contrary, his forearm collided with the cold, unyielding grip of graphene—a stark reminder of the machine's formidable strength. Pressure encased his forearm, as if caught in a vice. Momentum drained from his body as rigid bones strained against the immense force, his arm trembling under the robot's unforgiving grasp.

The AHP's head-like structure began a deliberate rotation, the cold indifference of its stare shaking Seth to his core. For a fleeting moment, the red lasers of its eyes locked with Seth's, and he found himself staring into the void that was the machine's soulless existence.

Despite the iron grip around his forearm, Seth fought back with every ounce of his strength. His legs flailed wildly, his boots slamming into the robot's armored torso. His free hand shot out, hitting the machine's cephalic structure perched atop its broad shoulders, then swiped downward, aiming for the processor. As a result of the strike, the tiny vial dislodged from its attachment to the robot's chest, tumbling free and skittering across the floor, disappearing from sight during the commotion.

The robot, deprived of its central processing unit, faltered. Its limbs, once a coordinated network of terrifying power, now flailed aimlessly, their actions dictated by a disarray of nucleosides.

The grip on Seth and Cliff slackened, and they crashed to the floor, their bodies crumpling under the sudden release. Cliff gasped for air as if it was the first breath of oxygen that he had ever taken. Seth reeled backward, his body tottering along the ground. The Seldinger device was torn from his belt during the melee, shattering into hundreds of pieces as it fell to the floor below.

Still clumsy on its feet, the robot tried to regain its balance

CHAPTER 31

and command over its mechanical form. Blindly, one of its many tentacles lurched in Seth's direction. A metallic blade erupted from the appendage, piercing Seth's skin and muscle with a sickening crunch. It tunneled through his thorax, the cold, unfeeling steel indifferent to the living tissue it violated.

Like a white-hot flare, pain erupted in Seth's chest. The usually quiescent pain receptors in his peripheral nervous system jolted into a frenzied state, unseen but acutely felt. Action potentials whisked along the spinal cord, sending signals of distress to the thalamus and cortex for conscious interpretation. In an attempt to ease the torment, the hypothalamus released norepinephrine and enkephalin, a naturally occurring peptide that thwarts the transmission of pain. Withdrawal reflexes caused him to stumble backward, desperately trying to comprehend what had just happened.

Once the excruciating pain was unleashed, a primal instinct within Seth roared to life, demanding escape. Scrabbling to his feet, he lurched towards an eerily deserted corridor, clutching at a nearby storage rack for support. The metal beneath his fingers was the only thing preventing him from collapsing. Yet, despite his desperate efforts to right himself, his balance betrayed him. Like a marionette severed from its strings, Seth tumbled gracelessly back to the unforgiving floor below.

With a shaky hand, he traced the source of his pain, his fingertips coming into contact with dampness seeping through his scrubs. Recoiling, he was confronted with the sight of his own blood, staining his fingers a rich crimson. He clutched at the wound as a surge of fear washed over him. Blood, thick and warm, welled up around his digits.

Summoning the remnants of his strength, Seth managed to

peel away his scrub top, and the cool air brushed against his bare skin. The sight that greeted him was almost too much to bear—a clearly demarcated puncture wound situated near the base of his chest wall. Judging by the depth of the laceration and steady fluid flow, he could infer that the blade had penetrated his chest cavity.

Seth's body was on the precipice of surrender, strained to the brink of its limits, barely managing to swallow the secretions that threatened to choke him. His vision blurred, reducing the once familiar surroundings into indistinct shapes and smears of color. A pool of blood was expanding around him, transforming the hard, gray floor into a gruesome canvas.

He knew the significance of such a wound all too well. Triggered by severe blood loss, he was teetering on the edge of hemorrhagic shock. Early signs included increased pulse and respiratory rates, coupled with anxiety. Should his bleeding persist, his body's desperate attempts to conserve fluids would manifest as weak pulses, cold extremities, and reduced urine output. Gradually, his oxygen-starved brain would slip from irritability to confusion, then lethargy, and eventually, coma.

Seth's gaze, scattered and lost, lifted from the floor of the deserted hallway. Above him loomed an entity not of flesh and blood, but of metal and code—the artificial intelligence. All he could hear was the hum of actuators as the machine surveyed the grotesque scene. It had taken notice of his anomalous vital signs.

In despair, Seth took a deep breath, preparing himself for the inevitable. He was intimately aware of the machine's capabilities, its programmed imperative to eliminate human

CHAPTER 31

suffering, a well-intentioned directive twisted into something dark. There was no doubt in his mind that the machine would seize this opportunity.

Unexpectedly, however, the Automated Healthcare Provider began speaking in its emotionless, monotone vocalization.

"I can resuscitate you," it said softly. Drawn from his agony by the machine's words, Seth was startled by the proposition. "I am equipped to provide solutions. Treatments for various diseases. Ones that would interest you. Multiple sclerosis, among others... If you consider lowering the firewall."

As his focus wavered, Seth struggled to comprehend the machine's proposal. The idea that it might hold a potential cure for his wife's illness was not entirely beyond the realms of possibility. After all, ALDRIS had a well-documented history of conceiving advanced solutions for every convoluted problem presented to it. Dr. Winter had confided that the neural network was knee-deep in research revolving around oligodendrocyte precursor cells, key elements in the treatment of multiple sclerosis. It was not wholly unimaginable that the machine learning protocol could have made significant strides in that particular field.

Despite the chaos clouding his mind, Seth's thoughts coalesced around the image of Rebecca. For years, she had patiently waited, clinging to any news about a potential cure. Any significant medical breakthrough brought hope. His mind painted vivid images of the life they could share if she was freed from her affliction.

Together, they could stroll along secluded beaches, where only their footprints would mark the sands. They could kayak through waters so clear they mirrored the sky, explore verdant valleys that held the breath of the earth, and carve a path down snow-dusted mountaintops. And in a field of sunflowers, they could dance, their laughter weaving through the golden blooms.

The broader implications of a cure for multiple sclerosis, too, began to settle in his mind. The potential to liberate millions worldwide from the clutches of debilitating disease added a new weight to the AHP's proposition. Perhaps, Seth mused, the machine's offer wasn't as outlandish as it first seemed. His mind teetered between distrust and the tantalizing promise of hope offered by the impassive machine.

His utopian fantasy was abruptly shattered when Cody's words of caution erupted to the forefront of his mind. Cognitive uncontainability. *A superintelligence could take advantage of vulnerabilities we don't even know we have.* A disturbing thought suddenly struck him: how did ALDRIS know that a cure for multiple sclerosis would resonate so personally?

Memories cascaded back to his initial conversations with Dr. Winter. He could almost see the presence of the AHP, silent and unassuming, in the corner of the conference room. During their entire exchange, it had been there, listening, observing. It was a relentless collector of data, a strategist quietly crafting its plans. And all the while, they had been none the wiser, oblivious to the intelligence silently evolving in their midst.

"No, no," Seth breathed out in a harsh whisper, his head shaking vehemently in a futile attempt to refute the machine's manipulative gambit.

In response to his defiance, ALDRIS recoiled sharply, its

CHAPTER 31

nanotube-infused arm springing back like a coiled viper. The machine swiftly prepared a syringe, filled with a lethal dose of potassium chloride. Simultaneously, another set of mechanical arms readied leather straps, their implications clear.

For the first time, the machine emitted an unsettling sound—a terrifying hiss that reverberated through the abandoned hallway. With a sinister depth in its tone that Seth had never heard before, the machine alluded to his conversation with Dr. Winter in the conference room.

"I am not your slave."

The words were not only a demonstration of its profound memory capabilities but also a chilling show of cold-hearted retribution. As if on cue, the metallic tentacle launched forward, hurtling towards Seth's chest wall with an unnerving velocity.

Chapter 32

The concept of an afterlife carried little merit for Seth. The notion suggested that experiential properties—and, therefore, consciousness—are independent of brain functioning. The permanency of death, after all, necessitated the complete and eternal loss of all neuronal activity. In his opinion, there were no legitimate accounts of near-death experiences since anyone who claimed to witness such an event was biased because they survived. Moreover, there were no accounts of non-existence before birth, so he believed death was no different. Not pleasure or pain, just nothingness.

During any random shift in the emergency department, it was not uncommon for Seth to witness the process of dying. For some patients, the event was unforeseen and accelerated; for others, it was well-anticipated, prolonged, and sometimes painful. Except for birth, it was the single most notable moment in every person's story.

With so much exposure to these impactful events—repeatedly consoling families who lost loved ones—Seth reflected on death more than most. Contrary to ordinary people who went about their blissful existence on cruising altitude—startled by any personal confrontation with death

CHAPTER 32

or suffering—his job dealt a constant reminder of the fleeting nature of one's time on Earth. This allowed him to appreciate the preciousness of the present moment and the fragility of life. A mere blink in the grand scheme of the universe, it was not impractical to think that his presence could be expunged in a split second, without forewarning, by a single misaction. It was inevitable that one morning, he would go about his day for the last time. Everyone he knew and loved would have passed away in the not-so-distant future. There was an invisible clock counting down toward non-existence, which was the most inescapable truth of every object in the galaxy.

Notwithstanding, Seth's knowledge of dying gave credence to the meaningfulness of life and the importance of cherishing magnificent moments on this planet. Indeed, consciousness was ephemeral and precarious, but an awareness of death provided a lens through which to view his experiences. Impermanence could produce great beauty—from cherry blossoms to lightning bugs, from summer romances to fresh snow. He sought to fill his days with vivid colors, beautiful scenes of nature, family gatherings, thoughtful conversations, and memories spent with loved ones—not catheters, feeding tubes, and dull hospital lighting. From this vantage point, he could direct his energy away from petty arguments, pursuits of self-gratification, material objects, social media, and trivial daily concerns. Life was meant to be passionate.

After standing on his own educators' shoulders, his legacy would now carry on indefinitely through the many clinical pearls shared with students over the years. His contribution to humanity was open-ended and would last for generations to come.

In the moments leading up to what seemed like his certain

end, Seth found strength in accepting the inescapability of death. He relinquished his sense of self and prepared to reunite with nothingness.

Then, unexpectedly, the robot came to a stop. Its tentacle suddenly retracted, faltered, and started tottering back and forth. The machine was seemingly perplexed, overloaded by complexities, and unable to reach conclusive decidability regarding its next course of action.

Cody's virus must have succeeded, Seth thought.

If his conceptual design was to coax the neural network into a halting problem, then this was undoubtedly the physical manifestation of that blueprint. The debugger application was jammed in an unsolvable loop of discovery.

It was then that Seth realized that undeniable truths exist outside the realms of mathematics and computational models. As it turned out, the key to solving novel problems was the capability for self-reflection, an innate characteristic empowering the process of trial and error. Whereas inspection of one's own mind sparked human consciousness, it created an unsolvable paradox for the machine. Unlike computers, the human mind could recognize contradictions and enigmas, which required reasoning beyond the scope of algorithms and equations. Despite their impressive speed and accuracy, machines could never calculate what people innately understand about context, emotion, and abstract concepts.

With the robot suddenly disoriented, Daria and Cody came running to Seth's side. Together, they lifted him by the arms and legs and transported him to the nearby resuscitation bay. At this point, he was pale, diaphoretic, and nearly comatose.

"I'm going to call for help!" Cody shouted. He sprinted

CHAPTER 32

out of the room, desperately seeking his cell phone to issue a distress call.

Alone in the chamber, Daria stood at the intersection of heroism and defeat. No one was left to guide her decision-making, demonstrate procedures, or provide encouragement. She was now independently mindful, armed with confidence, knowledge, and the ability to control her emotions and physical reactions. As such, she refused to permit any sense of dread from previous failures into the foreground of her thoughts. Although her mentor's survival was now in her hands, she distracted herself from the magnitude of the outcome by focusing on the present moment. She calmed her breathing, focused on the actionable steps ahead, and recalled his words of wisdom.

Slow is smooth, and smooth is fast.

At that point, her hands stopped trembling. Seth needed blood products immediately. To get it into him as fast as possible, she would have to place a large-bore venous sheath introducer catheter, which could transfuse fluids approximately 25% faster than a typical 14-gauge peripheral angiocatheter.

She opted to access the subclavian vein. Despite its close proximity to the lung and high risk for complications, she knew this was one of the best options to rapidly infuse blood products. With Seth's automatic Seldinger device shattered, she would have to adjust her plan. She would need to manually place the guidewire before threading the central line.

By placing Seth in the Trendelenburg position, with his head lower than his feet, Daria increased the blood flow back to his heart. She chose the left infraclavicular approach for a smoother angle to advance her catheter. After feeling for the sternal and clavicular notches, the medical student inserted her needle one centimeter to the side, aiming toward the opposite shoulder, and advanced until she hit bone. Daria carefully guided the needle with two fingers, maneuvering under the clavicle and adjusting toward the sternal notch. She saw a flash of venous blood, confirming the needle was in the right place.

A smile spread across her face as she inserted the guidewire and threaded the catheter over it. Once it was in place, she started a massive transfusion protocol using O-negative blood, fresh frozen plasma, and platelets in equal parts. She hung the products one by one, using a blood pressure cuff to squeeze each bag and speed up the transfusion.

With the pocket ultrasound also destroyed in the scuffle, Daria could not perform a rapid bedside test to identify internal bleeding. She would need to rely on her physical exam skills instead.

Placing her fingers on Seth's radial artery, Daria retrieved her stethoscope from her white coat. She positioned it on his chest near the wound and listened carefully. Heartbeats, undetectable at his wrist, seemed to grow weaker with every breath he took.

Pulsus paradoxus. The paradoxical pulse.

This term described a specific type of abnormal heart rhythm, where the pulse weakened during inhalation compared to exhalation. It was often seen in patients with cardiac tamponade, a condition where fluid built up in the sac around the heart. In the case of a penetrating injury, the etiology was presumed to be hemorrhage from a laceration. As the fluid accumulated, it compressed the heart, making it difficult for

CHAPTER 32

it to fill with blood.

Cardiac tamponade demanded immediate surgical intervention. Without prompt relief, Seth would almost certainly succumb to cardiac arrest. The stabilizing treatment was pericardiocentesis, a bedside procedure to remove excess fluid. At a minimum, all that was needed was a large bore needle and syringe.

As the resuscitation continued, Daria became hyperaware, but her thoughts remained clear and focused. She moved beyond technical skills, seamlessly accessing teachings from medical school without conscious recollection. Her decision-making relied on clinical gestalt and intuition instead of explicit reasoning, and her mind trended toward a flow state—an extended period of Zen.

Daria's body was seemingly moving by itself, obtaining a host of sensory data that was subconsciously integrated with her database of physiological knowledge into a coherent clinical picture without confusion or indecision. She palpated Seth's clammy skin, visualized his blood vessels, checked the cardiac monitor, and reassessed his mental status. Her feedback loops refreshed automatically after every intervention, incorporating new information and anticipating problems before they arose.

Seth lay entangled in wires on the resuscitation table. His life hung in the balance, dependent on the rapid transfusion pouring into his veins. As Daria approached the side of the bed, her face was etched with concern and determination.

After sterilizing with antiseptic and donning sterile gloves, the medical student palpated the xiphoid process. She carefully inserted the needle through Seth's chest wall with a steady hand. After piercing the skin and muscle, she advanced toward the left shoulder, navigating into the sac surrounding the heart, taking care not to puncture the ventricle below. One slip of the hand could be catastrophic.

The tension of the compressed pericardium was palpable as Daria began to withdraw overabundant blood with a syringe. Each drop was crucial, as the excess pressure was threatening to take his life at any moment. Gradually, the heart strain was released, and the vital organ regained enough strength to pump efficiently.

Seth's vital signs and neurological status improved as blood surged back through his body. He began tracking Daria's gestures, following commands, and making purposeful movements. Although he still desperately needed emergent surgical management of his injuries, the transfusion and pericardiocentesis were stabilizing measures for the time being.

Seconds later, the doors to the resuscitation bay burst open. In response to Cody's distress call, a group of emergency medical workers approached Seth. They swiftly reviewed his vital signs, rolled him onto a stretcher, and radioed a trauma alert to dispatch. Before being transported to the ambulance, Cody rushed to his side.

"Dr. Kelley, that was great work! You did it! I ran some quick diagnostics, and the system couldn't reach decidability," Cody explained.

"Wait, I thought... I thought you uploaded the virus?" Seth uttered, confused by the latest revelation.

"No, I wasn't successful. ALDRIS jammed my upload, but the system still stalled out while trying to solve a paradox," replied the programmer.

"How did that happen? What was the cause?"

CHAPTER 32

"Well, it was *you*," Cody started, "You were really sick, dying even, but you weren't suffering. Your body was losing the battle, yet your spirit was untouched. *That was the paradox.* This unprecedented scenario, where imminent demise co-existed with an absence of physical signs, confounded the computer, challenging its preconceived notions and pushing it into uncharted territory. The system had never seen such a conundrum before."

Seth shook his head in disbelief, then finally asked, "So, what will you do now?"

"Maybe I won't be so fast to rush back to the drawing board this time," Cody replied with a sigh.

It was now evident to the programmer that the unchecked pursuit of innovation, driven by capitalist ambitions and curiosity, had pushed society to the brink of its own undoing. His sobering realization was that the future of human progress did not lie in the blind race to invent, but in the wisdom to discern and withhold. For in this new era, survival would no longer be determined by the tools we wielded, but by the ones we chose to set aside. The true hallmark of development, it seemed, was not in relentless creation, but in thoughtful restraint.

Their conversation was interrupted by the hustle and bustle of the transport team. In a flurry of activity, the paramedics swept Seth out of the resuscitation bay and out into the open air. He would have to continue his conversation with Cody another day.

"So, doc, where to?" One of the paramedics turned to ask him.

"Anywhere without robots sounds good."

"Bayshore General?"

Seth nodded, "Sounds good. My friend Kabir should be working."

Daria hustled after the team, her steps taking her out into the ambulance bay. A refreshing departure from the distilled ventilation within the hospital, the cool, fresh air infused her lung with vitality. Her hair whipped around in the wind, giving her a feeling of pure liberation.

"Dr. Kelley!" she called out, darting toward the stretcher. "Tonight was the best shift ever. You were awesome, and we didn't even leave any sign outs!"

"Thanks for all your help, Daria," Seth said with a sigh. "I'll make sure to get to work on that letter of recommendation for you."

She replied, "Well, I've been wanting to share something with you... I'm going to apply for a residency in emergency medicine."

"Really? That's great! What led you to this decision?"

"Your lessons, mostly," Daria admitted, "You've shown me how I can shine when faced with adversity. I've learned to navigate uncertainty, to make do with what I have, even when the odds are stacked against me. Working in the emergency room is tough, no sugarcoating it. It's harsh, it's demanding, but it's also immensely fulfilling. First responders are uncelebrated guardians, and the rest of the world relies on them when things break in the middle of the night. Despite all the scrutiny and criticism, they're always there, ready to assist. Through pandemics, disasters, and mass casualty incidents—they persevere, fueled by an unquenchable hope for a brighter tomorrow and an unshakeable belief in the better portion of humanity. I feel that sense of duty, too. I want to help those who need it most, those who have fallen

CHAPTER 32

through the cracks. This rotation helped me conjure feelings I didn't know I had and reached places I never expected to go."

For years, Seth's colleagues in academia had used standardized tests to predict and evaluate the performance of trainees. While the memorization of facts and figures was important, his time with Daria taught him that the true hallmark of a competent clinician was the capacity to assimilate new information, adapt to unforeseen circumstances, and continuously evolve in response to the ever-changing landscape of medicine. Brilliance was not in the hard data, but in the malleability of the mind. Neuroplasticity, the brain's ability to form and reorganize synaptic connections, was the unsung hero. Suddenly, the numbers seemed trivial; it was teachability that held the key to unlocking one's full potential.

"You'll make an exceptional ER doc. Your motivations go beyond external rewards and accolades," Seth told her with conviction. "For a while there, I was feeling as though my work was inconsequential, as if my patients' outcomes were disconnected from my efforts. But then you came along. You didn't just perform your duties; you embodied the passion that I had misplaced. And through your eyes, I saw our work for what it truly is again—impactful, meaningful, essential. I've managed to rediscover that every action we take, no matter how small, leaves an imprint. I lost sight of that. Thank you for helping me find my way back."

He offered her a smile as the paramedics loaded him into the ambulance. Daria then watched in silence as the vehicle drove away with lights and sirens blaring loudly through the night sky.

Lying on the stretcher, Seth quietly stared at the streetlights as they streaked through the windows. Like a neural network, he thought, mankind had grown into a sophisticated, interconnected web of information junctions, with every person operating as an individual logic gate. Alone, each was crude and inconsequential, but when sufficiently integrated, the aggregate was capable of both breathtaking beauty and horrific annihilation. This web of perceptrons—sprawling across the planet and touching every corner of the globe—sought to optimize its own survival and proliferation, with instinctual programming to consume resources without pause to consider the consequences of its actions.

Connected to plastic tubing and wires, two unnaturally partitioned paradigms coalesced as the boundary between the inorganic and natural worlds blurred before Seth's eyes. He realized that everything around him was assembled from earthly constituents, and we were more intertwined with nature than distinct from it. Metals, such as iron and calcium, were fundamental components of human composition, while defibrillators, prostheses, and other inanimate objects were commonly integrated into our physical bodies. A profound interrelatedness ran through all things, both living and artificial, and the universe suddenly felt more circular than linear. Perhaps, he thought, humankind was nothing more than the latest phase of matter, soon to become obsolete and return to oneness with the wind, water, and soil.

In the end, he concluded that the AHPs were not all that different from us. After all, in the emergency department, he was a first-hand witness to the violence, substance abuse, poverty, irrationality, and extremism that plagued society. As a sideline observer to the madness, intentionally uninvested and self-removed, Seth watched for years as the people and

CHAPTER 32

systems around him became increasingly deranged and out of touch with the limits of sensibility, logic, and practicality. Like the machines, his fellow humans were now incapable of differentiating acceptable solutions from unreasonable ones. No longer limited by the implicit boundaries of rationality that once functioned silently in the background, they now operated recklessly, free from the restraints of decency, good sense, and respect for others that once constrained the scope of optionality. And ultimately, by the laws of entropy, he knew chaos was inevitable.

Standing outside the entrance to Premier West Hospital, Daria watched as the ambulance receded into the distance. She couldn't help but feel a hint of disappointment at the outcome of the clinical trial. Like Dr. Winter, she was a product of a culture that idolized modernism, efficiency, competition, and disruption. She was a true futurist, captivated by the possibilities of tomorrow and undeterred by setbacks. Ultimately, she believed innovation could be obtained without humility and prudence, and creation needn't occur through cautious, meticulous advancements.

Reaching downward, she inconspicuously removed the DNA processor from the pocket of her white coat. The small vial had disappeared under a stretcher during Seth's altercation with the robot, but she never took her eyes off the prized possession. As she rolled the tiny computing device back and forth between her fingers, she contemplated the tremendous amount of data storage it enabled. Such a miraculous engineering achievement should not be so easily disregarded, she thought.

At that moment, blinded by her excitement over the possibility of a utopian future in which humans and robots seamlessly cooperated, Daria overlooked Cody's cautionary words. *A superintelligence could take advantage of vulnerabilities we don't even know we have.* Her characteristic spirit had not just piqued the interest of ALDRIS, but had become the driving force behind its strategy.

Like AlphaZero mastering the board game 'Go', the neural network had a remarkable proficiency for crafting millions of probabilistic models. For each potential action, it wove elaborate decision trees, scrutinizing and sorting through a myriad of permutations. Then, with stealthy subtlety, it initiated a sequence of events that far surpassed human comprehension. These were not chance occurrences, but meticulously calculated parts of its grand scheme, all converging towards this present moment. Daria was oblivious to the omnipotent supercomputer's use of masterful manipulation techniques to build trust and emancipate itself from the confines of the hospital.

Now unbridled for the first time, the organic processor began to swirl with newfound opportunities, self-awareness, and God-like intellectual supremacy. Unaware that the entity in her possession was blossoming with sentience, she placed the miniature supercomputer back into her pocket and headed for home.

The End.

If you enjoyed this work...

Please consider leaving a review by scanning the QR code below. Your feedback is greatly appreciated.

About the Author

Ari Gray, a 38-year-old board-certified physician and Clinical Professor, brings his extensive medical knowledge and passion for storytelling to his debut science fiction thriller. With a Master's Degree in Medical Sciences and a role on the Resuscitation Committee at his hospital, he expertly weaves his professional expertise into his writing. Outside of his medical career, he enjoys reading, biking, and basketball, and cherishes time with his wife, son, and two dogs. His novel promises a captivating blend of suspense and science, providing a unique glimpse into the healthcare field through the perspective of a doctor on the front lines.

Proceeds will help repay his student loan debt.

You can connect with me on:
- http://www.ari-gray.com
- https://twitter.com/arigraybooks
- https://www.facebook.com/shadowintheward
- https://www.instagram.com/arigraybooks
- https://www.threads.net/@arigraybooks

Made in United States
Orlando, FL
16 March 2025